# The Paradise of Food

# The Paradise of Food

KHALID JAWED

Translated by
BARAN FAROOQI

🟊 juggernaut

JUGGERNAUT BOOKS
C-I-128, First Floor, Sangam Vihar, Near Holi Chowk,
New Delhi 110080, India

First published by Juggernaut Books 2022
Originally published in Urdu as *Ne'mat Khana* by Arshia Publications 2014

Copyright © Khalid Jawed 2022
Translation copyright © Baran Farooqi 2022

10 9 8 7 6 5 4 3 2 1

P-ISBN: 9789391165642
E-ISBN: 9789391165727

All rights reserved. No part of this publication may be reproduced, transmitted, or stored in a retrieval system in any form or by any means without the written permission of the publisher.

Typeset in Adobe Caslon Pro by R. Ajith Kumar, Noida

Printed at Thomson Press India Ltd

*For my father, Shamsur Rahman Farooqi, a treasure house of love and learning*

*Gali mein uski gaya so gaya na bola phir
Main Mir Mir kar usko bohot pukar raha*

– Mir Taqi Mir

*He entered her lane and departed, just disappeared without speaking a word
Many times I called out to him, "Mir! Oh Mir!" – but no answer ever came*

– Translated by Shamsur Rahman Farooqi

# Contents

| | |
|---|---|
| Introduction | 1 |
| Part I: Wind | 9 |
| Part II: Noise | 23 |
| Part III: Cold and Flu | 303 |
| Part IV: Noises | 359 |
| Part V: Dead Silence | 379 |

# Introduction

Khalid Jawed is an outstanding exemplar of the new wave of fiction writers in Urdu. There had been two paradigms for fiction in Urdu: the one established by Premchand and the Progressives and the other created by Intizar Husain and the Modernist writers by largely subverting the Premchand paradigm. Khalid Jawed represents the third generation of modern fiction writers in Urdu who have been trying to establish yet another paradigm for the narrative art in Urdu. His fiction is driven by powerful prose rhythms, heavy and pregnant with meaning, overshadowed by the consciousness of fear, disease and failure, spawned by the evil in human nature.

A philosopher by training, Khalid Jawed achieved instant fame in the early 1990s through his stories of lonely individuals growing up in an environment of ignorance, or of people with families, and not lonely in the conventional sense but still unable to come to terms with what life has been for them.

Contrary to the so-called mainstream of contemporary Urdu fiction writers, Khalid Jawed is passionately interested in looking into the psyches of individuals who are somewhat cut off from collective existence. His short novel *Maut ki Kitab* investigates the mystery of anxiety, the disease of the spirit fascinated by the death that surrounds it. In *Ne'mat Khana,* his novel published in Urdu, Khalid Jawed investigates the disease and squalor of domestic existence through the metaphor of the kitchen or the pantry. Food and sustenance make human life go, but they also corrupt human life.

Khalid Jawed has published three collections of short stories, and two short books on Milan Kundera and Gabriel García Márquez. He has been published on both sides of the border to great acclaim and critical appreciation. Born in Bareilly in 1963, Jawed now teaches in the Urdu department of Jamia Millia Islamia, New Delhi.

*Ne'mat Khana* is a remarkable piece of work by this third-wave Urdu fiction writer. It tells the story of an orphaned boy, Zahiruddin Babar, who is brought up in a typical middle-class Muslim joint family teeming with relatives from both sides of his parents' families. The novel is narrated in first person through the eyes of this little boy who eventually grows up to reach late middle age. The vast array of relatives from either side of the family intrigues the child. The author doesn't really explain this strange fact though the reader gets a sense of the custom of marriage between cousins in the Muslim community.

Khalid Jawed's work presents many challenges. I just mentioned above the departure from old paradigms and the establishment of new paradigms in fiction by the generation of Urdu writers which came into prominence in the late 1980s and very early 1990s. The three outstanding representatives of the new paradigm are Syed Muhammad Ashraf, Khalid Jawed and Siddiq Alam. Another name that occurs immediately as one mentions the above three names is that of Naiyer Masud, but Naiyer Masud belongs to an earlier literary generation and in fact did not influence the three writers I mentioned above. Masud created a world of his own: highly inward-looking, intense and semi-transparent, marked by a remarkably limpid but unadorned prose.

Having said this about the new paradigm and the strong outsider, namely, Naiyer Masud, who vastly impressed but did not much influence the three writers I mentioned above, one is led to another question: what exactly is the new paradigm and what does it do to fiction?

It is comparatively easy to answer the latter question. The new paradigm opened yet another vista over Urdu fiction. If the Progressives were obsessed with social change and revolution, and upheld the banner of hope walking warily around the seamier questions of life, the Modernists insisted upon an individual view, and a point of view not related to any identifiable individual in the fiction, but to an abstract entity brooding upon the scene of the contemporary world and holding out none of the formulaic propositions of action and hope; the third paradigm was marked by an attempt to look at life from many possible angles. They eschewed the intense, almost obscure manner of most of the outstanding Modernists and chose to write a prose not burdened by metaphors and symbols. It was basically in the mode of early twentieth-century narrators but investing their prose with nuances and layers which were not to be found and in fact were entirely foreign to the manner of the early story writers in Urdu. Thus they took narrative flow from their earliest predecessors but gave the narrative itself a depth and a variety which would have been unimaginable to the writers of the early twentieth century.

The trouble is that the similarity among the writers of the

new paradigm stops here. Each of them strikes out in his own way, on his own path or paths. I say paths because these writers are passionately interested in life but are not confined to any given mode or modes of existence. Thus they present a world of greater narrative variety, that was not available to their Modernist predecessors. Intizar Husain is a sole exception, but he is a writer who is almost impossible to classify.

Khalid Jawed presents a narrative personality drastically different from that of any of his contemporaries. The noted Modern critic Varis Alavi, said, 'Khalid Jawed's art is not confined to one level or one direction. It has many layers and many directions. His fiction is opulent because it travels from naked realism to symbols, myths and to cultural agendas and corners.' He also speaks of Khalid Jawed's 'imagination which loves invention and novelty'. While these observations are sufficient to give us a general understanding of the kind of fiction writer that Khalid Jawed is, it by no means presents a complete picture. There is, for instance, Khalid Jawed's interest – one might almost say obsession – with disease, sickness, filth and the grotesque. In some of his fiction this interest or obsession is so pervasive that one of the commoner views about Khalid Jawed is that he is a writer of the morbid and the diseased. For instance, in a review published in *The Dawn*, Karachi, of 28 June 2015, the reviewer Adnan Adil said:

> Khalid Javaid [sic] is obsessed with death and disease and has a gloomy outlook. His art lies in turning morbidity into fiction with a writing style so engaging and prose so polished that they make the reader stick to the story, howsoever, one may disagree with his depressing view of life.

Apart from the fact that Khalid Jawed does not necessarily present a view of life, gloomy or depressing, and he is not interested in giving the reader a 'message', the interest in the unsightly, even the filthy, and the mood of sickness and disease in his fiction is symbolic of something deeper about the whole universal scheme of things rather than a narrow infra-lapsarian rolling and roiling in the uglier things of life.

Doubtless it itself is an act of courage to feel and then observe the sordidness, and, one might almost say, negative modes of existence: eating, defecating, making love in a mechanical and unloving way, falling ill, a narrow environment of malodorous things and objects. There was a time when people wondered and admired the courage of Balzac for writing novels upon novels about moneymaking and filthy lucre. Somewhat later, one also admired the courage of Dickens, and then Zola, in plunging into aspects of urban life with the power that we had kept hidden under a thick layer of formality and respectability. But Khalid Jawed takes the process many steps forward and feels no shame, or shows no lack of courage in talking about human life as it is lived inside small, dinghy and basically selfish environments.

*Ne'mat Khana* functions on two levels. One is a kind of stark realism which takes account of the unsaid and unsayable things of human life. It is not just disease but blood and phlegm and stagnant water and small but repulsive minor beasts that live in the crevices of houses and their kitchens and storerooms. The observation of objects and situations is clinically pitiless. It lets nothing go; in fact it sometimes seems to enjoy finding unpalatable aspects of common phenomenon. These qualities of the prose in themselves make for a strong and compelling narrative, and in fact open our eyes to things which we were always prone to behave as if they don't exist.

Then there is the symbolic level. The implied and occasionally articulated motif is the perversity of food. Food is consumed by us largely to sustain existence and to a small degree for enjoyment. Then food converts itself to filth and also provides the kinetic force for sex. Thus the kitchen and the pantry are also, in the larger sense, sex shops, and since food and sex drive human beings, life becomes a struggle for not so much as survival, but a struggle for power. The beauty of the novel is that while most contemporary novelists look for evil and narrow-mindedness and violence and power struggles in the outer world, no one except Khalid Jawed had the courage and the imagination to see homes and families as the whole outer world in microcosm. Normally, households are presented in fiction, particularly Urdu fiction, as sites of passion, or friendship, or petty acrimony and animosity. In other words, these households are just like the ones we would like to imagine through our small imagination. Khalid Jawed goes behind the people and the locations of the households, comes back and tells us that the outer world is nothing but more of the same that he saw inside the doors and walls of homes and households.

Everyone has, to the extent they could, extolled the prose in which Khalid Jawed couches his narrative. Having been a philosopher for many years before entering the Urdu academic world, Khalid Jawed seems to find kindred spirits in philosophers of gloom, both among Indians and Europeans. The sombre rhythms of philosophical writing make their way through the narrative. But his are not philosophical fictions, his are human narratives given to us in generally extremely chiselled and many-sided prose with the sharpness of sight enabling the narrator to observe the details and minutiae of the domestic environment. Unlike Naiyer Masud, who too is strong on details, Khalid Jawed gives us details of small things. He observes them with hidden distaste, but also fascination, and both come through in this novel most tellingly.

It has been observed that Khalid Jawed is not interested in characters in his fiction, in the sense that he doesn't build characters who are 'round' in E.M Forster's terms, or characters that grow, develop and change, but this is the characteristic of all post-Progressive Modernist fiction. This fiction is always interested in events and things and the individuals in here come through to us via their ideas and through minute, static details of their lives. It is, however, true that Khalid Jawed betrays a certain misogynistic turn of phrase, if not turn of mind. Maybe, it is due to his revulsion from sex which is common to all middle-class and lower-middle-class educated Indians. The fact remains that in many of his stories, and especially in this novel, there are enigmatic women who don't lend themselves to admiration, much less affection, even when they are suffering. Yet it seems to be more than just portraying unlovely women, as these very women are or could be at some point objects of his desire.

It can be said that Khalid Jawed has established a unique voice in Urdu fiction. The danger with unique voices is that they tend to become repetitive, confined and don't always succeed in finding new patterns and subjects, but Khalid Jawed has enough strength of imagination to find new aspects of the same reality.

# Part I
# Wind

The wind was the only eyewitness to his entry into his own house like a melancholy thief. One didn't know if the house was under construction or falling or transforming itself into a ruin. No one knew this, only the wind did.

His melancholy fell to the ground through his feet, gathering in heaps. This sadness, what kind of sadness was this? It was like the melancholic gaze that rose towards the sky after peering into a closed well, and the sky was limitlessly cruel. Such limitlessness could only produce fear. All meanings, all connotations, all interpretations drowned in this limitlessness

It was just two chapattis, made with love, that were fluttering like flags on this large, ever-looming, frightening scene. But these chapattis were not meant for any stomach; they were not meant for digestion, conversion into blood and circulation in the body. Neither were they meant to be turned into excrement and flushed away into dark narrow drains. They were actually two pieces of evidence. Evidence of the spirit, like two pure and honest mathematical numbers. Like a chaste and immortal bindiya on the forehead of a plundered and dispirited-looking world. Even the embers of the chulha had become cold, but these were eternal and still warm.

And that's why the wind saw that he was just sad, not weeping; he might not weep at all, or ever. He will keep his salt with care and safety; corpses take longer to go bad in salt. There's still so much that he has to keep safe.

The wind had seen many shadows, in fact, had been witness to just shadows for a long, long time now. How many shadows had passed, walking into a deep, wide and dark river. Their feet left the sandy bank and slipped into the deep waters, and they became yet deeper and denser shadows. Every time one returns from a journey, one has to perforce walk towards the water. There's nothing called empty space, or vacuum; everything is water which can't be seen, but it is present in every place where there is love or hatred.

He wasn't alone; there were two more beings with him: the shadow of a limping rabbit with a jagged ear that kept following him, and a cockroach perched like a butterfly on the collar of his shirt.

The wind, the ancient wind of that house, or even that place, the eternal inhabitant of that place, was lying crushed and buried under a fallen tree, heavy and dry, almost fossilized into stone.

One knows not when the tree lost its leaves, its branches. Only some dry roots remained, totally absorbed into the ground in a meaningless and almost ridiculously pathetic manner. Oh, and yes, there was a trunk left too; it was very close to becoming a log of wood, the kind that is used to make the joints and frames of doors for a home.

It's not the kind of wind that actually blows. It can neither be felt against someone's body, nor does it dry the clothes on the clothes line. It is stony, it just peers from under the rubble. The rubble is that of the very tree from under which it emerged. It moved in the form of blasts; having travelled a distance of many miles, it reached the tree whose leaves and branches it touched and then stayed there. That was the tree I am talking about.

The mango tree which stood in the courtyard of past times, the wind knew that it had died a very long time ago. Still, it didn't desert it and go away. Like an unfortunate she-monkey roaming with the dead body of its baby still clinging to its pathetic stomach, just the same way, the wind ever lugged the corpse of the tree and that's why it had turned into stone under the rubble.

Could there be a bigger eyewitness than stone?

He was walking unsteadily, stumbling, yet trying to walk carefully so as not to hit something or fall. The wind realized, even as it lay on the ground, that the earth could now not stop itself from crying. The earth was weeping upon his canvas shoes which were slipping on the wet mud and sinking into it. The wind soon found out this secret too – that a dark and deep silence was also writing its story right there. The silence was pouring its story into the long ears of the wind.

And he? He filled his cold wet shoes with the dark and deep silence – perhaps he knew what was going to happen. A dreadful river was winding itself forward to prey upon a thin rivulet. Having accepted merging into the river as its fate, the rivulet was moving towards it gradually. This was a snare into which she herself was falling.

The wind saw that he was standing in a corner, like a shadow.

Exactly at that moment, the hundred-year-old snake, whose hiss would frighten to death the chickens of the house, wound itself away, almost touching him. This snake too was an inhabitant of that house, but he neither saw nor felt the snake. Neither did he see the innumerable shadows of the monkeys the house was overflowing with.

The wind saw his head hit an empty beehive that hung from the heavy, termite-infested wooden beam, but he remained oblivious of it. A hive in which no bee remained. It hung, abandoned, no longer golden brown but dry and white. Its bees had wandered off to some other planet. It was no longer a hive but the shroud of one. So weightless, weak and insignificant that it softly swayed and quivered even in the worst of the humid, airless atmosphere.

This hive, which was harmless to a disappointing degree, barely escaped falling after colliding with his shadow.

The wind saw that he had hopped over the dead dry trunk of the tree to avoid bumping into it. He had jumped exactly over the hollow in which Lucy and Jack used to huddle to protect themselves from the rain.

The hollow is yet another blanket of loneliness engraved on the loneliness of the trunk. An empty nest which is never occupied again turns into an iron nest. The tree trunk, separated from its flowers, fruits, leaves and branches, from everything, alone, and under it, a crushed but living wind. The wind never dies for it has always been alone. It can only turn into stone or ice. The wind was eyewitness to the fact that he was wandering around like the necrophiliac sadhus who roam the cremation grounds so that they may insert their spirit into some corpse and use it to their benefit.

Benefit?

Benefit? What was it?

To how much could the stony gaze of the wind be a witness?

Those eyes saw that he was wandering in his own house, an earthen pot in one hand and a yellowing, crumbling manuscript in the other.

He wanders but doesn't see a thing. Not even the crow on whose accidental death a large number of crows had arrived, God knows from where, flying long distances, and most surprisingly, perched in silence, their heads bowed, on the kitchen roof. That very dead crow sat silently on a fallen beam. But he didn't see it, regrettably, he didn't see it.

The wind saw that the rabbit with the jagged ear had left his side and was actually munching the grass growing on its own grave, and the cockroach had flown away from the collar of his shirt and was creeping with malicious intent towards the rubble of the walls and the bricks of the kitchen.

The wind knew that all sins, all gluttony and all greedy intent must go that way even if it had all been foolish little childhood games. All destiny is ultimately the same. Even after the checkmate and the closing of the game of chess, trying to drag back past time, time which is dead like a dead monkey's paw, results in terror and defeat, nothing more. The truth was nothing but becoming the dog in the stomach and then perishing. The journey towards total annihilation of the mental and corporeal continues, to such an extent that the annihilation of memory becomes the highest point of all.

The wind knows that other world too where no one recognizes anyone else. The chain of blood is just a memory. All worship, all religion, and all ethical practices are nothing but strategies for getting rid of memory. In that world, everyone will be rejoicing in their solitude. With dreadful shamelessness. Even a ghost doesn't have such shamelessness. This is because the ghost at least maintains some kind of relationship with this world; that this relationship may be full of ill intent, envy and diabolicality is another matter. But he doesn't rid himself of his memories. And he is punished for this with his sharp claws and the hollow pits of his eyes.

So, one will have to dismiss from the memory all worldly relationships, all emotions, all loves and hatreds, all lusts and desires, every one of them. What good will come out of going to a paradise where one wouldn't even remember who one's father was?

One will have to put up with this state of 'oh my soul! my soul!'. Bear it with patience.

The wind saw his face clearly for a moment. It was the tired face of someone who had experienced a long and uncomfortable journey. A very, very long journey, as long as the journey that the hot or cold winds perform. He had come home like a flowing wind.

Home?

Though home was perhaps not anywhere; there was just black water and a floating, frightening shore which seemed like rubble on which he was roaming around, stumbling again and again, like a blind and panic-stricken man. Once, in fact, he just prevented himself from falling like a dry leaf tumbling down on its own shadow. This was like a dream, but while dreaming you can't even see one of your eyes. If only he could see the misfortune of that eye, its dryness and its moisture, see the way the wind could. Pity that it wasn't possible that the eye which dreams, the same eye could also be visible to the person dreaming. See a face which looks like a sheepish, tired and broken railway engine hit by the fog, a railway engine which reaches its destination very late, and which continues sadly to emit smoke amid its absolutely silenced whistle.

The wind found him to be like herself.

The wind found him strange, something unique in its own self. He had come to the dead of the past and was devoid of every emotion, feeling or mood, just a spinning whirlwind. Or, he was a mummy whose brain, sucked out through the nose with great skill, is thrown away so that the body may not rot or decay. The brain wanders around in garbage pits and the body in the air.

Because of the eternal separation of the mind and the body, only shadows are born between them, devoid of emotions and feelings, just dark shadows. Certainly, they were nothing but emotions on whose river-like expanse he used to float the earthen pots of his sins and crimes and drag them with him as he swam. For of course, what else was it but the mind which devised the means of making and then pushing the pots under water. Now the pot could be pulled along comfortably, because it contained the creative power of the maker of the earth and also the force of the river's flow. An extra power, an external support.

But now he was a man, alone. Alone and hapless like the first man on earth, dependent upon the grace and mercy of God. For there was a long and deep abyss of sand where the river used to flow. He now carries the pot of sins like a headload, all alone on the sand. The wind is watching the downfall of Adam, and the wind also sees that the marks of his feet on the sand seem to form snake-like patterns.

'This is my snake! But where is yours? Show your snake too, you angels and decent, good-hearted people!'

He should have screamed this out loudly, protesting angrily, but he didn't. His lips were slathered with putrid honey and were glued together forever so that the silence would also putrefy on his palate and in his throat.

His cockroach reached the bricks of the kitchen. The wind saw that this was exactly the moment his left foot got stuck in the mortar of the earth, and it kept sinking. He held to an iron pipe. Otherwise, he would have fallen on his face right on his own shadow (though the shadow would not have been visible, he was himself a shadow). This thick and rusted pipe had actually conveyed the water in past times.

One could swear that however much the wind may have been crushed and trampled – it may become a fungus-ridden cliff, or by God's grace a stone statue even – it can always recognize the footfalls of rain from far, very far. The wind and rain are related in an eternal and mysterious fashion. A mystery, somewhat like the mysteries between human beings.

The wind could sense that the rain was arriving and along with it came another strange wind. A wind which didn't have any connection with this house was coming along with the rain. A wind which could drag out the dead.

Unable to walk, buried under the dry dead body of the tree, the wind smelt the alien, unfamiliar, fast and forceful wind and knew it to be brutal, merciless. The wind didn't feel any envy at this alien wind's presence. She knew that every wind had to turn into stone one day and be absorbed into stillness.

And certainly, it came.

The rain came riding the shoulders of winds from some other world. The rain was noiseless; it was wetting his head. The rain continued, drenching his head, and lice invaded his hair. He stood in the rubble, silent, with one leg stuck in the mud. He was somehow caught in the alien, dark wind. His red sweater, blue shirt and white canvas shoes seemed to have turned black. Even his eyes were filled with black wind. But not every decision is necessarily pronounced at the time of death. It can be declared later too. He stood on one foot, swaying in the black wind and getting drenched in the rain.

'Guddu Miyan has come! Guddu Miyan has come!'

The wind heard the sound of the cutting of the white sheet of still silence. It was the same sound that arises when you cut a sheet from a bolt of cloth with a sharp and ruthless pair of scissors. He wanted to wrap the two-metre-long scrap of the white and still silence around his body. He wanted to prepare an account of Death so that along with the entry of his name, he could in due course make entries concerning others. It was just like when one makes portions of roti and halwa. The rich sweet food, when prepared on ritual or other occasions, is made sacrosanct by saying prayers on it; the portions are then distributed among the deserving. So it was his portion to make: accounts of the deaths, so that he may not be treated as an absent absconder accused at the soon-to-be-set-up Court of Judgement, even if the court had no judge present.

'Guddu Miyan has come.'

The wind saw, with some joy and some grief, that his shadow, which was getting soaked in the rain, had recognized that child-like lisping tone this time. The wind silently heard the plodding steps of the dead. They were all going to come, their numbers couldn't be estimated by the sound of their feet.

Holding the old, rusted iron pipe with his left hand, he was standing at the same place, still and immovable, and his left leg was buried in the wet and slimy mud in such a fashion as if a hard, sturdy paste had been applied on it and a broken bone had been made entirely incapable of movement.

But the wind saw all this. She was the only eyewitness to this tragedy or comedy.

And if there had been a flash of lightning along with the rain, the wind would have been able to see that innumerable cockroaches had gathered on the crumbling walls of the kitchen. The court is in function.

The kitchen – it's a dangerous place.

# Part II
# Noise

My memory is a miracle. I remember everything – the only condition is that I should have seen it. Perhaps this is what is called optical memory. Although there's also some stuff I can't recall or can't clothe in words, for instance, I am aware of a dark world which you could call non-existence but I also think that this non-existence is merely a mistaken notion.

So I'm aware of that mistaken notion too, the shadows of a dark world, the objects there, which are like figures that quiver on the points of daggers and can never be seen. Maybe because the daggers have been used to gnaw lines on white paper?

And the eatables there, their aroma and their sweet, sour and bitter taste cause my intestines to experience a kind of distress which puts the left part of my brain in a state of dilemma.

I sometimes get fed up and try to get rid of this hassle, but my memory, that faithful dog, creeps upon me on tiptoe.

When I walked on streets as a kid, I often felt as if a dog was following me. It's only now that I have understood it's actually my memory.

Anyhow! A great many things have become clear now: the remembrance of death in life and the remembrance of life in death are mingled like spices in grilled chicken.

In any case, there's hardly a difference between life and death. You obtain in life whatever death has snatched from you and in the darkness of death you find all your lost stuff.

Which is why it doesn't make any difference whether you sprinkle the blood of living beings on the dead or the blood of the dead is spattered on those alive. You reach the same conclusion in both situations, which is, finding something after losing it or losing something after getting it.

An ordinary student of mathematics can form an equation from this. But it's very difficult to solve or prove this equation. This is an activity in which I'm constantly engaged and this equation keeps on expanding and getting longer like the devil's intestines. As far as I understand, the reason behind this is that, probably, humans have lost the road map of their spirit in this journey. At least this is what happened with me. I had kept the old and decaying road map of my spirit carefully in the pocket of my khaki pants during my childhood, but I don't know at which stage of my life and in which monsoon it decayed and turned into dust. I couldn't find it any more.

To get rid of my merciless memory, the faithful dog who would bother me constantly, I made this plan that I would suddenly turn back, catch hold of his collar and push him into the well of the novel. That is, I would place my memories into the mould of the novel and rid myself of this problem.

Me and the novel? It makes me laugh to think of it, but the fact is that I sometimes think of writing a novel. But, let alone a novel, I can't fabricate a story or even a single paragraph. One apparent reason for this being that I lack creativity and the second, perhaps more important, reason is that since childhood I've lacked any sense of grammatical rules. I can't distinguish between tenses. The remote past and the past perfect are the same for me. In fact, to my sensibility, the present and the past tense seem like twins. The same goes for the future, the future tense seems like past times to me. I managed my grammar tests during childhood by mugging it all up. I can at the most write the appeals or petitions of a case, and I tend to make mistakes over there too, which my clerk corrects later. If I hadn't been such a blockhead and so useless in this regard, I would surely have written a novel.

My novel would have been my home.

My house, my home.

Do you know which is the most dangerous portion of the house?

My tragedy is that on hearing the footsteps of my memory, frightened and uneasy, I'm running away. I live with those words which have yet not been written down. I throw my hands and feet about, walking in the din of those words as if I were deaf. I stumble in the darkness of my past and my forgotten faded memories.

Let it go, let everything go to hell.

I'm just not going to become a slave of words, in a world where every being is clouded over the life of another being like a deadly secret, writing about such a world and such people would have been an act of absurdity anyway.

Yes, but I do know about the true nature of human beings or I am aware of it, in fact, I would like to restrict this sense of their true nature to only awareness because the moment awareness turns into knowledge people fasten knowledge to their minds the way they secure pigs in a pen.

And this awareness is that human beings live inside their bowels. Their genitals are merely the possibility of their existence, the dwelling place of their shadows.

Mentally and spiritually, people live within their viscera. Flinging their viciousness, gluttony and appetites at each other's faces, their mouths slathered with the ugly red colour of hunger for swallowing up the other; it's a festival of colours, a Holi played with blood.

Blood?

Blood, the reek of which was in every circle, every triangle and every proposition of the geometry book I studied in my schooldays, like a secret sin, a grave error, which I could never resolve in my life.

And this is also a mysterious command that it is a human being's intestines that are his home.

Home?

Do you know the most dangerous place in the house?

Remember, Kitchen is the name of a dangerous and risk-laden place.

The kitchen is a dangerous place. Our house was somewhat like a mansion which had two halls. One inner, and the other outer. There was a veranda covered by a tin roof attached to the outer hall. Facing it was a large, wide, unpaved courtyard with a mango tree in it. It also had two rows of small plants and a sweet lime tree.

There were two tiny rooms attached to the outer hall, one in each direction. One room was full of trunks from unknown times in the past. The other room was full of books, most of which were old and tattered.

The tin roof of the veranda was supported by wooden pillars and curved wooden beams that had iron hooks fixed on them from which lighted lanterns were hung. To the east of the tin roof there was a hen coop and also a pigeon cote. There was a staircase close to the hen coop. There was nothing on the roof. Just low walls which became the playground for crows, doves and wild pigeons during the day and for stray cats during the night. We also had some pet cats at home.

The roofs, all made of small wooden beams, were in a state of disrepair and would leak at different places during the rains. Lizards and bats had made their homes in them too.

There was a handpump in the eastern part of the courtyard with a small tank under it. Clothes and utensils were constantly being washed there and wasps would collect there in the dry days of summer.

It was there right in front of the tap.

It – meaning Kitchen.

I had only ever known the wooden roof of the kitchen to be black from smoke. Even the cobwebs hanging from the beams had turned black and had a thick coat of dust and grime on them. Whenever they were cleaned with bamboo sticks (and this would happen once every few years), the cobwebs would fall to the ground like shreds of black cloth.

The spiders and lizards of the kitchen had also turned black, just like the women who spent a majority of their time there and because of this seemed more poisonous than they actually were.

The walls all around were black and so was every corner. But this sootiness created a feeling of familiarity and belonging. On rare occasions when the kitchen was painted with white chalk, the black continued to peep out from behind the chalk and emerge from its cover soon enough.

The floor of the kitchen was made of upright bricks which were coming off in places. It had crevices and holes which were inhabited by ants and centipedes. Sometimes baby snakes were seen disappearing into the crevices.

A forty-watt bulb hung from the centre of the ceiling on an electric wire. Our small town had been electrified but since the power situation was uncertain most of the time, a lantern would always be hanging on the frame of the kitchen door. I remember this lantern flickering most of the time. There was something wrong with it. It couldn't tolerate kerosene oil beyond a certain quantity and its chimney would often explode with a clatter. I don't know why, though the chimney was being changed very often, the lantern itself was never replaced. There was a problem either with its bottom part or the lantern had a quarrel with its own wick.

The electric wire that held the bulb had once been red in colour but it too had turned black later on. For some reason, flies were glued to it. There was a skylight on the southern wall of the kitchen which opened towards a palm tree. Sometimes, the leaves of the palm would peer into the kitchen or even try to enter it. These palm leaves were really great; the rain which leaked from the tin roof would pass over them and the water would acquire a different sound. The inanimate metal of tin and the living form of the leaves would engage in a music competition, a sad duet. When these palm leaves grew very big, they were sawed off the tree and thrown outside the house, where they would become interesting sport for the kids of the mohalla. One of them would seat themselves on this broad, green carpet-like leaf and other children would hold the stem and pull, dragging it on the road. I regret that I could never sit on the leaf.

The palm leaf and the kitchen are intermingled in my memory in such a way that talking about one without the other feels incomplete and is unsatisfactory, if not entirely impossible.

There was a brick screen on the wall on the other side which led to the staircase. If one sat on the fourth stair and looked inside the kitchen, it was like a black picture with a glowing red stain at its centre.

This was the chulha, plastered with pandol, a soft fine clay. Behind it, there was the aunla, a kind of hot hob. After cooking, dishes would be moved to the aunla which kept them warm. If the firewood was dry, it would burn with vigour but if it was moist, the entire kitchen would fill with smoke. The eyes of the women sitting in front of the stove would be watering all the time, dampening the black of the kitchen. After the food had been cooked, the stove would still contain hot ash. When it was scraped, the grey-coloured ash would reveal burning embers. Often the vessel containing milk would be left on the hot ash to keep it warm.

Our house did not ordinarily use cow-dung cakes for cooking which were used in somewhat poorer or lower-class households. But I loved the tea prepared on that chulha which used uplas or cow-dung cakes as fuel. The scent of milk in such tea felt very pure and motherly to me.

I've had such tea many times.

But we certainly had a sawdust stove in our kitchen. A man would appear every fortnight or so with a sack full of sawdust on his pushcart. He would heave it on to his back, bending almost double, and take it to the dark storeroom adjacent to the kitchen.

The stove required sawdust to be tightly stuffed into it, which was a very difficult and tricky affair. It wouldn't light up properly otherwise.

At a distance of two arm lengths, on the right, were a few masonry shelves which were used for storing utensils and spices for everyday use. Often there were rotten onions to be found there. In a corner there was a large brass basin for kneading the dough. A huge black iron griddle which seemed like the black sun to me was used to cook large round chapattis. The small-sized phulkas were not in vogue at that time, in fact, we looked down upon them.

The iron tongs and the blowing pipe could also be found lying here and there, close to the chulha. Both were black with soot and seemed to symbolize violence. There were many high and low wooden stools lying around on the floor which were used by the women to sit on and cook food. During winters everybody would sit on those stools and eat before the fire of the chulha.

The morning after Shab-e-Baraat – the festival of lights and prayers for the dead – when everybody in the house would come and sit on the wooden stools at breakfast time was truly a sight to behold. On enamel plates they would serve themselves heated-up halwa cooked the night before and eat it with chapattis, also from the previous night.

I forgot to tell you that in a corner of the kitchen there was a tiny dark room which was used to store grains, oil, ghee and other provisions. There was no electric bulb in it and one would require a lantern or a kerosene lamp to enter it even during the day.

The scene in the kitchen was one of disarray and chaos. If one were to think about it, there were not very many utensils or other handy tools for cooking there. Only the griddle, the blowing pipe, iron tongs, a stone slab for grinding, an iron mortar and pestle, along with some small and big spoons and ladles were all that were used. A piece of rag called saafi was used to handle hot vessels. Well, the saafi was so filthy, sooty and sticky that the women's fingers would often stick to it. In fact, experienced and skilled women would be able to lift the hottest of vessels off the chulha without the saafi. The skin of their fingers and palms had become hard and insensitive.

Most of the pots and pans were unsightly because their insides lacked the usual zinc polish. The coat of polish was always peeling off, either partially or completely, from most utensils. Most often, the pots, vessels and cauldrons were unpolished. As far as the utensils meant for eating food were concerned, all the plates in the kitchen were made of enamel, and so were the tea mugs. The good quality stuff was all kept inside a cupboard which stood in the veranda and would be brought out only when there was a formal lunch or dinner and then promptly washed and put back in their original place.

The chaos in the kitchen would heighten during dinners or festival days, particularly on the day of Eid when the brick floor was covered with china bowls of sewaiyan and the women of the household kept bumping into each other as they ran around in the kitchen anxiously, with the bottoms of their ghararas or salwars raised above the ground, jumping over the bowls.

Has anyone given serious thought to the fact that almost all the things in the kitchen have concealed within them the ability to turn into a weapon? Never mind if it is the knife used to cut vegetables, or the griddle, the iron tong, the blowing pipe, the burning block of wood, the lit-up chulha with the crackling, raging fire burning within it, the stone slab meant to grind spices, red chilli powder or the sizzling ash or simple kerosene. No other portion of the house had such things in such a large quantity. To the extent that the gun, hanging suspended on a nail on one of the walls of the outer hall, appeared insignificant and weak.

No other portion of the house contains such dangerous double-faced entities as those found in the kitchen and in no other section of the house do women appear so out of their wits, broken and envious, so full of violent energy and small-mindedness as they do in the kitchen.

The kitchen may be situated in any section of the house or face any direction, and however much the vastu shastra experts may give their solemn opinion on this, the quarrels of the kitchen do not cease. The kitchen is a battleground and the entire household, the whole clan or shall we say the entire human race's fortunes are decided in this small and seemingly pure and clean space. It's here that the court is held and the case fought. The whole house watches this game with silent eyes till the time the house itself turns into a ruin.

The hunger of human intestines and the two square meals of a day conceal a mysterious and frightening erotic charge. This charge moves only towards darkness and blood. And the final outcome is a vulgar and misleading covetousness. In the grip of its intoxication, dark, yellow and fair-coloured women, having become used to lifting hot vessels with their hard, insensitive hands in the kitchen, start behaving in the same way with the pots and pans as they behave with their husbands. Their men slowly begin transforming into big and small pots. All the women become extremely dominating and self-centred in the kitchen. The skin deadens. Women have sex with the pots and pans in the kitchen.

Despite priding myself so much on my good memory, I forgot to tell you that there was another problem with our house.

The kitchen in that house sometimes moved from its place and started creeping in all directions. Hanging from the wooden beam of the tin roof, a wicker or string food basket usually held the milk vessel (Sunbul's cage hung next to it, swinging). The food basket sometimes contained curry too.

A lantern hung at the other end of the wooden beam; it had a dim, sad glow. One could see the food basket swaying to and fro in the breeze and its shadow playing on the wall. At such times, vague and shadowy beings assembled mysteriously in the courtyard. On yet another hook, a hanging food basket had boiled meat. There was a wooden stool near a plant bed on which leftover chapattis were kept in a wicker basket. Used plates from the kitchen were in the little cistern under the water tap. There were no dogs in the house and they didn't worry about cats. After all, they were pure and clean animals.

The shapeless and unwieldy shadows of food, oscillating and trembling, somehow dematerialized themselves in a mysterious manner beyond their dark outlines. And there was a food cabinet too. On the inner side of the outer veranda, the food cabinet, which was aligned with the western wall, had a wire mesh on it that had turned black because of the dirt. The open spaces of the wire mesh were clogged with dust and grime. The wooden frame of the food cabinet was decaying in various places. The wood had been painted white at some point but even that whiteness had turned grey and blotchy.

The food cabinet had eggs, bread, large round biscuits and some fruits, mostly guavas and melons, in it. Apples and pomegranates were seldom seen and were meant only for the sick. I don't know why they chose to call it ne'mat khana, a container or small storage place for delicacies, creating the expectation of finding shahi tukda or phirni in it. But the ne'mat khana's fortunes were not bright enough to afford such goodies every day.

So it was food, food and only food. The whole house seemed to be constructed of onions, garlic, turmeric, dry coriander, hot spices and meat and bones rather than brick and mortar. The journey began in the kitchen and ended there too.

Emerging from the ashes and smoke of the chulha in the kitchen, all the love and affection, all the hatred, all kinds of attachment and all kinds of violence reached the outer and inner verandas, small rooms and doorways. The kitchen was that constructed text of humans which contained thousands of hidden meanings, in fact gave rise to them continuously.

Be it a wedding, a death or any other notable occasion, the kitchen had a singular role to play. It was in this space that festival offerings and prayers performed on food and dedicated to the holy ones had their most meaningful role. The gulgulas for all-night prayer ceremonies, puris for the Kunda festival, kheer, sewaiyan, the halwa for the dead were all obliged to this place for their taste and flavour.

The truth is that the rest of the house seemed weak and

helpless compared to the kitchen. It was the centre of power and strength. The contemporary kitchens of modern times don't seem to display any connection with the grand but frightful tradition of the primordial kitchen.

History bears witness to the fact that right from the times of Chandragupta Maurya to the end of the Mughal empire, the role of the cooking station has been secret but crucial in establishing or ruining dynasties. Even the Buddha's death was caused by a piece of bad meat given to him in alms.

The kitchen is connected to the process of cooking food, and food is connected to the human intestine as well as to hunger and slovenliness. Have you ever considered that speech organs, just like sex organs, perform two functions?

The mouth, tongue, palate and jaws chew the food. The taste of the food, its touch and aroma and its chewing, reducing it into tiny pieces and then throwing it into the gut after swallowing it is all dependent on the mercy of these organs.

Humans also speak with the help of these organs. It is these parts of the body that have endowed human beings with the power of speech. But why?

Why only these parts? Why not the eyes and the ears and the nose? Could it be that food too is a savage language unable to articulate itself, and hunger its meaning?

If there is one universal language in the world, it is hunger. These organs don't differentiate between chewing and speaking a tongue. Both these deeds deliver to them the same kind of satisfaction and satiation. One at the biological level and the other at the cultural level.

But no, what is being and what is culture – these are all rumours that have been spread by enemies. The real thing must be something completely different, and whatever it is, it must be macabre.

I could sense a strange and alien odour coming from the kitchen from my childhood. This smell was a result of frying turmeric, onions, garlic and chilli in mustard oil to add flavour and spice to the food, yet it was different. It was heavier, which is why the molecules of this smell formed a separate layer for themselves. It wasn't possible for them to dissolve in the smell of all those items.

What was that strange and unfamiliar smell?

Now that I'm almost an old man, it has dawned on me that the smell was that of predators and other beasts.

The kitchen was a huge circus tent after all.

Living life like a clown in this circus tent amid animal odours, I gradually lost the scent of my spirit.

I still live with certain animals perhaps. Though their ringmaster doesn't exercise control over me, I obey him. I am familiar with his face as well as his whip.

I'm spending my time with animals. My bread and butter lies with them as does my piss and shit.

I can't run away from them or from the kitchen. No one can. Humans don't go anywhere. All things come to them, just like the coming morrow. The tomorrow to come may perhaps not be for the body empty of intestines and liver.

This Hindu thought keeps striking me time and again, that the stomach is also a kind of sacred and holy furnace like the one into which we throw foodgrains. And hunger is a fire. You need food to quench the fire in the stomach. Eating is equivalent to a yajna.

I want to tell you that I shy away from metaphor. I like simile.

We were a strange kind of exemplary joint family. Everyone except my parents lived in our home. My mother had chronic tuberculosis and passed away a few months after I was born. My father was a policeman. I must have been about two years old when he was killed by a bullet while fighting some dacoits. So why talk about my parents; they are like a closed book with its content locked beyond access.

There was no dearth of members in the household, especially of cousins via paternal uncles, maternal uncles, paternal aunts and maternal aunts. Apart from my paternal grandparental family, my maternal grandparental family also seemed to be living there. I don't know the circumstances under which several members from my maternal grandma's household, like my maternal uncle and aunt, also came to live in the house I call my own. Who the house belonged to or in whose name it was registered were unknown to me, and never did I feel the need to find out. Who was rearing and tending me, who was responsible for my care and education, I don't know that either. Our land in the village stretched across acres and we got such a large quantity of foodgrains and other such produce from it that there wasn't enough space in the house to store them properly.

I could count and tell you the exact number of family members that lived in the house, agreed though that I have a wonderful memory, but why put it under strain? If one were to forcibly collect so many pictures in a tiny part of the brain and then count them by name, it would not benefit the pictures or the brain. It would be better to listen to the footsteps of the faithful dog which is following me, ignoring other unnecessary sounds.

Anjum Baji was my cousin from my mother's side. She must have been at least ten years older than me. She was probably the one who loved me the most in the teeming household. Up until I was six or seven, she carried me in her arms to the parrot's cage hanging from the iron ring of the wooden beam in the ceiling of the outer hall and say to the parrot, 'See, Guddu Miyan has come, Guddu Miyan has come.'

The parrot, Sunbul, was very talkative and excellent at mimicry. Sunbul observed us silently for two to three minutes, his eyes rolling, and then said in his childish, lisping, non-human voice, 'Guddu Miyan has come, Guddu Miyan has come.'

Anjum Baji handed me a green chilli and said, 'Here, feed Sunbul a chilli.'

He continued to look at us even as he held the chilli in his beak. Then Anjum Baji carried me close to the water tap and showed me the mud homes being made by the wasps on the wall adjacent to it.

Anjum Baji was a fair-complexioned, slim and delicate-looking girl. Not just then, but much later in those weak and mean moments of anger, when I tried to undress her in my imagination, I found myself completely unable to do so. Probably there was no corporeal body under her clothes, or maybe the moment her clothes were taken off the parameters of her body turned to smoke and drifted away.

Her body had a certain pale goldenness. Whatever the colour of her dress, it always seemed to me that her pale golden body was reflected through it in some mysterious way.

Sometimes you see only one quality in someone. After all, the eyes suffer from their own stupidities or unique tragedies.

My eyes could never see her eyes or her nose or her lips clearly, and as far as the portion below her neck is concerned, I did find the curves under her dupatta alluring, but the sight was as mundane as it was enticing. It is the difference that exists between man and woman, just as a chair is distinct from a table or a book from a grinding slab. Therefore, there was no curiosity in me regarding the curves of her breasts. You must remember, nothing definitive can be said about sexual matters.

And so all I could see was her fair, bright, neat and clean colour. I don't know if she was beautiful or ordinary. Why should I place my memory under duress? I wanted to remain in the embrace of her colour. How I wish that clean golden colour was not stuck upon Anjum Baji's skin. How I wish that hue would be independent of her, in some empty space, or in the air, or in the sky, and then the blackness of my sins would not have been so heavy. There would have been some sparkle in it.

I had fallen in love with Anjum Baji when I was a boy in shorts and hadn't even sprouted pubic hair, but I can say with confidence that the nature of my love was no different from the love of youth, or even that of a lusty old man, like raw meat not yet marinated in spices or been put into the cooking pot to boil.

There is a marked and dangerous difference between love and hate. The features of the face of love, its body, its contours and its details are not retained in the memory, but hate always maintains a body and a face.

I hated Aftab Bhai. Right from the beginning, never mind the treats of toffees and sweets he may have given me. Aftab Bhai was tall and strapping; he was fair-complexioned too, but that fairness was not like Anjum Baji's pure, pale golden fairness. The whiteness of his skin concealed a shade of red. Such whiteness is always patchy from within and smeared with the murkiness of violence. One may find this out only later.

His eyes were brown and cruel, and his mouth resembled that of a bulldog's. He considered all this to be the pride of his aristocratic family and a sign of his masculinity.

Aftab Bhai was Anjum Baji's cousin, her paternal aunt's son, so how was I related to him? I don't know, it is all very confusing. It is puzzling how so many cousins had gathered in this house.

Aftab Bhai did not have any quality that was independent of his body. He was a glutton and was always eating something, immediately after which he pressed a cigarette between his fingers and started inhaling deeply and continuously. One knew he was around by the smell of cigarettes.

My hatred for Aftab Bhai increased manyfold when I realized Anjum Baji's breath smelt the same.

I was growing in size, or one could say that the percentage of age was increasing in my body, causing it to gradually move towards old age or destruction.

Anjum Baji no longer carried me in her arms. My thighs had outgrown my shorts. I was growing fat and most of my time was spent in the kitchen. One day I was in the kitchen eating the previous day's chapatti with ghee and sugar when, from the fourth stair through the brick screen of the kitchen, I saw Aftab Bhai feeding Anjum Baji some cake.

The chapatti fell from my hands.

Anjum Baji was chewing. It was probably the first time I

ever saw her mouth open. She was swallowing the cake quickly, nervously. I saw the movement of her throat muscles for the first time. Intense grief and anger engulfed me.

It was a blazing May afternoon. The hot winds entering the kitchen from the staircase through the screen were weeping in bursts. I felt a kind of fear of Aftab Bhai, and also a sense of sadness at my failure to acknowledge that Anjum Baji's stomach too had intestines. I had eaten pulao cooked by her innumerable times. She cooked a very refined pulao, the colour of which resembled her own colour. And I ate the light curry she cooked with fanfare, serving myself in the white enamel plate. The day it was Anjum Baji's turn to cook, I abandoned my studies and loitered around the kitchen. It seemed like the most beautiful place on earth when Anjum Baji cooked. The griddle laughed colourful sparks when Anjum Baji made chapattis.

I had seen Anjum Baji eating countless times, but for some reason, I had never registered that her body (if she had a body) also contained a gut.

But on that day, that hot and deserted burning May afternoon, when the eagle was abandoning its egg in the skies, God knows from where, intestines appeared in Anjum Baji's stomach. For a moment, Aftab Bhai seemed to me that hateful eagle flying with a rotting piece of gut pressed in its beak.

This putrid bit of gut could drop on any neat and clean place or on some pure and clean human body. I sat near the hot ashes in the kitchen and began to cry.

I heard their hushed voices.

'Guddu Miyan is in the kichen,' Anjum Baji said.

'That fool is getting fatter and fatter. Why does everyone call him Guddu Miyan? His name is Hafeez and he should be called by that name.' Aftab Bhai laughed.

'He's still a kid, a child with no parents – he's Guddu, Guddu Miyan.' Anjum Baji's tone was affectionate.

'He's a kid . . . what can I say now, the other day when he was sleeping, I saw . . .' Either Aftab Bhai spoke too softly or allowed the sentence to go unfinished.

'Shame on you!' Anjum Baji spoke angrily.

There was complete silence after this. I was still sitting near the hot ashes from the chulha with my head bent. I wasn't crying any more. My ears were completing the lewd content of Aftab Bhai's incomplete sentence.

This is why I had said that hate has a body. And a face too. I am compelled to go on analysing my memories. After all, the body has aged and the cells of the brain, becoming weak, have begun to fade.

Aftab Bhai had become a rope of hatred with which I was bound. I cast plaintive looks at Anjum Baji like a wild animal tied with this rope. She couldn't make sense of anything, or pretended ignorance deliberately. It was around that time that she knitted a red sweater for me. I have never worn that sweater till date. It lies locked in the black iron trunk. I had come to know through hearsay that the trunk belonged to my parents.

I began to spend more time with my schoolbooks and did not go to Anjum Baji all the time.

I occasionally went to the parrot's cage and stood before it, depressed. The parrot observed me for a while, his eyes rolling, and then started chattering loudly, 'Guddu Miyan has come, Guddu Miyan has come.'

My eldest maternal uncle said that the mohalla in which the house was located had been built on a graveyard. This was the reason almost every home had a grave under it. If there was ever a chance that a house had to be dug deep, the labourer's spade was sure to hit some skeleton or the other. This was nothing unusual for the inhabitants of the mohalla. They had become accustomed to it.

Cemented graves, at whose heads good-for-nothing boys would lounge all day creating a din, could be seen in the streets too. People sat on those graves and gambled at night. Some graves were considered holy and people offered special chadors on them every Thursday. There was scented smoke from incense sticks and frankincense, roasted flower-like rice and batashas and qawwalis. Every household indulged in holy offerings and charity in the name of saints, and those who belonged to the other sect were categorically unwelcome here.

On the other side, after a long line of farming fields, was the mohalla where those belonging to the other sect lived. No one from that side could cross over and dare to offer namaz in one of our mosques, nor could anyone from our side go to their mosques. Several houses in our mohalla had girls who remained unmarried and grew old and shrivelled. It was preferred that these girls stay unmarried if a suitable match was not found among people of their own creed rather than have them married into households from the other sect.

Our family was one such household. Noorjahan Khala, Sarwat Phuphi, Shaheen Baji and God knows who all remained unmarried. Although I don't know much about these things, their old age must certainly have been miserable for them.

The house was always noisy, except for summer afternoons and that part of the night when it contained muffled voices. There was a deluge of female, male, young and old voices echoing in the house. There were no children's voices. I was the only child there, but at the time that I'm talking about even my voice would not have been a child's. In any case, I never regarded myself as a child. The kitchen and Anjum Baji's lap had made me aware of the existence of a malicious and dangerous male within me.

Every Thursday there would be a fateha between the time of Asr and Maghrib and invariably a mutton curry was cooked for it. Most of the time it was Bade Mamu who made the offering, with a towel covering his head. Sometimes Anjum Baji or Noorjahan Khala or Sarwat Phuphi did the cooking on Thursdays. Wives of my maternal uncles, the Mumanis, their daughters and some maids too could be seen doing something or the other in the kitchen. But a few special dishes, which were prepared on Thursdays with great care and respect, were the responsibility of Anjum Baji, Sarwat Phuphi and Noorjahan Khala.

Bade Mamu believed that every Thursday evening, before the Maghrib prayers, the spirits of our ancestors sit on their graves and wait for the food offerings. And the spirits of those who have been forgotten by their loved ones and do not receive any offerings undergo much sorrow and pain. Bade Mamu also said that at some time or the other on Thursdays the spirits of all the dead people of a household make a visit to the house.

I would sit near Bade Mamu at the time of the fateha. The curry kept in the serving bowls wasn't fully visible due to the smoke from the incense. One could hardly see anything clearly at that time. The two parts of the day were converging and the entire atmosphere was clouded in an unexplainable haze. I felt sorrowful when I heard the Maghrib call to prayer. There was sadness all around and I thought about the dead people sitting on their graves waiting for their food. Who all were there? Were my parents there too?

But amazingly, after a short while, this scene silently slipped into oblivion and the lantern on the wooden beam began to burn brightly. The whole house turned chirpy and the kitchen was flooded with the sound of clinking bangles.

I only liked the food cooked by Anjum Baji's hands.

Hands?

Hands have personalities of their own. I have come to know this only now – hands acquire the power of manifestation even before a person's brain does. Every finger has its own tale to tell. No other part of the human body has such a compact set of bones in it.

Hands are separate from the being, at times even strange and unfamiliar to the mind and the brain and the body. This is the reason different hands cook food that differs in taste, aroma as well as appearance. The kitchen was a museum of the movements and pauses of these hands.

I remember that we had once hired a chef. He used to peel garlic with his feet and everyone watched him in awe and amazement. However, when he expressed the desire to cook food with his feet, not one person approved of the idea. Food is a pure and clean entity. It should be treated with due respect, even if it becomes impure the moment it reaches the large intestine and transforms into a heap of shit.

The chef felt insulted, more so for his art. He immediately quit his job, but before leaving he said it was a pity they didn't know that sometimes people's hands descend into their feet. This could also be an illness, like when one's intestines sometimes get dislodged. Therefore, I am compelled to repeat that hands occupy a mysterious world of their own. They can perform any action. They can go anywhere, they can stroke someone's hair, wipe someone's tears and land a slap on someone's cheek. Hands can even commit murders.

Inside the kitchen, the same thing, never mind if it was the same jar of salt or dry coriander, was kept at the same place in a different manner by different hands. Red chilli powder or turmeric, each hand used them in a distinct fashion, be it the opening or the closing of jars, or just putting them away. If one hand were to sweep the brick floor, there might be some litter left behind. But another might make the floor shine like a mirror. Every hand had its own show and spectacle, and every show prided over its actors, and these actors were the hands.

The kitchen was a parallel world and the women fought among themselves to rule over it. They screamed and shouted and even attacked each other with kitchen utensils, and later wept or threatened to fling the hot ashes of the chulha into each other's hair. The hands on which bangles jingled turned into fists taking aim in the air. They were each other's friends, they were each other's enemies.

This little world of the kitchen was the scene of a pitched battle.

The men of the house were unaffected by this battle. They believed that if there were pots and pans, surely they would clash and collide. They were extremely proud of their ancestral zamindari, even if it had been snatched away, their ownership of land, their superior family background and the age-old tradition of the joint family system. They had no knowledge of the mysterious world of the kitchen. They were ignorant of scorched hands, numb knees and clouded eyes.

I was the only witness to the tamasha of the kitchen. I was a witness to the court set up there every day, and I had to stand in its witness box as the accused one day.

One can't escape one's destiny. Destiny walks up to you. Your jaw drops open in surprise to see your destiny appear before you, like an apparition that has sprung out of winding paths and blind alleys. Your feet turn to stone.

By the time I was twelve or thirteen, I developed an addiction for Urdu detective novels. Urdu popular fiction was at its height in the 1960s. I became a victim of this trend in literature thanks to Bade Mamu. I lapped up all kinds of romances as well because of my love for detective fiction. I also became fond of films. Though I seldom got to watch a film, we got film magazines regularly at home. Then there was the radio that played film songs most of the time.

Detective novels, cheap romantic fiction and four-anna movies and their songs have played a major role in shaping my personality.

Coming out of the house, if one were to turn left, there were three or four graves which were in a state of disrepair, and beyond them was Anjum Apa's house. Anjum Apa was a distant relative who was eight or nine years older than me. Her family had less money than ours and her kitchen was pretty small. It did not have an additional room and utensils were few. They mostly used cow-dung cakes to light the chulha. They also had a rusted and unwieldy kerosene stove. There was an abundance of kerosene oil at Anjum apa's place as her father was the owner of a government-approved ration shop which sold kerosene oil, along with wheat, rice and low-cost dress materials at subsidized rates. Those days were not like our present materialistic times and that small-sized city had many such shops.

Anjum Apa was quite interested in films and detective novels too. She borrowed novels and magazines at two annas from the mohalla library or the local shops. I began to get novels on rent for her from Mehboob Novel House. I'd spend a major part of my afternoon with her in her kitchen as both of us had similar tastes. She often prepared tea for me with the milk from her goat. Tea prepared on a chulha using cow-dung cakes seemed closer to nature, but destiny? Yes, my destiny was creeping towards me slowly. I don't know if it was the excessive reading of detective novels or something else that caused the development of a sixth sense in me. I had the dreadful revelation of the presence of a dangerous ability in me.

My intestines were the first to give me a signal of this dangerous ability, or shall we call it frightful knowledge? The grease of the intestines which came out of my mouth. Was that grease a blessing or a curse? I can't decide with certainty, but I have been repaying that blessing or curse with the interest accrued up until now.

I was quite weak at math and could understand neither numbers nor geometrical figures, or their relationships, ratios and entanglements. But this was a different kind of math. A problem whose solution required different kinds of dishes to convert themselves into geometrical shapes. The kitchen was that wretched space where this knowledge or sixth sense would begin to get ridiculous and unexplainable clues about disease and those suffering from the disease would begin to surface.

All this started one day after an incident in Anjum Apa's kitchen. This mysterious ability of mine came to light because of an unpolished cooking pot without a lid kept on the floor of Anjum Apa's kitchen.

I was talking to Anjum Apa about the latest detective novel to appear in the market as she sat by the chulha preparing tea. The haziness of dusk had begun to spread. One couldn't see anything clearly in the kitchen due to the smoke rising from the cow-dung cakes. The December evening outside had joined hands with the fog, its eternal friend. The only thing one could see clearly in the kitchen were the shadows of lizards. Despite the biting cold the walls were full of lizards who were almost as good as dead because of the low temperature. They were in the kitchen probably due to the heat of the chulha in the kitchen. Nevertheless, this was something strange and unbelievable.

There was a small weather-beaten aluminium vessel on the chulha's burner. There was no lid on it. The vessel contained milk. Anjum Apa extended her hand to pick up the vessel and poured a small quantity of the milk into the pan containing tea.

She said, 'I don't know why the milk turns slightly blue every day. This milkman is getting us really watery milk. I'll give him a piece of my mind tomorrow.'

I let out a loud scream just as Anjum Apa put the milk vessel on the floor.

There was a fat black lizard floating in the milk.

Anjum Apa too let out a scream.

Everyone at home came rushing to the kitchen.

'There are so many lizards here, blind girl, can't you see? All the utensils lie around uncovered all the time.' It was a woman speaking, but I felt as if the lizard floating in the milk had said this.

I recalled that I had had tea in Anjum Apa's kitchen yesterday too. In fact, I had had tea twice and she had mentioned the bluishness of the milk yesterday as well.

I came back home shivering and shuddering. I was sweating despite the severe cold and felt extremely nauseous. Soon I was dizzy.

If I remember anything after this, it is that I threw up again and again. It was so severe that I've lost count of how many times I vomited or how long it lasted. Exhausted, I had begun vomiting while lying on the bed by turning my face to the ground. I made unsuccessful attempts to see my face in the vomit. I didn't eat anything for very long. Bitter and vitriolic-tasting medicines were pushed down my throat. I felt as if my intestines would jump out of my throat and be strewn on the floor. There was a fierce anger in my intestines, and they had gone mad with rage. I heard them grumbling in anger. They threw their oiliness at me again and again. They cursed me and wished me ill in the course of their non-stop muttering.

I gradually became oblivious of time and the world and whatever was in it. The pain in my ribs rendered me unconscious. There was no night or day, morning or evening. I was rocking in the cradle of death.

When I regained consciousness, it was the beginning of a new life, or so people say. I was a kid who had played the dangerous game of touching the wall of death to come running back. I couldn't recognize myself in the mirror. I was a heap of disproportionate and pointed bones. The skin on my body had turned yellow and was peeling off at places. I looked shorter. I was in the throes of an attack of frightening dryness.

My memory was kicked around aimlessly in the winter winds like a dry leaf. I wondered, which age am I in? I searched for myself in all the three tenses described in the grammar book and found myself absent.

However, one day as I stood near the kitchen staircase, watching the December fog aimlessly, shortly before the Maghrib call to prayer, I felt as if my intestines whispered something in my ear. A kind of knowledge, like a mathematical formula, a principle of grammar.

But this utterance of my intestines didn't just stick to the ears; I saw it emerge from my ears and transform into a white light before freezing on the fog which enveloped the boundary wall of the house.

I felt very light for a moment, weightless like the wind or the light. I felt a distinct change in me, as if the tick-tock of the old, dusty clock hanging on the wall had suddenly grown very loud.

Something within me, my mind and my body had certainly changed. Who knows what had been poured out of my body through my countless vomiting bouts, but the winds outside had also brought in a mysterious ghostly entity and buried it in the depths of my being.

Some kind of strength had come into me. After all, weakness and loss of stamina were nothing but precursors of a new ability and power.

But my sixth sense told me that this power carried ill omen and was dangerous. I got the feeling that whatever it was, it would prove to be the prophecy of a painful curse for me. Yes! A painful curse without doubt!

I came back to my times. I saw my elusive memory reappear before me in solid form and I caught hold of it, as if to safekeep it in the spaces of my mind. At that moment the parrot spoke loudly from his cage, 'Guddu Miyan is here, Guddu Miyan is here, Guddu Miyan is here.'

Winter was over. It was March. The house was covered in heaps of dead yellow leaves. The gloomy blasts of the dry March winds caused the leaves to collect in the kitchen since it was in the eastern section of the house and these winds came from the west.

One of those afternoons I was seated on the fourth step of the staircase and peering into the kitchen. The staircase was full of fallen dead leaves that were crackling under my feet.

I heard a noisy rustle in the leaves on the stairs behind me. I turned to look. It was a tiny white rabbit with black ears, one of which was mutilated. There was no fear or furtiveness in the rabbit's red eyes, and he made me feel as if he had known me forever.

The fact of the matter was that the neighbours who used to live behind our house had moved. They had kept a pair of rabbits as pets. Anjum Baji would often lift me up when we were on the terrace to show me the pair of rabbits running around in their courtyard. The rabbits had a baby, and when our neighbours moved they took the rabbit pair with them but left the baby rabbit behind, abandoning him to the empty house. Noorjahan Khala had told me just a few days ago that the baby rabbit had come out of the drain of the house and was attacked by a stray dog. Though he managed to survive, he had lost a part of one ear.

It was that rabbit who had come to me after wandering in countless places, passing through dirty narrow and wide drains to save himself. He was now sitting on the steps of the brick staircase that was covered with dead leaves.

I picked him up and placed him on my lap. He had a festering wound in the torn ear.

I stroked the rabbit's head softly. He rubbed his snout on my leg in affection and with great familiarity.

I could see what was happening in the kitchen through the screen.

Sarwat Mumani was cooking something on the stove, with a copy of the cookbook *Rashida's Dastarkhwan* in her hands.

Every woman in our family could be seen carrying *Rashida's Dastarkhwan* or *Rashida's Embroidery Skills* in her hands those days.

I had come to know from Anjum Apa that Anjum Baji was getting married soon. This was possibly why various kinds of delicacies were being tried out in the kitchen.

Sarwat Mumani, her glasses firmly perched on her nose, flipped the pages of the cookbook till she arrived at the page she wanted to read. The ill-fitting spectacles with huge lenses slipped from her nose again.

I began to wonder about the dish for which she was reading the recipe – what was it? I descended the steps and entered the kitchen. The rabbit followed me.

Sarwat Mumani was a great cook, but the grains of the rice cooked by her were always a bit hard and uncooked. She could be cooking plain rice or biryani, she always took the vessel off the stove before the rice reached its proper level of steaming, resulting in the most attractive rice with each grain distinct like a white pearl, but painful to eat. Since Sarwat Mumani was quite ill-tempered, no one dared to say anything to her.

It was a curious scene. The day the rice turned out slightly uncooked, you could find everyone in the house walking around chewing coconut flesh like domestic animals chewing the cud. This was because hakims considered coconut the antidote to undercooked rice.

If there was one thing Achhan Dadi was wary of eating, it was hard and undercooked rice, otherwise she could gobble up and digest trotter, kidney, liver, lung, fatty meat and even the head without a belch. 'Move the jaws, avoid a thousand troubles,' she said.

But the same Achhan Dadi, chewing on coconut after eating the undercooked rice, mumbled, 'Point of broken rice, point of lance.' I find it ridiculous when I recall how all the members of the family quietly ate semi-cooked but evenly spread-out rice and walked around the courtyard trying to digest it by chewing coconut. Point of broken rice, point of lance.

But what exactly is the point of a lance? Only I knew then, and only I know now. I even know the ironsmith who had melted and moulded it.

'What are you cooking?'

Sarwat Mumani was a bad-tempered woman. She didn't reply.

'What are you cooking?' I asked again.

'Karela stuffed with minced meat,' she replied indifferently and focused her attention on the recipe book.

The oil in the vessel on the stove was burning and the few garlic cloves frying in it had turned black. The oil had begun to froth. A whitish froth which made me uneasy.

Sarwat Mumani began reading aloud as if she were mugging a lesson.

| | |
|---|---|
| 'Karela | 10 pieces |
| Finely minced meat | half a kilo |
| Oil of yellow mustard | half a kilo |
| Nagpuri onions | 2 kilo |
| Hot spices | 15 gm |
| Cashew nuts | 20 pieces |
| Raisins | 20 gm |
| Musk melon seeds | 15 gm |
| Chiraunji nuts | 25 gm |
| Red chillies | 10 gm |
| Turmeric | 20 gm |
| Coriander | 15 gm |
| Garlic paste | 50 gm |
| Ginger paste | 50 gm |
| Salt | as desired |

Peel the karela and immerse in water for some time. If the minced meat is greasy, try to remove the fat particles manually. The minced meat should be very fine . . .'

Sarwat Mumani was reading the recipe again and again as if to memorize it quickly. But I did not hear anything beyond this. I felt something happen to me. I was beginning to feel strangely ill. I couldn't bear to remain in the kitchen any longer.

The mango tree in the courtyard was shaking violently. Many of its leaves fell on my head when I went and stood under its shade.

My heart too was trembling like a dry leaf.

I understood a little later that my heart, which was trembling like a leaf, was trying to communicate something to me in its tongue. It was warning me, and I had understood this weird language of my heart.

'Not today, karela stuffed with minced meat should not be cooked today. This is not a good omen. This dish is a risky one for today. God knows the result of this.'

Slowly I was convinced that cooking that dish at that time could become the cause of some unfortunate events.

The food was prepared and eaten with relish. I ate it myself, but the feeling of unease was constant. A greasy light which had emerged from my intestines continued to dance before my eyes like a blot of shine.

It must have been around five-thirty in the evening when a commotion erupted in the house opposite ours and Babbu's hysterical shrieks shook the mohalla. Babbu's screams were a common affair and his family as well as the neighbours were used to his wild screams. Babbu's life story was weird.

He used to be a very stubborn and mischievous kid. One day when he was creating havoc in the kitchen, he escaped his mother's eye and sat down on the lit angithi.

From a poor family, he didn't wear briefs, even though he was six or seven years old. His pain was such that he couldn't even cry. It was as though his crying turned into an unending scream. His little innocent genitalia got completely burnt. His lower body was scorched.

But he didn't die, he stayed alive. People sometimes escape death.

They despise and reject a small-time and minor kind of death to embrace a respectable one.

Babbu was forty now. He had become insane after that incident. He roamed about the house naked and emitted such shrieks as if he was still sitting on a glowing angithi.

His mother had died long ago and his father, a carpenter, was sick and tired of his life as well as Babbu's.

Babbu was a subject of entertainment for the people of the mohalla. The mohalla urchins peeped into his house and shouted 'Babbu Angithi, Babbu Angithi' at him and ran away. Babbu's wild shrieks grew louder and his father chased after the children with a saw or a drill in his hand, swearing at them. The kids hid behind the scattered graves over there. The women of the mohalla also talked about his burnt sexual organs with relish and delight.

That day Babbu's hysterical screams were very loud. Extraordinarily loud. There was a din in the mohalla and people had collected at his house. Then the screams ceased abruptly, as if a mighty storm had suddenly subsided.

I ran to the terrace. One could get a clear view of Babbu's house from there. People were banging loudly at the door which was locked from inside. A mob of men and women broke it open and made their way into the house.

After some time we came to know that Babbu's father had strangled Babbu to death in frustration and then severed his own neck with the saw he used to chop wood. I remember a brownish liquid trickling through a drain. Though I could not at the time, now I can say with certainty that the liquid was blood seeping from the mutilated head.

The entire lane was filled with khaki-clad policemen in no time. I came down from the terrace. Everyone was busy talking about this incident. I wanted to go and look at Babbu Angithi but I was not allowed. I regret that I never saw Babbu Angithi from close quarters. I had seen him only once in my whole life when he had somehow slipped out of his house and the street lads were throwing clods of earth at him. He didn't scream at that time. He was wearing a filthy torn vest, the only piece of clothing he had on. I looked at the lower part of his body carefully and saw that there was nothing but a silent and deadly whitishness there.

I couldn't sleep that night. I was gripped by an unfathomable feeling of terror. In fact, the feeling of terror loomed over the house and the mohalla as well. My foreboding had turned true; in fact, my 'knowledge' had proved to be completely right. I became fully convinced that the reason for that day's incident was the cooking of the karela stuffed with minced meat in my family's kitchen.

I felt so terrified of this dangerous ability that I trembled in fear of the perception of it.

The secret of the frightful ability which had taken root in me after the continuous vomiting was finally revealed to me. Food and its different varieties were like complicated and difficult theorems of algebra which I could solve in the wink of an eye.

In those days I didn't know that the sphere we call earth began as an insignificant dot. I know for a fact now that the world is actually a dot made with a slate-coloured pencil on a white sheet of paper.

Talking about the shape and magnitude acquired by that dot and its expansion like the devil's intestines would be a complete waste of time.

Although the world is not some indecipherable puzzle for me, the people inhabiting this world are, I myself being one.

I have no interest in the expansion of a meaningless dot in a meaningless manner. It is like a disease, a kind of cancer. But the grey envelope of infinite volume that has formed within the dot is the place where men and women live. Animals live in it, insects live in it, and children too, if you please. And in the same world where there are mountains, volcanoes, seas, forests, rivers and deserts, there within the dot, there is a kitchen too. The kitchen is the name of, as I keep repeating (because I like repeating myself and so does the world), an extremely frightening and unpleasant place, yet it has an erotic charge for human intestines. The eroticism of the human intestines is even more alarming than the eroticism contained in the genitalia. And who knows if it is the satanic kitchen that has aided and abetted most in the expansion and enlargement of this insignificant dot. These days I seem to get all omens of the inauspicious future from nowhere else but the kitchen.

Therefore, despite having no interest in the growth, expansion or destruction of the world, I want to go and attach myself to this dot like a bloodthirsty louse. This is the reason I have always made efforts to reach that dot made on the paper. Like a cell that has been separated from its body, I want to fly around and observe the way the world treats humans. Or, how humans have cheated the world. Sadly, my memory doesn't go beyond my childhood and then I get into such a dangerous dilemma that the result is nothing but a severe headache.

My childhood?

I don't want to go back to my childhood once more so that I may live it again, rather I want to understand it. The way children want to break open their old toys to understand how the clockwork monkey lifts the bottle of milk and places it on its lips.

My childhood? Where is it hiding?

I tried to shave off the layers of my aged and discoloured skin to recover my lost memories with the sharp-edged blades of Mohammed Rafi songs from the 1960s again and again. I used the sharp-edged scissors of Ibn-e Safi novels to cut into pieces the thick threads made of jute which bound and concealed the memories I was searching for. I continued to hold conversations of yesteryear with old friends, but despite my memory aching for what I had lost, I couldn't find my childhood the way I wanted to. Though it was somewhere within me. Under my skin, in my bone marrow, stuck somewhere, like a broken piece of a plastic ball lying in some remote corner of the house. When I focus my attention on these broken pieces of my childhood, I realize that a certain kind of maliciousness was gradually taking birth in me. A dangerous kind of malice, which had a low-grade violence hidden in it. An unexplainable desire to cause suffering often rose in me. For instance, I often felt like poking a needle into someone sitting close to me, or spitting quietly into the food someone was cooking, or roaming around doing other such mean and unnatural deeds.

I'd like to talk about a particular incident as an example. I had noticed that Sarwat Mumani had begun to grow a little too familiar with Feroz Khalu. On the other hand, the quarrels between Bade Mamu and Sarwat Mumani had begun to grow more frequent and intense, to the extent that Bade Mamu had beaten Sarwat Mumani with his slipper one night. I was glad, since Sarwat Mumani was a very ill-tempered woman, and even though she had no children of her own, I always felt that she disliked me. There must have been some reason behind this of which I am ignorant. One should not get obsessed with reasons and causes. Rather, one should observe the flow of things and wait for further developments. Although I could not stick to this very useful principle myself.

That evening the aroma from the kitchen was of the spice paste in which fish is roasted. I am very fond of fish cooked in its typical paste of spices, but my sixth sense had warned me that cooking fish on this particular evening was not a good omen. Anything bad could happen to anyone. But I ate the fish with great relish that night. The fish had been cooked by Sarwat Mumani. If Anjum Baji had cooked it, the pleasure of its taste would have been even more. Dinner was had peacefully and no unpleasant incident took place. My sixth sense also retired to sleep.

It was probably early April. There was a small veranda to the side of the outer hall, the ceiling of which was made of wooden logs and beams. Bees were building their hives everywhere in and around them those days. There was a huge hive on one particular wooden beam of the veranda. A golden brown hive, built with extreme finesse and care, which could swing like a chandelier from the ceiling. No one dared disturb it.

The posterior skylight of the kitchen looked right into the veranda. The hive was clearly visible through it. It must have been around two in the night. I was lying awake, a little restless. My family lay asleep, scattered in different places around the house. I felt an urge to eat something sweet. I was in the habit of eating sweets late at night, quietly, which required my going into the kitchen. Thinking I could gulp down some sugar if nothing more, I get up, converting my thoughts into action, and reach the kitchen, walking stealthily like a cat. Very slowly and with great care, I open the kitchen door. I enter. The dark kitchen is full of the stench of fish. Without turning on the light, I make for the sugar container. A large frond of palm has made its way inside through the skylight and is swaying softly in the pleasant night breeze.

I open the sugar container. Holding the sugar in my fist, I am almost about to thrust it into my mouth when I hear a strange sound.

My jagged-eared rabbit?
Lucy or Jack?
A cat?
Or that black cobra?
I am frightened. My clenched fist falls open and the sugar spills on the floor in the dark. But no, these are human breaths and human whispers.

There was someone in the veranda.

I summon the courage to climb on to a large copper pan and peer out of the skylight. The palm leaf pricks my eyes and nose. My face begins to itch very badly but I ignore it and stand on my toes to peer out.

The soft moonlight revealed entwined shadows, as if they were wrestling. The light fell on their faces for a moment. I recognized them.

Sarwat Mumani and Feroz Khalu.

A powerful wave of loathing rose within me. The malice and ill intent in me started to cross all limits. I became a raging storm of anger, and the realization that I could do precious little to express it made me shake violently.

It was then that I saw it in the moonlit night. The hive which was hanging right over their heads.

I climbed down from the vessel with trembling feet. I reached the earthen pot which contained rocks of white salt. I got hold of a big rock of salt and climbed onto the vessel again. I wasn't trembling this time. Astonishingly, I felt very powerful.

Two dark shadows, in each other's clasp. I brushed the palm leaf aside with one hand, and with the other I took aim at the beehive. I held my breath and transferred all the strength of my body and soul into my right hand and flung the rock of salt at the hive. There was a light noise, after which echoes of a mysterious and strange buzzing began to fill the air. As if death were whispering in angry tones.

The entire family woke up on hearing their tortured cries. The furious bees had dug into them. The shadows of the bees were swarming and circling around in the moonlit night like horrible dark spots. I saw Feroz Khalu run towards the staircase. He was running around on the terrace, probably to jump from the railing into the adjacent house or lane. His shirt and pants were flung on to his shoulder. He was beating his hands about his lower half again and again – the bees had probably stung him on his private parts.

Sarwat Mumani screamed in agony and pain, rolling on the floor uncontrollably. Occasionally, she would get up and start whirling, her hair undone and falling up to her knees, then she would fall to the ground again and start rolling on it. I saw her taking off her jumper, her huge and heavy drooping breasts casting their shadow sometimes on the floor and sometimes on the wall. Her hair loose, her face hidden, she seemed to be dancing the terrible Tandava dance, like a chudail. Her screams ranged from loud and prolonged to squeaky short whimpers. She had taken a non-human shape. After some time she became completely quiet and collapsed on the floor like a heavy tree. I thought she was dead.

All the family members stood about here and there, hiding out of fear.

The terrible buzzing gradually came to an end. The shadows of the bees began to shrink. One could feel the April breeze blowing once again. Sarwat Mumani was lying on the floor, probably unconscious, and almost completely naked. Some family members began moving towards the kitchen. I found myself soaked in sweat. My heart was pounding wildly, as if I would die right there in that kitchen.

But no, a deceitful and cunning courage appeared inside me and I quickly exited the kitchen to join the others standing in a group on the veranda. In the chaos, nobody noticed me coming out of the kitchen.

It was lucky that the hive hadn't broken and fallen down; it must have only received a jolt from the salt rock, which is why the bees had begun to settle on to their hive after wreaking revenge. Noorjahan Khala had covered Sarwat Mumani's naked body with her cotton dupatta. But before that I had cast my eyes on Sarwat Mumani's bosom. There were no breasts there any more. They had swollen up to take the shape of a sack. I was reminded of the flour sack. She was carried inside. Her face was swollen like a balloon and her eyes were scarcely visible. Her lips were drooping like a beast's snout. Her face was red-hot like a live coal. I certainly had no idea that things could get so bad if one was attacked by bees. Someone remarked that she might even die if they didn't take her to the hospital immediately.

'Let her die, let the bitch die,' screamed Bade Mamu. Everybody jumped to silence him, but he could not be stopped. 'Ask that slut who she was debasing herself with. Who was it that ran away from the terrace?'

Anjum Baji caught hold of my hand and said, 'Guddu Miyan, you should go to sleep now. I'll come with you.' She brought me to the inner hall and lovingly asked me to go to sleep. I glanced at her face; it had a look of sadness on it. It was so intense that the purity and innocence of her face had also drowned in the shade of that sadness.

I went to sleep. I actually went to sleep. After committing such a horrible and mischievous deed, I slept like a log.

The next morning was extraordinarily silent and forlorn. It turned out that Sarwat Mumani had survived but she was no longer present in the house. I was told that she had gone to Bangladesh to some of her relatives for treatment.

I never saw Sarwat Mumani after that. Sometime ago I got the unverified news that she had died. She had probably migrated to Pakistan from Bangladesh.

Feroz Khalu, who was from the same mohalla as ours and was

related to us distantly, was not to be found either. He vanished. It was as if the earth had swallowed him! His wife had died before this incident and his children lived with their maternal grandparents.

Bade Mamu remained depressed for a long time. He then got completely absorbed in the life and cases at the lower courts.

I've recalled all this with great effort and written it down. And I realize now that it was all as ridiculous as it was frightful. Two people engaged in a sexual act and attacked by a swarm of bees! And a calamity of such magnitude falling on Feroz Khalu's sex organ just when that organ was busy enjoying an entirely different world. In any case, fear and ridiculousness are two sides of the same coin. The presence of one made the other inevitable. Take the case of a ghost. It is scary and comic at the same time, depending on the aspect on which you focus. The desire in me to cause pain and suffering to others was so intense in those days that there wasn't even a remote trace of guilt in me, and there was no question of conscience. There's the fact that even if I hadn't committed that act of malicious mischief, something or the other was bound to have happened. Cooking a dish of fish in spicy paste on the wrong day and at the wrong time was inevitably going to have dangerous consequences. This was my firm belief and faith.

It can certainly be said that the germs of criminality were in me from my very childhood. But I was a criminal whose court of justice, in which I was to be tried, had not yet come into existence. Therefore, I will roam around like a stray bull for a long time, maybe all my life. And I will keep myself covered with such a dense and dark cloak of secrecy that my inner self will turn into a mystery, a secret, a hidden mathematical equation.

And all this is not a long way off. If I had been capable of writing a novel my masks would have fallen off slowly and quite naturally. But appeals in a court of law, petitions and the arguments in courtrooms are themselves black masks, are they not? Every lawyer, every witness and every judge wears a mask.

Everything I am writing (I do not know if I am actually writing or only mumbling) is an appeal too, nothing more than a petition. I don't know yet in which court of law I will be filing this. I am just wandering around with it in my hands, searching for my court. Whenever I find it, I will file my petition and shed all my masks quietly. I will undress myself before that court of law. I will even cast off my body.

The scorching month of May arrived, accompanied by gusts of Loo. In this majestic summer, the heat was ready to burn everything to cinders, to purify it. This is what fire does.

Preparations began for Anjum Baji's wedding. The date was fixed. It was to be held after the rainy season. But she was not marrying Aftab Bhai as I had suspected initially. She was getting married elsewhere and her husband-to-be worked in Saudi Arabia. Anjum Baji was mostly in tears. I could see clearly that she did not seem interested in her wedding preparations. Somehow I felt very satisfied at this.

I asked her one day, 'I hope you won't forget me?'

She didn't say anything for a while. Then she picked up the jagged-eared rabbit sitting in my lap and hugging him to her chest, began to sob.

'You are crying because of me, no?'

Anjum Baji put the rabbit on the floor and looked at me with distant and vacant eyes.

I grew a little bigger by the time it was June. This is how it always happens. You suddenly grow up one fine day, or one fine moment, and you don't even realize that you have grown up or changed. The process of change is as mysterious as the earth's rotation, which humans don't get to see.

I grew a little more, and my body became bigger by an inch or a half. I had developed a great affinity for animals in those days. Along with Sunbul and the jagged-eared rabbit, we now had two baby squirrels that had arrived from nowhere. I insisted on keeping them as pets and had almost got my way. I kept them in a cardboard shoebox with cotton wool so they could nest there. I used to feed them milk and different types of grains in a small enamel bowl. Noorjahan Khala had given them names too – Lucy and Jack. But when they grew big they shifted to a hollow in the trunk of the mango tree in the courtyard and made their nest there, though they were well familiar with and used to human presence. They would sleep in the nest at night and frolic around the house all day, jumping on the beds.

When the rains arrived towards the end of June, the two discovered a new activity. The moment raindrops fell on the tin roof, they would jump off the wooden beams to scamper into the hollow in the tree, their beautiful, fluffy tails on their heads. They would watch the rain, peering from the hollow in the mango tree.

Monsoon hadn't yet arrived but the air was so muggy that my body felt sticky and greasy. I can now say that it was the first stage in the journey of human evolution. My skin felt like the scales of fish, the sweat refusing to dry out. Anyone who passed by me would cause my nose to revolt. At night most people left their rooms to sleep in the courtyards.

It was one such sultry evening. I had come down from the terrace after flying kites. A sweet and sour aroma, which I found distasteful, was coming from the kitchen. I went inside.

Noorjahan Khala sat by the stove, stirring the pot on it with a ladle.

'What are you cooking?'

Aam-ras, replied Noorjahan Khala as she continued to stir. I became nauseous at the smell of her clothes, which was a mixture of mango and sweat. I don't like mangoes or anything made out of mangoes.

The moment I turned to leave my feet began to tremble. It was the time of twilight when night meets day, which has its own significance. The sky seemed to have gathered a yellowish dust around it, as if a brewing storm had been stopped in its tracks. 'No, that's not right. It would be better if aam-ras isn't cooked today,' I murmured. It was my ominous sixth sense coming to life again. But I diverted my attention to something else. I started calling out to Lucy and Jack affectionately.

They came running to me, their tails on their heads. I played with them for some time, after which Jack proceeded to the kitchen, sniffing, and Lucy went into Chhote Chacha's room and scurried up and down the bedpost.

Night had descended and the lantern had been lit. I was hungry. The food had been readied earlier, but the completion of the cooking of the mango candy had been awaited. That too was ready now.

I could see that Noorjahan Khala had taken the vessel containing the mango candy off the stove.

Jack was next to her, nibbling on something he was holding in his forepaws. Noorjahan Khala extricated the burning log of firewood from the cook stove and extinguished it with water, sitting in her place all the while.

The action of pouring water on a piece of blazing wood

resulted in a loud hissing noise which resonated in the kitchen fiercely. Humans are familiar with this sound, but animals are not. Jack jumped up in fear and fell into the chulha full of fresh hot ash with burning embers underneath.

The squeaks were terrible and painful. Everyone rushed towards the chulha. I began to cry.

Chhote Chacha managed to pull him out of the chulha somehow. Jack was squeaking in pain, crying out loudly. He wriggled and fell to the floor. His tiny paws were completely burnt and looked like the tripe at the butcher's. The white stripes of Jack's fur were gone. His tail, burnt, had fallen off. He didn't look like a squirrel any longer, but a misshapen, scabies-ridden, dirty and tailless rat. He kept writhing in agony for a while, but soon he grew silent and exhausted. Chhote Chacha touched him lightly. I could see that his eyes were not in their sockets any more and the burnt skin of his head was hanging loose.

'Go get some milk quickly,' said Anjum Baji. But no, it was all useless; Jack was dead.

An eerie silence had fallen over the kitchen. Nobody ate any dinner that night. I wept the whole night lying on my bed. God knows where Lucy was.

No one dared approach me or try to console me. But it must have been around midnight when my rabbit came and sat near my feet. He nuzzled up against me. I don't know when I drifted off to sleep.

I woke up late the next morning. Chhote Chacha informed me that Lucy had died too.

When Chhote Chacha was returning home from the mosque after the early morning Fajr prayers, his gaze had swept past the electricity pole. Lucy was hanging there, swinging on the wire, her body dead and stiff, at the point where the electric wires pass through the pole and diverge.

I didn't cry this time. Instead I went to the terrace, climbing the stairs silently.

I don't know if animals commit suicide or not. But I was completely convinced that Lucy had done so.

I became very scared and anxious about this fearful ability of mine. I prayed to God that this strange power, this mysterious awareness be removed from my senses. I did not even look towards the kitchen for a long time. Even if I were to pass it, I would close my nostrils to avoid becoming aware of any scent or aroma that could lead to the occurrence of some undesirable incident or accident. But I can see now that my wish was childish and foolhardy, because this ability has become an ordinary and natural trait for me. Just the way someone is deaf or dumb or blind by birth, this dreadful ability is a defect or deprivation from birth, which has become a part of me, and living peacefully with it, without any trouble or difficulty, is something I have learnt to do. Truth be told, this ominous and evil ability has supported, strengthened and sustained the malice and small-mindedness in me.

And then came the rain. It had been present, hidden in the threads of humidity and mugginess. One night when I felt my wrists and face with my fingers, I knew immediately that it had arrived.

It must have been around three in the morning when it began to rain, with thunderclaps and lightning. The eternal companion of the clouds, the wind, was also blowing. The wall of humidity broke, and I found myself standing under the wooden beam of the tin roof in the outer hall. Sunbul's cage was hanging close by. A strong gust of wind extinguished the lantern hanging from the wooden beam. The entire house was plunged into darkness, interrupted by a vivid flash of lightning when I saw that the parrot had hidden his head in his feathers.

I too began to feel scared in the dark, in the terrible uproar of the rain. Water was flowing out of the drains on the roofs, making a loud noise.

I suddenly heard something different and mysterious in the din of the rain, a strange slithering and hissing sound coming from near the staircase where the hens were cooped. It then started coming from near the kitchen door, and then from near the mango tree, before becoming untraceable. This was certainly not the noise of the rain, which was getting heavier and heavier. I began to feel cold and terrified. I went inside quickly and lying down on my bed, I covered my face with a sheet. I immediately fell asleep.

It was raining when I awoke in the morning. There seemed to be some disturbance in the house. I came to know that all the hens in the coop had died.

Achhan Dadi told us that the cobra had passed this way at night. He was so poisonous and deadly that he only had to hiss for hens and pigeons to die. She also said that this snake was a very old inhabitant of this house and had been spotted slithering and sliding through the foundations of the house even as it was being built. Animals had died quite a few times because of him, but the cobra had never bitten a human.

Though Achhan Dadi had a reputation for spinning tales, this information was corroborated by other members of the family. I would have been scared if I had come to know all this at night, but at that moment I found myself curious to see the snake. This is exactly how day and night differ. Humans live double lives. One during the day and the other during the night. The rotation of the earth is not a trivial thing and needs to be remembered always. Forsaking this reality inevitably leads to dangerous consequences.

'Have you seen the cobra?' I asked Achhan Dadi.

'Yes, many times. Once when I was thirteen, and many times after that too. He has such long hair. He is very old and totally black. So black that a lamp won't light up before him,' Achhan Dadi replied with a shudder.

'He has also been spotted in the tiny store next to the kitchen many times,' said Noorjahan Khala.

My desire to see the mysterious snake remained unfulfilled.

I did not see it as long as I lived in the house. But now I have no regret for not having been able to see it, because I know that there resides an equally poisonous, equally black and equally ancient cobra inside my heart. These memories that I record in writing, or that I am narrating, are equal to placing my snake in his basket and performing before him, blowing the snake charmer's pipe. This is a very courageous and challenging act, however, I continue to search for my court of justice, or perhaps my trial court is sniffing me out like a hunting dog, but what are you people doing out there?

I have shown you my evil. Here is my snake. It is now time for you to show your respective snakes, your cobras, oh you kind-hearted and high-class people!

My memory is not obliged to try too hard or wander much at present. The recollection of the rain is taking my memory along in the fashion of a cloud carrying water. However dark the rain may be, it is an indelible illumination for the memories stored in the mind. Whatever I write now will stay written for some time, not with the ink of my pen, but it will come into existence on its own through the patter of the raindrops falling on the tin roof. The haze of the rain, its drops, its spray and shower, the sky covered with dark clouds, are all my pen and paper. Rain is the word that helps memorialize the seepage-ridden and wet times in my fluent and blemish-free tongue.

It didn't stop. Not a single day did the sky remain free of clouds. Heavy rain alternated with lighter showers. But the drizzle was persistent. Ten days passed. Rivers began to flow above the danger mark. The embankments in many places were opened and water ran over and submerged the surrounding areas.

The floods came, and in those floods, humans were carried away, along with their cattle. There was knee-high water on city roads. Ceilings and walls of many of the houses in the mohalla collapsed, and people died under these collapsing walls and ceilings. The rain did not relent.

Our house was built of brick and stone; it was pukka and strong. But the walls developed fissures in many places and the roofs of the storeroom and halls began to leak heavily. Beds and mattresses, trunks and tables, everything got drenched. The kitchen was the worst off. It was leaking so badly that it seemed it was raining in the kitchen just as it rains in the courtyard. The chulha was lying cold. Food began to be cooked on an angithi kept in the hall.

Everything in the kitchen – cooking oil, ghee, foodgrains and spices – was soaked in water.

One day the kuccha courtyard also got filled with knee-deep

water. The drains of the street were blocked; there was no way for the water to drain off. Since the kitchen was at the same level as the courtyard, the water entered it too. The kitchen utensils were swept into the courtyard by the water, where they could be seen floating. Cauldrons, big and small, pots and pans, ladles and spoons and griddles could be seen flowing out with the water. They wanted to get out of the house through the drain.

Everyone started praying for the rain to stop. It became difficult to walk in the courtyard. People slipped and fell all the time. A row of bricks was placed to serve as a path to the lavatory and to the main door. The bricks too were totally under water and couldn't be seen. Achhan Dadi inscribed the Urdu letter 'qaaf' three times on a white piece of paper and hung it on the little orange tree. There was nothing in the courtyard except water and wet moss. Dadi had hung the white parchment on the tree and was making her way back quickly into the hall, when she slipped and fell flat on her back on the green slush. Slathered in moss and slime, she broke her hip bone (for as long as she lived she was confined to the bed and to me she always seemed slathered in moss and slush).

Creatures of the earth floated into the house through the street drains. Frogs and earthworms, centipedes and slugs, and even baby snakes and earthworms. And one day, to top it all, little fishes too. The whole house reeked of green slime and damp. Each and every wall had turned black or green. The seepage ruined the paint on all inner walls. The lime and mud plaster started blistering and then falling off, and strange and ugly blots appeared in its place. Frightful faces that almost talked. Wild grass and weed began to spread across the tops of the walls. The sky had burst open and the earth too was probably going to slip and disappear from under our feet soon. I would crouch in the hall or in the tiny storeroom with my jagged-eared rabbit and watch the thunderous rain. Whenever there was a clap of thunder, Noorjahan Khala cried out, 'Ya Allah, khair.'

The sound of the rain became scary and mysterious at night. To me the rain falling on the tin roof sounded like the drums of Muharram played when the likenesses of the martyrs' coffins are taken out for burial.

The sound of rain gradually changed into a grim silence, like sad and mournful music which grows silent in the end or loses itself in a deep stillness. My ears had become accustomed to the sound of this rain by now. So there was no difference between the night's eerie silence and the sound of the rain for me. I began to sleep and, especially during such nights, I'd often be overcome with a wave of drowsiness and fall fast asleep. I wouldn't just sleep but also dream. Dreams that I haven't forgotten.

Some diseases, some habits and reflex actions and reactions are of genetic origin. Almost all members of my household suffered from the problem of biting their tongue while asleep, as if they were having dreams of pleasure and ecstasy, or of dread and terror. They would wake up in the morning rubbing their eyes, a stream of blood running down their mouth to their chin.

I had escaped this affliction up until now. But on those mysterious rainy nights, during which I had begun to sleep soundly and dream, I too would have a thin trickle of blood flowing down my mouth to my chin. I would often wipe it off with my index finger.

Those dreams always featured a girl, or maybe it wasn't a girl but the rain that had put on the robes of a dream. She would have a different appearance in every dream, but within me, in the subconscious mind, I was always aware she was the same girl. The same personality that visited every dream. However hard I try I cannot describe her. At times her face resembled every human face, but at others it bore no resemblance to anyone whatsoever. Some faces, some countenances are such that they elude getting captured by the eyes. They slip out after passing through them. And then transform themselves into a scent which pervades your soul. Now it is another matter that every scent does not necessarily make you happy; sometimes, in fact, it depresses you.

'Here,' she says and extends her hand, decorated with henna up to the wrist. I look carefully, and see a dry shami kebab is placed on her fair, bright, clean and delicate palm.

'Here, eat it.'

I pick up the shami kebab gingerly. It is cold as ice, and also sad. I take a bite of the kebab.

The manna from heaven goes and hides itself in a corner out of shame. The girl too disappears suddenly.

I wake up. The rain is beating down continuously.

'Guddu Miyan! What's your favourite dish?' asks the girl. Green bangles adorn her wrists this time. Her silvery voice makes the bangles clink.

'Korma,' I reply.

'And?'

'Pulao.'

'And?'

'Arhar dal.'

'And?'

'And . . . and . . .' I rack my brains and enthusiastically add, 'And most of all, kidney and liver.'

'Kidney–liver?'

'Yes! I really like that dish.'

'You like kidney–liver so very much?' The girl's voice sounds choked now.

'Yes! But they hardly cook it in our house. Only on Baqrid,' I tell her sadly.

'If you like kidney–liver so much, cut mine out and eat them.'

I look at her with wide eyes.

'Yes, extract both my kidneys and my liver,' she says in a sincere tone.

I go into the kitchen to get the knife with which we slaughter the goats on Baqrid.

I wake up. It's morning. The rain continues to fall. There's blood on my face from the mouth to the chin. My tongue is hurting badly after being cut by my teeth. After all, my teeth are becoming sharper these days, I thought.

The series of dreams continued till it kept raining. Then one day it stopped raining. At long last, the rain had stopped. Every rain has to stop some day or the other. That prolonged and dreadful rain which had been falling on this earth for millions of years had had to finally cease out of exhaustion.

The sun began to shine. The dark veil of clouds on the sun was lifted. Everything began to dry up. The house, the walls, the terrace, the clothes, everything began to heat up. But this heat was stricken by dampness. Food began to go bad. The smell of rotting food prevailed everywhere. The city was gripped by an epidemic of fever after the rains. This fever was the result of a dangerous infection in the stomach and intestines. Everyone in my house too was suffering from diarrhoea and vomiting. Having grown irritable, they were almost at each other's throats. Everyone's intestines were in pain, even Anjum Apa's (I was not so grief-stricken this time to realize that her stomach too had intestines). The only food being cooked at home those days was moong dal khichdi and it was eaten with curd by the entire household morning and evening. I had never seen such a large amount of khichdi being cooked in such a big pot.

I too ate the khichdi, but I did not develop a stomach infection; neither did my intestines writhe in pain nor did I vomit.

It was cholera. In those days it was common for this disease to occur after the rains, but this time it had acquired epidemic proportions. People were dying of vomiting and dysentery. Our own mohalla witnessed several deaths. Dr Iqbal was a quack and did not have a proper medical degree, but his clinic nearby, in a narrow by-lane, was flooded with cholera patients and overcome with the unpleasant smell of piss and shit. Patients were pressed against each other's backs and would often end up vomiting on the person in front of them, leading to scuffles, except they could hardly be called scuffles as all of them had grown very thin and weak due to continued dysentery, vomiting and lack of appetite. Not a drop of moisture remained in their skin, flesh and bones. Many of them died right there in the by-lane of Dr Iqbal's clinic, falling into the flowing drains.

The tamasha of human intestines was viewed by everyone. This was the punishment for our munching and chomping. The crime of human existence and the punishment for it lies hidden within its very foundation.

This is why I say human beings live in their intestines.

This epidemic too began to recede slowly, because the earth had not stopped rotating after all. The last days of September arrived and the winds which vanquish even a strong sun began to blow. It was a washed and clean sunshine. The blue sky began to seem bluer and the strong gusts of wind in the afternoon seemed to be carrying the sky and the sunshine away with them. The weather took a turn. The germs of cholera began to grow weak.

I have not yet been able to figure out if these winds were celebrating the departure of the rains or singing dirges of lament, but it may also be said that celebratory rituals and dirges are hardly different from each other, just the way life and death aren't two different things.

Those dreadful rains were over, but I was perhaps bigger and more dangerous now. There was a soft coat of down on my cheeks and chin. There was no trace of the indulgent girl in my dreams now and neither did I bite my tongue in my sleep. My exams were approaching. I was going to be staying up late and studying, so I kept my dreams in the upper-left pocket of my shirt, close to my heart, so that I could take them out and view them when I pleased. I wasn't dependent on sleep for my dreams.

I stayed up late into the night to study. I used most of the time to solve maths problems because it was the subject that scared me the most in high school. I was unable to answer many of the questions. I looked them up in the key provided at the end of the book and tried to reach the answers by applying my own methods and using incorrect formulae, before finally writing the answer at the bottom. It was obvious that my maths was going from bad to worse. Not to speak of algebra and geometry, where everything is 'supposed' from the very beginning. It was just a question of fitting the right answer to the question, like the rhymes of a doggerel. A blind route; start with a supposition, and then go on to prove it through a nonsensical, self-invented method (this is exactly how the existence of the world was proved, later negated after being labelled a mirage). These selfish and deceitful ways of the intellect and the mind and its philosophy have exposed themselves to me completely. But the subject of maths exhausted me in those days and thus, exasperated, I started looking up the answers in the key at the back. If the solution to a problem has already been found or is written somewhere, and if people are convinced about it, then what is the need to trouble and harass others over it?

But there was another, different kind of maths too. A death-dealing and mysterious kind of maths no one knew about except me. Only I possessed its terrible formulae. There was no book for me to turn the pages and find the answers at the end. Though I didn't know the answers, I knew the nature of the answers and between which numbers the answers would fall. More than mildly inauspicious and somewhere near middling inauspicious.

Surely this was a cheap and base weapon which had fallen into my hands, and I was proud of it at times. I am not the only one in the world who feels pleased at cheap and third-rate things. After all, how many knowers of the past and present, tantrics, astrologers, fortune tellers, politicians, mercenaries and contemptible, shallow people feel proud of third-rate things.

I solved one more question from this terrible subject very soon.

My first quarterly exams were over. I began reading detective novels again and would spend most of my time at Anjum Apa's place. Anjum Apa was dark-complexioned but her face was of a clearer hue than her hands and feet, which was strange. She was short and had a round face, like a chapatti, and the chickenpox marks on her face reminded one of the burnt spots on a chapatti. I always began to feel hungry when I saw that face and my intestines would start groaning. Her face seemed reassuringly familiar to me, just like the chapattis in the wicker chapatti basket at home. Anjum Apa always treated me with warmth, to the extent that at times I felt she loved me more than Anjum Baji did.

It was the month of October, when the sun shines brightly and a haze begins to spread in the evening.

I was talking to Anjum Apa about the character of a criminal in a particular detective novel when I caught the scent of something being fried in the kitchen. It was afternoon and I had been feeling very hungry. I flared my nostrils and took in the scent.

Anjum Apa began to laugh.

'Amma is frying parathas stuffed with dal. Have one before you go.'

'Parathas . . . dal-stuffed parathas,' I said.

Precisely at that moment I felt as if a needle had pricked my heart, a wet needle dipped in water whose cold prick had now crept up to my left shoulder. I was scared. A dangerous and secret mathematics question was before me. And I changed into a different person to determine the limits of its solution.

'No, I am leaving now.' I got up.

'Why? Can't you eat at a poor person's house for once?' The kitchen in the house had fallen into disrepair after the rains. Built with bricks, the walls had grass growing on them. 'That's not what it is, Anjum Apa. I have to buy some things from the market.'

I made an excuse and left their house, promising that I would return the next day. I seemed to have completely lost my appetite. 'Dal-stuffed parathas, dal-stuffed parathas.' My mind continued to whisper the words.

I must have barely reached the graves in my mohalla when I heard a loud explosion behind me. An explosion accompanied by a mysterious hissing. I turned around.

'The wall has collapsed, the wall has collapsed,' someone was screaming.

'Whose wall is it?'

But I knew very well whose wall had collapsed.

I rushed to Anjum Apa's place. A crowd had gathered there.

The dilapidated and crumbling wall of Anjum Apa's kitchen had collapsed. And her mother was crushed under it.

I saw this with my own eyes.

She lay still and motionless under the rubble of the age-old brick wall and the wild grass. Her body was covered in debris but her face was not. Her head was bleeding.

Perhaps the brick chulha was also lying buried somewhere under the wreckage, its fire having been out for some time.

'This is precisely the time houses collapse. The sun's heat after the rains makes the walls move from their fixed location,' someone said.

But I knew this was not why the wall had collapsed. A poisonous lizard floating in the milk had made me feel a little crazy and out of touch with the environment. Anjum Apa had swooned and fallen down, just like the kitchen wall. The crowd began to swell. The entire mohalla had turned up.

I didn't see the dal-stuffed parathas in the kitchen, but the aroma of them wafted over such long distances, carried by the wind, that I could catch their scent when I reached home.

I was disturbed and bewildered, enveloped in an unnecessary shroud of guilt. I went and stood near the parrot's cage. My jagged-eared rabbit came to me and began rubbing his face against the hem of my trousers.

I felt repentant. 'If only I hadn't gone there today at that time.'

'Guddu Miyan has come, Guddu Miyan has come,' said the parrot in an ironic tone.

A once removed niece of Noorjahan Khala's had come from a nearby tehsil to the city for treatment and was staying in our house. Her name was Anjum Bano.

She had arrived with her brother, who had brought a pot of rasawal for us. It was in an earthen pot wrapped in red kite paper. It was the custom in those days to carry a pot of rasawal while visiting a far-off village or township. Any relatives visiting us too would carry rasawal for us. This pot always seemed mysterious to me because of its shape and texture, but I was not very fond of rasawal.

Anjum Bano was my age. There was a shortage of blood in her body and so she had a pale yellowish complexion. It was possible that she was fair earlier but her skin had turned yellow. This yellow hue could not be compared to Anjum Baji's, which was a gift to her from nature. Anjum Bano's eyes were big and vacant and her pupils had a yellow tinge. This yellow of her eyes turned a slight red when she smiled, only to disappear immediately.

The rondure of her breasts could be discerned only after looking very hard at the shape of her body beneath her dupatta. It was otherwise a flat chest. I was now at an age where I was sexually attracted to women. And certainly, I developed a purely sexual interest in Anjum Bano. It was possible that this interest could have turned into love at a later stage because love and sexuality are tied with each other like rain before humidity or a yellow storm behind muggy weather. However, this couldn't happen, the reasons for which were incomprehensible to me then but can be somewhat understood now.

Anjum Bano's eyes contained thirst too. An intense thirst of a sexual kind which can be found in extraordinary proportion in any girl who has been suffering from a prolonged illness. In just about a week we had both read each other's intestines, pardon me, eyes, thoroughly.

I went quietly to the kitchen on a deserted afternoon one day. She was sitting in the outer hall cleaning masoor dal.

After entering the kitchen, I signalled to her. Initially she continued to clean the dal, then looked all around her like an alert cat, and holding the tray containing the dal, she tiptoed into the kitchen, treading like a cat.

I took her to the tiny storeroom inside where the sun's rays fell after being filtered through the skylight. I didn't have to make any advances; she clung hard to me as soon as we went in and began kissing me fervently. Her breath smelt of mango pickle. When I tried to feel her breasts, there was nothing there, or if there was, my fingers remained oblivious of them.

But she had lost any sense of restraint. She caught hold of one of my hands and pressed it hard against her chest. It doesn't make a difference whether a woman's breasts are swollen to the outside or are large sized or not. Probably the way in which some people have a tooth or two that remain buried inside the gum and never emerge. Similarly, the breasts of some women remain buried in the mysterious depths of their chests and become impatient and eager to expose themselves at a man's touch.

She was in a bad state of craving and her breath had quickened. She was breathing like a blast furnace and her lungs seemed to be about to burst. The odour of the mango pickle kept picking up. I used to, and continue to, hate the scent of mangoes. My pleasure began to turn into distaste. I gradually became scared too.

The sun's rays filtering through the skylight were falling on her yellowish face. I suddenly found her yellowish face and body very pure and pristine.

This was a diseased body unable to manufacture blood for itself. It is coarse, lusty and avaricious for a person to have too much blood in their body.

But Anjum Bano's lust was hidden within her spirit. Her illness-ridden, blood-deficient, jaundice-stricken body could not handle her frightening desire and was trembling and shaking like a decaying autumn leaf. The thirst of Anjum Bano's body was a thirst of many centuries and it was uncontrollable because her body was ill and unable to support it. The spirit continued to strike at the body again and again with its desire, lust and longing. It was about to destroy and break this weak, ill and pure body into pieces.

I moved away from Anjum Bano. She stepped forward in my direction. I shook her off. A yolk-like yellow settled into her large, vacant eyes. She looked like she was about to have an epileptic fit. She sat down on the floor with a thud. She clenched her teeth and her body stiffened. Her yellowish body suddenly turned an implausible shade of grey. Anjum Bano turned from yellow to black. Right before my eyes, yes, right in front of my eyes.

I can say with certainty that it was a sacred shade of black. The desire-laden spirit avenged itself on the pure body. But the body did not concede defeat before the spirit. I continued to stand there for some time, looking at her, and then left the kitchen hurriedly.

Anjum Bano stayed at our place for another three days. Neither did I look in her direction nor did she lift her gaze towards me. After three days, her brother came and fetched her. He had not forgotten to get the pot of rasawal with the red kitepaper pasted on it this time too.

Doctors had declared her illness incurable. She was suffering from a dreadful disease. There was no blood being made in her body and there was no option but to give her frequent transfusions.

Has anyone ever stopped to ponder that merely beating the drum about the chastity of the soul does not work? The real issue is the body, the chastity of the body. It is now necessary for man to understand that there has been too much talk of the knowledge of the self. Let us now talk of the infamous matter. Matter should also be given its proper rights. After all, for how long will the soul continue to punish the body for its sins?

Has the soul ever thought about what will happen if the body refuses to follow its orders and be its slave? The world's history will be written differently.

Many years later I got the news that Anjum Bano had died. She was given blood transfusions for as long as she lived. But a time came when her body refused every donor's blood. Whenever she received a transfusion, she bled from her mouth, ears and nose. Anjum Bano gave up food and drink a month before she died. Her intestines were clean and devoid of any previous signs of pollution, greed, gluttony or hunger.

Ultimately, Anjum Bano's purity of body defeated all of them.

How many things, how many memories do we have as excuses for sorrow, and how few as excuses for happiness. The past is strange. Even when one recalls the joys and happy times of the past, they too become a cause for sadness and despondence. The times gone by never come back exactly how they were – they assume the dreadful face of a ghost. Like the dead monkey's paw or bone.

October went by and November arrived. November is not really a month. It doesn't have a weather of its own. It is a month of decline. The November days strengthen the hands of the night. Already in line, waiting for the cold, thick and dark month of December with its roaring winds. These November days, saluting December, leave no respectable or individual imprint of themselves among the twelve months of the year and disappear quickly into oblivion. They leave their mark only on those unfortunate ones on whose chest has settled an odd rolling stone of November.

The body has to endure the punishment for the madness of the spirit.

It was in those days that a mad female monkey had started visiting our house. She would always be in her menstrual period and would bite someone or the other at the slightest provocation. I hadn't known till then that monkeys also menstruate, but when I saw bloodstains on her tail, I understood. After all, monkeys are our ancestors according to science. Humans experience all the curses of those beasts.

Everybody was apprehensive that the monkey would bite them while they were asleep. She had bitten many people of the mohalla while they were sleeping.

She scampered around the rooftops and parapets aimlessly all day, before disappearing into the night's blanket.

I had seen her. She was a large, heavy female monkey with a mad look in her eyes. They seemed to contain a relentless and unreasonable anger in them. She was probably suffering from some disease and menstruating all the time. This was not so shocking. The body has thousands of mysterious dimensions. Those early winter days were beset with panic because of this mad monkey,

The problem was resolved one day. She suddenly dropped down as she was scampering on the roof of the three-storey house opposite ours. The entire mohalla rushed to see her, including me.

She lay on the road, dead. A piece of bread was stuck in her mouth. The lower part of her body was soaked in blood. Her eyes still contained the same mad anger, now directed towards the skies. It was evening; the Maghrib call to prayer sounded in the atmosphere. I wondered if the monkey too had committed suicide like Lucy. It was possible, or maybe not? The growing darkness cast its cover upon the dead body of the wretched female monkey.

It must have been end of November or early December. I can't recall exactly. All the same, it was the season of marriages and niyaz. I cannot count the number of feasts I had. Since I was the youngest in the house and still regarded as a kid, anyone attending an event would always take me along, be it a wedding in the mohalla or at some relative's place.

It was a strange sight. Marriages were not performed in 'marriage halls' or hotels in those days. One of the comparatively bigger houses of the mohalla was used for the purpose. Three to four wooden tables were arranged in the courtyard or hall of that house. The tables would be covered with thick and grimy layers of dried gravy and oil on them. The tablecloths, if present, were wet and almost entirely stained with gravy. A row of discoloured and very uncomfortable iron chairs were put along the tables. The tables and chairs shook and wobbled.

People waited for their turn to eat, not so much by sitting around and talking, but mostly by standing behind the chairs, as if guarding them from disappearing. They counted every bite taken by the ones eating and showed their impatience by shifting their weight from one foot to the other. Those eating gobbled up their fare quickly, often swallowing without even chewing, devouring the food like hunger-stricken beings.

The food did not have much variety. Korma and chapatti were commonly served. If the hosts were of a higher status, they would serve pulao and zardah too. Biryani was not a customary dish in our region, although people have started referring to pulao as biryani these days.

The rotis were leavened or cooked in the tannur which was large in thickness and diameter. Those serving the food made it a very noisy affair, calling out to each other from all directions, generally out of their wits, the korma spilling on someone's head who was eating. A sense of mayhem prevailed.

The moment the serving dish was placed on the table everyone jumped to grab the better pieces of mutton or the rich and oily gravy. At times the serving dish overturned on the table in the clamour, but this hardly made a difference to the people eating. No one cared for the other, each one's intestines being their prime concern. Such a display of 'Oh, me! Oh, me!' would not even be seen on the doomsday plane.

Aluminium basins were placed near the tables in which the soiled plates were collected. The plates were either of aluminium or white enamel. The basins also contained leftover pieces of mutton, bones and pieces of rotis which were wet and swollen by now, flies swarming over them.

A similar large basin was used for storing drinking water. If it happened to be summer, a wooden board was placed over the basin on which slabs of ice were deposited. The melted ice trickled into the water in the basin to cool it. Water was collected from the basin using aluminium jugs and placed on the tables. Two or three glasses, also made of aluminium, were kept carelessly on each table.

People wasted a lot of food. They served themselves tonnes of gravy, bones and rounded pieces of mutton and filled themselves up to their nostrils, after which they got up from their seats, leaving the excess food in their plates. They stood up so clumsily that the chairs barely saved themselves from turning over and the table shook so violently that entire jugs of water overturned.

A large number of rotis were wasted and squandered in a very disrespectful manner. On many occasions I witnessed important men, of some station, with venerable beards clean their white beards covered in gravy and spices, use pieces of roti as napkins. Rotis were made use of to wipe hands, mouths, lips, chins and the watery discharge from nostrils on account of eating spicy hot food. They served as first-class handkerchiefs that cost nothing to wipe beards wet with gravy.

To top all this was the noise from the loudspeakers, fitted on the terrace facing the eating area. The loudspeakers would either be blaring out third-rate songs from some newly released movie or the qawwalis of Habib Painter.

(I don't find the feasts of those days very different from the buffets of today, where everyone serves themselves standing and eats standing as well.)

Wasn't this a battleground?

Yes! A battleground where humans fight each other with the help of their teeth, their jaws, their tongues and their intestines.

It is the wielding of these weapons that gives them the pleasure with which they prey upon each other's human hunger.

Who were those that tied stone slabs on their bellies to crush the feeling of hunger?

I never saw such people. In fact, what I have seen is humans tying stone slabs with their intestines and hurling them at each other like the noose of the hangman, one's neck entangled in the other's intestines. The length of those intestines, especially the length of the small intestine, God save us!

I too was part of this merciless game. On winter afternoons, maintaining the tradition of the zamindar households, we all ate black khichdi made of urad dal with oodles of pure ghee and then went to sleep under our quilts. When we woke up at the time of the Asr prayer, our faces were swollen and our eyes reduced to specks. The elements in the ma'ash dal and the rice, which caused the bloating and were the culprits.

I would look at myself in the mirror and feel ashamed. The mirror was fixed in a part of the hall from where it reflected the kitchen quite clearly, especially the stove and the huge black griddle kept to one side of it.

All this put me to shame and continues to put me to shame, but what does mere shame do?

Humans have been feeling embarrassed and ashamed for a long time, but this sense of shame has not succeeded in becoming the broom that sweeps away the world's garbage.

Guilt, shamefulness, the list of my sins, I continued to live my life accompanied by these. As my age continued to increase, the horrible incidents of my life also kept increasing. I have committed more sins than the sin of eating. Those horrible incidents which are inscribed on my soul and buried deep in my heart. Now when I experience the urge to break open my childhood toys and conduct a post-mortem on them, my memory will have to willy-nilly turn towards that mortuary.

My memory is being pulled towards the morgues of the mind by the scent of blood and the corpses shrouded and stored in the cold of cobwebs – as if a butcher were pulling a cow by the rope around its neck to take her to the slaughterhouse.

Let me first examine if the size of this noose even fits my neck or not?

December arrived. A majestic month in which fog-laden nights march on the streets like black platoons and the streets' soul begin to quiver. This is a month with high esteem. Sadness endows it with even more reverence and position. The dangerous histories of human destiny are written in the mad gusts of the cold wind. The December mornings are biting cold. The sun has to work very hard and takes time to gain its warmth, its heat, and by the time it does so, weakened by the severity of December, it is on its way back towards the abyss of the west.

Fog seems to be walking around on its feet in the courtyard. It acquires feet. The darkness has lost its wager to the fog. It was incapable of resisting the light to this extent.

Lumps of the black winter are descending all around. No warmth at all, and even if there was some, it lies buried and hidden in the black ashes of winter like a lone ember. The sky is not to be seen under the haze of the fog. The blue is nowhere to be seen. This is an incomplete sky without hands and feet. A torn and tattered sky, a weak and crippled heaven.

Anjum Baji's marriage will take place in this dangerous and majestic winter, according to her high status, but what about me?

I hadn't known till then that December would forever turn my life into a railway train, which remains immobilized at one tiny, deserted station, because it can't discern any signal in the fog. Neither green, nor red. And the smoke billowing whistles of the train would remain trapped in its throat forever.

The date and time for Anjum Baji's wedding had been fixed. The house was bubbling with activity. Some distant relatives also came to stay with us for the wedding. Despite all this, I felt a deep silence around me. The severe cold and the perpetually hanging fog might have been one of the reasons. There would hardly be any activity in the courtyard at night during such intense bone-chilling cold. But the kitchen would be bustling with liveliness late into the night. Girls from immediate and distant families, married women and elderly ones too would assemble together chatting and laughing before the hot ashes of the chulha. Loud peals of laughter echoed all around, but I noticed some hushed exchanges taking place between them too. I would constantly tread around the kitchen like a ghost haunting it.

Afternoons would be comparatively dull in the kitchen as most people would be engrossed in preparations or gone to the market shopping for dresses and jewellery. However, Aftab Bhai would visit in the afternoons sometimes and his cruel brown eyes would have a malicious and evil glint in them. His bulldog-like jaw would drop even further. I began to hate him even more, more than I had hated him earlier. Those were very curious days.

On the one hand, Aftab Bhai's stealthy and menacing visits seemed insufferable to me, and on the other, I had developed a silent but extremely hazardous complaint in my heart against Anjum Baji, which I haven't been able to define till date. Neither have I been able to find a reason for it. Obviously, the reason must have been something juvenile, but there must surely be some reason behind this juvenility.

I began to appear troubled and confused. I withdrew myself from the company at home. I would feel the need to piss again and again but the urine would flow brokenly. I would feel out of breath all the time, surrounded by an unfathomable restlessness. Anjum Baji would look at me once in a while with a wan smile. She seemed very forlorn and lost those days. I would get very angry and irritated with her sadness and begin to try and undress her in my mind, but I could never succeed in this obnoxious act.

I now realize that if Anjum Baji hadn't seemed sad and dejected to me those days, my life would have had a different direction. If Anjum Baji had not been grieving and sorrowful for Aftab Bhai and been lost in the dreams of her future bridegroom with joy and desire, the earth would have adopted a different route for rotation.

Aftab Bhai was the horizon of hatred for me. A loathsome and foul smell of stale, rotting fish. The odour of this hatred would crawl around every nook and corner of the house.

Why was this so?

I don't know. I really don't know. The biggest tragedy for us humans is that (at least this is my biggest tragedy) we don't discover what we need to discover about ourselves, and it remains a secret, a mystery, till our last breath. Just the way there is no deeper mystery in the universe than a dead human being. The ignorance of humans and their dead bodies are synonymous. One secret corresponds with the other. And then vanishes into the dark winter fog of this world.

But that, of which we need not have any knowledge, hangs over the stupid skulls of humans like glue or birdlime. Innumerable worldly conspiracies, loves, hates and desires, every unnecessary thing comes and falls on it, getting stuck, trapped just like the pigeons flying in the sky.

My anger crossed all limits one day. I tugged at my hair fiercely and grazed my nails against the kitchen wall. I quietly stamped my feet hard on the ground again and again when I was alone. Because I saw Anjum Baji weeping, actually sobbing, and that too in a corner, with her head resting on Aftab Bhai's shoulder.

How revolting and abhorrent such a scene was. No one can even guess.

The body of a chaste perfume riding the shoulders of a nose-destroying stench.

I couldn't tolerate it. I couldn't bear to watch a sacred sacred golden paleness lose itself in an artificial whiteness which had red inside it. The colour red. Too much blood in the body, having excess blood in the body was crude and a sign of lust.

Yes, a sign of carnality!

Anjum Baji had been isolated from the rest of the family as she was now in mayun – the ceremonial sequestration of the bride or the groom in order to prepare them for marriage. A screen had been created to put her in purdah using a few colourful sheets in the veranda of the eastern corner of the outer hall facing the screen of the kitchen. Anjum Baji sat on a string charpoy wearing yellow – a yellow kameez, yellow salwar and yellow dupatta – surrounded by women and young girls. Only a mahram of the opposite sex could go in occasionally and the na-mahrams were strictly forbidden from entering. Despite this, even the men very close to her in kinship, with whom she needn't observe purdah, avoided visiting her there.

A fair-complexioned nayin named Tameezan, who was very fat and somewhat past middle age, rubbed cosmetic unguents on Anjum Baji's body and massaged her morning and evening. Anjum Baji's complexion was actually acquiring more and more radiance every day. Professional female singers visited often and sang wedding songs accompanied by the dholak. They also sang a few cuss words to keep evil spirits and jinns away from Anjum Baji's person.

There was no purdah practised by Anjum Baji in my case. I

was a fourteen-fifteen-year-old lad who was yet to attain puberty. There was nothing to worry about and I was free to ensconce myself near Anjum Baji behind the curtains that had been put up for her privacy. I'm a little dark-complexioned, so I applied the unguents too. I still remember the fragrance of that paste.

Clad in yellow, Anjum Baji seemed like a radiant gold idol. She smiled only seldom when she was with her girlfriends, remaining enveloped in her permanent and sacred sadness. Sometimes I would find myself alone with her after everyone else had left. On such occasions, Anjum Baji would stroke my hair with her glowing, fair and yellow hands, brightened with ubtan, and say what she often said, 'Guddu Miyan, don't cry after I have left. Tell me, you won't cry, na?' Her voice too was pale golden.

'No.'

But she herself would begin to cry softly after this. A silent weeping, like the falling of a quiet rain on trees when the trees are still and inert and there is no trace of any wind around. The tears would stream down her face but she would wipe them so quickly with her yellow dupatta that one hardly saw them. Chances of their visibility were further reduced by the yellow striations on her dupatta which absorbed them and turned them yellow.

All this was bound to happen. After all, her hands were about to be coloured yellow.

Aftab Bhai called me to him affectionately one day. 'Guddu Miyan!'

I went to him, filled with loathing. He fished out two brown-coloured pills from his pocket and said, 'Guddu Miyan, go and give these to your Anjum Baji. Ask her to take these with warm milk.'

'Is she unwell?' I asked.

'Yes! She has a severe headache. Go and give them to her at once.'

Aftab Bhai had taken up the job of a compounder at a local doctor's clinic and often procured free medicines for the household for minor ailments.

I looked at the two brown-coloured pills with loathing and disdain. Once again I began to feel very upset with Anjum Baji. She could have told me if she had a headache. I would have pressed her head for her. What would these damn pills that Aftab Bhai brought do? However, much against my will, I had to deliver those pills to Anjum Baji. She was sitting with her head between her hands at that time. I don't know why but she looked thinner than usual.

'Shall I get some milk?' I asked.

'No, I'll take them later,' she said, securing the pills in her yellow dupatta.

But the mention of milk reminded me of milk with jalebis. I had always been somewhat of a glutton since childhood.

'Here, have some milk and jalebis,' said Anjum Baji, sliding the bowl of jalebis and milk towards me.

She was prohibited from eating salt during her seclusion for the mayun and permitted only sweets, that too milk and jalebis. Whoever came to meet her inevitably carried some milk and jalebis with them in a box or utensil, or else shoved some money in her hands saying it was meant for milk and jalebis. This was a custom I took maximum advantage of. I was eating jalebis with milk all the time.

December nights were extremely windy and the mayun curtains flapped loudly in them. The cold in the veranda chilled our bones to the core. Anjum Baji would lie with her knees folded or sit huddled in her quilt with yellow lining and yellow cover. Her friends too snuggled in their respective quilts, chatting away. They laughed and joked with each other late into the night as the fog in the courtyard began to intensify, to the extent that the light of the lantern hanging from the wooden beam began to appear black by the time they finally dozed off.

I would also begin to feel sleepy and get up and go to the inner hall to lie down in my bed. My jagged-eared rabbit would already be there under my quilt, waiting for me. But I wasn't feeling sleepy that night. Firstly, there had been meat korma for dinner and my heart began beating very fast when I saw it. I became as alert as a tracker dog. Korma might prove an ill omen tonight, I thought. Then I told myself that such dishes were often prepared on special occasions. Besides, my hidden sixth sense was not very active those days. All my physical and mental energies were directed towards the activities for Anjum Baji's wedding.

The wedding was in three days. I was tossing and turning under my quilt. There was complete silence all around, probably because everyone was going to stay up the next night for ratjaga celebrations.

There was silence in Anjum Baji's mayun quarters too. Her friends, tired, had gone to sleep.

Cold and menacing gusts of the December night's wind were blowing outside. The lantern suspended from the wooden beam rocked to and fro. The shadows of the various objects falling on the walls of the hall changed form continuously and each form seemed frightening and mysterious to me.

I sensed a sudden slight movement, as if someone had gone into the courtyard. I felt a little scared, but I couldn't restrain myself. Being an avid reader of detective novels, I had developed an unnecessary and uncalled-for childish curiosity.

I got up stealthily and saw a shape standing at the door of the kitchen. I could recognize even the darkest shadow of Anjum Baji. She was holding a vessel in her hands, which too I identified soon. It was a small container for jalebis and milk. She is going to keep it in the kitchen, I thought. But why is she relinquishing the customary purdah of the mayun, and that too to go into the kitchen?

I got my answer soon. I was rooted to the spot when I saw another silhouette at the threshold of the kitchen!

A tall and burly form, which pulled Anjum Baji into the kitchen with force. The kitchen door was then shut from inside.

I leapt towards the fourth stair of the staircase to see what was going on there.

It was dark inside the kitchen, but not really. A kerosene lamp was burning though the light it cast resembled the darkness to a large extent.

Aftab Bhai had Anjum Baji in a deadly grasp. He was all over her, like a man-eating beast.

'You are a dog, a dog, a contemptible cur,' Anjum Baji managed to say.

Aftab Bhai slapped her hard on the cheek.

'You cur . . . why did you feed me those pills?' Anjum Baji began to cry.

'Because I didn't want your husband to enjoy the pleasures of the first night with you. But I couldn't care less. I'll . . . right now, in this state.' I could hear the devil in Aftab Bhai's voice.

He knocked Anjum Baji down on the floor. In the dim light of the kerosene lamp, I saw her virginal and pure shape, scented with the bridal ubtan, clad in the sacred yellow of the mayun, lying still on the brick floor.

Aftab Bhai bent over this shape. The scene was not clear any more. Jumping up and down on the fourth stair, I tried to peer into the kitchen. I could not see anything, but I could hear. I could see the sound, no, not sound, but sounds, like someone was slaughtering a goat. Panting, stifled screams, which rose and fell in the cold December wind. The mango tree was swaying wildly in the wind.

I could not understand what was going on. I started feeling very cold. My teeth were chattering. From the desolate parapets of the roof the swaying wandering wind was crying. It sobs on the steps of the staircase. I experienced the savage attack of the wind on my back, as if someone were thwacking me in ritual mourning. A voice weeping in the silence.

The kitchen door opened after what seemed like an era. The tall and burly shape emerged and disappeared into the courtyard.

My freezing, numb feet stumbled down the stairs. As I approached the kitchen, my teeth started chattering loudly. My stomach began to cramp.

I reached the kitchen and in the ill-fated, dark light of the kerosene lamp, I saw Anjum Baji sitting against the chulha, her head between her knees.

Her long black hair had come undone and was touching the floor. Her yellow mayun salwar had stains of korma all over it. Did the pot containing the korma topple over?

Korma? No, I can see a little clearly now.

It wasn't korma, it was blood. Fresh bloodstains. Her dupatta, lying helpless, creased and crumpled on the chulha, had these stains too. And so did her kameez. The mayun dress was spattered with blood.

The container for the jalebis and milk was lying overturned on the floor. A trickle of milk had spread over the upright-brick floor and a cockroach was sitting in it. I deluded myself into thinking that the blood had mingled with the jalebis and milk.

The scent of ubtan mingled with the smell of blood in the kitchen.

Blood... what kind of blood was this? Whose blood was it? Was it the blood of menstruation that had arrived early? Or of the loss of virginity? Or of both?

The two kinds of blood perhaps had become one like the water flowing from hurting eyes.

I don't know anything. This is a secret unknown to everyone.

'Guddu Miyan!' gasped Anjum Baji in a hoarse voice.

Sobbing, she got up and pulled me in an embrace. The sound of her crying mingled with the sound of the cold wind blowing outside. It made my teeth chatter.

'You won't say anything to anyone, you must swear upon my life,' she said between sobs.

I stayed quiet.

'If you breathe a word to anyone, I'll die. Did you hear, Guddu Miyan? Your Anjum Baji will die.' She shook me violently.

I began to cry.

Anjum Baji picked up her yellow bloodstained dupatta lying on the chulha and wiped my tears. The dupatta too smelt of ubtan and blood, and this smell entered my eyes. But it did not stop there. There is a world beyond the eyes, and the smell seeped into it.

She held my hands and came out of the kitchen unsteadily. She hugged me fondly.

'Don't worry... I've hurt myself only a little. I'll be fine. This blood is a result of that injury.'

Anjum Baji had released my hand now. She took faltering

steps towards the bathroom and would probably go back to her mayun state after she emerged from there.

I stood silently in the courtyard, the cold mist surrounding me. I raised my head and look towards the sky. I could not see anything except blackness.

I could feel my hair. The fog had moistened it. My hands were moist too. I smelt my hands. They had a weird scent – a mix of unguents, henna, flowers, korma, jalebi and milk and even the smell of blood.

A stray cat howled in the dark narrow street outside.

I don't remember – I don't remember now. I don't remember any other detail of Anjum Baji's wedding except an extremely frail bride in a red shadi ka joda leaving the house crying and sobbing as I silently watched from the threshold of the house.

After a long time, probably after three years, when Anjum Baji returned from Saudi Arabia with her husband, she was unrecognizable. She had grown plump and rounded and seemed shorter than she used to be. She was laden with gold ornaments, but that is a separate story that I shall set aside for another occasion.

I hadn't felt as lonely as I had expected to after Anjum Baji's wedding. The reason could have been the dangerous rage smouldering inside me. I had taught myself to live with the anger concealed within the deeper recesses of my being. This anger was black, not fiery red or yellow. It blinded me but also provided me with succour. I was always accompanied by the black shadow of this anger that had befriended me, and I held on to it tightly, clasping it with both my hands.

Many months had passed. I was studying seriously. Aftab Bhai had begun to live in a room at the same doctor's where he was employed as compounder. He visited infrequently and was always smoking the same infuriating cigarette whose smell was so familiar and recognizable even in a crowd. It was rumoured that he had married someone secretly. I don't really know, because I never went to him although he had beckoned me more than a couple of times. I tried not to meet Aftab Bhai because I knew I would have to meet him one day. I obeyed the commands of the dark anger nurturing itself within me and was waiting for a signal from it to finally meet Aftab Bhai.

I visited Anjum Apa twice or thrice a week, but we did not talk about detective novels any more. I had lost interest in them and had begun reading translations from foreign languages, particularly translations of Russian masterpieces. Anjum Apa was neither interested in such writing nor did she have the ability to grasp it.

I had grown much bigger in just four or five months. There might or might not have been any visible difference in my looks or in my height, but the spirit residing in me had definitely outgrown my body, so much so that my spirit's feet would sometimes start peeping out of the ends of my body and I would anxiously clutch at the dark hands of my anger. It was anger that provided me assistance on such occasions.

I had always felt very close to Anjum Apa and it has often crossed my mind that perhaps she too loved me, even more than Anjum Baji did, but she could never disclose her feelings. There must have been reasons that I did not know back then, though I can guess now. However, speculations aside, let me just tell you that I felt close to Anjum Apa, or thought that I was close to her, because I was perhaps pining for someone's love, a girl's love.

Anjum Apa had become very dejected, troubled and sad after her mother's death and her father was in a hurry to get her married. I often thought of joking with her, say something humorous to her and make her smile, even if unwillingly, but I could not. Probably because I hardly remembered any jokes, and if I tried to recall some odd joke to narrate to her, my companion of those days, the mysterious dark anger, would start wriggling out of my grasp.

No, certainly not! I could not part with my precious anger at any cost. Full-throated laughter was taboo for me, which is why I never gave Anjum Apa any happiness even though I discerned a strange and pure glow of love for me in her sad, vacant eyes. A blinking glow that lit up, was extinguished, lit up again, was extinguished again.

But this affair could not move forward. Anjum Apa's nikah was performed one day, quietly and very humbly, and the round, chapatti-like pockmarked face, which was so familiar and known to me, went away from my world. The face, whose sight always made me feel hungry and my intestines to rumble, was lost in the palanquin, hidden behind that hateful red ghunghat, just as Anjum Baji's face had been.

I hadn't known then that faces return. People come back, even if their attitudes, their bodies and their spirits might have undergone change.

This has been human destiny since the beginning of time, and it will remain so till it ends.

Noorjahan Khala became obsessed with taking baths. She bathed for as long as six hours, refusing to emerge from the bathroom. We put up with it somehow, but then she began going into the kitchen with her towel and soap and a bucket full of water. She was dragged out of the kitchen with great effort, but she still managed to bathe in the kitchen two or three times. A doctor was consulted, who said that she had suffered a paralytic attack in a specific part of the brain. He prescribed some medicines and assured everyone that she would recover completely.

It was the time of strokes. Every second person seemed to be having one. To the extent that Ismat Chacha-Mumma (he was my paternal uncle from one side of the family and my maternal uncle from the other and so I called him Chacha-Mumma) who had come from the village about twenty miles from our place, carrying the pot of rasawal that he brought for us every year, had suffered a stroke by the time he reached our doorstep. He ran to the toilet every now and again with the pot of rasawal in his hand. When people caught hold of him and tried to restrain him, he screamed aloud, 'I will place it in the kitchen! I will place the pot of rasawal in the kitchen with my own hands.'

We were constantly receiving the news of someone or the other falling victim to this strange and outlandish disease.

The epidemic had spread to such an extent that I noticed a crazy rat roaming around the kitchen late at night, that never got caught in the mousetrap. His head hung to one side, and it was clear that the rat's mind was affected and its memory was not intact. It probably regarded the kitchen as a mousetrap and capered about meaninglessly in the silence of the night in order to get out of that trap. He might have believed the mousetrap in the corner of the kitchen, holding a piece of chapatti, was the kitchen, a space now unreachable to him.

I even suspect that the ants had lost their wits too, because they were failing to form proper queues when moving around.

Rehana Phuphi considered the magical pot of Diwali responsible for this ill wind. She was sure that the pot had flown over the townships of Muslims many times this Diwali. She had seen a lamp burning inside the pot clearly and had also heard a hiss emanate from it. I don't really know if it was true, but according to the reports coming to our house only Muslims suffered strokes.

I now think that the weather could have been responsible. February was coming to an end. Winter and summer were playing hide-and-seek with each other. All kinds of weird and inscrutable diseases begin to spread when winter and summer come together.

The cockroach population was increasing steadily in the kitchen. They remained hidden within and behind utensils during the day. After the work in the kitchen had been done for the day, they crawled out to roam around freely. Since I went to the kitchen at least once every night to gobble up some sugar, I knew best the condition of the crazy rat and the cockroaches.

Those were indeed strange times. People who had suffered strokes were everywhere, chattering away and behaving strangely, resulting in commotion all around. I was constantly lifting the lids of cooking vessels and examining the colour of the dishes. Red, green, yellow, orange, purple and even colours like white or shades of grey, but I have never came across blue-coloured food.

Why couldn't there be blue-coloured food too, I wondered. Probably because blue-coloured food is meant only for heavenly angels or devils. Poisonous food. It was probably for the best that blue-coloured food didn't exist in the human world since humans have not yet learnt how to distinguish between angels and devils.

Then one day it was announced over the radio that the cause for the strokes was worms found in the intestines and it was diseases of the stomach and the intestines that was making people lose their mental balance. And people from a particular community, religion, race and region were affected more than others.

I can't say how much truth there was in this. It is possible that this was partially untrue, or wholly so, and mere propaganda. Ultimately, it all boiled down to the same intestines, same stomach, same hunger and greed, same food, and yet again the same fire and the same kitchen.

The kitchen, the most dangerous place in the house.

It was the day of Barawafat. All the houses were lit up with candles. I lit candles in every dark nook and corner of the house. It was time for the procession. Ritual offerings and prayers began in our house and phirni was cooked and set in small earthen bowls. As I sat eating phirni in the courtyard at night, I thought about the phirni cooked by Anjum Baji. She would decorate the phirni so delicately and showed such precision with the silver foil that the earthen bowl would begin to glimmer and glow like the moon.

Instead of the moon, it was darkness that was rising within me at present. The dismal shadow of my anger, my companion, assumed a massive form. It became taller and higher than me, dwarfing me, wanting to emerge from me. But I was slipping into its grip completely with my dwarfed height. From my companion it was turning into my master.

'They shouldn't have cooked phirni today. Zardah would have been better.' My inauspicious, long, black tongue slithered over my ears. I looked at the sky. A paper balloon, red and bright, floated past slowly.

'I too will fly with the wind some day, like the balloon in the dark sky,' I thought.

Early in the morning next day someone rattled the chain on the front door. In those days someone rattling the door chain so early in the morning meant death, and death it was. We were informed that Ismat Chacha-Mumma had come to harm on the railway line in the village. It wasn't suicide; he was on his way to deliver rasawal to a relative's place but had confused the railway tracks close to the village for a road or a path. Ismat Chacha-Mumma's weak and ageing body was cut to bits and the earthen pot containing rasawal shattered and mingled with the earth again.

The news was distressing for everybody in the household and they left for the village quickly. Only Noorjahan Khala and Achhan Dadi stayed back. Achhan Dadi had become completely bedridden after she broke her hip and there was no question of her going anywhere.

She would relieve herself on her bed and her body had begun to develop bedsores because she couldn't even turn on her side in her condition. Food and other edibles she liked were kept near her most of the time, and she extended her hand and put them in her mouth whenever she wanted. Eating meals in a proper fashion had not been possible for her for quite some time now, but her intestines were alive, and a blast of stench greeted you the moment you approached her bed, which is why I always shied away from going to her.

Noorjahan Khala, as usual, was occupied most of the time in bathing or attempting to bathe. Sometimes she undressed and started bathing in the courtyard and was brought under control with much difficulty. She thought the kitchen was the bathroom and the bathroom was the kitchen. She made life extremely difficult for everyone at home. On hearing the news about what had happened to Ismat Chacha-Mumma, she rushed towards the kitchen for her bath, taking off her jumper on the way. She was gradually losing awareness of her nakedness and her sense of shame. She had to be lifted up by force and carried to the bathroom where she immediately began to pour water on herself, emptying mug after mug.

'Guddu Miyan, don't go to school today. Stay home,' said Bade Mamu as he left.

The house was empty, but I wasn't worried; instead, I experienced a certain freedom within me. A dangerous, uncontrolled freedom. An ever-expanding vast desert of white in me within which roamed black shadows in their actual shape and form. I heard a knock at the door. Since I had bolted the door from inside, I went and opened it.

Aftab Bhai stood before me, with his brown merciless skin and eyes. The same low-grade and stinking cigarette hanging from his lips. 'What happened? Is there no one here?'

'No.'

'Where have they gone?'

'Ismat Chacha-Mumma died.'

'Hmm . . . all right. Guddu Miyan, just check if there's anything to eat in the kitchen. I haven't had breakfast today. I'm famished.'

He had probably quarrelled with his wife, or whoever she was. He began to walk from the courtyard to the kitchen. I was walking behind him, but the bones of my feet were crackling under the awful weight of my revulsion and my kneecaps felt jammed. Aftab Bhai began to rummage through the pots and pans while I stood quietly leaning against the kitchen door.

He found the previous night's phirni in one of the vessels. He sat down on the floor on his haunches and began gobbling it up with a spoon. His back was towards me.

'Guddu Miyan, get me some water,' he said without turning to look.

I didn't budge. The heavy slab meant for grinding spices with a muller was lying close to my feet and my jagged-eared rabbit was jumping up and down on it. I saw that the crazed rat, which normally did the rounds of the kitchen during the night, was sneaking towards the chulha from behind the flour canister, its head lolling to one side in the daytime as well. The cockroaches too had emerged from behind the utensils and were crawling around.

All of a sudden the dark and huge shadow which had found sustenance in me transferred itself into my hands with all its might. My hands had transformed into the hands of a demon.

These hands now belonged to another world; they had a different mind and personality and a different nervous system. These hands were total strangers to the rest of my body and my mind.

The hands asked me to bend. I bent down and my hands picked up the heavy grinding slab, the way someone picks up a dry yellow flower from the ground. The grinding slab had the yellow colour of dried turmeric on it.

Aftab Bhai was in the same posture, on his haunches, eating

the phirni. Although I could not see his jaws moving as he ate, I could see an obscene kind of movement in his back again and again. I might have seen or felt this kind of an obscene movement somewhere earlier too.

Holding the stone grinding slab fairly high with my hands, I began to move towards Aftab Bhai very slowly, barefoot. I was right behind him now. The mixed scent of blood and ubtan entered my nostrils.

Holding my breath and applying all my strength, I lifted the slab higher and banged it on Aftab Bhai's head. He emitted a sound like a loud burp. It was certainly not a scream; he did not get an opportunity to scream.

His head hit the floor as he toppled to one side even as he was sitting on his haunches. A head which had been crushed completely.

The grinding slab slipped from my hands and fell to the ground. Tiny bits of Aftab Bhai's brain and blood were stuck on it.

The pot of phirni stayed in its place, but the phirni stuck in his mouth, throat and intestines had been evicted and was spattered all over the brick floor.

The crazed and nervous rat was disappointed on seeing this and went and hid behind the flour canister once again. He couldn't recognize the phirni as he had lost his memory.

But I saw clearly and distinctly, and I have no doubt about this whatsoever. I saw a cockroach sitting near the pot of phirni and staring at me. I think he had even laughed subsequently at me.

I don't know how long I stood there. A thick dark trickle of blood was making its way on the kitchen floor.

One could hear the nerve-racking sounds made by Noorjahan

Khala, pouring mug after mug of water on herself in the bathroom. She was lost in the act of bathing, oblivious of the world around her.

Then, even as I stood next to Aftab Bhai's dead body, it suddenly dawned on me that I had murdered Aftab Bhai. It was his white shirt and brown trousers that were the face of the murder.

It was almost afternoon. The sun was shining into the kitchen. A strong bright luminescence engulfed it. It engulfed my mind too.

I turned on my heel and ran to the inner hall to quickly put on my khaki school uniform pants. I was already in a white shirt. I wore my white sneakers, picked up my schoolbag, which I slung over my shoulder, and left the house, careful not to touch anything else. Leaving Aftab Bhai's dead body in the kitchen and walking away from the sounds of Noorjahan Khala bathing in the bathroom, I reached a small crossover on the highway, quite far from the house and on the same road as my school, and sat there. It would be at least another two hours before school got over. I climbed down from the culvert and washed my hands in the water flowing under it. I suspect that some tiny fish had probably leapt towards my hands, but there was no trace of blood. Neither was there any smell.

I made unsuccessful attempts to see my face in the water flowing under the culvert, but the reflection was unclear because of the weeds in the water.

School got over late in the afternoon, and when the children began streaming out, I too joined them and began moving in the direction of my house.

I felt a little nip in the air. My legs were trembling and my body was shivering.

As I approached home, I felt my feet dragging and my head spinning. I managed to walk by leaning on the walls of houses.

My schoolbag hung on my shoulders in a very unwieldy manner and I found myself unable to maintain balance. My shoulders began to sag and the weight of my bag increased so much that it seemed my back would break. My throat was parched. I tried swallowing my saliva but my mouth was dry. It occurred to me that I hadn't passed urine in a while; probably my kidneys had no urine in them. A dreadful dryness began to spread through my entire being.

I was finally in the lane which led to my house after turning left. A large crowd had collected there.

A police van with blue lights stood at the turn of the lane. I gathered some courage and continued moving up. Fear was my strength and support now and the shaking of my feet the stamina for walking. But for this, my feet would have turned into stone.

The house was swarming with khaki-clad people although the body had been taken for post-mortem by then. The police were recording each and every person's statement. Noorjahan Khala and Achhan Dadi too were made to give statements. In my turn, I said that I had been away at school since morning and had just returned. The police did not doubt my statement, or else they could have found out from the school whether I had been present that day. Luck was on my side.

Later, after the police had left, Bade Mamu did question me for not having listened to his advice and going to school, but at the same time, he heaved a sigh that I had done so. He might have been thinking that if I had stayed home that day, my life too would have been at risk.

'This is definitely the doing of the kanpati maar,' said Chhoti Khala.

Kanpati maars are professional thieves and robbers who load the corner of a large handkerchief with something heavy and hit unwary people on the temple with it. When the victim falls unconscious they rob him or her. Those days there was a mentally disturbed convict who barged into people's homes and murdered anyone he found alone using some kind of weapon. The police hadn't been able to nab him until then.

After some time a police inspector returned with some of his men in tow.

'It is possible for the kanpati maar to have done this, but his manner of committing murders is different. The weapons which he uses to kill are always strange and unconventional. However, he could have dropped or misplaced that weapon. We have searched the house for it, but you all should not ignore the possibility and try to look for it yourselves.'

The police had left but our house was overflowing with relatives and neighbours.

I began to feel very cold after some time. My teeth began to chatter. A quilt was placed over me and I heard someone say, 'He's a kid . . . has gotten terrified, he's getting a fever now.'

The fever was certainly coming. I heard the thud of his footsteps inside my ears. My temples turned into hot iron rods and my forehead became burning hot, so much that chickpeas could be roasted upon it. The sheet on my bed began to hiss and crackle with the heat of my body, ready to emit smoke any moment.

I began to lose consciousness. It seemed to me that I was lying on the road with eagles and crows flying above me. My memory had been blown into fragments in the hot blasts of the fever and those fragments were flying in the wind.

Has my mind suffered a paralysis attack? Is this a paralytic rain? A heat-pouring, burning and scorching rain? I only heard distant voices, which signalled to me that I was still alive.

'105.7.'

'106.'

Someone inserted a flabby needle in my mouth and underarms again and again.

'Cool his forehead with strips of cloth dipped in ice water.'

I sensed something cool on my forehead.

The portion in my geography textbook that described countries with very cold climates started floating before my eyes. I went and sat on that page like a buzzing housefly. I was a long-haired dog pulling a sledge on the snow. I slid down the snowy slopes where the polar bear of the North Pole eyed me threateningly.

'We'll try giving him an injection, otherwise we might have to admit him in the hospital.' I felt a lousy prick in my arm that travelled right to my heart, a needle, a needle pricking my heart directly.

I was sitting before Sarwat Mumani. She was doing her embroidery fiercely and angrily. She was working her needle on the hankie as if she were cutting it up. The handkerchief turned into rags and shreds.

After treatment I released rivulets of perspiration. My body felt moist and wet most of the time. But I experienced a slight shivering after a few hours and wanted to cover myself with a sheet. And I knew that this slight cold and shivering was a sign of its return. It was at a distance but I could hear its footsteps the way a dog can hear footsteps from a distance and begins to bark. And then it arrived. It, that is, the fever, then soaked up all the perspiration of my body in the grey dust of its frightful heat. The fever swirled around my body like a whirlwind. Fire spread to every inch of the body and burnt out all the damp, all the wetness from it.

I don't know. I don't know when I came back into the world from my encephalitis. I still had fever but it did not rise beyond 101 degrees. I was given only fruits and milk. I wasn't supposed to eat chapattis. I was weak but not so weak that I could not go to the toilet on my own.

One day, early in the morning, I developed a severe pain and burning sensation in my stomach. I went to the loo but didn't pass stool. Instead, I passed a huge amount of blood. I swooned on seeing the blood and fell backwards from the Indian toilet on which I was squatting. I banged my head against the wall and hurt myself badly. My younger chacha and Bade Mamu must have got me out of the loo after some time. Everyone became nervous and tense. I lay down on the bed and closed my eyes. A doctor from the hospital came to see me. He pulled my eyes open and said, 'It is jaundice. The blood was also a result of that.'

So, I had jaundice. By evening the house and every single thing on earth began to look yellow. The colour of my urine had turned turmeric yellow. It was as if a yellow powder had been smeared on my body, which then also rubbed off on my bed.

My stomach ached slightly all the time. It had also become quite swollen. In addition to the allopathic treatment, a maulana sahib visited me before sunrise to 'shed' the jaundice from my body with a piece of cloth. Along with that, he recited some chapters from the Quran.

I was strictly forbidden from eating greasy food and drinking milk. I was allowed only boiled rice and a mashed, almost liquid food made of potatoes, sugar and sugarcane juice.

The rice and potatoes were always white as they were devoid of chilli and spices, but they looked as yellow as tahiri to me. Raw sugar and sugarcane juice also appeared yellow to me. I was in the grip of a yellow calamity, a storm.

I constantly felt nauseous but did not throw up. It felt as if there was a flaccid, clammy substance that reached my throat from my stomach and went back repeatedly.

But my biggest problem was that I found everyone's face, their bodies and their clothes to be yellow, as if everyone were in mayun. I was also under the delusion of the presence of the sad, silent scent of the ubtan everywhere. The pupils of my eyes had become completely yellow.

I lay on my bed and watched the show of the yellow world all around. I felt a little proud that only I was witness to it. My eyes were distinct from everyone else's – they were capable of seeing the world in another colour and another light.

It was in those days that I heard about the arrest of Aftab Bhai's two brothers-in-law. It came to light that the brothers were against his marriage to their sister and often threatened to kill him. This was the time I, a jaundice-ridden patient, listened to the tales and small talk of policemen that revolved around lockups, remand, third degree, court cases, witness accounts, appearance and bail.

But things were back to square one. Nothing could be proved, in fact very soon something happened that cooled the affair down forever.

The police shot and arrested the dreaded kanpati maar even as he was fleeing after committing someone's murder. The bullet hit him in his leg. He confessed to every crime he had committed, and even confessed to having killed Aftab Bhai! Why did he do this? This remains a complete mystery to me.

One night when I was burning with fever, I opened my eyes to see him standing before me, completely naked. He was dwarfish and yellow, as if someone had coloured him with turmeric. There was a deep black hole in his temple that was oozing yellow blood which flowed down his neck to his legs and then spread to the floor. He smiled at me and moved ahead. A noose was swinging right in front. He looked at me again intently and laughed aloud. He turned his back to me and stepped towards the black rope which had formed the noose. Yellow turmeric powder dropped to the ground from his body and scattered as he walked.

The yellow kanpati maar hanged himself with the black noose, and turned black himself.

I suffered ups and downs in my sickness and recovered in about a month without much treatment.

I began to focus my attention on studies. I was now in class eleven.

Once I recovered I began to put on weight. My bones began to extend themselves and my appetite improved. My intestines wanted more food than before. The horrible incident was wiped away by my fever and jaundice the way someone wipes off filth lying on the floor with a wet cloth.

However, at that time I hadn't known that some germs and vestiges linger. They cannot be cleaned with cloth or soap or even acid.

My time was passing reasonably well when I came to know that Anjum Apa had returned.

I was happy. We'll spend some good time together, I thought. I decided to visit her that evening.

I was elated and my heart was full of joy. I began to think of some novels that might interest Anjum Apa.

With absolutely no concern for the fact that it was Thursday evening and the two states of time were in embrace, I was racing towards Anjum Apa's house, leaping over the graves in which lay the helpless dead waiting for the meals dedicated to them at the Thursday evening fateha.

I saw her in the kitchen, sitting on a low stool. Thin, and darker than before. She stood up on seeing me. She seemed shorter than before, like a stone statue whose feet and toes were eroding.

Her eyes wore a deserted look; perhaps it was the emptiness before the welling up of tears.

'Anjum Apa?'

'Guddu Miyan?'

'Anjum Apa, Anjum Apa,' I repeated.

'Guddu Miyan.' She spread her hands out in a vacuum to get a sense of where I was, and only then did I realize that her eyes were not just empty but static and immobile.

I went close to her. Her clothes smelt of spices, like the clothes of any housewife who spends the majority of her time in the kitchen.

She touched and stroked my hair.

'I heard you were very ill?' A certain familiar and intimate vibration seemed to be missing from her voice.

'Yes.'

'I'm sorry I couldn't sick-visit you.'

'Oh come on, Anjum Apa! Do you know of this new horror novel, *The Ghostly Cat*? I'll get it for you tomorrow.'

'No,' said Anjum Apa with a sob.

'Why? You were always so fond of those dreadful horror-filled novels?'

'You'll have to read them out to me.' Anjum Apa's voice seemed to be coming from afar.

'What do you mean?'

'Because I'm blind now.'

And it was then that I realized my foolishness for the first time. I should have figured out much earlier that she had gone blind.

'I'll come tomorrow,' I said, somewhat flustered as I moved back a few steps without intending to.

'All right.'

I walked back slowly from Anjum Apa's house. On enquiring from Chhote Mamu, I found out that Anjum Apa's husband had turned out to be an extremely cruel and violent man. He was a useless drunkard kind of guy with no income of his own and spent all his time gambling. He bashed up Anjum Apa to extort money from her father, and flung the tobacco from a burning cigarette into Anjum Apa's eyes one day. The poor voiceless girl became blind and no one could do anything about it. Anjum Apa's father was going to remarry at this age and didn't want to get involved in any police or court cases, or even a divorce. He was also averse to the idea of Anjum Apa staying with him any longer. Anjum Apa's husband was close to all the city goons and her father was scared of him too. Her husband often went to his ration shop and showered abuses on him while the husband stayed silent.

Chhote Mamu also told me that her husband visits Anjum Apa at her father's house surreptitiously and abuses and hits her over there too.

'Does no one object?' I asked.

'Who cares and why would anyone interfere in someone else's matter when her father himself is silent,' said Chhote Mamu.

It was the month of March, which was like a forlorn main door through which the winds would come and go. To me March seemed like the desolate, dusty and lonely entrance of a ruin somewhere.

I stood quietly for very long in this March silence. The only sound was of the footsteps of a receding winter.

Standing quietly in this manner, my earlier giant-shaped anger hissed loudly. The same black anger that had coiled itself like a poisonous snake and shrunk and hidden itself in the unseen nerves of my existence somewhere. It wanted to break out from the creases and compartments of my spirit.

I was frightened of the mysterious black snake within me, and recalled that it was just yesterday evening when I had found a cast-off snakeskin in the corner of the inner hall.

The month of Ramzan arrived at last. Everyone in the household used to fast except me. I fasted on but two days of Ramzan. One in the middle of the month and one on the last Friday, because I was not used to fasting at a stretch. I was very careful not to swallow my spit while fasting. This made me spit almost all the time, which was definitely a repulsive habit. I would fill the ground with my spit.

The sehri meal was an elaborate affair at our house. Milk, bread, pheni, khajla, paratha, kebab and fresh curry too. Cooking a curry without meat was probably prohibited during Ramzan.

The sehri scene appears in front of my eyes, before turning stationary the way a running movie pauses suddenly and one scene, just one scene, remains stuck on the screen, like a shrivelled-up dead lizard on the wall. Everyone rose from their beds with their eyes half-open, not in the dark of night but in the dark of predrawn, and shuffled to the kitchen to sit on the low stools kept there.

Since they had bitten their tongues during the night, there was a faint trickle of blood running from their mouths to their chins. They did not care to rinse their mouths as they knew they had to go in for a prolonged rinsing post this. This may have been an eccentric trait, but eccentricities are the fate of all living things, be they human or beasts (my jagged-eared rabbit was eccentric too). The fire was lit, food heated and served before everyone in enamel plates. They began eating, making huge morsels with the English bread and that morsel would get mixed with the dreadful blood trickling down their mouths and chin and assume a red colour.

After sehri they all rinsed their mouths at the tap near the kitchen, drank some water and then performed their ablutions as the call for the Fajr prayer was heard. The men left for the mosque to offer namaz while the women offered it at home on their prayer mats, following which they all proceeded to their beds silently at the crack of dawn. I don't know if they fell asleep or not, but I do remember that it was broad daylight by the time they woke up and engrossed themselves in daily activities.

This was the custom in every household those days. It is probably the same now.

I wasn't so interested in the iftar since it wasn't performed in the kitchen. A durrie and a white sheet was spread in the outer hall and different varieties of eatables and sweetmeats were laid out, but the most remarkable dish was the pakodi. I smile to myself when I think back on how inevitable the pakodis were at iftar time, as if iftar without them was forbidden or at least undesirable according to religious law. At such times, the pakodas and pakodis of India were no less in value and worth than the Arab dates.

I could never sleep after sehri. Once it was morning and there was light all around, I often went over to Anjum Apa's house. Her father also slept after sehri and woke up only around noon, but I always found Anjum Apa sitting with her sightless eyes in the kitchen.

That day too I was on my way to Anjum Apa's house as sunshine spread in the courtyard. Since it was early morning, the graves I crossed were also dozing. I didn't see any kids playing there. The graveyard was a bit too quiet and deserted. I walked gingerly, careful to avoid the graves.

I stopped short at the door of Anjum Apa's house. Someone was screaming and swearing inside. The kitchen, which was the source of the noise, was right in front of the dilapidated entrance door.

I huddled into a corner from where I could see half the kitchen clearly. Anjum Apa's kitchen had no doors.

I saw a man with cruel brown eyes and the mouth of a sinister dog. He was fair and had a spotted, violent face. His lips pressed a repulsive cigarette between them. Where had I seen this man and this cigarette with its revolting odour before? I racked my memory and then I remembered; I recalled everything.

He was swaying and stumbling with intoxication and hurling abuses at Anjum Apa non-stop. And then I saw her.

Anjum Apa was sitting on the floor on her haunches; I couldn't see her face clearly.

'Slut, you loose woman, out with the money you are hiding.'

Anjum Apa did not move.

'Out with it, or I'll cut off your nose and feed it to the crows and vultures. You haven't learnt anything despite having gone blind?'

'I don't have money.'

'Fuck your mother, but your pimp of a father has it.'

'I won't ask him for it.'

'Then take this.' He lifted his heavy, elephant-like leg in the air and kicked Anjum Apa on her forehead with force. Anjum

Apa toppled over on to the floor. She doubled up in pain and cried out in anguish.

'This time the kick will land on your stomach. The unborn baby you are carrying will come hurtling out from between your legs, like before.'

'No,' Anjum Apa screamed hysterically.

I see the man take out a knife. The obscene gleam of the knife's blade reveals Anjum Apa's face to me clearly for the first time. A face turned completely grey with fear and hate.

'Come, let me cut off your nose ... come here.'

His dreadful fist held Anjum Apa's black hair in it. He pulled her up by the hair, brought her face to level and tilted it towards the wall behind, built after the original wall collapsed during the floods. But the wall didn't collapse this time, Anjum Apa did. And a bright, sharp knife landed on her nose.

'Hahahaha.' I heard the devil laugh aloud. And it was revealed to me for the first time that the world of humans had been transformed into a wasteland.

'Abba.' A meaningless and helpless scream echoed in that ruin of a house.

I saw those misshapen legs stumble for a moment, colliding with the chulha in their inebriated state. The vicious knife fell to the ground with an emasculated sound.

Anjum Apa quickly got up and rushed to the door outside the kitchen, where I was standing quietly in a corner.

Panic-stricken, she ran out of the house without her dupatta. She did not see me but I saw her. I saw her running, crying, screaming and going out of sight behind the graves, and I ...

I even saw the blood dripping from her face, her nose. Even after Anjum Apa disappeared behind the graves, her face, her nose and the blood stayed before my eyes like a fixed entity. And I am aware that wherever the colour red is present, so is the colour black before and after it. And I am sure that a black colour was slithering somewhere close to the red blood.

I knew full well where this black colour continued to emerge from.

I felt a strange restlessness in my hands. My entire body stiffened, as if preparing to expel something from within. I had probably even stopped breathing.

Standing at the door in this condition, it seemed as if centuries had passed.

I came to my senses when I heard an unsettling sound caused by the stove burning in the kitchen. Like the anxiety-causing sound of rain. Anjum Apa's house began to get soaked in the invisible rain of that sound.

And just then I witnessed a dark, gigantic shadow come out of me and leap towards the kitchen.

I followed my shadow.

I reached the threshold of the kitchen and quietly stood there.

He was sitting on his haunches on the kitchen floor and preparing tea, remorselessly. His back was towards me. He probably didn't know how dangerous and harmful it can be to sit with one's back towards dark shadows mad with frenzy.

The brown tea was boiling in a small grubby aluminium vessel. I recognized the cockroach.

You may or may not believe it but the same old cockroach had miraculously appeared here. It was perched on an enamel bowl kept near the stove and was staring at me. It was probably going to laugh at me like before in some time.

I felt like I was re-watching an old movie, and just then I glanced at the tea boiling in the vessel again. Milk had not yet been added to it. The tea suddenly changed into boiling blood. Frothy and foamy blood.

A bottle of kerosene oil was placed next to some utensils on the cornice right above the stove. A glass bottle with a dirty rag stuffed in its mouth.

The harrowing hissing of the stove was my accomplice. He didn't sense any movement. His intoxicated head swayed from side to side.

I went and stood right behind him. He wore a grimy checked shirt and a lungi which was half-open and fluttering on the floor.

I stood on my toes and, with bated breath, extended my right hand over his swaying head, my left hand supporting the intentions of the right hand even as it lay in the pocket of my shorts. With great deftness and strength, I struck down the bottle of kerosene from the cornice in one go.

The bottle fell on the burning, hissing stove. I turned on my feet and swiftly ran towards the door. I barely crossed the threshold of the entrance door when I heard a dreadful blast behind me. The awful noise included his hysterical shrieks.

I didn't turn around to look. I ran and hid behind one of the graves. I saw that the entire mohalla was rushing towards Anjum Apa's house.

Someone was shouting, 'The stove has burst. The house is on fire.'

I felt a slight tremor in my legs. I sat down on the grave behind which I had been hiding, my feet dangling. I saw a black cloud of smoke rise behind the rundown houses at a distance.

The fire was brought under control after some time but the din of people refused to die down. Then I saw a black body being laden on to a rickshaw and taken away amid that noise and crowd. The body still had something alive in it, what was the sense otherwise, of taking it to the hospital? The black smoke was spreading in the air. I couldn't see people's faces clearly in the cloud of smoke. This smoky cloudiness was trailing the people and the rickshaw. Then it started swirling above the graves too. A piece of the sky turned grey with smoke.

The crowd started thinning, some people standing here and there talking. The women of the mohalla stood at their doors chatting among themselves, making guesses.

After a while, when ants began to crawl out of the graves and climbing up my calves and shorts, I coolly got up and started walking contentedly, swaying in my own breeze, towards home.

Nothing happened to me this time, neither anxiety nor doubt, neither fear nor any sense of having committed a crime. Had I turned into a seasoned murderer?

'Guddu Miyan has come, Guddu Miyan has come,' said the parrot as soon as I entered.

I slept peacefully in the afternoon after reaching home. It did occur to me though that if there had been no tea cooking on the stove the situation could have been different. The tea being boiled at that time wasn't a good omen. But what was surprising was that I hadn't received any indication of this ill portent, or it was possible that all my five senses had become so powerful there for a short while that the consciousness of the sixth one had been overpowered and buried under their weight.

I didn't contract jaundice or feel cold and develop fever or have bouts of vomiting this time. I had made a compromise with the dark shadow, the black snake existing within me.

Rehana Phuphi told me the next day that Anjum Apa's husband had died before reaching the hospital. The fire was so strong that the entire kitchen was reduced to ashes. If the neighbours had not swung into action within minutes the whole house would have burnt down. Anjum Apa's father had escaped being burnt alive as he was sleeping in the tiny room in the remotest corner of the house at that time. As for Anjum Apa, she had run to another house in the mohalla earlier that morning when her husband tried to kill her and attacked her on the nose with a knife.

'Didn't the police come?' I asked.

'They did, but what can the police do? An accident is an accident. You know that the rod of God's punishment strikes silently,' said Rehana Phuphi as she peeled onions, tears streaming down her face.

I never dared to go to Anjum Apa's house again. I didn't see her for very long, neither did she visit our house. I came to know after a long time that her father had got her married again, this time to a simple and decent man whose first wife had passed away leaving behind many children. Anjum Apa's husband was quite rich and his decency seemed evident considering he had extended support to a blind widow.

When I did see Anjum Apa, she was a changed woman. Laden with precious ornaments, she had grown fat and had developed a considerable paunch. Several big and small children were playing noisily around her. But that hair-raising story is for later.

Time passed and I grew up. My face was covered in a beard and whiskers and I had to shave every day. I was regarded as a young adult male, but deep inside I felt that my youth was over. The memories of my childhood and adolescence had snatched my youth away from me like it is possible only in a terrifying dream. I wanted to get rid of those terrifying dreams but it was not possible. Those memories were like a black flood that, after sweeping away my past with its waves, continues to advance towards me and is adamant on drowning my present and my future too.

If I had grown into a young man, everyone else in my family was nearing old age. Sunbul too was old and ailing. He wasn't keen on eating green chillies any longer. The jagged-eared rabbit too had grown lazy and laid-back. He didn't get up easily once he chose to spread himself somewhere and stared at everyone and everything, including the doors and windows of the house, with his red eyes.

Most people in the family were in poor health. They were always coughing and spitting phlegm and seemed exhausted even if they walked a little. Their stomachs were usually upset and so they were always irritated and looking for excuses to pounce on each other. They were like aggressive dogs and the kitchen was the site of their squabbles. They were hard of hearing and their eyesight had weakened. Their aged eyes were incapable of sighting insects, ants and other creepy-crawlies. Their intestines couldn't tolerate any oily food. Their ability to taste, smell, touch and listen and perceive was diminishing and being scattered into the air, or mingling with the earth, shattering into pieces. The same air and the same earth from which these five senses had once emerged, alive and youthful, with puffed chests. They could only taste water now. During summers their tongues lolled out of their mouths in search of cold water like those of panting dogs.

They were the aged leaves growing on an old tree that can't tolerate even a slight breeze and begin to fall off and crumple.

Noorjahan Khala's condition had worsened. Her hands and feet had to be tied up one day by relatives and friends and she was admitted to an asylum. I don't remember if anyone ever went to visit her.

And this was quite proper. After sweeping the house clean of dirt and rotting food, and collecting the peels and skins of onion and garlic and other vegetables and throwing them out, who on earth goes to see them in the garbage bin or grope for them in narrow and big drains.

Achhan dadi had reduced to a skeleton that still had some papery skin and flesh on it which had rotting sores full of worms.

I think if she had been devoid of flesh and skin and been purely a skeleton made of bones, she would have been enriched with a new beauty; skeletons, after all, have their own charm.

But most people have a very limited, in fact, prejudiced, view of beauty and grace.

By the time I grew into a burly young man, the smell of rotting or burnt food began to spread in the house. Dishes being cooked in the kitchen often got burnt and the food lying there began to rot, but no one noticed the foul smell. Chapattis burnt and turned black while cooking. But nobody cared. They had gotten used to eating burnt and rotten food. They added large quantities of salt and chilli in the food, complaining of its tastelessness and blaming each other for it. The women quarrelled with each other in the kitchen and even came to blows sometimes. The kitchen had turned into a wrestling ground.

They kept growing older and forgetting past incidents. A huge piece of the past had cut itself off from their memories and fallen into a far distance. If they still remembered anything it was the varieties of food, the delicacies they had eaten in the past and their names and flavours. The taste buds that made those flavours come alive for them had long been destroyed.

I need to make an important confession here. Though I was a dangerous murderer, who had committed not one but two murders with extreme cunning and cleverness, no one's suspicion fell on me even a bit. I had made a clean escape after committing two murders, but it has to be acknowledged that the lack of suspicion was also because I was a kid in shorts when I committed those two murders.

The significant point is that despite having committed two murders, I hadn't witnessed any death. Demise was strange to me. Murder and death are two separate subjects. I have seen the shape of murder in my inner self, in fact I have formed that image with my own hands. I had sewn the dress of murder with a needle and thread in my hand, but I was not acquainted with death.

What is death supposed to be, what does it look like, how does it walk, how does it come? I didn't know the answers to any of these questions.

But I was soon to become familiar with it, though I was completely unaware of this at the time.

People with experience can recognize the signals of the arrival of death early. For that matter, even dogs and cats can. But in those times I was completely and pitifully ignorant of the experience of death. My sixth sense, that I prided myself on, warned me in advance about the possibility of a mishap, but what mishap? Was that ill omen death, and even if it was, what did it look like? Did it walk on all fours or on its knees? The sixth sense had no knowledge about this.

Large ants began to appear in the latrine. No one paid any attention to them in the beginning because it was an old-fashioned latrine with tall bricks to squat upon and insects were always crawling in the cracks of these bricks anyway. Geckos and little snakes were often seen there but in those days it was nothing alarming or exceptional. People in the olden days were quite used to such phenomena.

But when the large black ants kept increasing by the day and it started becoming difficult to sit on one's haunches with one's feet on the rests, everyone became concerned. Nothing could be done because killing of ants was prohibited, but then Bade Mamu told us one day that the ants were jumping at his urine, attacking it with force.

I had also noticed innumerable ants crawling or stuck on the floor and in the small, narrow drain after Bade Mamu came back from the loo.

Bade Mamu had been losing weight steadily. His heavy face seemed pinched and there were dark circles under his eyes. He had had a big paunch earlier but his stomach seemed considerably flattened now. His clothes had become loose for him.

Ultimately, when he began feeling very weak, he visited his

family hakim and the mystery of the army of big black ants in the latrine was solved.

There was a large quantity of sugar in Bade Mamu's urine. He had developed a dangerous and severe form of diabetes. His pancreas had almost stopped working.

The hakim started treating him by giving him all kinds of herbal medicines and concoctions and stopping his sugar intake completely.

Bade Mamu was very fond of sweets. It was impossible for him to even swallow, let alone enjoy, simple food. Once he was diagnosed a special diet was prescribed for him and his food was prepared accordingly, which he sometimes threw in the air in anger and frustration. He began to cry like a baby if he smelt something tasty being cooked in the kitchen. The rest of the family members avoided eating in front of him.

One day Bade Mamu showed us a small boil on the left side of his neck.

'Just take a look, Guddu Miyan, what's happening here?' he said, placing his dry finger over it.

I looked carefully. It was a small red boil.

'Nothing much, it's a small pimple,' I said.

'Yes, but it's very taut. Can you just get me the mirror?'

I ran and got him the mirror kept on the cornice in the hall.

'Come, show me.'

I showed him the small and insignificant boil on his neck in the mirror. He was satisfied but kept repeating that it was hurting very badly. He later consoled himself saying that the pain was probably because the boil was right on the artery of the neck.

But the boil developed yellow pus the next day. And it swelled up considerably.

The hakim gave some ointment to put on the boil in a betel leaf but Bade Mamu got no relief, in fact the boil began to hurt and burn with such intensity that Bade Mamu kept groaning in pain all night.

The boil was huge in size by morning and he had developed high fever.

The family hakim was no longer in a position to help.

Bade Mamu was taken to the hospital where he was examined by doctors, who diagnosed that the excessive sugar in his blood stream had caused the boil. But the boil could not be surgically removed till the blood sugar was brought under control.

There were tiny wounds on Bade Mamu's feet too.

He was being given insulin injections. He cried at every small instance and my sixth sense told me that he wasn't crying out of a fear of death. As far as he was concerned, death was probably postponed for an uncertain length of time, the way everyone thinks that even if others are dying left and right their own deaths will remain postponed forever. People are perpetually queueing up to register their names in the book of life. It's a pity, however, that even as they remain in the queue, their names get written in the book of death in a blacker ink, floating in an invisible wind, and they don't get the wind of it.

I can tell you with certainty that Bade Mamu became restless and cried and fretted because he was being deprived of the eatables he relished and regarded as God's bounties.

Those were very hard times for the kitchen. If biryani or korma was being cooked, some radish bhujiya or cauliflower would also be cooking on another hob of the chulha so that its foul smell could drown the aroma of the biryani. In those days the kitchen had turned into a parallel world where everything elegant was subjected to being slathered with muck from the very beginning of creation.

The problem arose only on Thursdays when cooking radish or cauliflower or any such item is prohibited as it is the day of the fateha. Dal was never cooked on Thursdays and even if it were, there was no question of frying it with onion or garlic in hot ghee.

Right from late afternoon on Thursday, Bade Mamu perched himself on his jute charpoy and watched the goings-on in the kitchen carefully. He tried to decipher the aromas wafting from it by scrunching his nose from time to time.

Before sundown, when different kinds of food were arranged in a big round tray and fateha was offered, he watched from a distance and then began to wail like a child. The boil on his neck became larger when he wept. The redness around the boil spread further. The veins of his neck began to swell and it seemed as if the boil was about to burst, releasing all the blood and pus in it.

For some time everyone in the household felt guilty while eating biryani or korma. But how long could this last? After all, each one had his or her own intestines and his or her own teeth; they were all prisoners of the hidden spaces in themselves. Gradually Bade Mamu's wailing and crying became a matter of routine and everyone at home became indifferent to his tears. Bade Mamu began to be overlooked the way a poor cat sitting outside the kitchen is ignored as she watches food being cooked or people eating their food, blinking her eyes, a meek expression on her face.

Many months passed and then a miracle happened.

The boil on Bade Mamu's neck began to shrink. The pus inside started to dry up and the redness around it decreased.

Within a few days it reduced to a small pink dot. The doctors were puzzled. The boil on Bade Mamu's neck was the formation and destruction of a universe – the way the earth comes into existence with the help of a few substances, increases in size and sets out on the journey of growth and progress, before it starts to shrink one day and eventually returns to its constituent substances, which then scatter themselves far into the vacuum. However, Bade Mamu began to appear very old once the boil subsided. He was coughing continuously and his breath was like a hot furnace. His memory was failing him and his eyes wore the look of a stranger. Maybe no one else but I certainly found the colour of his eyes to be yellow too. I could have been imagining this as my senses were always dominated by the colour yellow.

After some time we came to know that Bade Mamu's kidneys were infected. He hardly moved around and his feet, which already had tiny blisters on them, were swollen. His face too swelled up. As a child I did not know but now I understand that his biggest illness was old age. The body is incapable of performing tasks and is more or less absent in sickness and old age.

I don't remember how much time had passed. Bade Mamu kept growing older and his illness became prolonged. It was probably winter again. I still remember the old quilt I had in my childhood. Its cotton wool had transformed into pieces of the fog and disappeared into the concealed occult spaces of the air. But a fistful of the warmth of the blood flowing through my body had remained stuck somewhere inside that cotton wool.

It doesn't take long for the weather to change. It deteriorates even faster than human beings. Humans, poor normal humans, on the other hand, take a long time to undergo change. By the time one reaches the other shore, one has drowned in dark waters, submerged and emerged, and only then become capable of surrendering one's memory. And change the colour of one's eyes. Forget people's names or call out to them wrongly. It is then that one's lungs can coolly rejoice at one's panting breath and take pride in one's cough. Bade Mamu felt no diffidence at asking someone for something sweet even in the middle of the night. This alteration in temperament and this change are purely the result of the permanent loss of ego. An eccentric, old body, almost always absent from all scenarios and ridden with illness, is actually the complete human. A body, fully psychological and shining in its own light like the mathematical digit one, crushing and abandoning the sins, the loathings, the loves and the friendships of the times past, all desires, all lusts covered by the white shroud-like curtain of just one 'desire' – to eat something sweet, the spotless white curtain of the grand desire for sweets overtaking every other emotion.

The black December wind blowing today was probably blowing during those days too. Pushing the people of this world towards the unseen shores of the other world, this black wind is turning the world black too. This world whose spiritual history has been written in a language I have now begun to somewhat understand. But I didn't know any of this then. Yes! How would I have known at that time that the world existed only to satiate the five senses of the people in it? That desire, that madman, that crazy person, that scarlet fruit wrapped in the taste of carnal lust, into which the world buried its teeth and bit off chunk by chunk. This resulted in the world's teeth becoming white, bright and strong. And then?

Then one day those teeth fell into a dirty and discoloured drain and were carried away, rotting. This was their real nirvana. Desire was extinguished one day. The body developed beautiful wrinkles and it grew old; all previous and future accounts were settled.

Those who died in accidents. Those who died in the prime of youth. Those who died before their time due to an unexpected disease. When did they really see life against the backdrop of its grand and terrifying expanse? When did they see a puny compartment gradually empty itself of its burden, its gravel, its dirty muddy oil on the ground and become indifferent to both joy and sorrow and the swaying of a cleansed and ritually purified blue shirt of the spirit on a grand huge rock?

Although the world will not come to an end. The awareness of this continued existence of the world can remain in the form of a beggar child's plaintive and urgent pitiable blabber. Anything is possible on this downward slope of awareness. Life and death slide on it like petty particles. Humans should have risen above these petty particles and thought of other things but it is a pity that they remained entangled in these very things, their heads only filled with these dusty, ordinary particles. Humans roamed the world with this dust in their heads and became robbers and saints, and this dust, dirt and mud – which polluted the oil of memory – turned the hair on their head sticky and grimy. This is my destiny too.

What a unique day it will be when the human forgets to take his medicines, forgets if he has eaten or not.

Dreams will dominate our logical senses. Except for some deprivations of childhood and youth and the decaying pieces of a few complaints or grudges, everything else will float in the clean and pure air of the silvery smoke of dreams. Freedom! Freedom!

To hell with memory!

Bade Mamu often forgot to take his medicines now. He also forgot that he had just had a full meal. The cells and filaments of his brain were decomposing and had become incapable of receiving messages from the intestines or the liver. He forgot people's names and referred to things incorrectly.

'Raees Miyan . . . oh Raees Miyan,' he called out loudly.

There was no one by the name of Raees in our house. He was calling out to me. I understood and went and stood near the foot of his bed.

'Get me something to eat on your way back at night,' he said with a vacant look.

'What?' I asked.

'Anything sweet.'

'But you are not supposed to eat sweets, Bade Mamu.'

'Your f . . . mother's not supposed to!' he roared, and started panting vigorously.

'Listen, bring me four annas worth of tilbugga,' he said, extremely short of breath. It had become a habit with him recently to ask me to get something sweet for him the moment he saw me leaving the house. He ignored all the advice against this by the family members and insisted on eating some sweet or the other, and then promptly forget about what he had eaten. If someone were to remind him, they were treated to the choicest abuses. I had never heard him abuse anyone his entire life before this.

My class twelve board exams were round the corner. I stayed up all night to study, and so I came to know that Bade Mamu had developed a tendency to talk to himself and grumble all night. I had probably heard him say 'Sarwat' only once in these ramblings. It was also possible that I had imagined it.

But his condition didn't remain the same. It changed continuously. One day he leapt up and wobbled towards the kitchen.

'What's it, what's the matter?' Rehana Phuphi and Kaneez Khala ran after him to stop him.

'Nothing, I need to piss.' Bade Mamu glared at them with his yellow eyes.

'But why here? This is the kitchen,' they screamed in shock and fright.

'Since when did this damn thing become the kitchen? The kitchen is there.' He pointed to the sky, where an eagle was flying with a piece of offal in its beak.

They stopped him with great effort and took him to the lavatory.

After some time he stopped getting up from his bed to use the toilet. His eyes remained closed and his mouth open. Flies were often seen squatting on his open mouth because of the sweets he had eaten the previous night, the remnants of which were stuck on his hollow molars and tongue. He was drowsy most of the time.

But that day when urad dal khichdi had been cooked in the afternoon, and while eating which the wind had whispered in my ears and my heart had begun to beat very fast, this drowsiness changed into unconsciousness. Bade Mamu's stomach was bloated and very hard. The doctor was called. He examined Bade Mamu and told us that he wasn't passing urine and his kidneys had stopped working. The unconscious state was a result of the impurities collecting in his blood. The impure and poisonous blood was gradually taking control of his brain.

'Bade Mamu, Bade Mamu,' I screamed into his ear. There was only a hint of movement in his pupils.

He started snoring very loudly by evening. I can never forget those snores. Alarming and scary, sometimes they sounded like the deep breaths of a beast and at others like the repeated opening and shutting of the old, creaking kitchen doors.

The maghrib call to prayer was heard. Bade Mamu's frightful snoring ceased. I didn't hear his hiccup. I didn't see it either, but Rehana Phuphi heard and saw it.

I saw his bloated and hardened stomach in the light of the lantern. I saw his closed eyes. I saw him submerged in a deep sleep. This time I didn't see his open mouth; his mouth was closed now – in this way, I saw the face of death. An old, experienced woman of our mohalla went into the house to pick up the leftover black urad khichdi and milk and threw it on to the street, thus making a formal declaration of mourning.

The only thing I remember other than this is the same black December wind which has still not stopped pursuing me.

Women from our locality and other relatives read the Quran, their heads covered with dupattas. Now and then a weak sob or wail was heard like a single stray note of music.

Thick rolls of incense were lit under his charpoy, and strong gusts of wind spread their mysterious and deathly scent all over the house.

Some woman (whose name and appearance eludes my memory now) got up, opened the kitchen door and began to make halwa. It was the day I came to know how deeply halwa is connected to the dead.

The dead body lay in the courtyard all night. Huddled in a corner, I watched the charpoy of death from a distance. I was hungry, but the chulha in the kitchen was cold today. What about the halwa?

The halwa was not for the family.

The sky showed the first streak of white with the appearance of dawn. Birds perched on the mango tree began to chirp like they did every day. But Sunbul was silent, sitting quietly in his cage with his beak hidden in his feathers.

I can't remember. I can't remember much. The left side of my head has begun to ache again. Pressing my memory so hard and counting the strands of the plucked-out roots of recall is becoming difficult for me at my age. This is agonizing for me; my being, my body, my mind, my intestines and my memory are all the same.

The sunshine descended from the fences of the roof to the courtyard. A board of wood had been placed near the tap in the courtyard. Preparations began to bathe the corpse.

But should I be writing all this? Why am I blackening page after page?

If I had been competent enough to write a novel it would have made some sense, but one shouldn't allow any opportunity to express one's inner being slip, even if it were as ordinary a thing as a leave application in school, or an appeal in a court of law, or a list of groceries to be done, and as for me, a part of my personal history was severed. Like the appendix without which one can remain alive, but still miss that little piece of intestine sometimes which is taken out of one's body and thrown into the garbage bin when it causes pain.

As a kid, Bade Mamu often took me to the circus or a movie or an exhibition.

But I wasn't watching a circus or movie that afternoon. What I was watching had the shadows of flesh-and-blood people in it. I was sitting on a small charpoy, a khatola, on the eastern side of the veranda in the outer hall.

It was almost afternoon. Bade Mamu was being given the ritual bath under the tap right opposite the kitchen before the zuhr azaan.

A prolonged ritual bath.

He must have never had such a prolonged bath full of rituals.

I could see the trembling shadow of that wash on the wall to my right. It was a bath of purification, and the freezing December wind was blowing the shadow to every corner of the house.

The shadow of this ritual wash could not stay in my moist eyes.

The sunlight started changing its direction and colour. Voices began to rise, as if from a deep pit.

Now it was a white shroud, wrapped within which lay Bade Mamu, asleep. People began to come and stand at the head of the bier to look at his face and ask pardon for their sins against him.

The bier was raised, and with it rose the sound of the weeping of women. The cries accompanied the body till the main door, after which the funeral procession went ahead indifferently, leaving the weeping voices behind.

This tall wall of a madhouse, a black and frightful wall through the drains of which madmen thrust their heads and peeped and that wide-spreading graveyard.

Inside the graveyard was a mosque where the prayer for the dead was read out for him. Amid the thickly growing wild grass, I found myself standing at the foot of his dead body.

Burying him deep under the soil, everyone left the graveyard.

Dinner was laid as soon as I reached home.

The food had been brought from a distant relative's house; I can never forget that meal.

Mutton and potato curry cooked in turmeric and huge, thick tandoori rotis. Everyone sat on the floor on which the chandni had been spread, and began eating the curry served in enamel bowls, merrily dipping the pieces of tandoori roti in the curry.

The food was delicious and I had a hearty meal, although I still feel amazed, and a little embarrassed, at having relished that meal. I remember that I hadn't even washed my hands properly after returning from the graveyard, and some of the earth of the grave was still stuck to my hands. When I licked my fingers clean, fingers that were slathered with the thick sauce of the turmeric-laced potato and meat curry, I found that I had swallowed with it some of the grit from the earth of the graveyard.

But the tragedy lies in the fact that the very things one feels embarrassed about are the truths of life; everything else is fake.

At night a lamp was lit at the spot where Bade Mamu had been given the ritual bath.

This lamp had to be kept alight every night till the fortieth day of his death, probably because his spirit would continue to flit in and out of the house for forty days, specially at the place where he was given the ritual bath. *This lamp, burning at the grave, may it not get blown out by the wind!*

One scene remains stuck in the membrane of my memory; let me pluck it with my nails and bring it here before you.

The kitchen came alive with the fragrant aromas of different kinds of food on the ritual of the third day of death, the seom. There was such a bubble of activity in the kitchen that had not even been seen during Anjum Baji's wedding. It was a noisy day right from the morning. Utensils kept clanging and the women were talking to each other constantly. One or two of them even let out a secret laugh now and then.

There wasn't a tear in anyone's eye now. All sorrows, all griefs evaporate and vanish like steam in the act of cooking food.

The preparations for the ritual offering, the fateha, began between asr and maghrib. A chandni was spread over the floor of the outer hall and the choicest of food items were laid out. An incense stick was also lighted.

People gathered and a maulana came and sat in front of all

the food, his knees folded, and began reciting some chapters from the Quran.

I stood next to the wooden beam, wearing a cap, watching the delicacies.

Large enamel plates, dishes, round trays and basins with pulao, korma, shami kebabs, spicy minced meat, dahivada and phulkis in them. There were tandoori rotis, chapattis, parathas and puris too, as well as halwa, kheer and shahi tukda for dessert. My eyes were fixed on the desserts. I could hear Bade Mamu whisper in my ear, 'When you come home at night get something sweet from Badawwan halwai for four annas.'

When my gaze shifted from the sweetmeats, I saw that there was paan too, arranged in a round tray, and some tea as well. Different varieties of fruits, such as guavas, bananas and apples, had also been sliced and placed there. Next to the food items was a brand-new kurta–pyjama set, along with a vest, folded neatly.

Maulana Sahib recited the fateha, and paused to ask, 'How many Qurans were completed?'

Chhote Mamu looked this way and that before replying, 'Two.'

Maulana Sahib made the prayer for the reading of two Qurans and the redemption of the departed soul. Then he prayed for the returns for all the food that had been provided to ensure the passage of the departed soul to heaven. He kept his hands raised in prayer for a long time.

Flies flitted from one dish to the other, particularly the sweetmeats and the cut fruit. Chhote Mamu waved a manual fan from time to time to ward off the flies.

The task of getting the portions ready was accomplished quickly. There were probably seven or eleven portions of food to be distributed among the poor and the underprivileged.

The time for maghrib was approaching and it was getting dark.

Bade Mamu must have been waiting in his grave for the food from his first fateha, I thought gravely.

All the relatives, neighbours and people from the mohalla ate the fateha food that night. The house was bustling with people and there was so much chatter that I began to feel uneasy. Why were people talking so much that day?

But late at night, after all the guests had left, a terrifying silence descended on the house. I saw that silence with my own eyes in the light of the lamp burning on the spot where Bade Mamu had been given the bath.

The fatehas were to continue for seven consecutive Thursdays, which would be followed by the fortieth day of death, the chaliswan.

I witnessed only three Thursdays. But I had now witnessed death and its proper appearance.

I can say with full faith and honesty that murder and death are two separate entities.

They are different in appearance, have different faces and wear different attires.

I hold this opinion to this day.

My class twelve results were announced and I came first in the whole of north district. My photo was published in the papers.

Chhote Mamu had a very serious approach towards education. Our city was really a small town and it lacked a proper degree college. Chhote Mamu did not consult anyone nor did he try to find out my views on the matter. He simply got a form, filled it for me and asked me to sign it, saying, 'Guddu Miyan! You have to leave for the big city in three days. You have been admitted to the largest college there. Start packing your things.'

'Arey, the child could have stayed till the chaliswan at least,' Mumani protested.

'No, it can't be helped. He'll miss the last date for admissions.' Chhote Mamu spoke in a decisive tone.

A train left for the big city at 2 a.m. each day.

Maqsud Khan arrived with his tonga at around 1 a.m. Almost the entire mohalla had come to bid me farewell.

After my luggage had been placed on the tonga, every member of the family hugged me. Their eyes were wet.

My jagged-eared rabbit was rubbing his paws on my feet. I saw his red eyes shining in the dark. He might have been crying. I suddenly remembered something. Rushing back into the house, I went to the parrot's cage. Sunbul looked at me crossly and buried his beak in his feathers.

When I turned around silently to leave, I saw the lamp burning on the spot of the ritual bath go out suddenly. The courtyard became very dark and desolate.

I screamed.

'The lamp isn't burning.'

Mumani and Rehana Phuphi came running and lit the lamp again with a matchstick.

The closed rundown door of the kitchen took on the appearance of an unknown shadowy entity in the light of the lamp, before which the handle of the handpump stood bowed. After I got into the tonga with Chhote Mamu, I suspected I heard Sunbul crying out from his cage,

'Guddu Miyan has gone, Guddu Miyan has gone.'

Chhote Mamu put me on the train after we reached the station. He stood near the window, his sherwani fluttering in the heavy wind. As the train blew the whistle to leave, he started crying. 'Study hard and make the family proud,' he said, as he ran alongside the slowly leaving train, 'Guddu Miyan! Study really hard, write home; you are the bright, shining lamp of the family's future.' His voice and his body accompanied the train for some time and then faded away in the roar of the train and the darkness outside. The derailed compartment of a goods train was lying sideways on the adjacent railway track, and I found it akin to a dead elephant at the time. So I was the lone bright star on the family's horizon! The lamp will keep burning on the bathing spot till the chaliswan and maintain its relationship with the December wind. These winds would be present in the big city too, I thought. Why did the lamp get extinguished just as I was leaving the house? Had Bade Mamu's spirit come to bid farewell to me? The train was now rushing through some deep forests. The cold wind was entering the compartment. I closed the glass shutters. There was darkness all around now. The jerking of the train began to sing a lullaby, rocking me slowly in the dark. I don't know when, sitting in that posture, I fell into a deep sleep.

Muhammad Sajid.
Yes, sir.
Abdul Moeed.
Yes, sir.
Shahkar Alam Warsi.
Yes, sir.
Anil Kumar Singh.
Yes, sir.
Sabir Ali Siddiqi.
Yes, sir.
Harsh Sachdeva.
Hafeezuddin Babar.
'Yes, sir.'
I stand up and respond.
Professor S.P. Yadav took off his spectacles and stared at me with bleak, red eyes.
'Your name is Hafeezuddin Babar?'
'Yes.'
'Father's name?'
'Zaheeruddin Babar'
'What does he do?'

'Sir, he's not alive any more.'

'Oh! I'm sorry to hear that.' Professor Yadav placed the spectacles back over his eyes.

I can never get rid of the memory of this scene. I am always accompanied by it. Always. In fact, I cannot even call it a memory.

Do I think about my knees, my nails, the wax in my ears? But they are with me, part of my body. In the same way, the scene of the first day of college in the city lives in my mind, without a reason or motive.

It was the BA Political Science course. This was the best college in the city. The Gothic-style building was of red brick. The college was an old one and had been affiliated to Calcutta University at some stage. This college's hostel was a renowned one and not many university hostels would be able to measure up to its standards. I was easily allotted a room in the hostel.

This big city wasn't very far from my home town. There were only two rivers to be crossed on the way. One was the river by the fort just outside my city, and the other, after some distance, the Ramganga.

But once I was here my home felt far away. Past incidents seemed like the nightmares that one either laughs off or forgets after waking up in the morning.

This was quite strange and surprising. I seemed to be in the grip of a storm that was carrying far into the distance, wrapped in the whirlwind of its mysterious dust, all the memories I had carried with me from my house.

And the reality is that I wasn't sad. This was probably my desire, hidden deep within my subconscious, to forget all that.

The truth is, new as I was to the city as well as the college, I began to forget almost everything mercilessly. After some time I even forgot that I was called Guddu Miyan at home. I was now

Hafeezuddin Babar or Hafeezuddin or Hafeez. I was Guddu Miyan to no one now.

The number of friends I made kept increasing. My personality acquired a completely different dimension. I became part of a group of a few smart and intelligent boys. The college also had girls, many of whom were in romantic relationships with the boys, but there were many restrictions too. Today as I write these lines (am I really writing them?), I think about how different the 1960s were and how quickly and drastically things have changed.

But wait! I shouldn't be writing my memoirs like this. These are just accounts. And accounts won't do for me. I shouldn't forget that I'm not writing an autobiography. I'm writing some petitions, some appeals and so on. My purpose is to find my court of law. And as I've said earlier, if I knew how to write a single line properly, or write creatively for that matter, I would have managed to build the grand main door of the novel. I wouldn't have needed to go anywhere else. I would have lived within my novel. My case, my court of law, my justice and my home would have been in the novel. The novel is such a thing. You should just know how to write it. After that, you'll find punishment, reward, heaven and hell, all within the novel itself.

But sadly, I'm completely infertile and unproductive in this field. As a result, whatever I'm writing is turning into applications and appeals. The petitions are piling up. But since every appeal and every petition has some or the other interior aspect to it, the fact is that the most important and decisive aspect is of the inner self of the writer. There is great artistic value hidden in standing pathetically with a begging bowl in one's hands, which is why I shy away from every testimony where the self doesn't play an active role. And the number of words is limited in petitions and appeals. If the words are too many or too few they tear up the pages into pieces and fling them in your face, and you can't do anything except pick up those torn pieces of paper one by one and throw them into a huge garbage bin. The affidavits and the receipt tickets pasted on them, they ended up inside the garbage bin because of one small mistake.

The garbage bin is gradually transforming into an archive, a record room.

Hence, I am obliged to avoid unnecessary details, although I am aware that earlier I have gone into unnecessary superfluous detail and indulged in meaningless nitpicking. But I understand that such frivolousness can prove very dangerous in such serious and legal matters.

My subjects for BA were Economics, Political Science, Philosophy and English.

I was becoming more and more brilliant each day. Why should I be modest? And that too at a time when I can see the evening of my life right before me, wrapped in dust and mist.

I hardly hung out with my classmates and spent most of my time talking and debating with MA students and PhD scholars, which had almost become an addiction for me. Despite philosophy being my least favourite subject, the logic in it had become the flame to my fire. There was nothing except random abstract thoughts there. Western philosophy in particular was nothing but a bundle of contradictions consisting of incoherent ideas and childish notions.

And yet there were some themes in Indian philosophy that attracted my attention, especially matters of the spirit and the body, theories of life after death and many such topics. In fact, the principles and arguments, particularly in the philosophy of logic, presented in Indian philosophy were so elaborate that Aristotle couldn't do even a tenth of the tenth of it.

The relationship between the spirit and the body has never been understood with any certainty by humans, which is why my interest has been in human beings rather than simply the study of unknown thoughts. I studied the other subjects with full dedication. My interest in detective novels had waned, but I have always regarded the connection between the spirit and the body as the plot of a detective novel, and as a student I wish I had understood all that I'm writing about now. I feel like writing the same lines that I have written before.

This world originated as an insignificant dot. But it has acquired a giant, demonic size and shape in which the business of life and death goes on. The spirit lives in the body like air. Then it abandons the body one day, leaving it remorselessly like a selfish and mean guest. It leaves its original home where it was welcomed and so well taken care of. It was given prime importance and was endlessly indulged and pampered. But the spirit is entirely lacking in affection and regard. It leaves the body behind, rejecting it like an incident from the past and leaving it for another world, the eternal one.

But his spirit will not do it. It won't forget its host's house, rather, its own house. It won't turn to the higher worlds, but will maintain its connection with this world, its home and its people.

It is possible that this is shameful and defamatory for his spirit, and he would be scolded and cursed for it or even subjected to black magic. People adept in matters of the occult may be called in for help and charms and amulets might be used on him.

But his spirit will convert this holter of curses into its cross and loading its sins and crimes on its invisible shoulders, will wander here. Yes, right here. It will never depart to an eternal world. It will acknowledge and accept its perpetual suffering, restlessness and unease as destiny and fly about the atmosphere like a balloon.

The mutual agreement between the spirit and the body has afflicted us with the fear of death. This world, which began as a tiny speck, has turned into a deep mystery for humans.

But it is not a mystery for him. It is not a riddle or a question – it is just like a disease, the irrational and haphazard expansion of an ugly dot, akin to a cancer.

This world, in which live humans, and children, and a kitchen too remains hidden within this weird dot.

Yes, the kitchen – an extremely horrible and dangerous place. It is possible that this very kitchen has majorly contributed to the growth and expansion of the bizarre and freakish dot. It was from here that he received evil forebodings of some future mishap like a severe torrent of rain.

But this is the story of 'him' who has yet not been cut off and emerged from 'me'. But this can at least be considered a sworn account in absentia of that 'me'. And the possibility of using this particular account for a legitimate purpose at the right time should also not be avoided. At present it is a little difficult to hear 'his' story or narrate it because of the commotion around. 'Me' has raised quite a clamour, a tremendous cacophony. Nobody will be able to hear the voice of the still winds and the sound of silences. It is noisy, very noisy.

And in the middle of this babble, there was this poisonous snake within me which, in a way, and in some matters, had illuminated the fourteen degrees of wisdom in my head. This snake wriggled in my mind and made me uneasy, making my legs tremble. This sickness and my misfortune did not leave me here.

I forgot two murders. I forgot Bade Mamu's death. But the one thing I didn't forget was the possible portent of a certain scent emanating from the kitchen.

I was never successful in getting rid of this strange and mysterious ability.

My room in the hostel was at the end of the corridor beyond which was the mess, or, in other words, the kingdom of the kitchen.

Different odours and aromas wafted into my room from the kitchen all day and I was obliged to keep sniffing them like a dog. Students hadn't been satisfied with the hostel food for some time now.

Tripathi and Idrees were sitting in my room sipping tea.

'Yaar, Hafeez, this can't go on any longer,' Idrees said, lighting a cigarette.

'What happened?'

'Those bloody fellows forced us to eat dhobi pulao in the name of biryani yesterday.'

Tripathi gave a loud laugh. He shoved paan masala into his mouth and began chewing it in a repulsive manner. Soon he would come up with a catchy phrase from the Upanishads or the Vedas regarding food. Tripathi had acquired a fair amount of expertise in ancient Indian philosophy. Just then I became aware of a rotting smell in my nostrils. As I flared my nostrils to smell better, Alauddin burst out laughing and said, 'Cauliflower, it's cauliflower.'

'Yaar, cauliflower smells awful when it's being cooked!'

'It is because of the sulphur. Cauliflower contains a good amount of *gandhak*,' said Tripathi, showing off his knowledge.

'Do you know, guys,' said Alauddin with a yawn, 'they also use fresh human excrement as manure to farm cauliflowers?'

'Look, brother, Alauddin – have you read about the food cycle?' Tripathi asked.

Alauddin shook his head.

'I had science as a subject in my high school. I've read about it. The whole game is of nitrogen and ammonia. Things begin from where they end. This is a journey from intestines to intestines. The food that goes into one's intestines changes shape and colour and emerges from them, destroying and putrefying itself to manufacture food once again for the intestines. Therefore, this yagya is of special importance in the Yajur Veda, a yagya in which the power of the mantra alleviates the hunger in the intestines and food becomes a series of symbols.' Tripathi elaborated on this further, but I wasn't listening.

My hands and legs were trembling.

The black magic had followed me here. Right from home to this city. I had crossed two rivers, but the magic hadn't waned.

I began to feel a wicked and mean happiness. This magic isn't my enemy. It's my strength. A dark strength that no one knows about. My sixth sense is of a magnitude that it will take over the blue sky one day. I remembered all the geometrical shapes, their angles and their mutual equations. My hands and feet stopped shivering the moment I experienced this wicked happiness.

'It is not a good occasion to cook cauliflower,' I spoke in measured tones, smiling.

'Arey yaar, cooking cauliflower is never a good occasion,' Tripathi said listlessly.

I kept quiet, gloating secretly.

'Let's go to the dining hall, it's almost two o'clock. I'm hungry.' Alauddin got up.

'You guys go. I'll eat in my room,' I said.

'Oh, you bloody idiot, you nerd, it is guys like you who are losers. Stop being a bookworm, stop it,' Tripathi began his lecture again.

I gave a yawn for his benefit and lay down, covering myself with a sheet.

Alauddin and Tripathi left the room. It was the month of November, which is no month at all. It has no identity, no image of its own, which is why it requires dreadful and evil events to create awareness about itself and draw attention to its dates. There was no sun that day, so it started getting dark by 3 p.m. There seemed to be a huge commotion happening in the dining hall. I pulled down my sheet and tried to listen to what was going on. This was not the usual bustle of students eating and talking about the food. I was slightly hungry by now. The bearer had kept the food on my table and left long ago. But I was waiting to hear some bad news, and eat comfortably later. I wanted to know if the news would be about a student or a professor or that tyrant of a principal, but this much I was sure of, that the cooking of the cauliflower in the mess kitchen at that time on that day was wrong and of ill portent.

The noise was now travelling from the dining hall to the corridor. I got up from the bed and went and stood at the door of my room. From a distance I could see Tripathi running in my direction.

'Hafeez, Hafeez, it's a disaster!' he started shouting.

'What happened?' I began convinced of my ability.

'Indira Gandhi has been killed.'

I began to go into a stupor. I had not expected the news to be of such great wickedness even in my wildest dreams.

I could see students and professors scuttling across in confusion. Many people were holding up transistors to their ears. We were informed that classes were suspended till the next day.

Before we knew it, it was evening. The sun sets so quickly in late October and November that it's almost imperceptible. There was an eerie silence all around. The streets appeared deserted and terror-stricken. People had either gathered in groups to exchange notes or were scurrying home quickly. All government offices had been declared closed. I kept wandering the streets near my college, loitering around the few bookshops there. I remembered someone back home once saying that when a great political leader or administrator of a country passes away, the whole country acquires a bleak and deserted look and there is a kind of wilderness all around. And it certainly was so. The prime minister, Mrs Indira Gandhi, was ridden with the bullets of her own bodyguards close to her house in Delhi, which was 450 kilometres away from where I stood. But the wilderness extended till there. It is quite possible that some part of the drab November evening might have added to the desolation.

I reached Prasad Talkies. Hoardings of Amitabh Bachchan and Dharmendra were on display. The film *Sholay* had been running in the theatre for the past eight years. And today, as I write these lines, it is still running there. I'm sixty-eight years old now. It is another matter that Amitabh BAchhan and Dharmendra also look old and pathetic now.

The cinema hall was empty and the door was locked. All the cinema halls of the city had been shut down. I hadn't gone there to watch a movie, but the lock hanging on the door of the cinema hall and the deserted look that it wore gave me a painful jolt.

I saw the burning rage of revenge in Sanjeev Kumar's eyes on the posters of the film and thought to myself that this evening Sanjeev Kumar's revenge will remain shut in the silent dark reels of the movie and not present itself on the silver screen. The way every revenge, in fact, every emotion flows within a time frame and then stops flowing, the way blood flowing through the veins congeals and the heart stops beating.

That was a period of revenge. The times of the 'angry young man'. Rajesh Khanna's era, the era of tragedies, sacrifices and love had just about passed and no signs of it remained any longer. Revenge had a unique flavour in those days. This individualistic revenge was not only popular among the masses, it received much appreciation and applause from critics as well.

Revenge, the product of which or the worm of the roots of which I too was, and Indira Gandhi's killing?

The revenge for attacking the Golden Temple and for not acknowledging Khalistan as a political entity.

Several police vehicles, their sirens blaring, passed me as I stood before the cinema hall. Section 440 had been imposed. There was news on the radio that Sikhs were being massacred in Delhi. Markets were being set ablaze and houses of Sikhs burnt down. Indira Gandhi's murder was being avenged.

The evening of 31 October began to change into a winter night. The sense of desolation, along with that of fear and terror, increased some more.

I came back to my room in the hostel.

My friends were waiting for me in the corridor. They all came to my room.

The terrible smell of cauliflower had filled the room. I covered my nose.

Friends kept coming to my room all night. Tea was prepared over the heater and political arguments and debates continued, although we were only old enough to have childish and immature ideas about society and politics. Nevertheless, once in a while, an opinion stood out, the relevance of which I can understand better now than I did in those days.

As far as I am concerned, I had no political awareness at that time and neither do I possess any now. There were other questions confronting me. I was accompanied by a past that smelt of blood. Though I had shamelessly forgotten that past, the fact is that no one really forgets anything. A leaf falls from a tree and sticks to the sole of your shoe. You hear the scrape of the leaf as you walk on the street, but the noise of the world around you drowns the sound and destroys it.

But there comes a day when you sit down to clean and polish your shoes. That day reminds you of your sins. That day reminds you of the number of dirty clothes you sent to the dhobi, you fish out that list from your pocket and examine which garment was damaged or torn at the dhobi's and which one has been lost forever. So that was all, and after coming here, to the city, the mere odour of cauliflower being cooked reminded me of the frightful ape residing within me. Everything came back with such a force that writing the word 'yaad' on paper seemed the most ridiculous thing to do.

My questions were not about political mistakes. I was not competent enough to discuss Indira Gandhi's political blunders. I agitated my left brain by constantly thinking about crime, punishment and justice and it started aching like a sore.

Who is it that commits crimes?

What is punishment like? Does the face of punishment resemble that of murder?

Which song does the hangman sing as he leads the accused to the gallows?

And justice? Which is the court that imparts justice? Where *is* this court? What is the difference between punishment and justice? Are the teeth of punishment as big and pointed as those of justice? How similar are the countenances of punishment and justice?

And most important of all, whose hand is it that dips its fingers in the blood-like red ink of justice to inscribe the hated numerals of punishment on the human back? Whose hand?

Whose hand is it?

Entire areas belonging to Sikhs were torched and gurdwaras were set on fire. Sikhs were being killed here there and everywhere ceaselessly. Much later, it was probably Rajiv Gandhi who said, 'when a huge leafy and shady tree falls...I don't know what he said after this. But recalling it now, that too by racking my memory, is merely a painful exercise that is futile and meaningless.

I changed my mind that night. The year after would be my second year of graduation in political science. My decision to get an MA in Political Science and follow it up with research and teaching in a university altered suddenly.

I made a firm decision to study law and seek admission for it the following year. I remember that the moment I made up my mind I felt a great amount of relief, albeit temporarily – the night had passed and dawn was breaking.

Everyone's eyes were heavy with sleep.

Even as I was falling asleep, I heard this news on the radio.

'Rajiv Gandhi has been made the Prime Minister of the country.'

This news was like a lullaby being sung to me. I was suddenly overcome by a strong surge of sleep. This unsophisticated November morning wind carried a tasteless and dry nip. I covered my face with the sheet.

The pursuit of my education continued and I also visited home off and on. I have reached a point in my appeal where talking about home in detail once again might weaken my case, however, there are a few incidents I need to talk about here, even if in passing. Based on my knowledge of the law, and the method of according a status of reliability and authenticity to a document that has been taught to me, this is what I should do, even if my mind and mood are not inclined towards it.

Everyone at home had grown weak and aged, and I no longer felt interested in them the way I was earlier. When my BA final exams were very close, I received news of two deaths simultaneously. Achhan Dadi had finally died, and two days before her my jagged-eared rabbit was found dead under the mango tree. Let alone be greatly affected by them, these two deaths failed to stir me at any level.

I don't know if this agrees with my temperament or not, but the fact of the matter is that when I was in college I had forgotten my home, my childhood, my pets and everything there like one forgets a nightmare.

News of deaths back home felt only as bad as one does on reading an obituary in the newspapers. When I came to know that my jagged-eared rabbit had become somewhat dull ever since I left home, I felt a little sad, but I wasn't sure if this report was true because Nasreen Khala always gave exaggerated and overdramatic accounts of animals. She thought every animal had a fever, be it a dog, a cat, a rabbit or a parrot. Pigeons, cows, buffaloes and horses were not spared either.

I was told that the jagged-eared rabbit was buried in the uncemented part of the courtyard.

But as I have said before, whatever we think we have forgotten, or what we actually forget, remains stuck to the sole of our shoe. It is only a question of when we will sit down to clean our shoes.

In those days at least I had stopped paying attention to cleaning my feet, let alone my shoes.

Summer vacation was upon us. I went home and stayed there for about a month, bored and uninterested. The house was constantly smelling of burnt food. The members of my family were almost deaf by now. They had nothing better to do than to stand at the door of the kitchen or inside it and squabble and argue among themselves endlessly. These arguments and quarrels included not just the women but the men of the household too, whose one and only interest in life was food and the process of eating and cooking it in the kitchen, even though their palates had gone numb with age and they had no taste buds left.

The salt tins in the kitchen were being emptied quickly as they required large amounts of salt and chillies to be able to taste anything. If there was any bounty of God left for them in this world, it was red-hot chillies.

The kitchen witnessed horrible fights over salt and chillies. The younger members of the household wanted a more restrained use of salt and pepper, while the older ones wanted entire tins of salt and spices emptied into the dishes being prepared. The fights got so out of hand sometimes that the ones with a hot temper were ready to throw chilli powder into each other's eyes. Those were dangerous times. Very dangerous.

The aged members' teeth had begun to fall, breaking into pieces. There were teeth on the ground, teeth in the drains. Teeth in the soiled utensils. Lifeless, brown teeth with huge cavities that lodged hot spices. When they cleaned and massaged their teeth at night with their fingers, the peppercorns, cumin seeds, cloves and red chilli seeds from the previous meal that they had eaten fell out and accumulated in the drain. They rinsed their mouths noisily but their mouths never got cleaned properly.

Their jaws also moved differently now when they ate. It was an unpleasant and troublesome but avaricious act, and ridiculous to some extent too. Their cheeks swelled and deflated in a strange manner and their throats let out sounds as if they were trying to make unsuccessful and pathetic attempts at singing some forgotten raga.

One blazing afternoon a rickshaw pulled up at our door. The month of June, gusts of the Loo, and a man and a woman. I remember this scene like someone drawing a line on a piece of white paper with a knife, where remembrance and pain, memory and bruise become synonymous with each other.

When the woman took off her black burkha, I was able to recognize her with some effort. Yes, I certainly had to try.

It was Anjum Baji, but she had grown very fat. Rounded and heavy, due to which she seemed shorter than she was. She was covered in expensive and ornate jewellery, to the extent that it seemed in bad taste. She was stooping a little, probably crushed under the weight of those ornaments.

She was visiting from Dubai after two years. Her husband was a foolish braggart who wanted to flaunt his wealth. Anjum Baji looked at me and smiled.

But the forlorn pale yellow of her personality was gone now, in fact I found her skin to have a reddish tone. Her body probably contained a lot of blood, a sign of vulgarity.

Anjum Baji saw me and smiled, but that smile had no meaning. It was a formal, worldly smile. She asked me, 'Do you like it in the city?'

'Yes.'

'It's your final year of BA?'

'Yes.'

Then she shifted her gaze from me and started talking to other members of the family.

If someone doesn't believe in the ironies of fate, they should come and see me. Not just the same day, but in that exact moment, Anjum Apa also showed up. She had heard of Anjum Baji's arrival and had come to meet her. That Loo-racked afternoon, that flaming fire.

It was a pity but Anjum Apa had grown fat too and was wearing many ornaments. Noisy children of all sizes surrounded her. She had a paunch that shook every time she laughed.

She looked at me and asked, 'Are you well, Guddu Miyan?'

'Yes.'

'You are in grade 14?'

'Yes.'

Then Anjum Apa turned her face away and started talking to Anjum Baji.

Once the sherbet had been placed before the guests, I went and stood quietly near the parrot's cage hanging from the wooden beam.

Sunbul spat the green chilli out of his beak and rolled his eyes in my direction.

'Sunbul, where is the grave of my jagged-eared rabbit?' I said, placing my mouth on the wires of the cage.

The parrot said, 'Guddu Miyan is here, Guddu Miyan is here.'

I felt like weeping loudly.

Anjum Baji and Anjum Apa returned to their respective homes in the evening, making some perfunctory remarks to me before leaving.

The tragedy was that both of them were blissfully unaware of the huge favours I had done them.

Such grand favours!

Two murders, not one but two murders, committed willingly by my hands.

But the two of them didn't know anything.

I was just an ordinary, timid boy of the family for them and nothing more than that, and the two of them had their own separate worlds that had no connection to my dark, poisonous and secret world. It was as if they had sat on a flying saucer and, with complete dispassion, reached another planet.

In vain I searched all night for the cockroach that was witness to my great favours, even as Sunbul kept taking jibes at me saying, 'Guddu Miyan has come, Guddu Miyan has come.'

I felt like wringing the parrot's neck out of anger and frustration. But these are bygone things. I have come to realize that life is the name of such a flat entity. Everything is routine. The past, the present and the future are all loaded upon each other. One riding the other. Eating, and eating to satisfy one's hunger is the real human principle. It is only the human intestines that at least provide her with a diminutive and broken vision.

This is the entire case. What can one complain of? Of what

good is complaining when all they do is stuff their mouths with food and copulate incessantly? How will they ever become aware of the good someone has done them? And they were not at all to blame in this regard. Who on earth had asked me to murder for them?

I never saw Anjum Apa and Anjum Baji again. I don't even know if they are dead or alive. I had no connection left with them. The relationships had turned into dried-up trees that no one ever watered.

Once that sad and painful summer vacation was over, I came back to the city. I topped the BA exam again and easily got a seat in the LLB programme.

While studying Law I often got the feeling that I would suddenly find a solution to my problems. But there was no trace of any such solution.

This subject was like religion, science or philosophy, where there are only some words and then some items that represent those words and some tricks about how to bide one's life. I began to study law with all possible attention and interest. Believe it or not, I was not studying law to make a career out of it. I didn't want to become a lawyer or even a judge. I was searching for that route, and trying to recognize the signposts on it which would take me to a point where I could find both, the advocate and the judge, as well as the huge Gothic building known as the court. I don't know why I always imagined a huge Gothic building spread over a large area at the mention of a court.

Although I know that courts of law also exist under the open skies, in the winds.

One day in September there was a strong wind, so strong that it carried the clouds away with it rather than bring rain. This strong wind had found some cloud of the past from God knows where, probably from the netherworld. I looked up now, and found the exact same cloud in the sky. A mixture of grey and light brown. It wasn't sailing with the wind; it was stationary in the sky. Like a frightening mountain or a deep black river.

I recognized the cloud. That horrible rain that had poured down ages ago. When there were floods, when Achhan Dadi wrote 'qaaf' on a piece of paper and went to the lime tree in the courtyard to fix the paper on it and slipped and fell. When she had broken her hip and become bedridden and developed festering wounds on her body with worms in them. It had been the same cloud then. Exactly the same. When I saw strange dreams in my sleep. Dreams in which I always met a girl who either didn't resemble anyone I had ever seen or resembled everyone. Dreams that always swept a broom over my existence. A melancholy sweeping that is only done three days after someone's death.

I went to the hostel terrace. I examined the sky again. Yes, it was the same cloud. There had been a prolonged and terrifying downpour when it had descended the first time. The same shade, the same shape, the same margins and the same smoky dimensions. The same light devouring malice in it, the same thick, ugly, huge black curtain casting itself over the sun.

So will there be a flood again this year, and will it rain menacingly? That terrible cloud was hanging right over my head, not budging despite the strong wind.

And then the expected happened.

It began to rain.

Everyone was pleased initially. Boys and girls in the college roamed around gleefully in the rain eating hot samosas. Newspapers and radio reported the good news of a strong monsoon. But I knew that there was no monsoon in September. In fact, the monsoon recedes in September. The radio, the newspapers, they all know how to lie. And these lies have deep economic and financial reasons behind them.

The average person remains clueless, never ever realizing that no weather office is autonomous.

My prediction came true in a week. I was in the process of studying the copy of an old, yellowed document. I knew that there would be floods and also that there would be tremors.

That is what happened, and it continued to rain, on the city, on the rivers, on the houses and on people's fates.

My room's ceiling began to leak. The floodwaters spread far and wide. The pitter-patter of the rain, the sound of my childhood, was back. It turned into the same old lullaby and I began to fall into deep sleep those days, dreaming the same forgotten dreams that were crawling out of the dark, old depths of the left part of my brain.

What did the floodwaters not wash away? There was a house flowing in them, leaving behind its foundations, leaving behind the busiest square of the small bazaar, floating along with its moss-covered walls and rundown doors. The house had arrived here, along with its broken turrets and its first-floor drawing room, having travelled hundreds of miles in hundreds of years, and come to a halt right outside my house, bobbing up and down in the muddy, black floodwater.

I heard the clink of bangles inside the house. A blue dupatta fluttering in the wind in the courtyard. The earthy, fresh aroma of hot chapattis was wafting out of the kitchen. All I needed to do was take a giant leap and cross the threshold, but just then the wind turned blue. This was an evil wind. The older winds were returning, leaving me alone and helpless.

She was sitting on the floor and burning waste paper and wood shavings in a large, shallow dish. It was very cold outside. I started warming my hands over the fire lit in the dish. My teeth were chattering with cold. I touched the ice-cold chapatti that she was toasting for me over the fire, and my hand knocked over half of the white chapatti into the dish and, turning into flour again, it began to burn. But she held half of it in her hand, like the moon divided into two.

She quietly extended the sliced moon towards me. The blood that had dripped on to the chapatti from her eyes had congealed and turned black.

A collective rain of stones of cold, insult and sorrow began to fall on me. I was staring at the fire burning in the trough. The debased, cheap tears fell from my eyes into the fire. No salt would evaporate on the burning of these tears. These tears were shameless and insensitive to the extreme and didn't even have salt in them. They could achieve nothing. The fire required a huge sacrifice. Smoke began to fill the room, making her cough violently. Her shadow, which had been on the floor, began to fall on the walls as she coughed. She placed the half-moon on my head and turned into smoke. The house began to fade into oblivion.

I woke up to the sound of the incessant rain. That girl was there in my dreams every day. Who was that girl? Or, who is that girl?

Wind, rain? Wilderness, crime, murder, sin or love? Who could she be of mine?

What does it matter who she is, but I continued to see her for as long as the rain continued. Feeding me something or the other, but sad, alone and full of complaint.

Those dreams revived some of the old wounds in my heart. When did I receive those wounds? I was not even sure of that.

But they were there. And I came across old sorrows when I searched my heart a little, they were all there, and I found them the way one finds a crumpled old piece of paper in the pocket of one's trousers. Or an old cinema ticket, or a railway or bus ticket. The print may have been erased but the ticket was still there.

The question that remained after washing and ironing one's trousers hundreds of times was that what was one to do with these sorrows and these wounds? The question was not of their permanence but of the use that was left of them. The sting, the pus and the redness of the sores was gone now, like the numbers printed on the old tickets.

So did I discard those crumpled pieces of paper, those washed-out shreds?

No, that was something I just couldn't do.

An incomplete attempt, a useless task remained.

This was just the beginning of self-mortification for me.

The rain stopped after fifteen days and I came to know through a letter from Chhote Mamu that, far away, that rain had virtually turned my house into a shambles. Every roof and every wall was in bad shape and my parrot, old and weak, got soaked in the water coming through the wooden ceiling and died, fluttering his wings loudly in his cage. When I go home now who will call out, 'Guddu Miyan has come, Guddu Miyan has come'?

Am I forgetting something?

It is occurring to me again and again that I'm forgetting my own story in the process of telling others' stories. I know it's natural to miss something or the other considering my age, but what I'm worried about is that whatever I miss may be of significance, and since I've developed this desire to file an appeal at this ripe age, I'm apprehensive that my mind's weakness will cause me to miss some important points and I will be unsuccessful in taking my court to the correct position and receiving my sentence at the right time.

But it is these stories of others that are the indecipherable signatures on the seals which will allow my writing to attain legal status, despite the fact that it's not really difficult to obtain fake signatures, stamps or seals. One would be justified in regarding every name featured in the appeal as fake. However, there is no risk of my feeling shocked or sad at this. Why?

Because I know now that all the battles fought in courtrooms are verbal. The limits of a person's existence and being are the limits of his or her words (I think Wittgenstein said this).

Besides, my court of law will probably be more exalted than even those high ones – the Indian Penal Code may not turn out to be very useful for me. In my study of law, I had committed the entire code and all its subsections to memory and tried to internalize them in my soul.

Therefore, it is dangerous for me to forget, for I will never be able to remove the burden of my debt. The thought of the presence of a different kind of language in this huge court keeps bothering me. If I forget something or convey it incorrectly or give something an inappropriate angle, I will lose the case, which is why I'm asking for my lost memory joining both my hands (provided I am forgetting something, that is) because hands have a personality of their own. Their own understanding, their own intent and their own emotion.

When one hand lifts a dagger to kill someone, no son of woman can tell what the other hand wants, or whether the other hand's nerves accept it.

There are veins all over these hands now. They have grown dark and thin. So thin that the metal strap of my watch slips off my wrist and slides to my palm repeatedly.

But perhaps these hands are quiet. In fact, they are deaf and dumb.

So then there is either the weak left part of my brain or my ill-fated huge eyes that look like boiled eggs, and I regard any scene trapped at whatever angle in them as authentic, and proceed with my appeal. I do this despite all my doubts, for I am helpless. I'm ashamed at having called my memory a miraculous one at some point though I would sometimes erase from memory incidents of my childhood and my home as dismissively as I am slashing off the margins of this paper with my paper knife and throwing them into the dustbin to give it an elegant and symmetrical shape.

Despite this, the shadow of my childhood had not abandoned

me. The red bulb of danger often flashed in my spirit, making me as alert as a dog that sniffs around and raises its snout to recognize heaven's curses and begins to moan and wail.

I remember the boys in the hostel bubbling with excitement as there was going to be chicken biryani for dinner that night. I don't like chicken biryani at all. I think it has a nauseous smell, which is why I wasn't in the best of moods since evening. But at around 7 p.m. when my nostrils picked up the smell of the chicken yakhni, the broth in which the rice was to be cooked, my heart began beating very fast. I started panting. It seemed my lungs had contracted fear and my breathlessness was a result of it.

In due course, dinner was eaten in the dining hall with eagerness, ravenously and noisily. I didn't eat the food as not only was I feeling uneasy, but I had developed acidity as well that evening. However, I gave my friends company in the dining hall.

Suddenly we heard a noise from the direction of the girls' hostel. We ran outside.

There was an ambulance parked at the gate of the hostel and wardens were running around in confusion. A crowd of girls stood at the gate.

After some time we got to know that Manorama had choked on her food. Before she could take a sip of water, she was overcome by shortness of breath and, in a horrendous turn of events, asphyxiated.

My breathlessness seemed under control now. The result was out. The result of cooking chicken biryani. Why would I feel uneasy now? Uneasiness occurs only before an unseen and unknown possibility of danger.

I turned to look at Tripathi. His face had turned yellow and he was trembling like a leaf. I realized that he was trying to slip out of the room unnoticed, and before I could say anything to him he disappeared into the crowd.

Can you believe that I have not seen Tripathi since that day? I was enrolled in LLB and he was doing his master's in Philosophy, but our friendship had endured and we spent quite a lot of time together every day. The entire college knew Tripathi was involved with Manorama. But no one had imagined that things would reach such a pass.

Tripathi's marriage had been fixed somewhere else by his parents, while Manorama had become pregnant with Tripathi's child. Manorama was also doing her master's in philosophy and had always seemed like a little girl to me, very short in height but very active and short-tempered.

I had read somewhere that alert and short-tempered girls tend to surrender their bodies to the men they fall in love with more easily than others. For them the body is like paan, which, if nothing else, should be placed in a tray and offered to a visitor coming home to give him respect and care.

There was a police case which was soon brushed under the carpet. Tripathi's father was a politician and very well connected.

Manorama's friends said that she hadn't actually choked on her food, but instead had wrapped the deadly poison arsenic around a piece of chicken and swallowed it.

Alas! The subject of crime and punishment had once again appeared before me.

During those days, a few of us had become addicted to roaming the city streets at night. The city seemed like a completely different entity at night. The sights, the sounds, even the winds that blew at night were different.

We walked for miles at night, stopped for tea, lit a cigarette and lolled around at some of the tea shacks that remained open all night. We wandered off towards the railway or bus stations sometimes and returned when it was almost dawn, lying to the warden that we were reading in the library, which stayed open all night.

One day I saw a graffiti artist standing below a flyover, bucket and brush in hand. He looked like a man carved out of the darkness in the night, an angry painting of a man.

Who was he?

But before that I should tell you about Ashfaq.

Evening comes before night arrives. It is when the two times of the day meet. This temporary evening scene is mysterious and smeared with the suggestion of sadness.

When the maghrib call to prayer was heard, the voice of the azaan always seeming to emerge from maghrib, the west, the covers of mist began to spread, and humans walking around started looking like shadows. Then he emerged, a wooden ladder on his shoulders, a black oily casket of kerosene in one hand and a dirty rag in the other. There was a narrow lane behind our house that led to the fields and had a last house at the turning, beyond which were a few ruins of houses and hutments after which the green of the fields became visible. No relative of ours nor anyone from our community lived on that side.

I had never mustered the courage to go up to the point of the last house as a kid. It was long afterwards that I went past that house and made vain attempts at listening to the clink of the chudail's anklets who resided in the tree and had reversed feet. I peered into the well under that tree but could see nothing except the dead bodies of dogs and cats or their skeletons.

But the memory of Ashfaq is from a long time ago, when Bade Mamu stood in that lane with me in his arms after the maghrib call to prayer. I don't remember now whether I used to feel cold or not but Ashfaq's khaki uniform often had a discoloured sweater over it, so I had probably witnessed this scene during the winters.

He set the ladder against the first pole of the lane and climbed up to pour kerosene into the lamp. Then he removed the chimney and wiped it with that black soiled cloth. He fitted it back on to the lamp and came down the ladder in the blink of an eye.

Bade Mamu had formed an acquaintance with him and made some conversation. The lane lit up after that. One could see the quivering faint outline of a girl dressed in red behind the fences of the deserted terrace of one of the desolate houses far away. The fog then started forming a circle of darkness and haze.

We found Ashfaq going towards the last turn of the lane with his ladder on his shoulders as we returned. The girl dressed in red was now visible behind the fences of the terraces of some other houses whose roofs were in continuity. Bade Mamu lifted his head to look at her. I got the feeling that the two had said something to each other, but the fast-descending thick fog and the whisper of the sudden cold wind, and then the passing of the peanut seller with his bag on his shoulder, ensured that I did not make out anything that was said in that quiet noise.

This was the lane that had a house on it in which grew a castor tree. It was from here that Bade Mamu had gone to collect the castor leaf with me in his arms for the sprain in my hand. I get the feeling now that Bade Mamu definitely had a mysterious connection with that house's darkness, desolation and silence.

Evenings in this big city are very lively. There are rows and rows of neon lights everywhere illuminating the city. There are innumerable lights under the flyovers too.

But the fate of humans is not so brightly lit. A person sometimes emerges from a coal tar–like darkness. An ill-fated painter who paints the slopes and walls of the flyovers at midnight, climbing a ladder, writing slogans. He hurls a black musical instrument forcefully at the illuminated walls. He dips a black brush into the black paint to draw figures on a white wall. He sings all the darkness collected in his lungs like a scream. A black song, whose notes slip away from below the flyover walls like a ghostly wind.

This artist, this graffiti artist, emerging from the darkness is today's Ashfaq. He was born again to blacken this illuminated city. Because this is justice and this is protest, and this is among the official duties of his position, along with his moral duty.

The lights make the city cruel. Such spotlessness, such glitter is inhuman. The ladder will now be used not for lighting the kerosene lamp but to blacken this profligate, covetous and cruel city.

As far as I am concerned, I know this city ends in a jungle just like all other cities. A jungle where there is a ditch. A ditch that might have been a moat at some point. There must have been a war across every trench. There must have been a fire. And some evil humans must have followed the victorious army, trailing behind them so that they could search the heaps of dead bodies later. Strip the bodies. Steal.

It has always happened this way. Behind the young and adventurous, the bravehearts, the fearless and the martyred, there has always been an army of two-bit rascals and mysterious small-minded people, and eunuchs present mysteriously. Then the cities become debauched and profligate with the treasures looted by this evil community from these wars. Politics comes into play and leaders come into existence. Bars, malls and nightclubs crop up. The city starts becoming beautiful in an inhuman, cruel and shameless manner. The layers of fat on the buttocks of the women of such cities come from the female cats thrown under flyovers. The lips and mouths of these vulgar women remain open in the same manner perpetually, as if they are ready to suck at the organs of impotent males.

Then flocks of impotent men are seen frequenting massage parlours in the city with their impotent weak penises. Those guys with no sexual potency, petty thieves who are members of the group that specializes in snatching away the clothes from the dead bodies of the brave and the honest. I have always felt that there is a pond in this city everywhere whose water source is now dried up.

But be careful! Don't even imagine that I had felt or experienced all this during those nights when I roamed the streets as a student. It is now that I have come to feel like this. I wasn't capable of such thoughts at that time, but having emerged from the darkness, that painter had compelled me to once again ponder over the question of unseen crimes and invisible punishments. I wanted to relate law to every issue, every moment, every event.

Was this city also undergoing a sentence?

But I haven't been able to understand that approach to punishment even today, according to which you are not being punished because you have stolen the sheep but so sheep may never be stolen in the future!

The sinner was the sacrificial goat!

Ashfaq was a judge. The punishment for darkness was light. He illuminated the lanes of the small cities. And this graffiti artist too was a judge. The punishment for light was darkness. He will write justice with bright black coal tar.

After all, what was the difference between darkness and light?

And punishment and reward?

Law books contained only technicalities. The sections sometimes began to seem like mathematical formulae. Right from the ancient iron laws of Rome to the latest ones of the highly modern countries of Europe, law has been written in a manner that can be understood very easily by some people, but there is an entire population that can't make head or tail of it.

How ridiculous is it that one has to acquire a degree for law just like one acquires a medical or engineering degree. The question is how something as common and mundane and natural to human life as a sneeze or a toothache, or crying or smiling, can be turned into something so unnatural?

Full of heavy and long law terms and artificial efforts to organize them into a system, these huge legal tomes!

How many nights have I spent trying to make sense of these books, but believe me, I couldn't make out the meaning of sin or retribution or justice. Allow me to say that I wanted to solve the fundamental questions of my inner self through the study of law. I wanted to understand the sense of terror, the anger and the uneasiness in the deep recesses of my being. I wasn't going to be satisfied with any superficial explanation of the sense of guilt. I was also not convinced by the kind of analysis of lawyers that Mahatma Gandhi had made in *Hind Swaraj* and the construction of an ideal social system. A set-up where there was no crime. It seems like a very populistic ideal.

The reality is that crime is the backbone of society. No social system or human race is possible without sin and without crime.

Crime is like the brick-dust and lime stuffed into the cracks of the bricks of the structure of society, and this is a normal, natural thing. All this fuss and these degrees seem like a waste of time to me when it comes to talking about crime.

Who but I could be a better and bigger example of this? I who had flung a pebble at a beehive, I who had committed two murders.

And I, Hafeezuddin Babar, also acknowledge the strange and dreadful ability in me that recognizes the aroma of a particular food item being prepared and converts it into a terrible event or mishap taking place somewhere in this vast universe!

But all this seems as routine and ordinary to me now as the simple act of rinsing my mouth in the morning.

This is the reason I'm wandering in search of my punishment, my court of law and my justice provider. Because I can't understand the equation between human destiny and justice, and if law can't explain and expand on human destiny then death sentences or life imprisonments seem like jokes to me. But that invisible court of law!

No, I'm not a religious person, and having recently read Marx thoroughly, I've become absolutely incapable of discussing any matter from a religious perspective.

In any case, what does this slipshod petition have to legally do with religion? I have wandered for long, and in this aimless drifting, have also acquired a degree in law in my student fervour. But perhaps my court of law does not lie within all this gathered knowledge but resides in some kitchen utensil instead, like a cockroach.

Be it in ancient Greek philosophy or the present day, there have been innumerable debates on crime and punishment, justice and fair play. So much discussion, but it always goes back to square one.

There is no unanimity of opinion on death sentence in the world as yet. And even if the revenge aspect of punishment is now redundant, the horror and repentance angles remain. Those who regard crime to be an illness are victims of their own sense of greatness and superiority and are unsuccessful in presenting the natural dimension of punishment properly.

Justice, by the way, for any state is the rules it imposes upon its subjects, which means that justice is always in favour of those who are in power. It is another matter that one can present any argument or explanation in the interest of hypocrisy.

Which requirement of justice does the death penalty fulfil? (Someone repeatedly whispers in my ear, 'Indian Penal Code, Section 302.')

There was a time in England when the punishment for picking pockets was death.

Now, if one was to consider for a moment that picking someone's purse could result in a death penalty, it would seem like a frightful and illogical, albeit hilarious, equation of algebra, and one feels inclined to pity the people that coin such laws. According to Arthur Koestler, some cutpurses may have been picking people's pockets right there at the time when other cutpurses were being publicly put to death.

But sometimes I feel that the most natural is also the most complicated. However difficult and beyond the understanding of common people law may seem, it is actually a pretty simple affair. Law imitates algebra or geometry or mathematics. How can law hope to have human nature in its grasp when the great philosophies and religions of this world could not accomplish this task.

Bacon said something very stimulating and enlightening in his essay. (And I recall that Camus and Borges have almost repeated this thought.)

Bacon said that no human emotion is so weak as to get warded off by the fear of death. Revenge, honour, love and grief eradicate the fear of death.

Who would know better than me about how an emotion can overshadow all other emotions in the struggles and conflicts of life and loom large like a mountain or a ghost.

This is why, to me, the spread of both public human rights and personal human rights appear the same, immaterial, even ridiculous. Be it full democracy, limited democracy, direct democracy or indirect democracy, regulated democracy, or even socialism or communism, the question of punishment and retribution remains unanswered the same way everywhere as it had been at the very outset of creation.

The law of every country and every race is ultimately nothing but Euclidean decoration.

Another thing is that punishment sometimes becomes reward. As I write appeal upon appeal and wander in search of my court of law and my case, know I want to procure my reward and I have a vague intuition that I will definitely get it unexpectedly, just the way one sits down to have the poor man's simple dal masoor and there arrives at the doorstep a bowl of fine paaya curry, or someone lands up with an earthen pot of rasawal.

Alauddin had joined LLB with me. He had a sharp mind and there was no doubt that he would make a successful lawyer.

Alauddin made fun of my ideas. He often said, 'Hafeez! Learn the sections. Just mug up the sections and theories. Don't concern yourself with anything else. The practice of law is a profession, not a philosophy.'

I bickered with him and tried to explain the difference between punishment and reward. Alauddin said, 'Reward gives pleasure while punishment gives suffering. This is so obvious.'

'Not necessarily always,' I said, but my statement remained incomplete. I continued to muse over the fact that someone can inflict punishment on his own self if the present government were unable to decipher his crime or failed to punish him at all as an oversight. He may be acquitted too. The punishment will then turn into a reward. And I wanted one or the other of the two at all costs because both Anjum Baji and Anjum Apa had cheated me.

I kept studying law, or shall I say mugging up law. I secured good marks but neither could I make sense of Aristotle's corrective measures of justice nor could I understand the preventive approach of punishment or the policy of compensation.

Besides, there was the forbidden approach to punishment and the natural outcome and vindictive point of view as well. All these had messed up my mind completely. I was quite sure that if the dust of punishment, retribution, justice and fair play were not to settle in my mind, I would never be able to set up a practice.

If a student of medicine is not familiar with someone's tear-filled or smiling, bright and blinking eyes, he will not really achieve anything by poking his fingers into the sockets of the skeleton's eyeballs, except for the right to fool his patients. Before I proceed any further, let me also tell you that though I am not capable of writing a novel, it was during those very student days that I read some of the best novels of the world, which directly concerned my subject – for example, Dostoevsky's *Crime and Punishment*, Tolstoy's *War and Peace* and Stendhal's *The Red and the Black*. And a few other books too. However, despite the greatness of these novels, the way human beings and human life had been presented as all-dominating and the philosophy of good and evil had been simplified and explained did not satisfy me. Moreover, the questions of crime, punishment and fair play, and their essence and relevance and all other discussions about them would acquire a Christian colour by the time things reached their conclusion. I had no interest in religious explanations, but these novels are the masterpieces of the world. You may include Flaubert's *Madame Bovary* in this list if you like.

The question of Kafka remains. The same problems exist in his works too, right from the beginning to the end, but as a novelist, and despite his greatness of art, he seems even more confused and troubled than me on these matters. And as I've said earlier, giving a commonplace explanation of punishment and retribution will never be able to satisfy the craving of my spirit, or else I would have puffed up like a pig after reading Manto's short story 'Thanda Gosht'. Freud's one-sided intelligence has badly messed up things for literature in certain areas.

No, no! I'm not competent to comment on literature, how I wish I could be a creative writer!

Now the one recurring thought I have is that being born is a punishment, the crime being the love and desire that men and women feel for each other and the sexual relations they indulge in. Sexual intercourse requires the participation of human beings, which means that human birth and existence is necessary. Then what is the original sin? And what is the original retribution? Desire, according to Buddha?

The desire to be born or the primordial sin or the Fall of Adam?

This is the problem once religion comes into the picture with its religious interpretations and religious tales.

Well, all these have come in very useful in affording me anxiety-free and undisturbed sleep.

But I don't want to sleep undisturbed. Not today and not even then when I used to laugh and joke about the legal world. And my house in my small town, which I had left behind, was growing more and more battered and news of someone or the other's death had become a frequent occurrence. Each time I was warned by my sixth sense through the news of some or the other food item being cooked, and I would drown in an unexplainable, irrational feeling of criminality. Then it wouldn't be a book of law but something located within me which made me understand that crime and punishment are actually twins, each other's clones, or perhaps punishment is the shadow of crime. It comes into existence through crime. Punishment is a victim of the eternal desire to be born into this world. It inserts its seed into the belly of crime. Evil or immoral action is only a means to the creation of punishment. But don't forget that punishment is the illegal and forbidden seed that is nurtured in crime's belly, and therefore, later, crime or evil and immoral action has to nurse punishment secretly. The darkness of crime and sin illuminate the punishment. Then a court of law is set up where justice is meted out and some ill-fated, innocent person is awarded punishment.

The human being, the poor human being, who in his substance was neither crime, nor sin, nor even punishment. The human who is the sufferer of his own fate, crushed by love and hate, whose spirit is badly bruised and wounded by the gashes of revenge and grief – that human, bearing his sentence on his shoulders – walks the distant dark wilderness. Despite this, he finds this sentence a reward. And then, death, life, and hate, love.

Antithetical words start seeming synonymous with each other.

Will this petition of mine, my appeal even reach where a silent court is in progress? I've heard that the court of law is set up in a deep dark cave. If I don't lose my way I will reach that cave, with this sheaf of papers in my hand, but before that I will have to tease every drop of pus and yellow discharge out from the abscess of my memory, pressing it again and again. This is no easy task.

Another one and a half years passed. I cleared LLB with very poor marks. The reason was that I used to forget the numbers of the sections. Converting numbers or figures into a theory of any kind or forming a principle out of them or even creating a section had always seemed unnatural and childish to me. Issues that had to do with human emotions being given a meaningless shape and design through figures – how legitimate was that? I spent the whole night learning all the sections by heart, but messed up everything when I was writing the papers. Section 320 turned into Section 304, Section 415 became Section 420 and so on. However, it was imperative that I acquire an LLB degree, so I continued my efforts at learning by rote. I used to think of my dead parrot very often. If he had been there with me, I would have made him memorize all the sections and then taken him along to the examination hall, and even to the court of law.

My friends gathered in my hostel room late every night. Alauddin, who was part of this group, had topped the first year of LLB. We were all dunces engaging in discussions and debates just to prove our flair for good conversation. Rajinder Kumar Misra mostly liked talking about food. He watched the cookery shows that aired on the TV in the hostel lounge with great interest.

'Yaar, the question that arises is how the human palate senses and understands every new taste and flavour,' he started a discussion one day. I felt uncomfortable when there was a conversation about food, since the stage for the tragedy of my life was set on some unfortunate food items. The strings of that tragedy, concealed in my ill-fated soul, were actually the black ability about which I'm tired of writing.

'And when modern science has proved and established that there are special cells in our tongue meant to pick up every variety of food taste, does it mean that these innumerable tastes and flavours of different kinds of food are already present on the tongue? Or is the palate creating new sensory cells after anticipating the process of the new varieties of food being invented?' There was a short silence, after which Anil said, 'I think only three basic kinds of tastes or flavours exist – sour, sweet and bitter (you can include salty in bitter). The rest are shades of these tastes and flavours, like you have in the case of colours. Just the way some people are colour-blind, there are some who are taste-blind. They don't care what they eat. They can't distinguish between sweet and sour.'

'Don't compare these things with colours. All colours are concealed in sunlight, and–' Rajinder was interrupted by Anil, 'Listen, I've studied some science too. The question is that the way all colours are concealed in the white sunlight, are all flavours deposited somewhere too?'

'Yes, they are!' I said.

Anil lit a bidi.

'The vulgar and violence-prone greed and hunger residing in human beings' body, in fact, spirit.'

'There . . . there . . . hahahaha.' Alauddin laughed crudely.

'This young fellow always takes quantum leaps, bringing scientific issues to a philosophical level.'

'You are an ignorant fool, Alauddin!' I lost my temper. 'Where do you see philosophy in this? However, I admit that I would like to see science moving closer to a more human, problem-oriented approach.'

'Well, well, my dear sir! I may be an ignorant fool but when you were devouring the pulao like a hungry hog and chewing and sucking the chicken bones yesterday, why were you not reminded of the vulgar greed of human beings?'

'Oh yes, I was gobbling up the food but for your kind information, it was biryani, not pulao. I absolutely hate pulao.'

'What on earth is the difference between biryani and pulao!'

'Go and read Sharar's book *The Lucknow of Yesterday* and you'll understand,' I replied indifferently.

'I think Sharar is a fraud. His historical novels are tolerable, but this book is nothing more than a compendium of jokes as it is difficult to figure out if he is poking fun at the downfall and decay of the culture of Lucknow or praising the city.' Muqim Ali had been silent for long, and he opened his mouth to speak then. I didn't want to get into a discussion with Muqim, especially on a subject like pulao and biryani. Muqim Ali was a serious young man and spoke only within limits.

But the subject this time was food and I knew that this issue was going to get as prolonged as the devil's intestines.

And so it was. Rajinder Kumar Misra almost sprang out of his chair and began in a declamatory tone, 'Listen, please listen carefully. Hippocrates said that food, I mean nutrition, is the real medicine and the kitchen the real clinic. But then the question that arises is which disease or entity is food the treatment of?'

'The treatment for life?'
'Or the treatment for death?'
'The world's?'
'Or when the gods fall ill?'
Everyone, except me, guffawed at Rajinder's lecture.

'And it is not without reason that we Hindus believe eating meat enhances the evil in us. It is the food of the ogres. Although one finds mention of cow sacrifice too at places, that sacrifice is not in terms of its meat but of milk and ghee – the purest of foods.' Rajinder would have continued his lecture had Islam Sabri not sprung out of his chair right then. Islam Sabri was an orthodox Muslim. Jamaluddin Afghani was his idol.

'Shut up! What is this nonsense about pure and impure? A mind with such illogical and poorly formed ideas and beliefs despite having studied law . . .' Islam Sabri roared. 'All the superior foods, the ones you are ready to die for, are ours. Did you know that the original name of the samosa is qutub? This is actually sanbosa and the Muslims brought it from Iran. Meat broth, kebab, stew, dum pukht, naan, chapatti, phulka and plain rice came here from Turkey. Roti and puri also came here from West Asia. Khichdi is a Mughal dish and there is no mention of it in history before Humayun's time. Only the Muslims know how to cook and invent food. It is in their genes.'

Islam Sabri was trembling with excitement. Finally he sat down.

'I think we should avoid dragging religious communities and cultures into debates on food, or else they will soon announce a clash of foods too.' Muqim Ali said 'clash of foods' in English and Urdu. 'This could prove to be the final flashpoint of the last decisive world war,' he continued in a cool voice.

But Anil Singh ignited the bidi again. Whenever he lit the

bidi, he had something to say. He took a very long puff and blew some smoke out of his mouth and nose. Coughing slightly, he stood up from his seat. 'No, I'm going to respond to Islam Sabri at all costs. I can read out a list hundred times longer than this punitive list of foods you have mugged up and recited here. Tell me, what would have been the worth and value of your dishes or anyone else's dishes if there were no spices? Spices are the pride of India. They don't just enhance flavour but also cure diseases. Black pepper, red chillies, fennel, asafoetida, cumin, carrom seed, mace, bay leaf, ginger, turmeric, coriander seed, cinnamon, nutmeg – these were more precious than gold and diamonds. Before the birth of Christ, merchants from Rome and Greece came here and took away spices in exchange for diamonds and pearls and other precious stones. The same was the case with merchants from Arabia and Iran. A sack of black pepper was equivalent to one human life and these spices were kept under more secure vigil than gold and other treasures.' Anil took another long puff at his bidi and looked at me, smiling. I signalled him to keep quiet, and he went back to his seat. For some reason, Anil always listened to me and agreed with what I said. I still think of him fondly. But the argument didn't seem to be coming to a close.

Muqim Ali got excited again and said, 'Look, there's no point in talking so animatedly about different dishes. Everything is being eaten. It is just that religion has put prohibitory instructions on certain foods, otherwise every single thing is ready to be consumed. One is under attack by the other. Each one is ready to swallow the other. I've heard that horse meat is becoming very popular in Europe. There was a time when empires rose and fell for the sake of a horse. That same horse is now being served on our plates all dressed in spices . . . and what is there to find fault with? It is better to domesticate anything that can become dominant over you. It's easier to gobble up something after taming it, and this is supposed to be more socially acceptable too. The fact of the matter is that taming and eating are one and the same thing. A story about my dada is that one day while eating a biggish piece of rohu fish, its bone pricked his jaw and got stuck there. Blood began to literally spout from his mouth. It was very painful. He finally managed to extricate the bone from his mouth and used it as a toothpick forever after.'

'Hoho hoho.' Alauddin laughed his crude laugh. Others too could not avoid smiling. But I wasn't amused at all. Muqim Ali's ideas had affected me seriously.

I realized that every crime can be attached to food, even murder. The way Proudhon declared all private property to be robbery, I believe eating to be a kind of murder. How many times have we heard of humans eating other humans, in fact parents eating their own offspring, out of hunger? And the way they first prepared cooked food.

'What are you thinking, Hafeez?' Muqim Ali asked.

'Nothing.'

'Listen, Hafeez, white ants also eat wood, and a relative of mine developed a strange disease. Food rotted inside his large intestine for ages. He rarely ever passed stool. Ultimately that putrid food, that shit consumed his large intestine and destroyed everything. It was an extremely shocking and filthy death. It was extremely hard to stand the foul smell when he was being given his ritual funeral bath.'

I took a deep breath and said, 'Muqim! If one was to think about it, the whole world is under the attack of various kinds of food. Look at the cookery shows on TV. Look at the columns on food in newspapers. These dishes, in fact the whole world's greed and gluttony, are the weapons that are gradually destroying humans. They are domesticating humans so that instead of humans consuming 'food', the 'food' can consume humans. And if this happens, believe me, the foundation of a new world will be laid. This new world will be created not out of layers of soil, mountains, seas and trees but with meat – regions of meat, mountains of meat, rivers of blood, grounds of bone. Humans will crawl around on all these the way insects and reptiles do.'

'Hoho hoho, hee hee hee hee!' Alauddin's cruel laugh filled the room again. 'Hafeez's half-baked philosophy has taken off now,' he said, doubling up with laughter. 'No, he's not wrong,' Muqim Ali challenged him. 'In this universe, as each and every being is waiting to turn the other into "food", they themselves are waiting to be turned into the "food" of humans. This will be the destiny of the universe. Can't you see the vultures, eagles, crows and ants coming from afar even now? Therefore, if you eat pork, eat it like pigs eat and if you eat buffalo meat, devour it the way buffaloes graze on the grass. We may only be able to maintain a balance then.'

'Muqim, you probably haven't read anything about the food cycle or the nitrogen cycle. Neither have you read Darwin or Spencer,' said Rajinder Kumar, making a face.

'But listen, Muqim,' I said, not paying attention to Rajinder Kumar Misra's scientific overtures.

Everyone, including Muqim, turned to look at me.

'The actual problem lies in the bawarchi khana. Or in that place where the fire was first lit to cook food.' (There was a hiss in my ear that only I could hear, 'Who knows if the fires of hell were also ignited by the two pieces of stone that were rubbed against each other to create fire, and the same stones and hellfire will burn the grinding slab that used to be in Anjum Baji's kitchen, and the fire that had erupted in Anjum Apa's kitchen will also be flung into this hellfire.')

'Bawarchi khana? Do you mean the kitchen?' Rajinder asked like a dunce.

'What is the kitchen's status quotient? What history does it have? What you call the kitchen did not even exist in Europe before the eighteenth century. It has come into being after water supply and the cook stove were made available to us. Bawarchi khana used to be the place where a fire was lit with wooden logs inside a chulha. Its walls used to be covered in soot and would turn black. Stark black,' Islam Sabri spoke.

'Don't we have such bawarchi khanas now too?'

'We do, we do,' someone was screaming within me, 'and there are lizards on the walls. There are baby snakes, there are stone grinding slabs, there are kerosene canisters, and . . . there . . . murders happen there. The bawarchi khana is a murdering ground.' But no one heard me.

But I said *this* loudly, 'There is fire inside the kitchen. It cooks the food and also warms it, but sometimes it burns humans alive too.'

'This doesn't really matter, because there is fire in the kitchen too in one shape or the other and accidents happen there too. The Western equivalent of the bawarchi khana is the kitchen, according to me.'

'No, one can't equate this two-bit modern kitchen with the bawarchi khana. It doesn't have anything to do with the deadly tradition of the bawarchi khana. This lowly kitchen has come into existence only after the breakdown of the joint family system,' I said bitterly.

Anil Singh, a hardcore 'comrade', cleared his throat and lit a bidi. He spoke haltingly. 'According to me, the centre for the real productive forces is this. The bawarchi khana is the real production house or "factory" present in every household. This includes everything from the ordinary roadside restaurant to five-star hotels. The roadside restaurants are closer to Marxist ideology, both in the aesthetic as well as the social sense. They are just bawarchi khanas, and nothing else, because the bawarchi khanas of those restaurants are not hidden from view. There is no curtain hanging in front of them. What was the need for a screen to shelter the bawarchi khana? It's not a bathroom or a latrine and neither is a newly married couple going to sleep there. Therefore, the concept of "sanjha chulha", the common kitchen, is a completely Marxist one. It tears bourgeois socialism to shreds.'

'Don't talk about Marx. He was a fraud too . . .' Muqim Ali shouted. 'He had relations with his minor girl servant, and she even conceived once.'

'Yaar, Muqim, just shut up! I know you have read Paul Johnson's *The Intellectuals* recently. But Paul Johnson is another fraud and doesn't deserve to be regarded as anything more than a yellow journalist, and in any case, we are talking about Marxist ideology here, not analysing his character or judging him for it, neither are we suing him in a court of law for his deeds,' Anil Singh responded zealously.

'No, Muqim, you are absolutely right. Marx was a very evil man.' Islam Sabri got up, his fists clenched. He went on, 'Marx had developed the dirty and repulsive scabies disease in his later years. This was god's vengeance. He was an atheist, an atheist.' Anil Singh's face turned red with anger. He dropped his bidi on the floor and stubbed it. It was impossible for him to hear even a word against Marx. It looked like he was going to punch Islam Sabri in the face. His breathing grew fast, but when I signalled to him with my eyes he heeded my request and, after giving Muqim Ali a hard glare and throwing a murderous look at Islam, went back to his chair and sat with his head bowed. The only sound in the room now was the clatter of utensils coming from outside. There was an unpleasant smell coming from the direction of the mess.

Anil Singh got up suddenly for a second time.

'Listen, Hafeez!' he seemed oblivious to any other presence in the room as he locked eyes with me. 'The productive forces and their interwoven threads are deeply embedded in the filaments of human intestines, not his brain. This entire business is completely material, but it's an extremely subtle materialism in which the fat content in the human intestines includes the worms residing inside it. Also, the puke and smelly retching and eructation that erupt from his throat, due to his hyperacidity. It is here that the material aspect of hunger becomes most apparent, and so does taste, greed and gluttony. This materialism might be of a subtle and sophisticated nature but it has the ability to sweep up your spirituality into its circumference. The food at charity dinners in shrines and monasteries, fateha and niyaz, the bhandaras at gurdwaras, the charity dinners dedicated to the gods at the stairs of temples and the food offered at the shradh ceremony of a departed soul, donations and sacrifices – what is it that is free of this materialism? Therefore, I say with full confidence that the bawarchi khana or the rasoi should be public property, far removed from the home, otherwise we'll find a battleground right inside the house. A dialectic conflict followed by a ridiculous revolution. The remaining bones of the joint family will turn to dust and get scattered. Then the eternal loneliness of humans, the ill-fated humans, will mingle with their hunger and become their destiny. What is all this supposed to be?'

'Food, food, food and only food. Marx will have to be discovered once again.'

Anil Singh fell silent. This time there was a tangible, deep silence in the room. In fact, I felt like I was speaking in Anil Singh's voice.

I suddenly caught a whiff of the unpleasant smell again. I screwed my nose and looked at the clock hanging on the wall.

Half the night had passed in this discussion. It was three-thirty in the morning.

'Let's go somewhere for tea,' Rajinder Kumar Misra proposed. The use of heaters was prohibited in our rooms in order to save electricity.

I don't know why that unpleasant smell was troubling me.

'Smells like putrefying honey or vinegar being made,' I said.

'Yes, there certainly is a bad smell,' some of my friends agreed.

'I hope those rogues, the bearers in the mess, are not guzzling country liquor in the middle of the night,' Islam Sabri mumbled.

'Oh no, their kitchen is very dirty. They don't empty the garbage for days. Egg shells, fruit peels, tea leaves, green leafy vegetables, and the sticky, foaming white worms of those leafy vegetables. Lizards licking the garbage bins. Go and take a look right now. All you'll find is this. India is a warm place and chemical breakdown is fast here, which is why food rots aplenty here,' Muqim Ali tried to explain.

Alauddin opened his mouth wide and laughed his repulsive laugh.

'What's there to laugh about?' I glared at Alauddin and asked.

'You all are fools... putrefying honey... vinegar... country liquor.'

Alauddin had a slight paunch that was shaking wildly as he laughed.

We all looked at him in astonishment.

He controlled himself with some difficulty and said, 'I had requested Kallan yesterday to cook beef trotters for me for breakfast. I gave him twenty rupees to fetch the trotters and promised to give him more later. These trotters are being boiled after being soaked in hot water so that the black skin and hair of the hoofs can come off. This is what they smell like – rotten.'

'Saale, glutton. You want to eat beef trotters for breakfast. That too alone,' Islam Sabri said. Everyone started laughing.

But at that moment I felt as if something wet and slimy was crawling over the left side of my chest. It was a winter night. Why was I sweating? And that too on only one part of my body! I put my hand inside my shirt and touched the area that seemed wet, but it was warm and dry now, almost burning, as if in a fever. The wetness had now shifted to the right.

My hands went cold. I was feeling very restless.

Anil Singh noticed my uneasiness.

'What happened, Babar?'

'Nothing.'

'No, there's definitely something.'

'No, just that in my opinion the boiling of buffalo legs and hooves is not something great,' I replied listlessly, and then asked Anil Singh for a bidi.

Anil Singh had just picked up the bundle of bidis when we heard a strange commotion in the mess – hysterical screams over the voices of several people. We ran out of the room towards the bawarchi khana of the hostel. The hostel's guards and other employees were running helter-skelter in the chaos. The warden had also heard the noise and was running towards the mess.

'What happened, what happened?' I was the first one to ask.

'The cauldron!' said someone.

'What happened to the cauldron?'

'The cauldron overturned, Sahib. The vessel containing the boiling legs and hooves fell off the stove and on to Kallan.'

And then we all saw it.

Kallan was rolling on the wet floor in a mad frenzy. He tried to get up a few times but failed and kept screaming hysterically.

The kitchen smelt of something similar to strong turpentine resin and the burning of organic matter.

It was then that I looked more carefully.

Kallan's body was forming bubbles filled with a whitish fluid at a very fast rate. These were blisters. His shirt and vest were torn to shreds and sticking to his body. Then I saw clearly the bits of fat from the buffalo hooves, splintered bones, cartilage and black hair stuck on his red skin.

We heard the siren of the ambulance approaching from afar.

Kallan was taken to the hospital after a while, the ambulance sounding its siren once again, and along with it one could hear Kallan's terrible and hair-raising screams, which grew faint as the ambulance vanished from sight.

I looked at Alauddin. He was standing there looking guilty and seemed to be trembling violently.

I stepped forward and placed my hand on Alauddin's shoulder and said, 'No, Alauddin, you are not to blame for this.'

'I was the one who had asked Kallan to cook those paaye,' he said sadly.

'No, it's not your fault. The timing of cooking the paaye is to blame. If something else had been boiling in their place, this accident wouldn't have occurred.'

'Meaning?'

I didn't reply. What reply could I possibly give to anyone? I was speechless before the wetness of my chest.

I am standing helpless and hopeless before this evil knowledge hidden in the depths of my soul since I can remember.

Bark, you dog, bark. Or chew up my hand if you want to. But I'm not letting go of your collar now. You have been following me for ages; you've made my life hell. Pierce my wrist with your sharp, pointed teeth, maul my body, but I will not rest till I have pushed you into the blind, dry and foul-smelling well of my writing. O my disgraceful memory, I have heard your evil footsteps following me right from childhood. Now I have inflicted myself on you like an evil spirit. I will write, I will write, I will write.

I'm quite aware that simile, metaphor, suggestion, symbols and whatnot are tumbling into what I write. I know that an appeal or petition cannot make use of these techniques, and not only is it wrong to do so, it is also punishable by law. It is possible that the subconscious desire to write a novel may be spoiling the effect of my appeal, making it ridiculous, but you don't have to worry. After I've written my petition, I will pick out every obnoxious mention and discard it the way the large intestine is thrown into the garbage once it is removed from the stomach, or how tumours of the stomach and kidney stones are thrown into the trash.

Every reader should also know that I use blue–black ink, supposed to be the most suitable for a written record. Although plain black ink might have been better for writing these petitions as it dries faster, it has a stench and also ruins the pen by drying up inside it.

I'm not using a new kind of pen. I dip the nib of my black pen with the white cap in the inkpot and write, because I consider myself to be old school, an ancient fellow, in fact, an eternal human being. A wild and dangerous human for whom crime and sin hold no meaning. And murder is equivalent to merely waving one's hand. This blue–black ink is also suitable for my account to come in useful as a reliable piece of evidence and proof.

I have lists of pains. Life can't be managed without making inventories, but we should also keep in mind that in order to reach the innermost hidden recesses of the human body and mind, we have to find out the secret language of nature. Although I am able to use this secret language, which is free from all ornamentation and figure of speech, only in a disjointed manner, I can claim to be an expert of this language. I still have to write, for not writing would be akin to that suppressed sneeze which causes the eyes, nose and ears to bleed and maybe cause death. I don't want to die. I don't want to die yet.

Time is moving ahead, trampling everything. I remember it was the last year of LLB when Alauddin's elder sister joined our college. Her education had been suspended for a long time for some reason and now she was resuming her studies.

You may be surprised at this or find it completely unbelievable, but her name was Anjum.

The moment I came to know her name I was sure we would have a purposeless connection. I am convinced that if I was in a truck with a thousand women, they would all be named Anjum. I'm unable to give you a cogent reason for this, because the reason is also concealed within that secret language I spoke of earlier.

Alauddin used to address her as Apa and I had a feeling that he was a little afraid of her. Though I was different from Alauddin in many respects, we were sincere towards each other, and I also knew that however selfish and stupid he might be, Alauddin had more faith in me than he had in his other friends.

Anjum was not able to get a room in the hostel, so Alauddin left his room in the hostel and rented a small two-room apartment where the two of them began to stay. Alauddin came from a wealthy family of a town in eastern Uttar Pradesh. He could have rented an even bigger apartment if he wanted.

Alauddin often called me home for tea. I observed their kitchen that had more varieties of pickles and fruit preserves than pulses and spices.

When I commented on this, Alauddin laughed and said, 'Apa is very fond of pickles and preserves. She can pickle almost everything.'

Anjum laughed only rarely. She didn't even offer a smile out of politeness at Alauddin's joke. Her face had a severity to it. She was fair-complexioned, but the fairness did not cause a stir in my heart. I found this whiteness similar to that of split milk. I studied her from behind when she walked. This was because despite wearing pretty short kameezes, the curves of her hips did not seem at all feminine to me. Even the thinnest of women's hips have some femininity to them, and I always suspected that I was not observing her from the right angle. After ascertaining quite a few times it became clear to me that Anjum's hips had yet not swelled properly on the outside, the way some people's teeth remain embedded in the blind depths of their gums despite attaining adulthood. The stage of life at which they would come out was something that defied any kind of prediction.

But the surprising part was that Anjum was fairly healthy

and had heavy breasts too. The disproportionateness of her body seemed to endow her personality with a mysteriously cruel element, just like people with disabilities or people who have a missing body part. If one looks carefully one will find this aspect clearly.

But there was something curious and worth mentioning about her eyes. Though they weren't very small, they seemed small due to her habit of squinting to look at anything, the way women with weak eyesight squint while cleaning rice or pulses or trying to figure out the quantity of spices to be put in the vessel when cooking or examining a piece of meat for tenderness after it has been cooking in the vessel for some time.

I often saw Anjum squinting while picking up the pickle container too. But the funny thing was that she looked at humans the same way, as if they were something to eat, or something edible was being cooked inside them and she was waiting to put a ladle into them and start stirring the pot. But it's possible that this was the product of my imagination, although it has been a part of my tragic destiny that the vaguest of my suspicions have been truer than truths. I have almost stopped believing in real and tangible things now. Instead, I have more faith in the black snakes of suspicions which find nurture within me.

'Apa, Hafeez is a very nice guy.' I don't know why Alauddin said this in an entreating voice. Anjum squinted to look at me. It was a look one would give to a piece of raw mango that was being considered for immediate pickling by putting inside a jar full of hot oil and spices. I just didn't like the way she squinted her eyes. I turned my face away whenever she looked at me.

Time seemed to have grown wings in those days. It was flying. The final exams for LLB began. I began to mug up my law books. You may or may not understand or make sense of it, and you may or may not be in agreement with any crime and its punishment, but if you want to clear the exams, just rely on rote memory. The examination system in this country is highly inefficient.

It was the month of April which sometimes experiences a pleasant breeze and at other times gets stuffy and humid followed by a yellowish dust storm. Nevertheless, it is a comparatively better and decent, well-balanced month. Free of any dimension of extremity. It feels good to write exams in April.

I forgot to mention that our college had become the breeding ground for students with criminal inclinations for the past one or two years. There were two or three villages on the banks of the Ramganga. The sons of the Thakurs living there had made the college their preferred destination. All of them were very rich and mischievous and also had political connections. These Thakurs played a massive role in the local elections and the success or failure of a candidate depended on their whim and fancy.

Jitender Kumar Rathore, Nanhe Singh, Rajju Chaudhury were all highly dangerous people and surrounded by dozens of other miscreants and scoundrels all the time. All of them were enrolled in the LLB course, the reason being that since childhood they had spent time with criminals and witnessed crimes and murders being committed. What better profession for them then?

Not only the college administration but the entire city, including the local police, was shit-scared of them.

I often saw Nanhe Singh riding a horse to college. He raced his horse up to the college campus and all of us felt terror in our hearts at the sound of the horse's hooves.

All these boys entered the exam hall chewing paan, a cigarette dangling from their lips. They cracked obscene jokes and sat on any seat they wanted, placing their knives and revolvers on the seat next to them. They then fished out their books and proceeded to copy in the examination.

The invigilators in the examination hall were terrified and thought it better to make themselves scarce on such occasions.

I took advantage of their presence to some extent, quietly fishing out the Agarwal series key I had hidden in my underwear and copying the numbers of the sections. In fact, in some papers I completely copied from sources. My friends were also able to surreptitiously do some copying. Everyone except Alauddin, because he had no need to do so. He had probably learnt all the numbers and other details of the sections and read everything about law while he was still in his mother's womb.

Please pause for a moment now. Quite a few things are getting muddled up in my memory. Let me focus and then proceed. But no, I can recall now. I can remember everything.

It was the day of the final paper. The exam was to be held in the second half, which meant it would start at three and end at six.

The pleasant April breeze was blowing till afternoon, but by the time it was evening, the wind had completely disappeared. The exam ended at six. We all decided to go to the canteen and celebrate the completion of our exams. Although I had been in favour of watching a movie for the evening show – Imperial Talkies was pretty much next door – I had to give in to the common consensus to celebrate in the canteen.

We were moving towards the canteen talking and discussing the day's question paper. The canteen was in a far corner of the college. There were large bushes and tall trees around it. Opposite it was a swimming pool, which was closed most of the time. All it afforded was a flock of crows sitting above it, cawing noisily, and a few monkeys scampering here and there. If one climbed the stairs next to the swimming pool, the view one got of the college, with its Gothic-style building, was very mysterious and a little sad too.

Entering the canteen, we saw that all the chairs and low stools were full. The canteen was jam-packed as exams were over.

I noticed Anjum seated at one of the tables. Meena Rani, Shashi and Suman Suri were sitting with her. There was a huge charcoal oven on which tea was boiling and a pan was placed next to it to fry samosas. The canteen counter had glass jars full of coconut biscuits, cream rolls, savouries and toffees.

We decided to stand and have some tea and samosas.

Suddenly we heard loud laughter behind us.

I turned to look and froze in fear.

Those scoundrels were coming this way. Jitender Kumar Rathore, Nanhe Singh and Rajju Chaudhury burst into the canteen with their entire gang.

Many of the students vacated their seats.

The owner of the canteen was a Sikh. He swiftly ran up to them, welcoming them into the canteen, but I noticed that they seemed interested only in the girls, who probably wanted to leave but remained glued to their seats out of fear.

Just then the sky outside turned yellow. I saw eagles flying at a distance, high in the sky. There was no wind at all, but a thick yellow cloud of dust was fast approaching from the north-west.

'It's a storm,' I thought to myself.

And it really was one. A yellow storm raining yellow dust. It became dark.

Soon it was pitch-dark. The strong gusts of wind were causing trees to sway and flap like paper flags. The wind was whistling loudly, so loudly that nothing else was audible. The power went out in the entire campus, no, the entire city. The darkness grew thicker, and after a while I sensed that accompanying the dreadful noise of the storm was another suppressed but heart-rending sound. The noise of the cauldron rolling over, utensils falling down, jars breaking? No, embedded within, or under it, a muted wailing noise! I couldn't fathom anything. There was another noise too in the canteen. A completely different noise in the darkness, a second storm.

Samosas and cream rolls were flying around with the dust from the storm. They hit us hard on our faces. The embers from the oven were also dancing in the wind, glowing and blowing out.

God knows when the storm abated. Extremely tall shadows came looming out of the canteen and moved swiftly into the darkness outside, disappearing into it.

We remained rooted to our spots, like mud statues, covered from head to toe in dust and scraps of other materials. The power was back – how I wish it hadn't been restored then.

I saw in the bright light of the high-power bulb hanging in the canteen that the four girls were half-naked. God knows where their salwars had flown off. Their faces were full of scratches that were bleeding. They had covered their faces with their hair that had fallen loose and were cowering on the floor, sitting on their haunches to cover their bare bodies and reveal as little as possible.

The college proctor must have come after this. The police too must have arrived. All the four girls must have been taken somewhere. All of us must have stepped outside the college. They must have questioned us and God knows how many more students about what we had witnessed. But Alauddin must not have been with us. He must have left us in that dark silence and the cool April breeze must have begun to blow. But I have no interest in recalling those details at this juncture.

The local newspapers were full of this dreadful news the next day.

'The biggest and most prestigious college in the city witnesses a mass rape of four girls . . .' but what was strange was that the truth and other details of the situation had been distorted in those reports. According to police sources, the rapes hadn't taken place in the canteen but in the swimming pool, where the four girls were bathing. There was no trace of the real names of the culprits, neither was there any mention of the criminal students coming from the lowlands of the Ramganga. Anyhow, the way it generally happens, this affair too was suppressed completely by the joint efforts of the police and the college administration. This was easy, since those four girls belonged to respectable households, and this terrifying reality converted itself into mere rumour and speculation.

Yes! Although I do know this much that Meena Rani, Shashi, Suman Suri and Anjum left not only the college but even the city with their families.

Alauddin didn't show us his face after that evening. He had also probably left the city for the time being.

But there was something which crossed my mind again and again. Where had that mysterious sixth sense of mine disappeared that day? Why had my sinister ability been asleep? Did the storm cause this? Or was it the wind? Or was my ability waiting for a particular smell of food – and that smell, say, the smell of samosas frying in oil, didn't reach my nostrils just then.

Was my nose blocked? And incidentally I also hadn't heard the word 'samosa' being uttered by anyone, otherwise seeing, hearing or smelling, any one of these could have set off the magical forces in me. So I came to the conclusion that there is definitely some other invisible force which has the real control. We are all merely puppets, and the string is in someone else's hands.

So what do crime and punishment mean? If what is to happen has been written already, then everything is meaningless, even life and death. Each sheet of paper in the coir inscribed by fate is under the command of an unseen finger. Everything is written on the paper. The full geography of a man's soul and its suffering and also the recipe for masala biryani. But this writ becomes visible only when it happens. The inscriptions of fate are not made up of words but of events.

Vacations had started after the exams. The hostel too began to get empty. Everyone could be seen going towards the railway station with their belongings, their holdalls. Anil Singh, Muqeem Ali and Islam Sabri, they were all leaving. And at this stage we didn't even know who would return and who wouldn't. I too folded up my things, but much later than everyone else. The train would leave at four in the evening for my very small town, the town where flowed the river of the fort and where my house was. Home, where Chhote Mamu lived (Mumani was dead now). I set out for the station in the middle of the afternoon.

Am I forgetting something? I am liable to forget, and what I forget could be very important and miss being entered into the ledger book, resulting in my failure to find my court of law at the right place and receive my punishment at the right time.

Who knows the size of that court of law? Bigger even than the Supreme Court. I have now realized that all the battles fought in the higher courts are verbal. Incorrect words and bad grammar can have harmful consequences. And, of course, wrong pronunciation turns everything into a joke. Merely using the wrong word, spelling or pronunciation can land me in hell, where there will be an alien and completely strange court of law for me which will have no connection with my sorrows, my joys and my afflictions. How will I find justice in that case – why don't they start a movement to make a formula for words? Up until the time that does not happen, the world will not be able to know whose heart is innocent and whose is sinful – only God is aware of these things, but what difference does that make after all?

It was nearly morning now. The train passed the river making the familiar noise it always makes while crossing the bridge.

I was home. When I hailed a rickshaw after getting down at the station, I saw a strange kind of destruction all around. The entire town seemed to have been dug up. There was dust and debris everywhere. The roads, the lanes and the footpaths, all of them broken or dug up, and the rickshaw puller had to carefully wind his way through them. Every joint in my body began to ache from the jerks I received each time the rickshaw's wheels descended into a pit or depression.

'Bhai, why have all these roads been dug up?' I asked the rickshaw-wallah.

'Arrey, Babuji! Can't you see, they are laying sewer lines,' he replied.

'Sewer lines!' Then I noticed the huge cement pipes lying on the roads haphazardly.

'Babuji, none of the houses will have manual latrines now. Here, you have reached your mohalla. I can't take you any further than this.' The rickshaw-wallah halted the rickshaw. This place was known as 'Pehelwan ka Akhada'. I could reach home in about ten minutes walking through several narrow lanes.

I paid the rickshaw-wallah and sending him off, I began walking on the uneven streets, my holdall lugged on my back.

The morning was setting in. I saw a strange morbid light spreading in the sky. Nothing around me seemed familiar, as if I had reached a strange and alien planet. I don't know how long I spent leaping over the fat pipes, stumbling, hitting myself against boulders and pits in those desolate lanes. My shoes were caked with mud and dust. Finally I reached the door of my house. The wood seemed more rundown than usual. I put the luggage on the ground, panting and sweating.

I beat the iron knocker on the door. It was so old that it was almost crumbling with rust. A monkey scampered into the lane and vanished from sight, jumping over the fence aligned to the door. A very weak and old man, with an extremely thin stream of blood running down his mouth, opened the door. It was Chhote Mamu. Nobody said, 'Guddu Miyan has come, Guddu Miyan has come.'

The wooden beams were vacant, and the wood, which had become weak and loose, was almost swinging from the ceiling.

I felt a strong wave of sleep overtake me. It was as if I hadn't slept for ages. My eyelids grew heavy and my eyes began to swell and become watery. My hands and feet seemed exhausted to the bone. I didn't bother to change my clothes and collapsed on a small, worn-out jute charpoy in the outer hall.

Burning hot gusts of wind woke me rudely. It was afternoon. A harsh sunlight filled the courtyard. I got up, rubbing my eyes.

I went to each nook and corner of the house, the tiny storerooms, the rooms. I felt the mango tree with my hands and pushed the handle of the handpump till it started spouting cool water in place of the hot and the wasps came and collected on the cool stream of water emerging from it. I put my feet in the shallow tank under the tap and looked up at the small food cupboard towards the inner side of the outer hall. Potatoes and onions lay rotting in it. The wire mesh was broken in many places.

And then, I went *there*.

It was more dilapidated than before, in fact, it was almost a ruin. Its walls were completely black now.

The bricks of the chulha were chipped off at various points. The hob was almost gone, it had broken so badly. The bulb hanging on a string from the iron rings of the roof was entangled in cobwebs. Everything lay scattered. The tongs, the griddle, the iron blowing pipe, the vessels, the large trays, the cups and the ladles. God knows how long the curries had been lying in their pots, stale and rotting. Flies were buzzing over them.

Two black poisonous lizards were staring intently at me from the skylight.

I recalled the days when this was the brightest part of the house, including being the place where women chatted and laughed among themselves, occasionally fighting furiously over trivial things. But everyone was dead now. The days of cooking, eating and drinking were over.

Finally I gathered the courage and ran my eyes over the place, searching for it. I didn't see it in the first glance. Right then one of the lizards stuck to the skylight plopped down on the floor. I retreated, scared, and I saw it was right where the black lizard lay, surreptitious, still.

It – the heavy grinding stone slab. It had become smooth and completely yellow. There were no ridges on it any more. It must have been ages since the ridges were rechiselled on it.

I knelt down on the kitchen floor and began to examine the grinding slab. The bloodstains and the white shreds of brain – they were there. I felt that they were definitely there, beneath the thousands of layers of turmeric, pepper and coriander seeds. I bent further down and sniffed at the very old smell of blood. The black lizard, now very close to my hand, suddenly slithered away. At that moment, I sensed a frightening movement, not in my ears, but in my heart.

I turned to look, and I couldn't believe my eyes. I recognized him. I could recognize him among thousands of cockroaches. That cockroach was sitting right behind me, laughing.

'They all died, Guddu Miyan, they all died.' Chhote Mamu had become eccentric. He followed me around everywhere.

'They all died, they all died. Your Mumani died too. Only Rehana is alive. Even our distant relatives are dead; the entire clan has been wiped out.'

'No, Mamu, the relatives' kids are around,' I said.

'No one comes. No one comes here. Neither does anyone call us over. They don't call us over for neyaz, nazar, fateha, weddings, or anything else. People's blood has changed colour, turning white from red. How many years have passed since we received the pot of rasawal from Rahmat Miyan's. Chhamman does his yearly prayer and offering of food for gyarhveen. The entire mohalla and all the relatives relish the beef korma and the tandoori roti made of fermented flour, but neither does he invite us nor does he send us any food. He has even forgotten Rehana, who is the adopted sister of his paternal uncle's daughter, his cousin.' Chhote Mamu had a veritable treasury of endless complaints.

Just then Rehana Phuphi came in and sat down, flurried and panting. I heard a chain rattle as she sat down.

'Hafeez, my son, should I cook urad gosht for dinner?'

'Yes, please.'

'Then let me go and stand at the door.'

'Why?'

'I will entreat some boy roaming in the mohalla to get me a quarter seer of mutton.'

'Why? Does Bhura the butcher not come to deliver the mutton now?'

'Bhura... He died God knows how long ago. That unfortunate fellow was addicted to eating raw liver. Ultimately, his heart began to enlarge. It became bigger and bigger and burst one day,' said Rehana Phuphi ruefully.

'Rehana Phuphi, what is this sound I hear every time you get up or sit down?'

'My bones.'

'Bones?'

'Yes, my son, what is it . . . in the blood . . . I don't know its name. The quantity of that substance has increased and is wearing out and softening the bones of all the joints in my body. Offering namaz has become an ordeal now. My entire body rattles when I bend or prostrate. It sounds like mice scurrying around in the garbage can, and sometimes it is like the clink of chains. The lubricants of the joints are exhausted. What do I tell you, life is so difficult. Going into the kitchen and working to feed the stomach's oven is like going into hell. So be it, life is almost over now, who knows when God may call me to him.' She continued talking. I had understood that raised uric acids had led to the softening and wasting away of Rehana Phuphi's bones. I knew there was no treatment for it. The bones in Rehana Phuphi's thin and frail body actually clinked under her skin. Very soon these bones would break and scatter and Rehana Phuphi would get eternal freedom.

But I didn't say any of this to her. Instead, I offered her advice, pretending to be wise. 'Why don't you guys employ a servant? Someone who can cook and clean? He can do outside chores too. I think this is something you can afford. How much do two people need to eat?'

'No, no,' Rehana Phuphi and Chhote Mamu spoke in one voice.

'Why?'

'Stop, Hafeez, stop. You have no idea of the state of affairs here. If you employ a maid or a cook, they'll slit your throat in the night and run away with all that is there in the house.'

'What are you saying, Mamu? We don't have riches here in the house. No jewellery or anything. We have already sold everything and consumed it. What treasures are lying buried here?' My tone had become a little bitter now.

'I keep saving a bit from my pension. That is how I am funding your education.'

'That process is over now. I'm through with my LLB. I'll fight cases in the courts now.'

'Cases?' Chhote Mamu's eyes turned vacant. He was staring into space.

'What happened, Mamu?'

'We had a fairly big estate in Sangrampur which was illegally occupied by Rahim Baksh. Sixty years have passed. His descendants have now occupied it. We fought cases against him many times, but always lost. But now, now we have you, Hafeez! God protect you from the evil eye, a great lawyer!' The vacant and desolate look in Chhote Mamu's eyes disappeared and his eyes began to sparkle with hope and happiness.

'Tell me, Hafeez, speak, Guddu Miyan, will you fight this case? It's not a question of the land, it's a question of our honour.'

'Yes,' I said in a weak voice.

'Yes! Then we are bound to win the case and retrieve our land from them. We will get wheat from there, and rice. We'll get pulses too. We'll sow the basmati variety of rice. What can I say about the basmati of that region . . . it must be cooked with goat meat, and . . . the arhar pulse, cooked and then topped with garlic and red chilli fried in pure ghee and . . . Say, Rehana, you know how to cook the arhar pulses?'

I was staring at Chhote Mamu in amazement. Was he mentally okay? He seemed extraordinarily old and weak. His eyes had sunk deep into their sockets. His wrists seemed like dry sticks and the skin of his neck was hanging loose up to his chest.

Chhote Mamu continued talking.

'What can I say of the mutton cooked with gram pulses. We'll cook that dish on the seventh day of Muharram.'

'Mamu, it's food, food and only food. Can't you think of anything else?'

Chhote Mamu's face darkened suddenly.

'Hafeez, I'm very ill. Whatever I eat is of no use to me. It's been two years now and I'm growing thinner and shrivelled by the day. At least allow me to "talk" of food.' His voice seemed to be emanating from a deep well.

'What's wrong with you?' I felt bad and was suddenly reminded of all that Chhote Mamu had done for me. Whatever I was today was because of him.

I shook him and asked forcefully, 'Mamu, what are you ailing from?'

'I have worms in my stomach. Innumerable worms. So many that sometimes the whole lavatory overflows with them. And sometimes if they come out in my vomit, it becomes difficult to get them to flow out through the small drain. These white worms are forming pockets in my stomach. They hog up all the food I eat. All the food.' Chhote Mamu began to weep loudly.

I stood up. I was nervous and confused. With nothing better occurring to me at that moment, I began to pat Mamu's back, the way one reassures children.

Chhote Mamu was crying violently now. Rehana Phuphi started crying too. As she shook while sobbing, her bones began to creak loudly.

'Be quiet, Chhote Mamu, don't cry,' I said like a fool, as he continued to cry.

'Have you seen a doctor? What does he say?' I asked finally.

Mamu continued to sob for some time and then, wiping his tears, said, 'All the doctors recommend surgery, but they are not sure that they will be able to prevent the worms from appearing again, because it's my blood which is generating them . . . No,

Hafeez, I won't get the operation done. I feel scared. No one has ever had an operation in our family. This is some evil force which is pursuing me, some curse, which I don't know the cause of. The doctors ask me to keep eating and eating. My stomach should always be full, which is why I always keep munching on something or the other. But these evil white worms gobble up all the food. I always feel nauseous. I keep vomiting all day and these worms keep spouting out of my mouth. All the flavours of my tongue have vanished like a ghost. I can't taste salt or pepper. I cannot tell bitterness from sourness. My mouth seems to be full of some kind of air which has no taste, no flavour in it.'

'Don't worry, Mamu! I'll take you to the city and consult an eminent doctor, and you'll get better.' I tried to console him.

But just then Mamu got up, looking flabbergasted. He ran to the drain next to the courtyard and began puking. I went to him and started stroking his back. I saw a yellowish fluid coming out of his mouth, and swimming in it were innumerable white worms that were now swarming in.

I closed my eyes in fear.

Mamu looked like he was feeling better after he had puked. He started talking to Rehana Phuphi about fetching bread and milk. Rehana Phuphi was mumbling to herself, 'It's actually the crow's meat – nothing else – which he had eaten once that is causing all this.'

I gradually grew used to Chhote Mamu and his illness. His vomiting had become a matter of routine now. I stayed home most of the time and I went and sat on the fourth stair of the staircase from time to time, sometimes roamed the terrace, spent time in the kitchen and sat under the palm tree sometimes. It was the month of May. I liked the gusts of Loo. This season at least spares us the malicious humidity in which the sweat doesn't dry at all and one's body gets ridden with prickly heat.

I roamed the courtyard in the heat like a ball of fire. The Loo would be calling out, making its presence felt in all directions. The sunshine seemed bent on drying up even the blood in our veins.

When the throat and the tongue became parched, I poured some water from the earthen pot kept on the stone floor in the courtyard to drink.

I roamed the house which was now a wilderness like a ghost, restless and without a proper resting place or abode. As far as Rehana Phuphi and Chhote Mamu were concerned, they were ghosts too, weren't they?

I stayed home most of the time. One reason for this was the sewer lines being laid outside which had transformed the streets into deep pits. The other reason was that there was hardly anyone left in town whom I could go and meet. I had never really socialized with the people of the mohalla when I had lived there anyway.

So what remained finally was the graveyard where I could go and offer prayers for the dead, but I didn't know how fateha was offered and I didn't want to enter the house with the dust from the graveyard caking my shoes. It was said that if dust from the graveyard were to somehow enter the house, it would cause the death of someone in the house. I'm not a superstitious person, in fact I have a scientific temperament. I'm very intelligent, very clever, but who knows better than me that the connection between disease and the diseased is so delicate that it cannot be understood by a healthy mind. It's a mysterious thread which becomes clearly visible at times, and at others it becomes so blurred and indistinct that it can only be sensed. And so I didn't go to the graveyard. I had a feeling that Chhote Mamu would die any day and then I would have to go to the graveyard in any case, although one can never be sure who will accompany whose dead body to the graveyard.

The month of May was over and the grudge-ridden and malicious month of June arrived, full of wet and sticky summer rain, permanent sweat and rotting body odour. Mosquitoes and bedbugs in the house were increasing by the day. Chhote Mamu and Rehana Phuphi spent the nights beating the jute charpoys with rods and a pile of bedbugs collected under them. They crushed the bugs with their slippers and the bare brick floor became stained with their blood. The blood that was actually theirs and the bedbugs and mosquitoes were their offspring. I also spent the nights tossing and turning in bed, scratching myself. The house had not been whitewashed since God knows when. The age-old lime on the walls was crumbling under the moisture and falling to the ground. The walls wore a strange look due to the patterns the moisture and the seepage had created on them. It was as if dead people's faces were peering through the walls. The faces of the people who used to live in this house. The faces of all those who were no longer alive in this world.

It was the first Friday of the month of June. A strange, lonely and forlorn Friday. There was no sign of life in the house. Chhote Mamu was the only man left. He was no longer fit enough to go to the mosque for the Friday prayers. He performed the ablutions in his own confused manner and offered the namaz, probably incorrectly. Well, Allah knows our intentions.

I recalled the bright Fridays of my childhood and their hustle-bustle and felt sad. I thought to myself, Hafeezuddin Babar, alias Guddu Miyan, will go to the mosque from this house. It was eleven-thirty in the forenoon. There was one and a half hours left to go for the Friday congregation. I began to prepare for my bath. What preparations, I just put on an underwear and sat down in the shallow tank under the tap and began to push the handpump and allow the water to pour on myself. Yellow-coloured wasps began to buzz around the stream of water. I continued bathing without any care. I knew they wouldn't sting me.

When I was leaving for the mosque wearing a white kurta–pyjama and a black cap, a sharp smell of something cooking in the kitchen hit my nostrils. I wondered what was being cooked.

Just then Rehana Phuphi called out from the kitchen, 'Guddu Miyan, come straight home from the mosque, I have cooked mutton tahiri today.'

My legs below found themselves shaking slightly.

'Mutton tahiri,' I repeated under my breath. Although I had always been fond of mutton tahiri, I felt myself shuddering at the thought of it for lunch today. My heart began to sink. No, this isn't right. It isn't right for tahiri to be cooked for lunch today. But it had been prepared now. The rice was boiled and had almost softened. I controlled the trembling in my legs and came out. The call to prayer had been made. If I delayed any longer, I wouldn't get a proper place in the mosque.

I didn't get a place in the mosque, but on its terrace. A shamiana was hitched there to protect from the sun those who had come to offer namaz. The domes of the mosque were right in front and clearly visible from where I was. The dome which was made of burnt brick had cracks in it in places. Grass was growing out of the cracks. A loose conglomeration of naked electrical wires was hanging above the domes. I don't remember how many times I must have offered namaz in this mosque on the occasion of Eid or Baqrid. I grew sad, recalling those days.

I noticed that the number of kids in the congregation was more than usual. Children on whom namaz was not yet a religious duty were also there. It was a custom to bring little kids along for the namaz offered on the days of Eid or Baqrid, and even that was not followed strictly. But so many little children together for the Friday prayer, wearing their skullcaps and kurta–pyjamas? I couldn't figure this out. Why on earth are these boys not taught how to offer namaz at home?

The congregation was now ready for prayer.

Those kids made it difficult to offer the prayers smoothly. One of them burst out laughing in one corner and another one followed suit in the other. They were pushing each other and whispering to one another. The people offering namaz began to get distracted. They forgot the rukuh and went directly into the sajdah. Most people made some mistake or the other in the process. I myself was not really offering namaz. I was furious and felt like thrashing these ill-mannered and mischievous kids. I felt even more angry with the adults who had brought them along and were not reprimanding them. It's possible they were of the opinion that a time will come in the future when these children will be the flagbearers of Islam and so it's important for them to get into the habit of visiting the mosque and offering namaz. It wasn't wrong to have such expectations from children or the new generation.

Finally, the namaz got over. The June sun was pouring hellfire over our heads by then. Everyone was drenched in sweat. The door to the mosque was a little narrow and a minor stampede broke out as people jostled with each other to find their slippers. They were putting on each other's slippers in the killing heat which was bothering everyone, making them irritable and quarrelsome. To add to this were those irritating, noisy children who were stepping on people's toes and tearing into the crowd.

I managed to get out of the mosque somehow and began walking on the street, avoiding the sewer pipes and the pits and ditches. Pandit, the churan seller, passed that way with his box. He sported a long tilak on his forehead and was always dressed in a snow-white kurta and dhoti. I bought lots and lots of churan from him as a kid. Everyone knew him in our mohalla. The pomegranate seed churan made by Pandit used to be very tasty. He often gave me churan for free. He was kind to all the children of the mohalla. It was common knowledge that those who were fond of eating and filled their stomachs right up to their throats gulped down his churan regularly.

I looked at Pandit's face carefully. He seemed old. But his fair-complexioned forehead still had the gleaming red mark of the tilak . . . I suddenly noticed two children standing close to the wall of a house with stones in their hands. I recognized them from the mosque. They were the naughty ones playing mischief who had stood close to me in the congregation.

Before I could make any sense of the situation, the children took aim and threw the stones at Pandit. Pandit's little trunk slipped out of his hands and fell open and the different coloured churan balls scattered far and wide on the road. Covering his forehead with his hand, Pandit flopped down on the street. The tilak on his forehead was covered in the blood oozing out there.

Those little mischievous urchins ran away, making strange unseemly sounds with their mouths.

Pandit was badly injured. He was losing consciousness, partially due to the extreme heat and scorching sun and partially because of the excessive bleeding. It wasn't clear where the stone had hit him.

Some people came forward to help and took him to Dr Iqbal's clinic. I was shaking with anger. If I had my way, I would have torn those urchins' bodies into two. I reached home in this state of rage and sorrow. Rehana Phuphi served me an enamel plate full of yellow-coloured mutton tahiri. I must have taken two or three mouthfuls when I heard a noise outside. I left my food and leapt towards the door.

Pandit had died in Dr Iqbal's clinic. He had been injured in some sensitive part of the brain. The Hindus were pelting stones at our mohalla now from the Maliyon ki Puliya area.

I shut the door.

I knew it, I knew that cooking the yellow mutton tahiri was a bad omen today. It was possible for riots to break out in the town.

And this is exactly what happened. By evening the town was ravaged by horrible riots. Police vans could be heard passing by, their sirens blaring. A curfew was imposed midnight onwards. The entire town was covered under the blanket of a dark silence.

I said to Chhote Mamu, 'All this has happened because of those uncouth and ill-mannered kids.'

'Kids?'

'Yes, the mosque was full of them during the Friday prayers today. They created such a ruckus. Two of those children threw the stones at Pandit.'

'I haven't been to that mosque since God knows when. I used to go to the Budh mosque when I was in good health,' said Mamu.

'But what's wrong with the administrator and the leader of prayers of that mosque? No sense of discipline! Why should so many small children, for whom namaz is not even compulsory, be allowed inside the mosque? It's a place of worship, not a playground. Believe me, Mamu, it became difficult to stand properly. And after all, this mosque was built by our ancestors. You should make them accountable for this. Why aren't the administrators taking any action in this regard?'

'Guddu Miyan! This is the new generation. It is not one for obedience. The old generation is gone. People have come from different places and settled here. Nobody really knows anybody. People are becoming more and more rigid and orthodox.' Mamu spoke uneasily, stroking his chest. He was probably nauseous. The worms in his stomach were attacking his food.

'No.' I shook my head in denial. 'Not at all. Aren't you orthodox? Our entire family has remained orthodox by religious standards. It's a person's private matter, a matter of someone's faith. This isn't religious fundamentalism. This is something else. Something dangerous. When religion reaches the hands of the underage, these will be the consequences.'

The police were patrolling the street outside. The sound of their heavy boots turned the atmosphere eerie.

'But . . . but, Guddu Miyan, the environment of the town has been deteriorating since long. Prejudice and ill feeling is on the rise. Why are you only blaming the children? What can kids do, after all? Unh unh.' The puke had probably reached Mamu's throat. He got up and leapt towards the drainlet.

A poisonous laughter resounded within me. What do you know? What can children not do? Children do everything. Children commit two murders and no one even gets to know.

Beware of children, Chhote Mamu, beware!

There is no living thing more dangerous than a kid.

Someone kept laughing a deadly laugh within me and the worms kept coming out of Chhote Mamu's mouth along with vomit and flowing out of the drainlet.

No one will ever find out anything. Nobody will get to know. The most dangerous of incidents will find their way through the narrow drains of time and pathetically flow down them in this manner. The way these poor worms are floating away.

Many days and nights passed in the curfewed environment. The house had a full stock of potatoes and spices, ghee and oil and pulses. Milk was not available because of a rumour that it had been contaminated by the people who live beyond the Maliyon ki Puliya with poison or some substance that causes Muslims to lose their fertility, or else the milkman would have found a way to reach our homes during the curfew. Rumours started spreading rapidly during the riots. These rumours had their own peculiar psychology and sociology. One rumour can outweigh the biggest of truths in times of riots. A rumour suddenly acquires an uncontrolled character of truth, which is impossible to deny, and even solid realities are converted into elusive dreams and mirages. People use rumour as an intoxicant during riots; the way a drug addict cannot live without drugs, in a riot nobody can survive without rumours.

One day there was a rumour that the police would be conducting searches in every house. And they would not enter from the main door but jump into people's houses using ladders, and then look for weapons. All the people in the mohalla were very intimidated. I saw many people throwing away kitchen knives and fruit knives into the sewer pipes surreptitiously. Another rumour doing the rounds was that any young male found in the house would be nabbed and taken away.

I was the young male in my house. I was hoping for this rumour to be true! Let the police nab me for the crime of inciting riots. Let me be held responsible for some crime at least. A foolish sense of criminality began to build in me.

That night I had a dream. I saw innumerable mosques, the mosque with the twelve doorways, the Naumela mosque, the Mirzai mosque, the Domni's mosque, the red mosque, the mosque of the Bibiji and even the mosque of the graveyard.

Every mosque was packed with children. They were four to five years of age and wore white kurta-pyjamas with caps on heads. There was no one else in the mosque. I found the scene very frightening. 'Where have all the adults gone?' I ask in the dream, surrounded by a strange wilderness.

Just then a small boy whose face bore no trace of innocence wrapped his arms around my shoulders and began swinging. Did he want me to take him in my arms?

I tried to shake him off very hard but he held on to my shoulders so steadily and was swinging on them in such a manner that his feet were lifted off the ground.

My shoulders began to ache. And I suddenly woke up. I realized that Chhote Mamu was shaking me by the shoulder violently.

'Hafeez, Hafeez. Get up, wake up.'

I woke up hurriedly. 'What happened? Are the police here?'

'No, but they can come any time. They've just passed our lane. Listen, come with me . . .'

Chhote Mamu began to move towards the bigger storeroom adjacent to the hall. I followed him, bewildered.

It was pitch-dark all around. The house seemed empty and uninhabited. We entered the storeroom.

'Here, Hafeez, light a candle.' He handed me a match.

I lit the candle kept on the shelf. The room was full of trunks and old books. The books were being destroyed by white ants from within. The dampness in the air began to make me nauseous.

Then Chhote Mamu produced a small spade from behind a trunk and gave it to me.

'What are you doing?' I felt irritated.

'Dig, Hafeez, at this spot.' Chhote Mamu was sitting on his haunches on the worn-out brick floor and pointing to a spot under a big black trunk.

'Yes, here, just push the trunk a little.'

I obeyed. The trunk wasn't heavy. I could shift it easily. A small mud-coloured snake frisked out from beneath and disappeared under another trunk.

Mamu did not pay attention to the snake. He was trying to recall something under his breath.

'Hafeez, dig here, at this spot. Take out these four bricks,' he said, running his hand over the bricks. He didn't hear what I said.

'No, tell me the reason behind all this.'

'Listen, all right, listen. A dangerous riot had broken out here thirty years ago too and the police had really misbehaved with Muslims. They entered our homes and seized tongs, griddles and iron blowing pipes saying they were weapons, and arrested all the members of the household except the women. The police have inflicted innumerable cruelties on us. Those days we had many hunting knives and daggers to slice up hunted game. Bhai Miyan and your Bade Mamu had buried them all deep in this spot and placed a trunk over it for fear of the police. They have been lying buried here since then. But I heard from someone today that the police are actually digging up the floor in people's houses. Hafeez, I'm worried about you. How I wish you had not come home during the vacations. If they were to dig up this place, it will be the last straw.'

'So, what do we do now?' I asked.

'Pull out these four bricks ... these four. There is a line drawn with coal around them. He bent down and took a closer look and then said, disappointed, 'It has probably gotten erased.'

'Hafeez! Dig up this place and take the knives and daggers out. I will go to the terrace quietly and deposit them into the pipes for the sewer line. Dig, see, there should be four big knives with no hilts and a very big hunting knife. It has an ivory handle, just check, there are five in all.' Chhote Mamu was trembling with suppressed fervour.

Outside, somewhere in the distance, someone was giving the call to prayer, which was being answered by several other calls to prayer coming from different directions.

'What calls to prayer are these? It's two-thirty in the morning.'

'Could be the Hindus laying siege from across the Maliyon ki Puliya. These calls to prayer are made to provide encouragement and for safety too. Or it could be the jinns. You just move the spade.'

I began pulling out the bricks from the floor with disinterest. Though they looked weak and worn out, it was very difficult to move them from where they were set.

There was the earth here, wet earth, which was letting out streams of ants which were now running helter-skelter.

'Dig. Keep hitting with the spade right here. Those knives are buried here. We'll find them shortly. But be careful, there might be snakes here. Take care not to cut up a snake.'

'Why?' I stopped working the spade. I was panting and my whole body was wet with perspiration. 'A snake had appeared a short while ago. I should have killed that injurious creature right then.'

'What a shocking thing to say! Don't you remember today is Thursday? One shouldn't harm a snake or a lizard on a Thursday. They are actually in disguise on Thursdays. Amma used to tell us that our grandfather, Dada Miyan, had once killed a snake on a Thursday and it bled so much that the blood filled the whole house. The same night Dada Miyan dreamt that he had murdered the prince of the jinns who had come to our house for a simple jaunt in disguise. Dada Miyan had seen the dead body of that beautiful prince wrapped in a shroud. The shroud too was wet with blood. The blood didn't stop flowing from the dead body. This is a sign of martyrdom. And do you know what happened afterwards? Dada Miyan was gripped by high fever and he lost his mind forever after that. He became insane. He wasn't even afforded the kalima at the time of death.' I was scared for a while after listening to this tale by Chhote Mamu. Then I picked up the spade and resumed working.

As I continued to dig, mounds of damp earth, which became higher and higher, began to collect all around.

The pit became deeper, and deeper, and deeper, but there was no trace of any knives.

'Chhote Mamu, the knives aren't here,' I said, tired and annoyed. I threw the spade to one side and sat down on the ground on my haunches. I was out of breath and my throat felt absolutely parched.

'They should have been here. I remember quite distinctly, right at this spot. Under this blue trunk.' Chhote Mamu peered into the pit I had dug as if he were looking into the underworld.

The candle kept on the shelf began to quiver a little. The shadows cast by our bodies huddled on the floor, on the discoloured, seepage-ridden walls seemed ridiculous in the hazy flame of the candle. Chhote Mamu took a sad, deep breath as he straightened himself and said, 'The knives have gone from here.'

'What do you mean?'

'If you bury weapons made of iron under the earth, they stay there, waiting for a certain time period for their owners, but later they move to another place underneath, swimming in the mud. After this, if the earth were to release them, they are found, otherwise they stay out of reach and are lost forever.'

I couldn't possibly believe this nonsense, so I remained quiet.

'Hafeez, the same thing happens with maya's pot. If you fill a copper pot with gold and silver coins and then don't take it out for a long time, maya begins to grow feet and one day it walks away to some other place in order to enhance the fortune of another.'

'Chhote Mamu, you are telling me such weird things.' I was amused even though I was irritated.

'Hush, Guddu Miyan! Don't laugh. Believe me, it's true. Have you seen the rear wall of the kitchen? The one we share with Akbar Ali's house?'

'Yes.'

'Have you seen a big round mark on that wall at about four feet near the chulha?'

I tried to remember but couldn't.

Mamu continued, 'There is a maya pot buried in the kitchen. It is a copper vessel weighing twelve sers. It's a treasure that belonged to our unknown ancestors. That poor vessel waited many years, and finally one cold dark night, when the winter rain was falling and lightning was striking and hailstones and the wind was blowing very fast, the vessel broke the rear wall of the kitchen and departed from our house. The wall developed a gap the size of a twelve-ser vessel used for cooking pulao. Nobody heard the wall breaking down due to the roar of the rain and lightning at that time. Everyone only noticed it in the morning and they were struck with despair, but what could one possibly have done? The gap was filled with bricks later. That round mark is due to that gap. It was then that our misfortunes began. They say Akbar Ali's paternal grandfather was a rickshaw puller, but he started acquiring an astonishing amount of wealth after this incident. Today, Akbar Ali is the wealthiest man in the mohalla.' Mamu started feeling very pukish even as he finished saying this.

I thought the disgusting worms in his stomach had started consuming the food again and began filling the pit I had dug.

Chhote Mamu went and sat by the small drain. A large number of dogs were barking in the lane outside. One could hear religious slogans at a distance in frightening and inhuman voices. Once in a while the noise of firing or an explosion was also heard and the western corner of the sky showed a brilliance spreading over it. Then many police vans were heard passing, their sirens blaring.

'The atmosphere is deteriorating. God have mercy,' Rehana Phuphi mumbled as she lay on her bed.

I looked at the time. The night was over. It was four in the morning. My head was aching and my eyelids felt heavy. I went and lay down on the charpoy in the courtyard. Prickly heat had erupted on my body and the bedbugs were biting me, but I still felt sleepy. I had grown used to Chhote Mamu vomiting. I could hear him puking for some time, after which I fell into a deep sleep.

It was true that I had developed a kind of insensitiveness towards everything. My heart had turned to stone. This was the house where my navel-string had been buried. This was the house where so many people, so many relatives had lived that it was difficult to recall all their names. This was more an assembly than a house. Today when all the members of this household were lying buried under tonnes of earth and only two members remained, and death was fast approaching them, amazingly I didn't seem to be affected by it. I had lost interest in this house. I was bored, kind of fed up. Riots were raging in the town and news of people dying kept pouring in. There was curfew everywhere. Within myself, however, I felt disconnected from all this. It's possible that this was a function of my age at that time or the shadows of my dreadful childhood that did not want me to live peacefully in this house. I wanted to get out of my house.

But there was another thing, a little puzzling and troubling as well.

I often got the feeling that I will make a grand return, trailed by fans and followers. On that day this house will once again be alive, full and vibrant. All the members of the household, who are not here at present, will be present then. The kitchen will flourish once again. My parrot, Sunbul, and my jagged-eared rabbit will also be there. Then I'll come. Then my coming here will hold meaning. This was a promise I had made to myself.

What sense did it make to live with two old people on the verge of death?

A day came when the riots ceased. The curfew was lifted. Every curfew has to be lifted one day or the other. Peace committees were constituted in different parts of the town. People sang songs of Hindu–Muslim unity. Local political leaders had a field day. The atmosphere of the town was restored to normal, although the stench coming from the pipes of the sewer lines and the ditches remained for quite some time. Dead bodies were rotting there. And they kept getting discovered for many days.

Arrests were made on a large scale, but 'they' remained safe.

'They' – the young but dangerous kids with whom the mosques were teeming.

This is how it happens. Children always escape. God is particularly kind to them. Even if they are dreaded devils in reality. I didn't find this surprising at all. Who knew this truth better than me?

The month of July arrived. Monsoon clouds appeared and disappeared without any rain. It was a hide-and-seek between sunshine and shade. I came to know that my results were out and checked my roll number in the newspaper.

I had cleared LLB with a third division.

I began making preparations to go back to the city. I would have to go to the college first to obtain my degree and then–

Then what?

It was decided that I would set up a legal practice. I had to fight others' cases for the time being. So that one day I will be able to walk the hazy and mysterious path leading to my own trial. I should file a case against myself and also understand the intricacies of the case which has been filed against human beings' intestines. But I don't know from whose side I will fight the case? The human intestines, in this mysterious instance? And who knows whether I will be chosen as one of the lawyers for this case or not.

Every lawyer doesn't have the good fortune of being able to showcase his language skills in a case of his choice. To offer arguments in favour of his choice of criminals and murderers. And to be able to take boxes of sweets home after winning a case or pull a long face after losing one and putting the entire blame on hostile witnesses.

I had put my suitcase in order. My train was to depart right at the stroke of midnight.

Chhote Mamu had a sad countenance and Rehana Phuphi had been shedding tears since morning.

'Hafeez!' said Chhote Mamu in a weak voice.

'Yes.'

'You are going today.'

'Yes, Chhote Mamu.'

'Come with me to the back of the kitchen, near the palm tree.' I felt mightily irritated at this desire of Chhote Mamu's. God knows what cock and bull story he'll come up with, I thought. He's become completely eccentric. Anyhow, I went with him to the palm tree so as not to be disrespectful. Just then a dense black cloud appeared in the sky and the green leaves of the tree turned dark, almost black. Since the wind was blowing hard, I knew that the cloud wouldn't stay long and would disperse quickly.

'Just check that Rehana is not here,' said Chhote Mamu, glancing around. I found this strange. I saw Rehana Phuphi lying on a mat in the inner hall half asleep.

'She's inside, but what is the matter?'

Chhote Mamu retched lightly as if he was about to belch. Surely his mouth must have filled up with a sour liquid that smelt of the meatball curry he had had for lunch; the smell might have been good or foul.

He brought out a roll of old, worn-out papers which he had tucked under the drawstring of his pyjamas and sat down right there on the kuccha ground.

I sat down too and leaned forward to look at what he was holding.

There were some names written on them as well as some designs and maps. The papers were inscribed in the old-style shikasta hand with a reed pen.

'What is this supposed to be?'

'This is your family tree. I have worked very hard to save it from white ants and wastage.' Chhote Mamu's voice was shaking.

'Family tree?'

'Yes, family tree records. I'm now handing it over to you. You are, God be praised, a big lawyer, and can very well understand this document.'

'I haven't understood a thing. And how will my understanding this help?'

'If you were to understand it, it would become clear who the legal heir to this house is, although this is a very complicated matter. So many relatives lived in one single house, this house. One couldn't find out who was the actual owner of the house. Or maybe if the house were to be divided, everyone would have got property the size of a pin, and some might have been made ineligible for any share in the property.'

'Why?'

'I couldn't figure it out, Hafeez, I couldn't figure it out. The older generations would know. I do know this much that every member of the family married at least thrice. Many women among them were widows or divorcees and brought their children along. There was no restriction on producing children like there is now; it was a common practice for everyone to have six or seven kids. The generations kept progressing this way and recognizing or classifying relations became a very tall order.'

'I got it, Chhote Mamu,' I interrupted him, fed up.

'To cut a long story short, what you have to do is understand the family tree and get the papers made. Now it's you who is the heir to this house.'

'How do you know that I am the only legal heir? What proof do you have for this?'

The black cloud sailed away, sprinkling just a few drops of rain on the palm tree.

'Because I'm a lamp which has burnt through the night, my flame is weak and pale. May you live a hundred years, God willing. The one who stays alive becomes the successor.'

'But how much one owns or has inherited can be known only after partitions and divisions have been made. It's possible that I may not be eligible to inherit even the smallest portion of the property.'

'That is why I'm saying this. If the family tree were to be made public, all kinds of people will emerge from all kinds of corners to claim their share. One might have thought that everyone lived here and shared the same kitchen. But the truth of the matter is that the kitchen was always a battleground. I have seen women pull each other's hair over fights on salt and chillies. It was kitchen warfare that separated hearts from hearts and bones and nails from bones and nails. I haven't even told Rehana that a son of her first husband is alive and is a businessman in Nepal.' Chhote Mamu was rubbing his chest, he must have been feeling nauseous.

I was watching him silently. Chhote Mamu continued to stroke and rub his chest uneasily as he tried to restrain himself from vomiting, applying all his strength, as a result of which he spoke with a gurgling sound.

'Guddu Miyan, please keep this safe. I'm giving it to you just like my elder taya gave it to me when I was your age. It was passed on to him by his Mamu and . . .' Chhote Mamu was elaborating on this ridiculous account of the past. I thought that its last link would perhaps be an ancient, emaciated monkey. This house too had now become so decrepit that it might turn into a monkeys' abode after a few years.

'Here, Guddu Miyan, take these and keep them safe, hidden from view in your bedding case. Go to the city and get the legal papers ready claiming you as the sole inheritor. It will be good if this happened in my lifetime.' He handed me the bunch of papers and went to the edge of the drain to throw up.

I raised the papers to my nose – they had a damp, earthy smell.

A brownish cloud appeared again at around four in the evening. There was a slight drizzle and a pleasant breeze was blowing. I had acidity; perhaps my lunch was not properly digested yet. I went and lay down on the old large wooden bench in the outer hall. The drizzle-laden breeze put me to sleep.

Someone knocked on the door at midnight. Everyone in the house was asleep but are now awake. All of them have bitten their tongues in sleep. There is a trickle of blood on everyone's chin. Who's there? I get up to open the door. Who is it?

I unlock the door.

Bade Mamu is standing outside, at the crossing, in the moonlit night.

There are two people with him.

'Here, these are your guests,' Bade Mamu says disinterestedly.

'They have been searching for the house since long. Wandering here and there.'

'Please come in.' I welcome the guests, showing them the way indoors. All the members of the household have now come to the front door.

'Come in, come in,' everyone says to the guests. 'You have come after a long time.' The guests walk in smiling. They have earthen pots of rasawal wrapped in red paper in their hands.

Bade Mamu is still standing outside, his manner aloof. I close the door indifferently.

I don't know if he has left or is still standing there. I don't care. He seems very distant from this house despite having shown the guests the way here. He's unconnected. Almost a stranger, although an unending dusty haze of anger, complaint and the sorrow of some unknown compulsion is visible outside in the moonlit night through the chinks in the door. His silent shadow trembles slightly in the dusty haze. I can see it, but I don't care. The dust which has accumulated on the doorstep sobs under my feet. I don't care. I turn back inside.

'Guddu Miyan, Guddu Miyan, get up. It is the call to the maghrib prayer.' I woke up hurriedly. Chhote Mamu was standing near the wooden platform. The pleasant drizzle had stopped, so had the breeze. The clouds had dispersed in the sky. Only in the western corner, where the sun sets, had a red cloud spread over it. Like a sheet drenched in blood.

I started finding my house unbearable. I had to leave from here at eleven for the station. But it had become very difficult for me to pass four hours. I didn't want to stay here any longer. What was I to do with a house where distant relatives are shown the way and brought till the door by a member of the family but he himself returns from the threshold? Unconnected, aloof, no one asks him to come in. Who is it that prevents him from crossing the threshold of the house? Is this the destiny of every dead person? They reach out to people wandering around in lane after lane, looking for the right address. Living people do not allow the dead ones to come in. This is a compulsion for those who are alive, and up until the time there is a living person in the house, the dead will bring those wandering for the right address to the threshold of the house at midnight, and after that, return to their own respective darknesses.

What will I do in such a house where the dead don't get a share in the family property?

I should run away from here. I should run away as soon as I can.

With the yellowing and decaying bunch of papers in my hand, I came out of the house quietly at ten in the night. The lane was deserted. One or two stray dogs lifted their heads to look at me, and then lost interest.

I looked around and then quickly shoved those family tree papers deep inside the pipes of the sewer line.

No one saw me, no one ever spots me doing anything. I felt a criminal sense of pride.

These papers recording the family tree will be destroyed in the dirty, foul-smelling water of the sewer line like the white worms squirming in Chhote Mamu's shit that swallow up everything he eats.

I left the house with my luggage exactly at 11 p.m.

Chhote Mamu, with his retching, and Rehana Phuphi, with her dreadful jingling bones, came up to the front door to bid me goodbye.

'When will you come again, Guddu Miyan?' asked Chhote Mamu in a voice choked with emotion.

'I'll come soon,' I lied.

'Yes, come soon and take me to the city this time to consult a doctor.'

'Yes, yes, certainly.'

'Do remember to get the recipe for the biryani cooked with spices. That place is very well known for its biryani.'

'Yes, yes, for sure.'

'And . . . and the pot of rasawal too.'

'Yes, yes, surely.'

'God protect you. May God keep you in his safe custody.'

Once again I crossed the rough and broken streets with my bedding case on my shoulders. I hailed a rickshaw after some time.

My train departed from the station exactly at midnight. Up until the time we had crossed the river of the fort, I continued to feel uneasy. Once the wheels of the train had crossed the narrow rails of the old bridge over the fort river with a familiar slight rumble, I was at peace. Such peace as is attained only after hundreds of years.

I was leaving behind the lit-up areas and the darknesses of my small town and I was forsaking both of them with equal speed.

After some time the sound of the train started putting me to sleep as if it were a lullaby. I covered my eyes with both my hands and drifted off to sleep.

The wedding happened soon enough. I've avoided including the details of it in my memoirs as they are of no use and my fingers are tired from writing. If I was really writing a novel, a frivolous, cheap one, I would have noted these details from the outset, but I want to retain some garbage in the sieve of my memory so there is proof that I also omitted something which I took with me as a secret when I left this world. Why should I bother you as well as demean myself by writing about what doesn't concern this case?

I had mentioned earlier that Anjum's complexion was like curdled milk. And I must tell you now that her body smelt of stale curd. She seldom laughed. But when she did, it seemed like the buzzing of thousands of bees. She spoke in a nasal tone, which gave her an air of being indifferent towards everything. I can even say with conviction that she didn't care about the horrendous incident that had happened with her. Alauddin seemed far more troubled than she did.

Anjum was miles away from any kind of coyness. Such people spend a more successful and better life in this world, maybe because they have very weak memories, and when some faculties are weak in humans, they develop other strengths. I had no love for Anjum earlier, neither did I develop any for her after the wedding.

In earlier times people were simple enough to believe that real love happens only in marriage and is at its best in old age when the couple becomes inseparable. According to me, this is nothing but a misunderstanding. The truth is that when the rest of the world begins to look down upon their agedness, they have no option but to rely on each other for succour. This is merely selfishness; giving it a romantic angle is nothing but foolish. I won't say that love has never been part of my share in this world, but the kind of love it was doesn't make me want to talk about it for the time being.

Nevertheless, I will confess that there was buried deep down somewhere in me the wish that Anjum would love me madly, or that at least she would be grateful to me. Then it occurred to me that I had never committed a 'murder' for her, and neither was there any chance of my doing so. Committing a murder and obliging someone are one and the same to me.

They never came to know of their obligation, the ones for whom I committed murders, the result being that I went missing.

But my wife, Anjum, could never love me, and so there was a perpetual feeling of homelessness in me. Despite living in a grand apartment, I continue to feel till today that I have only roamed the streets or stumbled upon the open pipes of the sewer line, fallen down and gotten up, and fallen down again.

This is obviously the smallness of my mind. When I didn't love Anjum or have any sympathy, concern or regard for her, wasn't expecting her to love me a very base kind of injustice? But I don't want to be ashamed of the injustices I have inflicted on others, rather I feel sorrowful and ashamed of the injustices I have borne silently. After obtaining a degree in law and reading all those thick tomes of theories on justice, punishment and crime and the rest, I still believe that the person wreaking injustice should not be put to death by hanging, rather he should be subjected to the same injustice that he has inflicted on others.

So, this may be said to my satisfaction, that though we did not love each other, we were, nevertheless, being honest to each other. However, this life is nothing but a conspiracy against honest people. It makes a mess out of the lives of honest folks. I can't say about Anjum, but as far as I am concerned, I know it is my honesty that has ruined my life. What bigger proof of the mean conspiracies of the world can there be than the fact that it has produced cockroaches. A cockroach, which never dies. A cockroach, which has no blood in it. A cockroach, which will remain safe and sound even after the destructions of the atomic wars. I know a cockroach that watches the blood and filaments and fragments emerging from a head crushed under a slab of stone used for grinding spices. He watches the stream of kerosene falling on a blazing stove, and then looks at me and smiles at my honesty, laughs at me, yes, believe me, he laughs at me, the sound of his laughter is safe and secure in my ears. On hearing his laughter, I become a wild horse and shying again and again, roam the streets like a wastrel. I loaf around in the high court, so that these wandering and straying feet of mine should take me to the cave where a dark and dingy court of law awaits me. When will my honesty, my obligations on others, my murders, take me there? Six months had passed since I got married, but the feeling of the passing of time cannot be recorded on paper. Time is the biggest art, the horrific art of the world's many disguises. Every art can be brought on to paper, to the extent that even music can be written down, but not time. Time is a coin which has 'distance' written on its reverse side, but it is impossible to determine the extent of these distances from the distances between my words and sentences.

My memory is helpless here. It can't regurgitate itself fully even if it may want to do so. Despite not trying to conceal anything at all, I can't inscribe the feeling of time having passed on paper. Just the way someone suffering from the common cold cannot bring himself to express the suffering and torture of this ordinary disease, human beings cannot rid themselves of the realization of time having passed. They haven't managed to invent a vaccine for the common cold till date.

Alauddin came home to meet us one evening. Anjum asked him to stay for dinner.

Anjum's cooking was tasteless and unsavoury. No food is worth anything without the addition of spices. The curry cooked by Anjum, which used to be served in enamel bowls, looked so colourless and was so devoid of flavour that the intestines stopped functioning beforehand. Let alone make the mouth water, her food caused the mouth and palate to dry up to an extent that I started feeling like a thief who was fearful of his thieving being exposed, causing the saliva in his mouth to dry up, at a time when he was being asked to swallow dry flour.

Whenever Anjum cooked food in the kitchen there was no scope of good or bad aroma spreading to any part of the house. But that night, strangely enough, a familiar smell reached my nostrils, having distilled itself through the walls of the kitchen. I found this very surprising.

I screwed my nostrils and sniffed.

'What are you doing?' Alauddin laughed. I forgot to state that Alauddin's stupid and irritating laughter had resurfaced immediately after my wedding to Anjum.

'There's a scent in the air, what's cooking?' I said.

Anjum entered the room for some work.

'What's being cooked?' I asked.

'Everything's done, I just have to fry the eggs,' she spoke in her nasal tone.

'Eggs, eggs, eggs.' I felt the hair on my wrists stand on end. Ants seemed to be stinging all the pores of my body. I felt an insect crawl on my back. I tried to shake it off using my left hand. I began sweating profusely. It was the month of May. The ceiling fan was working at full speed. Why this sudden perspiration then?

I understood then that the limits of my awareness and sixth sense had reached a dangerous point where red warning lights were blinking.

'What was the need to fry eggs today?' I asked in a peeved voice.

'Why? What's it to you? You need not eat it,' said Anjum, swaying rudely and in this swaying movement her buttocks got sucked in further, like a tortoise retracting its head.

'It's not about my eating or not eating.'

'Then what's it about?'

'I'm getting a feeling that something wrong is about to happen. It's an ill omen.'

'Because I fried eggs?' Anjum jeered.

'Yes, but you both won't understand.' I spoke with icy coldness.

'Why, are you some godman who spews prophecies?' Anjum spoke angrily and screwed up her eyes to look at me as if she were scrutinizing the chutney that she had just ground and kept in a bowl.

At that moment a utensil fell from the kitchen shelf on to another.

'Arey, arey, why are you guys squabbling, this is nothing to fight about,' said Alauddin, forcing himself to laugh even though he appeared fazed.

'Ask your friend, did I commit a sin by cooking eggs tonight?' Anjum began to flare up, seemingly uncontrollably for no reason.

'C'mon, Apa, let it be. Hafeez must have had some kind of suspicion.'

Food was served at the table after some time. I didn't even as much as cast a look at the fried eggs. The food was tasteless as always. I ate barely a morsel or two.

Alauddin left after dinner.

I lit a cigarette as I sauntered in the balcony. I was felling distressed.

Suddenly there was a knock on the door. Anjum got up to open it.

Alauddin was back, his face terror-stricken.

'Hafeez, Hafeez, where are you?'

'What happened?' I asked.

'Switch on the radio,' he said in a trembling voice.

'But what happened?'

'There's a crowd on the street outside. There was this news on the radio.'

'What?'

'Rajiv Gandhi has been killed.'

Perhaps I have already written about Anjum's facial features. When I saw her for the first time after the wedding, she was still in her wedding finery but there was no change in her looks or her health. But after a while when she opened her mouth to say something (I don't remember what it was that she said – must have been something ordinary), I found an unpleasant change in her appearance. When I looked carefully, I realized that one of her lower front teeth was halfbroken. It was not so earlier.

It is possible the tooth had chipped off when she suffered that dreadful rape in the college canteen.

The half-broken tooth had enhanced the cruel line of her mouth, and I have often thought of telling her to either get the tooth removed or get an artificial whole tooth fixed in its place. Vacant spaces don't carry so much dread as the wind passes through them. But half-finished or incomplete things are mysterious to a frightening degree, and one cannot say anything at all about them with certainty. The terror and cruelty of this world is concealed in its being incomplete. An empty world in its place would certainly have looked better and even beautiful to some extent.

But such things don't affect sexual hunger at all. This hunger is free from all restraints – of love, as well as of hatred. And as far as revulsion is concerned, the two are bound together inseparably. And so Anjum's half-broken tooth never caused me any hindrance in copulating with her, not even when her mouth fell completely open exposing her half-broken tooth, a thin film of yellow lime over it, and she stared with malicious eyes at my lascivious face bending over her's.

All those fancy stories about women's bodies are total nonsense. The dimensions of a woman's body, its curves, its touch, all these are nothing but rumours. These rumours have mostly been spread by poets and writers so that men can rule over women's minds. This is a serious conspiracy hatched by poets and writers against women. The more they sing praises of women's bodies, the more they continue to slice up women's souls. God created even the cockroach in pairs, but it is impossible to find another example of this dangerous conspiracy that humans have hatched against the female of their species among any other living creatures of this world.

The bodies of men and women are like food spread on the table for each other, the sight or smell of which is enough to raise the appetite. One starts feeling hungry but greed and hunger are related to a man's or woman's own blood and intestines. The taste too is dependent on one's own mouth and tongue and the scent depends on one's own nostrils.

The question that arises is what is eaten and how. What difference does it make whether you sit before the spread with your legs crossed or on your haunches? The loud burp that you let out after eating to your heart's content exposes the truth about you. Comparing women's bodies to a flower, a bud, kneaded dough, butter or cream is completely meaningless. What better evidence is there than the fact that I have seen men rubbing the lower part of their bodies against hard black iron poles to derive pleasure, attaining the kind of satisfaction and satiation they do by rubbing their bodies against women's bodies. What, ultimately, was the status of a poor woman's body? Everything was an illusion, merely air. What was solid was reaching that point, which could not be impeded by Anjum's half-broken tooth nor her inward sunken buttocks nor her bee-like buzzing, unattractive laughter, nothing – they all sway in their own wind and drink the wine drawn from their own blood.

I was certainly doing this and Anjum too was probably doing the same.

And what was all this?

In an inevitable moment drawn out of the twenty-four-hour day, two savage and empty vessels rolling around directionless, colliding with each other, producing vulgar, violent and cheap noises, causing pain while rubbing against each other and desiring to fill their bodies to the brim with an unseen soup and finally, tired, realizing their respective emptiness to be their destiny once again, fall to their respective sad corners, silent.

Anjum wants to hog all the food in my intestines and I want to enter her intestines like a snake and lick everything there. Anjum treats me the same way she treats the soiled utensils she scrubs in the kitchen and I regard her as a plate in which I have my food and then lick clean with my tongue.

This is not love – this is sexual intercourse, which has its own rules and its own maths. It's more honest than love but it's the victim of a grave misunderstanding. Love is a thought, a word and a metaphor wrapped in mist. Love doesn't have hands or feet or nipples, and if love had kidneys or a liver, it would take them out and sacrifice them, whereas sexual intercourse is an honest equation of mathematics, but the deception of which is dependent on its sum. The sum that is nothing more than a blank, zero.

But stop, it would be wrong to conclude that I never got my share of love in life. I have entered love with a faded ink in my account book somewhere, and now that you have read the disorderly tale of my childhood you must be aware that whenever love came into my life, it was a love polluted by grains of trash. These were not grains of trash and tiny particles of rubbish that enter the rice from outside. They had germinated within the love itself, coming into existence through some mysterious germs during a moment of humidity.

Nothing could be done now. The rice had been consumed. The teeth were unpleasantly gritty because of the fine particles of sand and tiny stones lodged in the gaps and cavities, creating plaque and caries. The teeth ached. They ached badly.

My heart was aching too. A little piece of scab had peeled off. Such huge spots ... Such huge spots ...

The stream of my thoughts went astray. I should exercise objectivity but there are times one can't do something despite wanting to. Sometimes I feel a strange, unseen pressure on myself as I write these petitions and a thick darkness begins to emerge from within my being. Just as the turtle is forced to put his neck out under the pitiless pressure of a heavy foot. You'll have to forgive the turtle.

The existence of the kitchen and various kinds of exotic food were also necessary for complete honesty towards each other during sexual intercourse.

Anjum took great care to feed me a particular food item in a very organized and systematic manner. She didn't care a fig about what I liked or did not like. She did not even come to know if my hunger was satiated or not – she was never concerned that I felt weak and tired all the time, fed up of doing my regular rounds of the high court but remaining unemployed. She found making tea for me to be a bother and kicked up a huge fuss about my smoking.

But there were a few things she never forgot to feed me regularly. I hadn't even tasted these before marriage. For instance, she soaked dry dates in milk at night for me to eat in the morning. The hard shreds of the dry dates got stuck in the gaps between my teeth and I suffered from toothache for hours. She soaked urad dal in water overnight and I had to eat it raw the next morning. I was also forced to consume milk and almonds. I had a problem digesting milk since childhood, so I began suffering from a perpetually upset stomach.

Such foods were supposed to be effective in enhancing male sexual prowess and appetite. I was sometimes not in the mood at all but my wife, despite her quarrels and fights with me, was very generous when it came to sex and God is witness that she did not allow a single night to go to waste.

Once it so happened that I came home late on a winter night.

'When you come home so late after loafing around outdoors, you might as well bring that sometimes.' Anjum gave a fake coquettish look and screwed up her eyes.

'What?' I asked.

'That which they sell on pushcarts on the big bazaar street.'

'What . . . I don't know.'

'Shakila was telling me that her husband gets it every day on his way home from work.' Anjum had now turned her lips also into circles.

'What does he get? Why don't you tell me?' I was getting irritated.

'I feel shy to tell you.' Anjum turned her back towards

me. I understood a little late, but I do understand everything ultimately.

'The cot-breaking halwa?' I asked coldly.

Anjum said yes and began to laugh. Bees started buzzing everywhere.

'Why do I need to eat it? Yes, it can be had for the taste of it.'

'No.' Anjum turned around to face me and started running her fingers lovingly through my overgrown stubble. 'They say one has a boy if one eats it. You don't realize, Hafeez, you have grown weak.' Anjum was trying to please me.

Then she gave a look that made me feel like a vessel on the cook stove in which mutton was being slowly prepared.

I went to the bathroom quietly to freshen up. I had begun to sense for the past few days that Anjum was not satisfied by me. The lava inside her was seething and had turned her skin numb, or it was possible that she had become a sadist after the gang rape and wanted to experience through me the dangerous criminals and their wild galloping horses who lived in the fertile marshes of the Ramganga.

It was a wicked thought and I felt deeply ashamed of myself for harbouring this cheap sentiment about her, so to compensate for it I tried to bring some semblance of love for her, albeit unsuccessfully. How I wish food hadn't existed, perhaps pure love would have existed in the world then, but for these wretched foods, which are prepared in the kitchen, the kitchen, which is the most dangerous place in the house. Let someone ask me about the destructive power of foods and dishes. These dishes which fulfil the dangerous task of strengthening and sustaining the low-grade entity that is life. These foods which enhance sexual desire, the body's lust. They led Adam and Eve astray and became the cause of the expulsion of Adam from paradise. These dishes which become the cause for producing a male offspring, the males who grow up and ride horses, coming out from the alluvial land of the Ramganga into the world to rape their mothers, sisters and daughters. But Anjum doesn't understand. She doesn't understand anything. Why doesn't she understand? These dishes which are the root of worms inside the stomach and the dirty, putrid faeces in the intestines.

And me? I too have been the adulator of a tea made with poisonous milk. I have become poisonous myself – I have a dangerous ability in me Anjum knows nothing about. I am aware of the dangerous qualities of those food items. Anjum doesn't know anything. She doesn't know that I have more strength than the criminals and their horses who live with their faces covered in the alluvial soil of the Ramganga. I can have intercourse with Anjum which can cause her head to splinter and spread over the grinding slab. Anjum doesn't know anything, she is only in the grip of desire, and I am in the grip of a cockroach who lives in a sooty kitchen.

Anjum became pregnant two years after the wedding. It was the first month. I began to experience an unexplainable tenderness within me. Anjum's face suddenly appeared pure and innocent to me. The day I got this good news was the day I first became aware of the meaningfulness, value and worth of the union of man and woman.

I spent that entire day eating sweets and fried snacks outside the high court. I don't know why the whole day I heard the voice of a little girl lisping childishly into my ears, 'Papa, Papa, my Papa.' My spirit began to cleanse itself. I was in a hurry to reach home. On entering the house in the evening, I went to the kitchen directly. Anjum was usually in the kitchen at this time. It was better to describe it as a kitchen rather than a bawarchi khana because it had a gas range and running water. There were other gadgets to help in the process of cooking too. There was no soot or filth. There was no grinding stone or mortar and pestle. There might have been some mice and lizards but I had never seen an insect. In any case, the kitchen doesn't achieve completion by just one woman. Anjum was crazy about cleanliness. She got the floor mopped twice a day. There was no question of any dust or even the tiniest cobweb anywhere. Such inordinate stress on cleanliness is also a kind of violence, which is why it is difficult to make a connection between this kitchen and the ancient and mysterious tradition of the bawarchi khana. However, I will refer to Anjum's 'kitchen' as bawarchi khana only out of habit and necessity so that the word doesn't lead to any confusion in my case later on, the advantage of which maybe accrued by some agent kind of lawyer. After all, I should always remember that I'm writing petitions and appeals based on memory.

I wanted to sneak into the kitchen and take Anjum into my arms. I could even imprint a kiss on her half-broken tooth.

But the kitchen was empty.

I turned and went to the inner room.

Anjum was lying flat on the bed and staring at the ceiling.

She didn't try to get up on seeing me.

I sat down at the edge of the bed, smiling.

'It's good that you are resting. Be careful not to lift anything heavy.'

'Heavy?'

'Yes, like a pail of water, or a heavy chair or table.'

'Why?'

She didn't even know this much. I smiled pleasantly.

'It can cause harm to the expected baby.'

She didn't say anything and turned on her side, away from me.

'What is it? I hope you are well?'

'I'm feeling very weak. I won't get up. You can prepare your tea and have it.'

'I hope you didn't lift anything heavy while cleaning the house?' I was worried.

Anjum got up suddenly with a jerk.

'You can't tolerate the sight of me lying quietly. You've eaten up my head. I went to Dr Ranjana's,' Anjum replied in an unpleasant tone.

'Why? Why do you need to go now? Is everything okay?' I stared at her.

'I've got a cleaning up done,' she spoke quietly, avoiding my gaze.

'Cleaning up? I didn't quite get it.'

'I mean abortion. Did you get that? Abortion,' she exploded, like a beehive bursting open and falling.

Her sharp and cruel nose was runny and her half-broken tooth seemed ready to pierce my flesh and suck my blood.

The glass on the window which opened towards the west suddenly turned red. The whole room was covered in a terrible redness.

Far, far away, the sun set, drenched in red. The call to the maghrib prayer was heard.

*Allah-o Akbar Allah-o Akbar*
*Ashhado Alla Ilaha Illalah*
*Ashhado Alla Ilaha Illalah*

I felt sick. My eyelids grew heavy under the weight of a frightening and unknown tiredness. The blood in my body stopped circulating.

Was my head spinning? No, maybe I was sleepy.

Or was I about to die? A part of my body had died.

I tried to control myself. Forcing my eyes open, I asked in a cold and dead voice, 'Why did you do this?'

'Because it was a girl. I did a sex determination test. 'I don't want a girl. I want a boy.'

'Why?' I summoned up all the strength in my body and asked.

'My wish. It's a matter of pride to be a mother of sons. I don't want to produce a mouse of a baby girl,' she spoke with utmost cruelty.

'Shame on you, you base woman. Without my permission…' I got up, trembling.

'You should be the one ashamed, you impotent fellow. It is your fault. You couldn't give me a son.'

'But I needed a daughter. A small little innocent girl. My blood, a piece of my liver.'

Finally my eyes began to shed tears.

'I am a woman. I have the right to choose if I want to have a baby or not. I don't want to get into this mess at present, and if I were to get into it, I'll do it only for a son. I want to become the mother of strong, burly sons. I got this test done two days ago. When I came to know that it's a girl I first gulped down a large quantity of dill seeds, swallowed four raw eggs and moved around a bucket full of water in the bathroom, but nothing happened. The idiot was very stubborn, very hardy, I had to go for a clean-up finally.'

Once again, after ages, I felt the dangerous, Herculean shadow begin to emerge from within me. I wanted to murder Anjum. My legs had begun to shake as they had already sensed my murderous intention. But right then I heard that innocent lisping voice in my ears, from a great distance this time.

'Papa, Papa, my Papa.'

A strong wind began to blow outside. It was the season of fall. My heart heard the sound of a large number of leaves falling to the earth.

The woman's shamelessness made my head hang in remorse. The huge shadow shrunk into a single dot and got lost within me.

Far away in the distance, Muharram's tableau coffins were being taken out. I heard the mourning drums play. It was the seventh day of Muharram.

I dragged myself out of the room, turning to look once I was at the door. Anjum was settling her salwar. Her hair lay scattered on her shoulders. Then she picked up a huge piece of cotton wool.

My drooping eyes saw it clearly. Her salwar was stained with blood.

'Such huge spots, such huge spots.'

I went out on to the street. The street lights had come on. Leaves were getting crushed beneath my shoes and the yellow blood stuck to their soles. Just like that, without any intention or direction, I kept walking on my exhausted legs.

Casually, for no reason, I raised my head to look at the sky. There were only a few stars. It hadn't been long since sunset. A sad and fading redness of the dusk covered half the moon.

Blood had congealed on the half-moon.

I came across the Muharram tableau. My swollen feet enclosed in my dusty shoes were moving ahead singing a mourning song along with the mourning sound of the drums.

Walking thus, I reached the highway.

'Ya Husain, Ya Husain, Ya Husain.' There was a large procession of black-clad knife mourners in front of me. Weeping and lamenting loudly for Husain, they were hurting themselves with knives such that their blood flowed freely. Their chests were soaked in blood. It was the first time in my life that I had seen a mourning of this kind. Like a madman, I joined the procession, beating my chest with both hands.

Those were rapidly changing times. New economic policies were being floated in the country. The market economy had turned welfare economy into a thing of the past. Multinational companies entered the country with their respective brands like ants. Government jobs had become almost extinct. Hundreds of private colleges for engineering, management and medicine set up shop all over the country. Inflation was reaching the skies. The rich were getting richer and the poor were becoming poorer.

The middle class lost its balance, slipping out of control at the introduction of private television channels. The inferiority complex of the middle class resulted in a flood of consumerism, skin exposure and vulgarity. Everyone was being carried away by this flood.

This was the time when the Babri Masjid was demolished. Riots gripped the country for a long time. Another issue raised its head by the time the riots were brought under control. The new generation became fascinated with religious fundamentalism and orthodox ideology, which began spawning religious terrorists. Young boys were finding faults with their parents for not fulfilling their religious duties and were ready to kill them for this sin. Any limits left to be crossed were taken care of by technology. The market of hatred and bitterness began flourishing with the arrival of mobile phones and the internet, and eventually Facebook and Twitter. The world had shrunk into a village. A village where the game of loathing, fire and blood was being played all the time. And everyone was participating in this game in their eagerness to be called modern.

Poor farmers were committing suicide even as a multinational cosmetics firm aired fashion shows on television with half-naked girls walking a sexually provocative walk like cats, sashaying from one end of the ramp to the other before turning around.

Movies were becoming more and more obscene. Rajesh Khanna's era was long over and Amitabh BAchhan's slightly tolerable era was also a thing of the past. Music was turning into cacophony. Dancing, read gyrating one's hips, had almost become a religious duty. Under the influence of TV and cinema, everyone, even infants, seemed ready to dance. They jumped around as if there were wasps in their pants.

Art had never seen worse times and such superficial and shallow readers had never existed before. One had to place everything before them on a platter. They had become habituated to even chocolate being offered to them without a wrapper. Even a child takes the trouble of removing the wrapper of a chocolate before eating it, but readers now seemed hell-bent on getting art to remove its clothes to resemble the nude bodies of women they were used to seeing in TV serials and fashion shows. They didn't like ambiguity in art. They were readers of sensational news items in cheap newspapers.

The market entered the home through TV channels and the language of the market became the lingua franca. This market did not even spare religion. Religious channels were selling daily short prayers to be chanted on rosaries, predictions or judgement of the future through omens or augury, tantra mantras, astrology as well as amulets from these shops. Religious speakers of the political kind had no need for a mosque or a temple or tents and microphones any more. They had entered every home. The wares were being sold from all quarters. The clash of cultures was raising a din which was making people quake in their shoes.

The 'death of God' had been announced quite long ago, but the announcements these days concerned the death of the writer, the death of the cold war, to the extent that even the death of history had been announced. The only announcement that remained was of the 'death of the human being', but that had probably happened long ago and humans hadn't even come to know of it.

I was, however, not surprised that I was alive despite all these deaths. All those born in the '60s were the witnesses of this ridiculous destruction. They had spent their childhood on one planet and their death was destined on another planet. Everyone from the sixties had seen these two planets clashing with each other. They were ones witness to both, the old and the new. No other generation has seen the times change at such a dangerous speed. A train caught fire and one of the states broke out in riots, killing members of a certain community. The killers were projected as national and community heroes.

There was a time when there were only newspapers but something called the 'media' had been created now. I don't know what this word is all about. Anyhow, this media turns every event, every issue into a 'product' or 'brand'. It starts following something with such vulgar enthusiasm and tenacity that it completely spoils the real essence of things.

As for me, I could never find what they call love in its pure form, but the people of our times did not believe in love, they believed in making love. They made love like they made food; they made it and ate it up. Their hearts descending through their intestines had made a home in their private parts.

Such poisonous winds have blown during the last twenty years that all human beings seem blue to me. I'm alive in this poisonous air and fight a case or two in the high court sometimes. I lose those and wander around the streets aimlessly. That dangerous ability of mine surfaces only rarely these days. For instance, news of Rehana Phuphi's death arrived but no food cooked on that day or the previous day gave me a hint of what had happened or was about to happen. The guy who lived across the street from us, Bashir Ahmad, wrote a second letter to me. Chhote Mamu was dead. But I had sensed no danger when I saw food, any kind of food, being prepared. I felt no sorrow at these two deaths, in fact, there was a kind of relief.

My ability had probably gone to sleep when these two deaths occurred because they hardly mattered to me. These were probably not incidents for me but something routine.

However, I definitely underwent a change after the deaths of Rehana Phuphi and Chhote Mamu. I had started missing home now. Because they were all dead and gone now. I have never been a religious person nor am I one now, but an irrational desire to continue the traditions established by my elders began to take root within me.

I learnt how to offer the ritual prayer for the dead, the fateha. I offered the fateha every Thursday and also made ritual offerings of food or the niyaz on special days like Muharram, the fortieth day of Muharram or the Chehlum, the Gyarhvin, Barawafat and Shab-e-Barat. I began to feel troubled about losing some unknown possessions. I wanted to regain ownership of those lost possessions through the fateha and the niyaz.

I continued receiving letters from Bashir Ahmad with requests to come down and inspect the house which was fast falling into ruin. He advised me to either get it repaired and put it on rent or sell it off and get a substantial amount of money for it.

But I always tore up Bashir Ahmad's letters after reading them. Let alone home, I never even visited the graves of my elders to recite the ritual prayer there and neither did I regret not having had a chance to see Chhote Mamu before he passed away or not participating in his funeral procession and accompanying his body to the graveyard.

It was not that I didn't want to go home, but I knew very well that the appropriate time had not yet arrived. I'm aware that whatever I have written up until now resembles a report. I wanted to write about the changes in time and the changes in myself in an uncomplicated manner. I know that these things will count a great deal in my appeal. After all, the court will have to take notice of the changes in the times and the changes in me. When values change, beliefs change, people change, the heart changes, the noose swinging to and fro also changes its direction. The noose can't possibly avoid the direction in which the wind blows.

I may have cleared my LLB with a third division but I am treading the path of my court of law with caution and proceeding very carefully. I have placed the meanness of the world and my meanness parallel to each other. Two parallel lines!

We both continue to live our lives.

The only difference is that I have to reach my court of law before I die, and if that's not possible, then after I die.

And the world?

It sets up its court of law every day and adjourns it. The world is eternal and permanent. It doesn't even know the spelling of the word 'death' while my entire battle is with my death. If I were to fall into an eternal sleep, my court of law will be lost forever.

Someone once said, 'You can't step into the same river twice.' Everyone knows that a human being's blood is renewed entirely in a span of four months. New blood cells are formed and old blood cells are destroyed and disappear.

It's not just humans, but birds and animals and even inanimate things are afraid of the mysterious action of change. Therefore, despite having vowed to myself a million times that I would not unite bodily with Anjum ever again, the process started again, I don't know when. It's possible that it happened because we stayed together. It might have been possible to abstain had I broken up and separated from Anjum after the abortion, but I didn't do anything of the sort. This had nothing to do with my cowardliness or selfish interest, but with my desire to deepen the hatred I had developed for Anjum. Love and loathing are the same in this context. Both increase with close proximity. I wanted to convert my loathing into a dry and prickly acacia tree. I wanted to experience the gashes of the thorns of that tree in my heart. I could find peace only through those gashes of hatred, which is why I continued to stay with Anjum in that house.

If you are engrossed in something, be it writing or reading or even watching TV, and in front of you or by the bedside is kept a bowl of roasted peanuts or gram, you begin to snack on them now and then without thinking. The same way, yes, exactly like that, I had intercourse with Anjum once in a while. But do believe me when I say that this was a different kind of intercourse. It didn't contain any love or lust or sexual provocation. It had neither enthusiasm nor any emotion. It was worse than masturbation. It was merely an involuntary act comparable to blinking your eyes or moving your legs needlessly. This was not sexual intercourse, just a clumsy imitation of one.

Every time after we had intercourse my being was enveloped in a dangerous and filthy shadow of loathing and the scratches from the thorns of the acacia tree grew deeper. I began to hate not just Anjum but myself too, and, even more so, my sexual organs.

I sneered at myself in disgust and the echo of my sneer lost itself in Anjum's vagina.

The result of these involuntary intercourses was that Anjum became pregnant again. She gave birth to a son and to another son fifteen months after that.

Anjum stopped caring about me completely after the second son was born. She hardly ever oriented her mind towards me, not even as a formality. Her face had acquired a cheap kind of vanity upon becoming the mother of two sons. Her buttocks finally swelled a little, but her breasts began to sag and looked like a pair of dirty rags. Her voice became a little thick; the bees' stomachs were full of nectar now. A black spot appeared on her half-broken tooth. She stopped having intercourse with me.

It was good that I got rid of this filthy practice. There was no bowl of roasted peanuts by my bedside now.

However, despite such a degree of disconnect, our quarrels didn't cease.

As far as I am concerned, I hate foul-tasting food.

Only someone sitting in hell can unwillingly swallow food cooked by Anjum's hands. She didn't use hot spices at all and to make the curries attractive she only found red chilli powder in the market, which had more colour and less flavour – they were merely dead chillies, fake and artificial.

It's a pity that I was addicted to spicy foods. Anjum's intestines may have been suffering from acidity but mine were perfectly healthy, so healthy that if there was ever a case filed against them and the verdict was death by hanging, there wouldn't be even a moment's delay in the event as the doctor examining them would find no excuse of any kind of illness for them.

I was irritated by the insipid taste of food prepared for a sick stomach and screamed and shouted at her, and she responded with equal ferociousness and alacrity.

I spent Thursdays offering niyaz and nazr and performing fateha. My instructions at home were to cook mutton that day. Anjum didn't approve of such things as was natural for her not to since she belonged to another sect. She had no interest in animal flesh and hated washing mutton, feeling a sense of revulsion.

I've told you earlier that Anjum was crazy about cleanliness. She could clean just about anything. As for me, whenever I entered the home, my shoes were worth seeing for the filth they had accumulated.

I either did not know how to walk properly on the road or unconsciously chose such routes which were extremely dirty. As a result, my shoes had banana peels, pieces of rotten vegetables, muck, worms and insects breeding in garbage, rotting animal intestines, wrappers of sweets, biscuits and other snacks and pieces of waste paper stuck to their soles, which I then brought home with me.

You shouldn't feel shocked at this as the roads of every big city in our country are overflowing with such things.

Please don't take what I wrote sometime, I mean a few pages, ago, during the hearing of my case, lightly. I wrote about them in an informal way because of my weariness, but these are all very serious and profound things in actuality. There would be no greater injustice to me were they to be ignored.

'Take off your shoes outside,' she screamed, 'when you get home.'

'I won't leave them outside, do what you will,' I replied complacently.

'The house gets dirty,' she screamed louder.

'The filth is already here,' I replied even more complacently.

My smugness was the reward of my hate. If my hate had not been so strong and far-sighted, I would have murdered Anjum long ago, having lost control over my temper. Murder and swatting flies are one and the same for me.

She turned mad with anger and started pulling her hair. She had begun losing hair. Balls of her hair were found lying here and there. They reached all kinds of nooks and corners and I wouldn't tire of spitting at them lightly when I found them.

'Look, look, I'm just waiting for my sons to grow up, tolerating everything. See what happens then,' she yelled threats at me.

'Are they only your sons?' I faked a laugh. She started screaming even more loudly, and both the kids were terrified and began to cry.

It is true that they were my sons, the spring of my blood.

It is also true that instead of healing, the wound that Anjum had given me had grown and become as big as my hate. Anjum, for whom my hatred had grown and become an acacia tree full of thorns. And though the acacia tree doesn't need to be watered, I was continuously watering my tree with the blood of my memory and the poisonous manure of my maliciousness.

But these two were innocent and hadn't come into this world on their own. They were my children. How was I to take the revenge for my wound from them? But I confess that I wasn't able to love them very much. I did not even feel fulfilled and satisfied at becoming a father. There must be a reason for this, but I don't know it as of now. Yes! I used to often feel on seeing them that they were ninety-nine per cent Anjum and one per cent me.

If sometimes I tried to hold one of the kids in my arms, Anjum stopped me.

'Put him down, don't make him accustomed to being held, put him down,' she would say ill-temperedly. 'In any case, I don't trust your hands, God knows what all you might have touched on the way.'

I would put the child down dejectedly. The kids too didn't ever show any attachment towards me.

Time, yes, the same old time. There is no way out of talking about time. Time was passing. The elder one was already six. Both of them had started going to school. I had begun to get some cases with the help of Alauddin and Anjum's father. But I lost all the cases. It doesn't really affect the lawyer. He has already extracted his fee from the client.

My business was growing. I had appointed a munshi too, who often questioned me about my memories and kept suggesting that I use his services to write my memoirs, although he often dozed off. I was able to earn enough to keep myself going without asking for help from anyone. I didn't care about the expenses of Anjum and the kids. Alauddin and Anjum's parents were there to take care of that. They had an abundance of money. As for

Alauddin, he was now one of the prominent lawyers of the city. He hadn't lost a case yet. He was master of this profession. He changed colours like a chameleon in the courtroom. He changed his tone. He could laugh his stupid laugh when he wanted to and give it up when he wanted to. Alauddin was all brains. Nothing like involuntariness existed in him. He first measured crime with a meter, and then sized up the criminal or the client. He then measured the distance of the accused from the limits of all punishments the crime could attract. And then very nonchalantly in the courtroom, he crushed the heads of innocents. He put innocents to such a death that they didn't even get a drop of water to slake their thirst at the time of death.

Alauddin came to my house one evening. He was accompanied by a man approximately my age, thin, lean and with a yellowish complexion. It was the month of September when the common cold and accompanying symptoms spread very fast. If it rains, there are floods. If it doesn't, there are earthquakes. The person was suffering from a cold. He held a grubby handkerchief in his hand. He was breathing through his nose which sounded like escaping steam – shoon shoon – and he wiped his running nose and eyes with that hankie.

'Do you know him?' asked Alauddin, signalling towards the yellowish-complexioned man.

'No,' I replied, looking intently into the person's eyes. His watery, mud-coloured eyes had a strange, wild look about them, as if crabs were swimming in them.

'His name is Narendra Kumar,' Alauddin said with his customary laugh.

I remained silent.

'You have to fight his case; I can't due to some reason. But I'll tell you all the intricacies and everything you need to do. Believe me, Hafeez! Don't refuse him. He'll pay you any fee you quote.'

I fell into thought for a while, and then said, 'What's his crime?'

'He hasn't committed it yet, but is going to soon.'

'What do you mean?' I asked, astounded.

'Narendra Sahib, why don't you tell the esteemed lawyer?' said Alauddin.

'I want to murder somebody,' Narendra spoke coldly.

His voice and intonation sounded similar to mine.

'Why do you want to commit murder?'

'He has raped my beloved . . . shoon shoon.' Narendra wiped his nose with his hankie.

I felt an earthquake within me. I gripped the handrest of my chair firmly.

'How will you commit this murder?' I asked softly.

'I will either crush his head with a stone or set his house on fire. I don't want to shoot, stab or poison him. I want him to have a violent death.' Narendra's voice had a familiar cruel tinge to it. He continued in the same cruel tone, 'I will be doing this within the next two days. It will be difficult to get a chance later. Now you tell me, advocate sahib, how will you protect me? It's possible that I get caught red-handed.'

The cliffs moving inside me came back to their original position and I replied coolly,

'I will face the prosecution in your place. I'll stand in the dock.'

My voice was the same as his. I don't believe in counterparts, but if this guy wasn't my counterpart, who was he?

'You are making fun of me, advocate sahib, shoon shoon.' Narendra's watery eyes became more fearful and strange.

'No, I'm serious. I will put the noose around my neck in your place.'

'Hafeez, what are you saying, this is not the time to joke.' Alauddin found himself unsettled.

'What difference does it make, Alauddin. Every punishment wanders around in a vacuum like an unclaimed object and can be found by anyone. Anyone can lay claim to it. What does the punishment have to do with all this? All it needs is a body to inhabit. It could be Mr Narendra's body or mine. The poor homeless punishment can have no objection to this.'

Narendra got up suddenly from his chair, still producing the shoon shoon sound, and said to Alauddin angrily, 'I didn't know you were bringing me to a mad lawyer to make fun of me and waste my time.'

'Oh listen, please listen, Narendraji! Where are you going?' Alauddin leapt in Narendra's direction as he was about to go.

'If you thought the money was less you could have told me,' Narendra spoke loudly.

'Arey, that's not the case at all, you misunderstood.' Alauddin was trying but failing to pacify Narendra.

Narendra looked at us, annoyed and angry. Then he opened his mouth and closed his eyes. He sneezed violently, letting out a volley of tiny droplets, some of which landed on my face.

He went out of the house stomping his feet loudly, with the shoon shoon in full volume.

Alauddin stared at Anjum foolishly, who walked in with a tray of tea in her hands.

Then Alauddin looked at me and said, 'Hafeez, the little philosophy you have read will ruin you one day. Were you lecturing him on philosophy or were you serious?'

'I have never been more serious and alert in my life,' I said as I lit a cigarette.

'That means you have lost your mind. You have no idea how well known and wealthy a person Narendra is. Had you accepted his case your deprivations would have become a thing of the past.'

'You are talking about the case; I was ready to take his crimes upon myself.'

'Are you mad? Look, Hafeez, your children are growing up. It's true that I never allowed your wife and children to feel any want. They are living a comfortable life but real happiness for the wife and children is when the man of the house earns wealth for the family.'

'You have the cheek to talk to me in this manner, Alauddin?' I spoke frostily, looking into Alauddin's eyes.

Alauddin's face drained of colour. He remembered his obligation towards me.

He laughed and said, 'I was just joking. It's entirely up to you whether you fight his case or not. No one can force you. But yaar, you have such a terrific sense of humour, I had no clue about it. You really pulled a fast one on the poor fellow.'

Today when I write these seemingly meaningless appeals with the help of my memory, I think that if the world regarded such a highly serious and meaningful thing as a sign of my sense of humour, then it is likely that with a peal of laughter loud enough to reach the sky, someone will tear these appeals to shreds in the courtroom after dismissing them as a bundle of cheap quality and unbelievable jokes. As far as my opinion on the same is concerned, my writing is full of that secret deep seriousness which can be regarded as my sense of humour and overlooked or heartily made fun of.

But I shouldn't lose heart at all this, after all, who knows anything?

Who saw it?

Who had known it?

It was not Alauddin's fault, nor was it Narendra's, except that Narendra's sneezing had spread his cold to me.

My eyes and head were aching and my nose was itching.

I was feeling hot inside the room. The nights in September aren't usually so warm. There were many lizards on the wall; they had appeared out of nowhere. 'Apa, there are too many lizards in your house,' spoke Alauddin, taking the last sips of his tea.

'I don't know from where they have appeared today; usually there are only one or two,' replied Anjum.

'All right, I'll take my leave now.' Alauddin began to get up.

'No, have dinner with us before you go.' Anjum detained him.

'What have you cooked?'

'White urad dal fry, potatoes with cumin seeds and brinjal fried in fenugreek seeds.'

Once again I felt an earthquake in my being. My heart, lungs and intestines began to shake violently, as if rocks were hurtling down within my body. I started perspiring.

'Brinjal fried in fenugreek seeds should not have been cooked today,' I thought.

'What happened, you seem to be sweating profusely. Shall I increase the speed of the fan? Open the window,' said Alauddin.

I didn't respond as it would have resulted in a spat with Anjum, and I didn't want to create a scene before Alauddin.

The dining table was set for dinner. Purple brinjals, fried in fenugreek seeds – they looked very attractive served in a white enamel dish. But that attractiveness frightened me. The purple colour of the brinjals seeming to be soaked in poison to me. I began to feel pukish. Nevertheless, I gathered some courage. I had barely broken a morsel of chapatti when I began to tremble and shake.

No, this was not the usual trembling of my being; everyone was shaking.

Anjum, Alauddin, the tables and chairs, utensils, sofa, bed, everything was dancing.

'Arey, it's an earthquake, earthquake,' screamed Alauddin, petrified.

'Run, run.' I could hear a stampede outside.

Everyone was running out of their houses towards clear land. The iron almirah to the left of the bed began to shake noisily. The dishes and plates kept on the table clinked against each other loudly. The white urad dal, the cumin potatoes and the spicy brinjal, all got mixed up with each other.

'Run, Apa, run,' Alauddin screamed again and quickly left the house, as if the angel of death were pursuing him. Anjum followed him, screaming hysterically. The power went off.

There was a strange uproar. Hearts quailed at the loud rumble and the sound of collapsing rubble. People were yelling. I was the last to come out of the house. There was a huge crowd gathered outside in the open space. I saw some houses collapsing at a distance. Doors and windows, glass, iron beams and wooden logs were falling with a loud disastrous din to the ground. There is no sound more frightening and terrible than that of falling rubble. My eyes began to close in the haze caused by the mud, cement and sand. I couldn't see anything. I was feeling suffocated. Someone somewhere in the haze was crying loudly and saying, 'My children, oh my children. They got left behind.'

Although my ears were almost dead in the doomsday sounds and the uproar of people like on the day of resurrection, I could discern and recognize Anjum's voice.

I was reminded of my children now. They had been playing in the other room. A strange kind of old strength reverted in me. I had to combat that dreadful, deathly noise which was crushing my body under its weight. The veins in my head were about to burst.

I opened my eyes wide and tried to see.

The house was there, behind a frightening cloud of dust, sand and haze.

I made a big leap and entered the house like a flying football kicked by a strong foot. I reached the kids' room, falling, stumbling and getting up again.

The roof had developed cracks. The white lime-painted walls had become crooked and bent. The square room had transformed itself into a triangle and was becoming smaller.

Both the kids lay unconscious on the swaying floor. I stooped and picked them up and was about to fling them across my shoulders when the deadly grating noise stopped. I looked at the walls. They had come back to their original position. The floor had also stopped shaking. The roof was not plunging any more – the earthquake had ceased.

The earthquake ceased, leaving behind a few scratches of its demonic nails on the walls and the roof. I didn't go outside. I sat down, next to the children, on my haunches. The noise outside seemed to subside a little. I don't know after how long the kids' mother came into the room crying and wailing, and almost went numb on seeing the children safe and sound. Then she came back to her senses and, holding the children tight to her chest, began to smother them with kisses. After some time, she lifted her face to give me a grateful look, the first and the last from her in my life.

I crouched on the floor silently. My throat, nose and ears were all blocked. They were full of dust. I suddenly felt a sort of moisture inside me. God knows from where a fluid was entering the dry, burning dust which had penetrated every pore of my body. I don't know from which hidden areas of the body, which tunnels in it, trickled a thin line of liquid.

And then I sneezed very hard. A second, third and fourth time – the sneezes continued.

My nose and eyes began to run. The glands in my throat began to ache. I felt a fever arising in me. I began to wheeze through my nose like Narendra.

I felt a strange intoxication developing in me. The noise outside, police and military wagons bleating horns, wailing voices, houses reduced to rubble, crushed and buried dead bodies, everything began to lose importance under this intoxication. Everything was flowing away.

It was a surging river whose banks were terrifying. On both the banks the river was flowing with full force and it took the earthquake with it.

Did I find out which intoxication it was?

I was in the clutches of a dreadful cold.

# Part III

# Cold and Flu

There is a swell of water into which the shores of time fall and are carried away. God knows what all has passed and what all is going to pass.

These are the times when my memory, being transformed into the fluids of the cold in the left part of my brain, is flowing out of my nose and eyes. It's difficult for me to restrain and control it.

Which, among many, are the waters I'm supposed to restrain? How many waters am I supposed to control?

The sewer line outside has become dysfunctional. Its dirty water is mixing with the water in the pipes of the house. The dirty water entered the house but Anjum couldn't see it. She thinks I'm imagining it or that I have gone mad. I stand with a broom in my hand to locate the dirty water and sweep it into the drainlets of the house.

This water is humiliating me. But I'm not so weak as to be unable to combat such a situation, to not be able to fight a lowly, dirty body of water. I know that nothing comes to you on its own. It's you. Your time and space, your intellectual and physical locations are the deciding factors. Even if you were to stand fixed in one place like a solid iron pillar, that place will decide your fate.

I am the bridge which has always stood over that malicious and frightening river into which dirty drains from innumerable sources flow. I never saw a clear, pure stream falling into it. Its pillars and arches are always submerged in dirty water. This water which contains soap suds that washed away the dirt and perspiration from human bodies, the solid black film of urine and faeces, and a frightful smell.

It follows that whatever I have done, I have to pay for. Why was I present at this ill-fated point in history?

Why did I sit in Anjum Baji's lap?

Why did I read out detective novels to Anjum Apa?

I could have refused. I could have refused to listen to the kitchen, refused to become a murderer. But one can't refuse it, the way one cannot refuse one's destiny, the way one can't refuse to be born or to be destroyed. The echo of the crystal-clear and pure spring of the mountain reached my ears from afar, and my spirit continued to swim in the whirlpool of dirty, mud-coloured rivers, so that I could once again convert into rotting and foul-smelling water.

But I have sworn to myself to fight this water. I have my cold to fight this water, and the catarrh from the cold which runs ceaselessly from my nose and eyes. My eyes and nose are both red, and I sway intoxicated with the power of the flowing cold.

I'm not even aware of time now. I'm alone but my dog is with me. My memory is with me, like a group of friends, a committee or council. I'm not the only one who's a victim of the cold. It's everybody. The cold is spreading everywhere. Anjum too has a cold. She coughs and sneezes all the time. Both the kids have the cold too. Their noses are always running. The children have grown big now. It won't be long before they become full-bodied youths. Both are becoming very religious – they have been going to the mosque from an early age. I don't know what they do at the mosque. Anjum has given them religious instructions right from the beginning. This is a good thing. It's important to learn about one's faith along with general worldly teachings. I never got to properly. But Anjum is a good mother, and why shouldn't she be, she's the mother of *two* sons, not of a she-mouse.

But why can't Anjum see this dirty water entering the house? The same smelly water flows from the tap of every tank in the house.

Why doesn't Anjum see that this roaring water is following me menacingly, tenaciously? She regards my running cold as dirty water and feels repulsed by it.

The drains on the streets are choked. All the water has reverted to the drainlets and is entering the house, especially the kitchen. Vessels float in that water. The rotting water and its putrid smell have spoilt the kitchen utensils forever.

Both the kids don't pay me any attention. I'm a bad father. They feel ashamed of me. I don't offer the namaz regularly or fast during Ramzan. By now I have become a complete stranger to these practices. I know that my children will begin hating me one day. Intense hatred.

I have started running a slight temperature too these days. This is nothing alarming. It's usual to have low-grade fever when one has a prolonged cold. Almost everyone in the city is suffering from it. Everybody suffering from cold and congestion, coughing and sneezing and breathing through the nose and making a sound like escaping steam – shoon shoon. They all sway to the intoxication of the flowing catarrh. The cold opens new doors of mental awakening in me. It has just occurred to me that water has a memory of its own. Modern science has proven this.

Water never forgets anything it touches. It never forgets the prayers read over it or blown into it, even those of ill intent and malicious emotions.

Now I have finally understood why such a large amount of dirty water is after my life.

It's taking revenge. With its elephantine memory dissolved in its dirty waves, it is clearing its previous accounts with me.

In how many mean and wicked people's kitchens did I eat? And drink water?

With what emotion was that water given? And my sins? The water of my sins, which is mingled with my blood. Everything remembered me. The dirty, mean waters, bearing malice, stayed with me.

The pure and good waters carrying memories of love and affection appeared only rarely on the forehead of a hard-working person in the form of crystal-clear droplets. They shone like stars once in a while and then became dull and faded. There might have been times when I forgot my sins and those huge stains, but water didn't forget. I sometimes get the feeling that I am in the clutches of an elephant's memory, I can't fight it, but I am ready to bear every attack that it makes. My own memory is my shield.

I have my dog with me to protect me from the elephant's attack.

So, in order to develop my appeal further, I am compelled to acknowledge that this dirty water is just a figment of my imagination. Let it be that, but I have to write more, even if that court of law were only dirty water. I can't see anything under the intoxication of the cold. Either my eyesight has been damaged or my power has increased.

I become sad whenever this happens. What will happen to the lenses of my spectacles? All a waste.

The unkind spirit, which makes everything its abode and habitation, humiliates it and goes off. The spirit of the eyes exited through the frame and its lenses. Only burning water remained in the eyes.

But my spirit – it will never do such a thing.

I preferred to become a ghost after my death rather than accept such indifference, such disloyalty and such shamelessness of the spirit that it should roam around in the pure and expansive atmosphere of the skies leaving behind the body to rot and putrefy.

Anjum was getting the kids ready for the Friday prayers. The water for their bath was ready. All three were looking at me weirdly. Me, who is picking up the shards of memory carefully from the floor. The droplets emerging from my nose are freezing themselves on those shards, causing them to sparkle.

I have started remembering people from the past. All the members of my house who are no more. All the people from my mohalla who are no more, as well as distant relatives. I have started recalling all my lost objects. I want to reach all of this once again.

In the grip of this cold, I don't remember which season it is or which year and month. It must be the month of June because the humidity has increased. The wind is ridden with algae and fungi. It can only be cut with a knife.

I recall those days. On one occasion I had met a slim and dark-complexioned but very beautiful girl in the kitchen of a house. She had kept a plate of pulao before me and then looked at me with keen affection. I can't recall her name. I was very small, God forbid if her name had 'Anjum' added to it before or after, God forbid!

She has entered my mind today dressed in blue, like a shining housefly. Her eyes looked like orange honeysuckles which could be sucked. Up until the time she stayed with me, she was glowing so much that I continuously felt I had accidentally swallowed the bulb which had been hanging in the kitchen. When she laughed, her protruding teeth seemed ready to bite off a thread.

But I knew. I knew in that moment too that I didn't have any connection with her. She was not related to me. And just like the shine and glitter of a festive occasion ultimately changes into darkness, she too gave me the slip through all the shine and glitter and suddenly vanished into the deep darkness. Forever.

I miss them intensely. I also remember my kitchen, which is a murdering ground, a battlefield.

Long ago when there lived in my house cousins of all varieties, maternal aunts and uncles and paternal aunts and uncles and their children, together. I feel like crying when I recall those times today. I don't know what's come over me these days; otherwise I'm pretty thick-skinned, unkind, selfish and bad.

But I don't want to cry. I want to keep my salt safely. Corpses take longer to rot in salt. I have kept quite a bit in safe custody and I'm afraid that this cold might sweep away everything in its flow. The entire city is in the grip of this cold and is roaming around making shoon shoon noises.

So, long ago, when there used to live in my house innumerable cousins drawing from maternal aunts and uncles and paternal aunts and uncles. Those days a Khala often dropped in and went straight into the kitchen. Chhakkan Nani got very irritated with her because the old Khala immediately conducted a survey of the kitchen shelves. These shelves were the sole property of Chhakkan Nani. This was even before my memory had formed; I'm managing to get by with the help of some guesswork and by recalling some scenes in my head.

On that kitchen shelf was kept a small faded box with two of Chhakkan Nani's teeth which had perhaps fallen off in February. It is the time when leaves fall off from the trees.

Some yellowish snakeskin, a bottle of rotten water from hailstones, a broken pink soap case, a pumice stone and a dead honeybee which might have been fresh at the time I saw it, and God knows what other rubbish.

Wearing a burkha, old Nani looked like a bat. And when she took off her burkha! God save me, even under a thin kurta, her breasts seemed to be flying in the air, like a dreadful giant bird. The shadows of its wings were immensely frightening. Seeing her breasts, I got frightened and started crying. Sajju Phupha, who I remember vaguely, was fond of talking to children and cracking jokes which were often of a vulgar kind. He told me that when she sat on the floor and bent over to eat her food, her breasts reached the floor and rested on it as if a wild animal were resting there.

I don't remember seeing this. Sajju Phupha used to narrate this chuckling to himself. I can't help tugging at my memory with the help of another person's the way one pulls a vehicle broken down on the road with the help of another vehicle's engine that is working smoothly. But this is necessary. If I don't pluck out all the insects crawling in my subconscious, either my crime or my punishment will lose their way and will be written in the shape of a 'wrong word'. In any case, the cold has started to cause my memory to fade. So, sadly enough, I have to make do with many impressions, sights and sounds. I can't claim that they are a hundred per cent correct, at least till the time this blessed epidemic of cold continues in the city.

I don't know how much time has gone by since this epidemic. It's uncontrollable. Yes, so what was I saying? No, what was I writing?

Let me wipe my nose with my hankie before I try and recall. Yes, now I remember! But before telling you anything let me clarify that I could have written these appeals differently too. I can turn my socks inside out and still wear them. The inside-out socks are also my size, but I have adopted this method because although I can't write a novel, I can at least follow some of the rules of the poetics of the novel by moving my pen on paper with the help of a masculine melancholy. It is certain that this work can be done only with the help of a masculine melancholy, or else legal appeals are drafted using another method too – whining badly and begging for pardon.

Nobody in the house had any love lost for the old Khala because her eyesight was very weak. The vessel containing milk either fell to the ground or the milk turned sour whenever she went into the kitchen. Nani said that once when old Khala had stared at the milk for some time, it had turned into blood. I hadn't believed this at the time, but I have full faith in it now. The world is nothing but another name for inscrutable and illogical happenings. Look at Anjum for instance. She's become really vain these days. Both the kids have grown up, and they are strong, well built and healthy.

There was no salt in the food yesterday, and, as always, I gave my wife a piece of my mind. My wife used to talk back to me and had a reply for everything I said, but this time she continued sitting there, smiling with pride and complacence, because both her children were ready to take me on on behalf of their mother and warned me of dire consequences if I found even the slightest fault with the food she cooked.

Anjum looked at me with eyes filled with scorn. I was like the cumin seeds she added to her curry while cooking. I saw something new in her eyes for the first time, something like the glint of lust in the eyes of a blind woman. It could be the effect of the cold on me, but whenever I see her the organs of her body seem to be hanging out of it in a pathetic manner, and her spirit has nothing to do with them. Is it only one intestine that is extra in the human body? The looks Anjum gives and her condition are very dangerous. If I'm not mistaken, the other day she squinted her eyes to look at the plate of rice put before me, and the spotless white rice grains spread on the plate appeared soiled in blood after a few moments.

Had you been able to see my face at the time you would have thought someone had slapped me hard. It was no longer one face now but two. Two different ragas or notes flowing in one time frame.

And as far as I am concerned, I feel my skin has been peeled off. It is as though I am hanging upside down before the children in shame and ruination, the way skinned goats are suspended upside down and displayed in a vulgar manner.

However, there's one difference which can make this comparison meaningless. I'm not dead. I'm alive and I'm not a coward either. I just happen to be in the clutches of a cold. I'm running a slight temperature and my throat is sore.

I don't feel like doing anything while I have this terrible cold. Neither hate someone nor get angry at someone or take revenge on someone or even murder someone. It's probably raining somewhere far away. There is no suffocation or mugginess. I'm feeling cold. Has winter arrived? Is it true that it's winter now?

The wind has changed direction. A train is passing through the darkness somewhere in the distance and no one sees it. I hear it from afar, the rain, it is falling into deep trenches and no one sees it. I hear the sound.

I overlook everything. I postpone everything and no one sees me. Nobody ever sees me doing anything.

All I want is the shadow of my lost possessions. All my dear ones, all my dead ones.

I'm not reconciled to my insult. I just happen to be wearing the garments of my dead ones. The moonlight is spread outside. My eyes have begun to hurt at the white glimmer of the moonshine. This is how cruel white light is.

I wished, irritated, that at least half the moon be covered in blood, which when it dries turns black.

My dear ones! Have you forgotten all the joys and all the sorrows after dying?

Will you return?

Will you happily (or with a heavy heart) sit in that kitchen and eat together?

Will you bicker and squabble?

Or will you come to the earth only after transforming your memory into particles of white light and tying it to a stone and drowning it in a dark sea?

Do people change like you have after going into the far, vacant distance? Or is there a kitchen, at least a Hindu-style rasoi, there too, through the skylights of which they come like white light?

Or do they change into cockroaches and crawl in their own utensils?

It's raining. Water is flowing under the kitchen window, and there, four hundred and fifty miles away, in my city, close to my house, it's raining on your graves too.

The cold has suddenly become more severe. My ears are hurting terribly. I am beginning to go deaf. The water in my nose and eyes has reached the ears.

Their memories keep coming back. Their memories keep coming back. And there was a miracle today. The girl who used to visit me in my dreams when I was a young boy, the same girl who doesn't have a face, probably not even a body, came in my dream after several years.

I was very sad before I went to sleep. My eyes had emptied out. They didn't even contain the fluid of the cold. I suddenly fell asleep, as if some invisible hand had fed me a sleeping potion. Although I know that sleep does come eventually. I had once slept through a dreadful sandstorm. When I sleep, I dream too. Dreams are usually black and white but they acquire colour sometimes, which is definitely the consequence of the awakening of some unknown part of the brain. I know that even the blind dream.

The only colour I ever saw in my dream is of that girl. My one and only colour, different from and beyond the greens, yellows, reds, blues and oranges.

When she came to me, the jamun seller was selling jamuns on a cart outside.

'Should I make the rotis now?' she asked.

'Yes, make the chickpea flour roti.'

'The gram flour roti, and chutney made of red chillies and garlic, along with pure ghee.'

She had no body, no clothes, but somehow seemed to have a chest covered by a dupatta. The dupatta slipped from her chest and love came out of her heart silently, passing through every dark corner of the room, licking my forehead and lips, following which it returned to her heart. I saw everything clearly. Love went and sat to one side of her heart on its haunches. Sheepish, helpless and sinful love.

My eyes opened. The water of the cold had reappeared in my eyes. My left cheek had sunk into the pillow like an ill-fated foot stuck in a mire.

Believe me, I'm unable to tell you how much time passed

without the cold showing any signs of letting up. The moon had many eclipses, the sun had many eclipses. I don't know how many shooting stars headed towards the earth like balls of fire and got extinguished. I don't know anything, caught in the flood of the cold, I don't know anything. I fear that this cold may become the cause of my death. I don't want to die. I don't want to leave this world. I want to stay here. Like a tree or a rock or the sweep of water in a river, or even like a demon. I'm game for anything to stay alive.

Even after cleaning my dirty, cold-filled eyes, they remain disappointed and sad. The eyes have imprisoned their sights within themselves. Wilderness stands guard over them. Let it be clear that this is not a metaphor. Literature uses metaphors to fool us but not law or legal petitions and appeals – I'm not writing a novel or a long poem, which is why in my writing repetition is no flaw, rather it is an extremely important and indispensable element. What is law but reiteration of crimes and punishment. And no case in the world can be fought without repetition. It's a huge act of impotence to describe the inherent criminality and degradation within human beings through metaphors, and if I happen to do something like that by mistake, I feel a terrible fatigue in my heart. I want to record all the degradation and conspiracies only descriptively, like one were preparing for a court case and this was an unbreakable witness account which can never shy away from the truth.

I know full well why I'm missing the people of the past. The end of the thread of my blood is getting dimmer. I stand at an unknown place in time holding the noose of my memory over the mysterious, hidden thread of my blood. Time is motionless and still here, this noose of memory is the noose of the gallows. I start measuring my face with it. I will become eternal and immortal once I put my neck into this noose. Death will flee from me like a person with rabies flees from water.

It's the same dirty water again. But why does Anjum, who is obsessed with cleanliness, not clean it? Why doesn't the bad smell bother her? Has she lost her olfactory powers despite having such a straight and thin nose? Or has the cold deprived her of her sense of smell?

My nose is working properly. My sons and their mother have begun to bathe in this dirty water. Yesterday both my sons performed their ablutions with this unclean water and went to the mosque. I even checked them but they accused me of falsehood. They think I am hallucinating. An eccentric, foolish man who keeps having suspicions and apprehensions.

This is what happens, this is what happens always. And the world gets divided into two sections. But one shouldn't falsify the truth! The three of them can't see that the water from the drains is pouring into the house. The narrow drain in the toilet and the bathroom are bringing in all the filth and muck from outside. Maybe I'm the one to blame.

This happens when the chain of your cistern is out of order, and your own toilet bowl is in disrepair and likely to lead you astray, when something inside your toilet is weak or broken due to decay. Then it requires just a little bit of rain to cause the filth from other people's homes and the muck and excreta from the drains on the roads to enter your home. Fearless, undaunted, spitting in your face. Then the home doesn't remain a home. You can see dirty, muddy water collected here and there. Your bookshelf, bed, chairs and table, all get submerged in it and you see their shadows trembling in that filthy water. God knows from where black as well as white polythene bags come flying through the air and collect on the stagnant water in the house. They look like unrecognizable, repulsive birds dipping their beaks in the rotting water.

Yes! You'll have to acknowledge that it's your toilet bowl which is broken. You were not able to adjust the restlessness in your bowels to the geometry of the commode and its aesthetics. You always knew that a human is nothing but his intestines. One doesn't live in one's heart, mind, teeth or eyes. He lives concealed in the intestines. His body is only but a shadow of the real human being. It's a pity that soft-tempered, sophisticated and foolish people regard this secret as either a joke or bury it in the obscure clothing of filth and the cleanliness 'myth' and dismiss it.

It happened this way also because I didn't see my desires and wishes slithering in the garbage bin. It's a pity I never noticed that the drain of the kitchen in the house of my childhood was often blocked, which is why stale pieces of red buffalo meat slathered with vegetable ghee got stuck and remained there (just as their threads rotted in the intestines) and the grains of rice and dal moved very slowly in their midst. The kitchen reeked of rotten eggshells. The falling salt-and-pepper hair of ageing quarrelsome women also choked that drain. The kitchen became the centre of shocking blasts but you just kept looking at Anjum Baji as she cooked the food, and after that, just a stone slab. All you remembered was a crushed head and a blazing stove.

You will have to note all this down here. In the account book, you will have to make the entry of something as tiny as a cricket or an ant's egg – you want justice, don't you! Then first be just yourself; recall now, with all your strength, everything that you may have overlooked.

But the cells of the mind that have died will never come back to life. They will go and lie against other cells that are useless so that the weight of the mind stays around one and a half kilos.

So we have to make do with the remaining living cells of the mind. Recall everything and write – writing is as important for you as dying is for others.

Anjum served the food with an air of disinterest. She does this much like any hypocritical woman from the east would do.

All sides of the chapatti made by Anjum are half-cooked. It's a strange, thick, wet kind of chapatti. The sides are not chewable at all. My teeth have started decaying. The cold must be affecting them – I have to dip each morsel of chapatti in the dal for a long time to eat it. Some of the dal drips on to my white kurta-pyjama before it reaches my mouth, just as blood seeps and drips from a bleeding wound on to one's clothes. I try to see the reflection of past times in this watery arhar dal. But the grief and loneliness of God knows which unseen times was already staring at its reflection there.

I was feeling a little grief-stricken, although I wasn't so really. You require a lifetime to get buried under the burden of grief. Early youth and youth don't contain grief. They carry just the disguise of grief. After a long time all the disguises suddenly appear from nowhere and assemble together. They change into a dreadful reality and climb on to the back and shoulders of the spirit weary of the burden of age. All the sorrows we have borne change course suddenly and overtake you from behind, like a cunning and malicious leopard. This happens when your body has started to grow weak, when the strands of your curly hair have flown out of the drain after getting entangled in your comb, your facial features, your looks have been swept away in some flood. Something has fallen off from your cheeks, your ears and nose, your forehead. A thick film of fat is congealed on the pupils of your eyes, all their light is now dimmed and the cataracts have started to develop. Your smile is devoid of brightness and your tears are ridiculous. At such a time, sorrow prevails on your body and doesn't leave you, like the old man with thread-like legs in the story of Sinbad the Sailor.

Age, age!

The punishment of staying alive. A school which prepares you to go mad.

I'm not so old yet. I'm neither ready to go mad nor to die.

I will write my own pain. If I ever get the chance, I will prove wanting in expressing and narrating my pain. I will never take the aid of professional weeping women. I know that if I happen to die before my wife does, she will weep and cry for the benefit of the world and also to salve her own conscience. At heart, Anjum is a professional weeping woman; she has already gained the profit in exchange for her weeping.

I don't want to die before Anjum, which is why I have stopped eating red meat and deep-fried food. I only eat boiled vegetables and plain dal. Anjum has seen through my trick and she's always furious when she cooks such food.

I firmly believe that if all kinds of food were removed from the world, nobody will die. Everyone will achieve everlasting life; birds and animals and all the creepy-crawlies of the earth will also stay alive. The heart of this world which is grievously injured and carries wounds all over will begin breathing again with fresh lungs. All the wounds will heal. The world, which started from a dot, will start expanding – I have heard that this universe is as yet incomplete and that all the time there comes the sound of 'Be' and 'Things begin to happen.'

However, it's possible that all this is my defective power of reasoning. I can't even understand a simple section of the law. I'm not eligible to discuss or ponder such scientific and philosophical subjects. I haven't even been able to understand this insignificant ailment of the common cold. Sometimes, for short intervals, I do feel lighter. I get out of the house. The sunshine is spread all around. This is a different kind of sunshine. Poor romantic Chekhov would never be able to fill his hat with this sunshine. This sunshine falls on the skull like droplets of fire, which then enters the eyes and the nostrils. Right at that moment the cold starts again. It just doesn't leave. I don't know about others but I get this cold again and again. As if I peeped again and again into a well which is overgrown with plants and rubbish.

And one becomes more and more hollow inside just like the well. One doesn't grow upwards like a tree.

I feel that if we were to understand the world in the true sense, we would have to read it backwards. All history should be read from the bottom up and from left to right. True meaning may be lying buried somewhere under a heap like the remains of something. To return from old age to childhood is true evolution. I will have to walk again towards the school which is across the bridge of the gardeners. I'll have to walk back to my ancestral home, return where my umbilical cord is buried. Like the empty paper bag of the condiment seller, like a tattered rag of the flying dust and soil, like a dust devil, we'll have to move against the water that always flows from its source to the sea. We'll have to catch hold of all those winds and stick them back upon the leaves of the trees. The winds which have blown from them and are wandering here and there.

And in the end, we'll have to bear the peril of going into the most dangerous part of the house, that which they call kitchen. The kitchen, where the fire of hatred, anger, greed and ill intent begins to blaze so quickly that even the chulha made of wet mud is covered in flames.

Loathing and anger!

These are the two most pure and spiritual emotions of human beings. Only these emotions have the power that can cause the faces of plates, cups, bowls, serving bowls and platters to become crooked like a witch. The half-lipped ghosts come and sit on the utensils, their teeth protruding. Brimming over with anger and loathing, these dark vessels leap up with a complete but unfathomable power and a large quantity of a terrible kind of curry spills on your face. This curry has the stench of the unseen flesh of wild animals. Your face is wounded by the invisible pieces of meat containing hard, stringy threads and sharp bones and becomes inflamed. Your snout hangs in a sorrowful manner like that of the Stone Age man when he sat with his knees bent and thought about the 'fire' that was yet to be invented, the fire produced by rubbing two stones against each other.

So all human evolution happened through the route of burning human anger and loathing. Walking this route, human beings sacrificed themselves on the altar of anger and hatred.

I should remember that sacrificing has a history older than that of the black goddess's red tongue that hangs out of her mouth and the blood-drenched headless goats.

I should also not forget that before the leaves shed themselves in the autumn season, they turn yellow because they give up their share of nutrition and vitality to the new leaves that will unfurl themselves in the future. They are happily and wholeheartedly ready to fall to the ground and get crushed under a heavy, merciless boot.

I feel that my evolution is a singular evolution. It moves left and right and back towards the darkness as much as it moves forward.

In this darkness to the left and right, there is a quagmire

under my feet within which, underneath, innumerable rivers join each other, losing their existence. But out of all these, I'm searching only for the river of the fort. My foot is alert even within the mire. Alert and agile like a dog's eye.

I remember the people of the past. Only they can save me. I, who am in the grip of the slaps of a wind which is wet with a continuously running cold. I, who am being chased by a swarm of honeybees. I, who am being chased by street dogs drenched in dirty water barking at me.

My crimes, my sins, my mistakes, my failings lie within my pockets like coloured glass marbles. I can feel them with my hands. But I can't take them out and see them. At such a moment I only want to embrace tightly the rubble of old times. There is a kitchen in this rubble. There is a pantry cupboard and a vessel containing milk suspended from a food basket. There is a canister of kerosene oil. And there is a spice-grinding stone slab on which sways my immature shadow.

I live with animals now. My subsistence is with animals now. I can't even go anywhere by fleeing from the kitchen.

Tired, or rather fed up, of my situation, I want to go towards the food cupboard, towards the shahi tukda, the bowls of phirni, the shirmal, the bread, the eggs, the gulab jamun and the peda, the apple, the pomegranate and the grapes; towards the sweet, white batashas of the manna and the quail meat of the salwa.

But alas there is no food cupboard here! There is a fridge and inside it are cold, stale and all kinds of unnecessary tasteless food items. Food items are cooled nowadays to prevent them from getting spoilt. Cold as ice, there is a layer of ice on the foods. These are not living food items. These are the dead bodies of those foods. My wife heats them over a gas stove at mealtime. The fire of the gas stove is cold and blue too. The food doesn't regain its lost flavour on heating, the way vigorous rubbing of a dead man's chest to give heat and energy doesn't do anything to revive him.

But I am obliged to wonder if food cupboards have become extinct from the world now. Is it possible that the whole world has been reduced to a vast food cupboard, where one thing is a prospective delicacy and an item of sustenance for the other? What difference does it make whether one eats up the other raw or by cooking a high quality and delectable dish out of him or by swallowing him up as a concept or presumption?

With all these chaotic thoughts running through my mind, I light a cigarette and cough violently after the first drag. The lungs cannot tolerate the smoke of the cigarette during a cold, but I certainly can. I can even stay alive comfortably underneath the rotting, fermenting food in a garbage bin or under the pieces of fungus-ridden bread, with the sense of satisfaction that this is where we were born. We came into existence via this temperature and putrefaction.

The smoke from my cigarette spreads in the room very quickly. Is there some sort of wind here? No, it's completely still outside, then what kind of wind is this?

I know that this strange wind is the wind of pain in my heart. This wind has not just stayed in my heart, but it also blows over my torso and my hands and legs, and travelling away from my body, it also pervades the walls and the floor of my room. It enters the dusty, dull bed sheet and pillow covers and the mattresses and the termites under them; this wind saddens me, and leads me astray. It's a pity that it's impossible for me to access the geography of my spirit; if I could just get the map for it, I would have made some necessary emendations to it. I would have chopped off the jungle mushrooming at the mouth of the silent volcano's crater. Where waterfalls flowed in the map of my soul, I would convert them into symbols of the desert. I would assign geographical spaces to all the rivers, mountains and deserts in my soul according to my own sweet will.

I suspect that I had found a map of my soul long ago, in a forgotten time. I tucked it in the back pocket of my worn-out pants but then I lost it, and it turned to pulp due to my carelessness in a terrifying rain.

I'm recording these submissions as if they are the wet clay of memory and you should not be deceived into believing that this is the book of my life, and even if it were, it should be clear to you that a whole chapter which could have endowed this book with a reliable identity is missing. The white ants devoured that chapter. And these white ants roamed in my courtyard laughing at me – do white ants have teeth? Believe it or not, but I have seen white ants baring their repulsive and ugly teeth. They spat at me scornfully, just as the rancorous dust cloud of the yellow tempest spits scornfully at the azure of the sky. Yellow spittle flies off the yellow teeth of the tempest.

The very white ants, which convert the wood's marrow into sugar and fill their stomach, had long ago eaten the most important chapter from the book of my life and fulfilled their spiritual hunger – yes, spiritual hunger, white ants possess spirits too; it's a different matter that their spirits are tiny and frail.

The spirit of the ant is much smaller than the spirit of the elephant. The bigger the body, the bigger the spirit.

Therefore, you must not regard these memories as the book of my life. There is a difference of large and small between the two, and as I have said a thousand times, these memories have a specific purpose, which is why I'm writing them in a particular manner. I could have jotted down these memories differently too, like a raga or any other musical note written down on paper. Then you could have read this text as a commercial publication in a book of cheap jokes titled *Guddu Miyan's Dining Cloth*. But that would have weakened my argument. My judge, who is sitting in the courtroom (if there is a court of law), waiting, might have laughed out loud at my appeals and dismissed the court. Not treating me as a criminal but rather an insolent joker, he might forgive all my impertinence, but I am not willing to accept this; I'm not yet clear on what I'm willing to accept. In any case, time will tell you a few things.

The cold is persistent. Doctors and hakims are having a field day making money. The clinics are so packed that there is no room left to stand. I have stopped using all western medicine. I take the Hamdard cold infusion these days, although there has been no improvement. I don't know what I look like now after having been slapped by the cold again and again. I haven't looked into the mirror in a long time. It is pointless to look as I'm wearing a mask anyway. A mask made of banana peels. I have picked up this shameless mask of banana peels from the ground. People will never get to know what I am. Not only their glances, but their entire wisdom will lose its footing due to this mask made of banana peels.

Let someone finally get to know that I'm a murderer. A knower of the secrets of ill omens and a criminal (although there are many other crimes which have been attributed to me, they are merely rumours.)

I remember the people of the past. There was probably a dog's spirit in my body which only protected and looked after ghosts. That unfortunate dog which only opened its mouth wide and howled at humans. It can't bark at anyone else. Not even at its own shadow. In a deserted ruin of a house, ghosts threw their chewed and sucked bones at him. He roamed around, the bones in his mouth, and guarded the ghosts and sprayed the poisonous foam of ill omens at humans and stared at the sky.

I have often wondered if I am the source of all those ill omens. Different varieties of food were defamed unnecessarily.

My quarrels with Anjum over some dish or the other continue as usual.

In this interminable duration of the cold, I heard about the deaths of many people. Some old friends from my college days passed away. I came to know that Muqim Ali and Tripathi died too. I also got the news of the passing of two or three professors from my college. Some of the neighbours from my ancestral home are no more. They were several incidents and every dish cooked at home alerted me about some mishap, but I happen to be so wretched and unfortunate that I can only spot an ill omen slinking out of its hidey-hole, not stop it. I can't even figure out whose house the ill omen will strike.

It was yesterday, or day before yesterday, or maybe a few days ago, I don't remember (it's difficult to remember anything with this cold) when I got into an argument with Anjum over salt. Nowadays she cooks the food lightly salted.

I told her, 'The cold has spoilt your taste.'

'There is adequate salt in the food,' she responded sharply. I felt like wringing her neck, but I restrained myself and asked her to add more the salt in the future. My younger son retorted, 'There won't be any more salt than this. Eat if you wish to or else you can make your own arrangements. You are not going to say anything to Ammi.'

I would have slapped him out of anger if my older son had not attacked me even more disrespectfully. 'You chew your food vigorously and the kind of ugly sounds you produce are evidence of greed. You don't deserve to sit among decent people to eat.' Whom should I slap out of the two? I was undecided, and droplets of catarrh began to drip into the bowl of masoor dal. Humiliated and ridiculed, I got up quietly and left my food. Children are bound to favour the mother. 'Mother' is in vogue these days and has been turned into a brand name. 'Father' is just a supposition. He's in a very weak position because the 'father' is never fully sure of being the 'father' of his 'children'. 'Father' doesn't have any proof except for a weak conviction. For those who are not very religious, it cannot be said that the universe was created by 'God'. 'God' and 'father' have both been marginalized these days.

So it is vulgar to chew one's food vigorously? The salt in the curry does not spread upon the tongue but gets lost in the walls of the jaw and the depths of the gums. I wander far and wide in search of my share of salt, like a distressed elephant who has strayed from his herd travelling up to the cliffs of salt far away in the distance to lick the salt. Elephants make a silent and sad trip in the form of a procession to be able to lick the salt. I, a useless wanderer, was not able to make it to any cliff of salt concealed behind dark, thick forests. Therefore, my tongue flits in and out like a malicious serpent. Deprived of salt, this tongue is ready to sting just anyone.

So the yellow curry which had spilt on to my white kurta–pyjama contained only turmeric, red chilli, coriander and fat. The salt had vaporized, or else I would have chewed up those clothes.

Let it be clear that in a legal battle, emotions do serve as weapons to some extent. I want to give my memories the shape of a legal document used for a court case. I have no evidence except words, which is why my writing has become a bundle of similes. These similes are my only precedents and my witnesses too. If I were not to explain my condition through precedents, how else was I to explain it? Metaphors won't prove useful in fighting this legal battle. They are capable of only bringing into existence masterpieces of literature and poetry, not a proper petition. However, if some metaphor were to appear by mistake, I will pick it up and keep it aside the way one picks out black peppercorns from pulao and keeps them aside on the plate.

One more thing must be made clear at this juncture: everything that I'm writing may be required to be spoken aloud in the court of law, which is why I'm trying my best for the 'expressions' on my face and my body language to serve as commas and full stops, and the length of a line to be equivalent to the pause between breaths.

Nevertheless, I'm sorry to say that many of my sentences are actually circles, vague to the extent of being boundless, or perhaps just dots that have as much possibility of being boundless as of getting obliterated. Controlling this aberration is beyond my means. But the world is also a dot which is endless. Although I rarely take the world seriously. For me this world is like those soiled utensils lying in the kitchen sink weeping in protest for not having been cleaned. I remember Tameezan Bua used to say that unwashed utensils in the kitchen sob through the night.

It began to rain heavily. It became cooler. The cold will aggravate now. It will produce phlegm in the lungs and fever in the body; my cough will echo even more loudly.

I am missing all the people of my house, all those who died, even more so in the rain. I thought about my ancestral graveyard. It must be raining there too. God knows where the rainwater must be taking the soil from the graveyard. The rain must be falling on the graves of my dear ones too. In the grip of this cold, I forgot that it is Eid today. The whole day went by and I didn't do anything. I didn't bathe, nor did I go for the Eid prayers. Partly to spite both my sons and partly because Eid can only be celebrated in one's ancestral home.

It was night now and it was raining in the graveyard. The shrouds were lying crumpled inside the graves. All those who used to celebrate Eid together, made new clothes for Eid together, those close relatives whose clothes touched each other's – they were all dear to each other (even if superficially so), but their shrouds were very far from each other. They lay away from each other soaking in different rains, decaying, rotten and wet. Was there a tunnel somewhere which could open its bright mouth in a strong wind to make these shrouds cling together? The shroud of one loved person should cling to that of another even if their bones lay scattered far from each other or worms ate their bodies.

But?

There was a time when I used to visit the graveyard very often. Although I did not offer the ritual prayers or the fateha (I still remember Anjum Apa's house), I had been to that graveyard so many times that it had started seeming like a part of the house. Very familiar, as if it were a tiny storeroom constructed away from the main house where broken furniture and other unusable items are kept in semiorganized manner. And then a huge lock is fixed on the door.

Listen! O my dear ones! My relatives! My family members! I descended into your graves searching for you, but you weren't there. There was only ice. But I know very well that every grave has a window which opens into a kitchen.

I want to use your wet shrouds like paper, till the day every corpse in a grave develops heat in its body by going near the warm stove in the kitchen and eating its share of halwa. I can recognize the changing scent of the incense that passes through the outer and inner halls and both the tiny rooms, reaching the courtyard and then the kitchen to finally disappear. I will have to visit that kitchen once again.

Is this pessimism? Yes, I have certainly experienced a supreme sense of dejection. Perhaps there's nothing left for me to do now, or maybe the cold doesn't allow me to do anything. Only the past remains with me. A dead ancientness which is invisible and can only be felt around the dead or those close to death. This is not remembrance, this is not the past either. This is just an old, bruised and decayed idiom. A redundant treasure of words which is not used by anyone any more, but which the white ants are very familiar with.

How I wish I had loved somebody in my life. Then these lines would have been written differently. But I always kept the piece called love in the wrong house on the board. I wrote the right word on the wrong sheet of paper or the wrong word on the milky white trunk of the eucalyptus tree with the true point of a knife.

No, I never loved anyone. Not Anjum Baji. Not Anjum Apa. Not Anjum Jaan. Not Anjum Bano. Not even Anjum!

Then what did I do?

All my life I stood in a wretched kitchen trying to cook the wrong dish using the right method and with utmost honesty. I used the recipe for korma in khichdi and ate slices of apple like the liver of a quadruped, dipping it in lemon juice and spices. Everything went wrong; everything was chaotic. The ship of my life sank and I lost everything. And one day, it so happened that all the pots and pans in the kitchen found themselves on the top of a mountain, lost in pouring rain.

So it all turned out to be my fault. It's me who'll have to bear the cross. I dumbly hear my verdict in a silent courtroom.

A decision full of gladness . . . my noose – the noose around my neck.

This is the month of February. The month when teeth move from their positions.

My appetite is stuck in the gap between two teeth. I eat liquid food nowadays. This liquid food is actually the negation of food. It is the dismantling of food. The next stage is particles of food value in it evaporating into empty space. This is the month of February. It is the terrible, painful weather when teeth leave their place in the gums and drop into dinner plates like leaves in the fall, ants dragging them away into unknown spaces. But none of my teeth ever found the right place for themselves. They tore out from the gums at the wrong spot. Many of them are still buried in the gums and haven't come out yet.

My wife and my sons are gulping down their food at incredible speed. Porridge, the food of dogs and cats, has been placed before me. A thick whitish mash. I don't eat it; my mouth only makes eating sounds.

I have resumed biting my tongue in my sleep. Long ago in the rainy seasons of my boyhood, when I used to dream of that faceless girl, my tongue got stuck between my teeth and cut itself. This stopped as I grew up. But nowadays I get up and first taste my blood, salty – at least there is salt here. I can now proudly enter my name in my family tree. This was bound to happen. Am I now equal to my ancestors? They lost their memory before death but I'm sure my memory will remain intact until I die. All the words dance before me to my command. I can force the toughest of feelings to bow before words. I can write, which is not easy. It is equivalent to cracking a walnut with an aching tooth, but I have managed to do it. I'm writing down all that happened in the past. When a man dies, his future and his present don't leave him. Only his past does. The only loss in death is of memory. I'm alive, much more alive than others. Once again I say that . . .

All relatives – brother, sister, mother, father, son, daughter, husband, wife and cousins – are tied together only with the string of memory. The chain of blood is merely a memory and every form of worship – the pujas and recitation of mantras – and all moral deeds are tricks to get rid of the memory. There in the upper world no one will know the other. Everyone will rejoice in their aloneness, with a horrible shamelessness. Even a ghost is free of such shamelessness because he maintains at least some relationship with the world. He doesn't forget humans, even if the relationship may only contain lust, envy and evil. He doesn't give up on his memory under any circumstances, and the punishment he gets for this is pointed nails, hollow eyes and terrible teeth. What is the use of going into paradise after plucking from the memory all relationships, emotions, love, loathing and food? On doomsday there will be cries of 'my soul, oh my soul' and no one will know each other. What is the use of going into such a heaven where you don't even recall who your father was?

The fingerprints of all my sins are etched on my body. One under the other, again, layer by layer. I will reach my court of law, lugging my body along with these fingerprints; in my hands will be this heavy bundle.

But will there really be a court of law? Will the members of his family and their sins be produced before one? Will someone who administers justice see these fingerprints and then make a note in his book of justice?

Which court of law? I don't want a court of law where a person's memory will not be with him. Nobody knows the other. The criminal doesn't recognize his action and the sinner doesn't recognize his deeds. How will punishment for one's actions and deeds be meted out without memory? I don't want such a court of law. I am in search of a court of law where the fingerprints of all the sins on my body will begin to glow suddenly, just as darkness begins to glow sometimes. A black hole absorbing every particle of all kinds of light in its thick and complete blackness. This court of law may be somewhere between reality and dream. My body flows along touching the shores of both reality and dreams. I don't want my punishment to shoo my crime out of the court of law scornfully, which is why I'm reading correctly the incorrect text written by others. I add diacritics in some places and remove them at others. I add a dative marker at one place and erase it from another.

I have to be very careful. The cold causes me to make mistakes sometimes. I don't have time to correct these mistakes, but I promise you that I will amend this flawed text before presenting my case in the court of law.

I fall asleep sitting on my broken chair outside the courtroom. Sleep drags me towards my grave. Sleep is a mail train and its destination is the grave; it's another matter that the train's wheels get stuck in the mire frequently and the journey is postponed.

I descend into my grave in my sleep. It's just like a tandoor. The warm smell of the glowing red-hot earth, sweet like that of parched chickpeas, and large, round white leavened bread skewered on black iron rods. The scent of the earth is mingled with the scent of flour.

A burning rod moves in my direction. There is a round white leavened bread at its tip. I am frightened of the rod and stand against the burning red-hot wall of the tandoor. The white bread flies off the tip of the rod and hits my face with full force – a terrible slap of bread. I mourn and cry in pain and want to hide my slapped face with the bread itself. My face sticks to half the bread. In the red-hot oven, the round white bread now looks like half of a full moon on which black blood has congealed.

I begin to sob.

Such huge spots, such huge spots. My clerk holds my hand and moves it up and down. No, he's waking me up. I have woken up. The fluid which flows out of my nose has collected on the hairs of my moustache. I walk to the water tank in front to wash my face. A crow perches silently on the tank. He has already washed his face.

I remember the people of the past. Today I miss even those who don't belong to my family, who were not even from my neighbourhood or part of my extended family, those who didn't belong to the world of decent people.

Bade Mamu actively participated in every function that took place in the mohalla. It could be any event. A wedding, wedding reception, aqeeqa, chhatti, bismillah, milad sharif, rozakushayi, qawwali or a nautch girl's performance. All of these were organized in a compound opposite our house, and Bade Mamu, along with some other people of the mohalla, were busy all day making arrangements, fixing the tents, spreading the carpets, durries and white sheets to spread upon them, tables and chairs. If there occurred a death in any of the houses of the mohalla, the dead body was placed in the same compound before it was taken away for the ritual prayer for the dead before the burial. This was also the place where extremely large cooking pots called deghs were put on the chulhas to cook food for weddings and wedding receptions. Deghs of pulao, zardah and korma. In order to cook the oven-baked rotis, an underground oven or a tandoor was placed in the circular patch of land. Food for feasts on the occasion of the third day or the fortieth day of mourning were also cooked in this compound.

What was this gher? It was a big patch of earth, square in shape, right in front of our main door. It had a drain full of dark water on each side. As a kid I used to spend a long time standing on that square patch. I didn't think of it then, but now I often wonder how our intellectuals engage in philosophical hair-splitting about the circle but pay no attention to the four equal sides, which I will not call a square nor will I tell you why.

It's very mysterious to be equal on four sides. Square-shaped faces have an unexplainable dignity. It's not easy to disrespect such faces. The stone of insult flung on them collides with this dignity and immediately ricochets with the same speed and strikes the face of the one causing the insult, turning it bloody.

Things with four equal sides ensnare you in their magic. You can't even make rounds here since this is not the circle which is correct and appropriate for dancing or circumambulation. Equal on all sides, the length equal to the breadth, but you have to pause at every angle, every joint. There are shining red geometrical bulbs. Beware! Take every step with caution. You can't go round and round inside an equal-sided object.

I don't remember whose wedding reception it was in the mohalla. There was going to be a performance by nautch girls at night as part of the celebrations. I must have been around seven years old at the time. Bade Mamu appeared very enthused and happy since morning. It was the dead of winter and the evenings were foggy. They were two women. One was called Kallo Jaan – she was very thin and dark – and the other was Anjum Jaan, plump and extremely fair.

It must have been barely 8 p.m. when the musicians started playing in the gher.

Bade Mamu entered the house and whispered in my ear.

'Guddu Miyan, do you want to see the dance?'

'Yes.'

The other members of the house were displeased. 'You are teaching the child to become frivolous too.' But Bade Mamu never listened to anyone and feared nobody. He held my hand and took me outside. The door was closed and locked from within. Everyone was upset and had started getting into their quilts early, pretending to go to sleep. According to them, it was a reprehensible thing to watch prostitutes dancing. Bade Mamu was the only one who was fond of such things. In the square-shaped gher was spread a snow-white chandni over the mats. People who had come from far and wide were sitting on them, some were jumping, even putting their feet inside the drains to peer into the gher. Some of the terraces in the mohalla had shadows of women hovering over them. The focus of everyone's attention and curiosity was our gher, filled with bright gas lanterns.

Bade Mamu tore through the crowd holding my hand and made me sit right in the middle of the gher.

I saw them now. They were sitting in front of me. Clad in blue, there were huge jhumars adorning their foreheads and their wrists were full of bangles. Their eyes were lined with kohl and their lips were crimson red, soft and delicate. Their cheeks seemed to be shining with a golden dust.

'Here, Anjum Jaan! This is my nephew, Guddu Miyan. We will begin with a song of his choice.' Bade Mamu spoke with such affection and familiarity as if he had known Anjum Jaan for ages.

I felt shy and lowered my head. The musicians began to play some unknown music. I could hear some vulgar phrases and abuses – the crowd was rowdy.

Then they touched my chin with their soft and smooth fingers.

'Guddu Miyan! Look at us.' It was the sweetest voice on earth. I looked at them shyly.

She had a face equal on all sides. I hadn't, and still haven't, seen such an even-shaped face. I spotted a black beauty spot on her fair chin. She covered her head with her dupatta.

'What would you like to hear, Guddu Miyan?' Her tinkling voice seemed like music to my ears. I was a stupid little boy of six or seven, what could I possibly request? But her awe-inspiring countenance forced me to think about the film songs of those times.

'Please tell me what you would like to hear. I will sing whatever you ask me to.' It was perhaps out of respect for me that she kept her dupatta carefully over her head and looked at me intently with her large kohl-rimmed eyes.

'Bahaaron phool barsao mera mehboob aaya hai,' I said shyly.

'Oh, okay.' She smiled softly and signalled to the musicians, who began to play the tune of this supremely beautiful song sung by Mohammed Rafi. She stood up slowly. Her blue ornamented gharara, made a gyration. I couldn't bear to look at her square, dignified face. She began to sing. The mysterious and attractive quality of her voice made me want to cling to it in a fast embrace. She was dancing slowly to the rhythm of the song. A halting, alert, pure and proud square dance.

I lost all sense and forgot where I was.

Then the song got over. The dance got over. The music stopped. The entire assembly fell silent.

But she didn't sit down and kept standing before me silently.

Bade Mamu fished out a five-rupee note from his kurta pocket and handed it to me.

'Give this to her, Guddu Miyan.'

I wasn't feeling brave enough for this but I timidly offered it to her, looking in the other direction.

She suddenly bent down, and sitting on her knees, accepted the note from my hands.

She lowered her head and offered her salutations. Then she took the note and circled it twice over my head before giving it to the musician sitting close by.

She cupped my face in her hands. Her hands were warm, as if she were suffering from fever. I looked at her face closely. Her huge, droopy kohl-lined eyes had tears in them.

She bent down to kiss my forehead and said softly, 'Now you can go home and sleep, Guddu Miyan.'

Bade Mamu took my hand and brought me to the door. I don't know who opened the door and pulling me inside, quickly locking the door. Bade Mamu was left standing at the door and I went and hid inside my quilt. The house was dark but there was a pure, sad light, emanating from the gas lanterns burning in the gher, scattered over the boundary wall of our house.

One could hear noises coming from outside. Time and again the sound of some musical instrument would be carried by the wind, only to fade away. I was feeling cold. I curled up into a ball. Gradually the quilt became warmer and I fell asleep.

When I woke up in the morning, the household was buzzing.

I came to know that many scoundrels and rogues of the town had turned up at night and a fight had ensued in which they pulled out their knives. The police arrived and caught many of the ruffians. They also stopped the dancing and caught hold of Anjum Jaan and Kallo Jaan by their hair and dragged them to their jeep, after which they whisked them away to some unknown destination.

I cried for a few days, hiding behind the door, thinking of Anjum Jaan. I felt tempted many times to ask Bade Mamu about her, but I couldn't sum up the courage to do so.

It's a pity that she vanished from my mind soon enough.

This terrifying cold has revealed to me today that the mysterious element in her voice was the presence of motherly love. Today the cold has also told me that she was probably the first woman in my life who had shown me any respect. She had saluted my innocent childhood, and then asked me to leave that debauched place.

But I have a complaint. Why did she never come to see me again?

Why did she not kiss my forehead again? Where did she go away? Why did she go away?

And the kind of times that befell me! The same innocent childhood that she had bent down to salute became sullied and blood-soaked so soon. And she didn't even get to know. I hope she didn't forget me because her name was also Anjum. How I wish! Were she to come before me now, I would leap up, coughing and sneezing in the grip of this cold, and show her the stains my spirit now carries. 'Bahaaron phool barsao mera mehboob aaya hai.'

Such huge stains, such large stains.

So to whom should I show these stains? I know God can see them but I want to show these stains to another human being too. This is my last desire, but then I wonder whether all human beings' spirits carry such huge stains on them. It could be that all human beings are as mysterious as I am. Every human being is a thug for another human being. Apart from the outer or visible religion, every human being spends his life carrying a secret religion within himself. A murderous religion, like the secret but probably real and terrible religion of the thug. We are all thugs. Who orders whom and when to perform jhirni katori or tobacco (code words used by the thugs directing a chosen member of the tribe to commit murder). Concealed in each one's hands is a noose to be put around the other's neck and each one of us is busy digging the other's grave. Even love is helpless and powerless before this murderous religion. It follows the command of jhirni. It sneaks up from behind and throttles the victim with the rumaal.

Who was a bigger thug than me? I continue to walk on the blood-soaked ground, like a thug who has strayed from his group, where everyone is in pursuit of the other. The shadows of the thugs keep getting bigger and the earth keeps getting filled with graves. Rotting and decaying bones underneath lush grass and plants and flowers. Human skeletons. More and more skeletons.

These are not mere words. This is history, a history bathing in blood again and again. At some point in this history, I begin to suck at the hollow bones of a goat like mad. Instead of marrow, those bones contain the fluid being secreted from my nose during the cold. I feel like flinging these hollow bones at Anjum's face. It now takes me hundreds of years to chew half a roti and the soiled food in my plate remains unfinished. My fingers, their tips, the margins of my lips, all get soiled with this spoilt food. The enamel bowl from my childhood in which I used to have my bread and milk is kept at the boundary wall of the terrace and all the milk has been polished off by the ghostly cats roaming there.

If my hunger is not satiated, and if I were not to find salt in my food, I will certainly strangle my wife one day.

Many a time the tall dark shadow of the anger which resides in me has wanted to fling the handkerchief noose around her neck from behind, but just then an innocent lisping voice has turned it back on its heels. 'Papa, my Papa.'

But nobody knows all this. This is my secret which no one is privy to, except the dead people.

We often dwell in the mistaken notion that secrets are small in size and therefore can be concealed. Like small little objects, such as a diamond, a pearl or some pointed stone or a knife. But no, a secret is actually very big and remains hidden from everyone's eyes because of its expansive nature and magnitude. The way the sun, despite being visible to the earth, remains a mystery.

I too am present in this life to a frightening degree with this huge and expansive mystery, and the interesting thing is that nobody knows me. Nobody knows my secret or my mystery. I don't want to die but if ever death were to recognize me and choose me as its victim, I would opt for a collective death over an individual, lonely one. I would like to search and find numerous such human eyes to share my dead silence after the terrible hubbub. I seek many shares in my death. I had flung the family tree of my ancestors into the gutter long ago, but I want to see everyone's names written on the papers of the property of death in a bright, black ink. I'm searching for many such witnesses who can collect all the evidence for me.

The cold has increased, and my cold has descended on my entire body. Like a piece of rubble. I'm under the rubble now. My feet have been trapped and crushed within my cold.

I get up in the morning and prepare to leave for the court with those crushed feet. In fact, it isn't morning but midnight when I prepare to go to the court. My mouth smells of sleep and the blood trickling from it introduces me to the first and last salty taste of the day. My cheeks smell of the running cold of the night. The breath that I exhale from my mouth carries the smell of sleep along with the gas that has been produced by the particles of undigested food from the previous night. The smell begins to fall on to the cold dark floor where I search for my slippers. In the toilet, the acidic smell arising out of the stream of my urine mixes with everything. This urine, which is passed in a state of sleepiness, is no different from the urine passed while dreaming. And my dreams have always been of this kind. They passed through toilets or deserted houses as I stood on the crumbling footrest of the toilet, like a naked criminal, all my life.

I was made into a sacrificial animal for crime and sin; this was my destiny. I am the sacrificial animal that has a mark on its forehead. But no one knows that this sacrificial animal contains within itself a malicious flaw. However much you may push your hand into his mouth and try to count the number of teeth, and however many times you may pat his back and try to estimate the amount and weight of meat in him, he keeps a mysterious spot of malice hidden in the red flesh of his gums, behind his teeth, from where arises a heavenly curse which collides with his tongue and jaws to be released with the breath he exhales into space, where it mingles with rotten and stagnant storms which have been there for ages. The layer of fat over his stomach contains a silent poison which only the sacrificial animal knows of.

Crime imitates punishment and sin reward. I'm brought into the sacrificial ground to show this game with a kettledrum in my hand. This whole world is a similar kind of game and has been formed as an imitation. Human beings tried to behave like God and became cruel and autocratic. Animals tried to imitate human beings and they became degenerate and shameless. Children tried to be like adults; they sprouted pubic hair before time. Women tried to imitate men and men tried to imitate women and both turned into eunuchs.

The nautanki of the world continues to play out in the sacrificial grounds. Intestines stuck on the blade of the knife, dripping and flowing blood, the red earth, the red water flowing and stopping in drains, the crowd stands and watches the fun. The spectacle of slaughter, a magic which is beyond compare, no other magical game can come close. The way the head of an animal is severed from its body, and how from a distance, lying at the margins, it witnesses its own body being cut into pieces. The eyes on the severed head are astounded at the spectacle. Here are the kidneys and this is the liver, soaked in fresh blood. The heart, the lungs, the intestines and the viscera, the trotters, the brain, the ears and the jaw – all organized into different compartments. Under the tent of knives, this is a different sport, peaceful and quiet, like a weak advertisement strip running at the bottom of the television screen on which some other show is being aired.

This process of imitation of an imitation has become prolonged. It's difficult to figure out now whether the punishment was an imitation of the murder or the murder was an imitation of the punishment. If there's anyone who knows it's the God sitting in the distant blue sky or a cockroach. A cockroach who weighs even more than that grinding slab which might still have the filaments of Aftab Bhai's brain stuck on it. Even now I can't bear the weight of that cockroach's existence, but I wish a day arrives when that ill-faced cockroach flies up to the collar of my shirt like a butterfly and perches there.

I wash my face when I emerge from the toilet. I don't bathe when I'm in the grip of a cold. Dirt has accumulated on my neck. But not caring about that, I go straight into the kitchen. I look for food for my shaking teeth, food which is actually the negation of food. Anjum is used to waking up late. Both the children are leaving the house to go to the mosque for the fajr prayers, looking at me the way someone else had looked at me hundreds of years ago. Anjum had perhaps looked at me in this manner before we got married, squinting her eyes and inspecting me as if I were a piece of raw mango which she was going to pickle in a pickle jar with hot oil and spices.

I don't feel bothered by these eyes.

I set out on foot for the court. This city has become so crowded that it won't take long for it to become a megacity. Everyone is suffering from the cold but is running towards some unknown destination. Since when did this country come up with so much work to do? I walk on the road, avoiding the pushes, sneezes and coughs of the public.

I reach the court, the Victorian-era building which is still enveloped in fog though it is eleven o'clock now. This fog won't dissipate before afternoon. And God knows when this afternoon will arrive.

The scene in the court is also one of chaos. Lawyers can be seen running here and there wearing black robes which extend below their knees, sneezing, coughing and rubbing their noses with a piece of cloth. There is a rush of clients behind them. Some lawyers who are sitting idle and in search of new clients cast hawk-like glances on all who come and go. I go and sit in a court. The ongoing hearing is regarding property. Feeling bored, I go to another court where the case in progress is about a rape. I flit from one court to another in this manner, listening to one case after another. I'm waiting for the afternoon which seems to be stuck somewhere in the skies.

The judge sitting in each court is also wiping his nose with a handkerchief and producing sounds of shoon shoon. His eyes have been dimmed by the water of the cold. He is flipping through the pages of the documents placed before him in a disinterested manner. He then postpones the case to a date in the future.

I finally return to my scribe. He and I don't have anything

to do these days. We either sit there swatting flies or we roam around the massive building of the courts aimlessly. Yes, I have recently begun to think that I will soon start frequenting the court library. The library is good and contains books on almost all subjects. It's been a long time since I read a book. I'm in fact in the process of forgetting all my science, all my philosophy and all my tantric knowledge and classical texts. As far as legal books are concerned, I have almost rid myself of them now. Or one could say that legal books have become so disappointed and weary of me that they have moved away.

I rarely got cases, and even if I did, I promptly proceeded to lose them. This is nothing important, but I've often suffered many ironies of fate. For example, a petty thief got rigorous imprisonment for life because of my weak argument, or a dacoit of the opposite party was acquitted because of my folly and the party ended up thanking me for my role in the case. Once it so happened that a poor fellow whose crime was no more than selling movie tickets in the black market barely escaped being hanged on the gibbet because of my incoherent arguments and my quoting of entirely inappropriate sections of the law.

Obviously, in such conditions it became difficult for me to manage even my personal expenses. I had never bothered about home expenses since Alauddin always took care of the needs of my wife and children. Alauddin had immeasurable wealth. He had many bungalows in the city now and if one were to look at it this way, I was trying to extract my pound of flesh from Alauddin for the favour I had done him.

The court is not very far from my house (Anjum's flat). I don't know why but when this hateful fog did not dissipate and the afternoon did not arrive, I began to feel extremely hungry. Although my teeth ache and are shaking the way an old autumn leaf trembles in the wind, I feel a strong desire to eat arhar dal khichdi. I know that Anjum cooks only arhar dal khichdi for lunch during winter. She eats this with various kinds of pickles, preserves and chutneys and also feeds it to her young robust sons. I salivate at the thought of pickles and preserves. Ever since my teeth had grown shaky, I had become a little greedy. It's difficult to predict when a man's powers of smell and taste will break into pieces and scatter.

I begin to take long strides towards home for the love of arhar dal khichdi.

But can a human being ever escape his bad luck?

There is spicy goat brain for lunch!

'You didn't cook arhar dal khichdi today?' I ask Anjum peevishly.

'No! The children wanted to eat goat brain today. They fetched it from the butcher's in the morning itself,' Anjum replies coldly.

I feel enraged. 'So you'll do only what the children want?'

'Yes, of course, and goat brain is eaten in winters,' Anjum begins to argue.

'Where are the two of them? I'll explain to them that eating goat brain is not a good habit. It contains worms, tiny poisonous worms which are invisible. They produce germs of madness and cause the human brain to go topsy-turvy. Goat brain was never consumed in our home.'

'So you think you are sane?'

'Tell me where the two are.'

'I don't know, they have been out since morning. By now they must have gone to the mosque for the Friday prayers.'

Just then I experienced an acute attack of the cold. An extraordinary kind of cold. It felt as if a large quantity of phlegm had collected in my throat and someone was thrusting an iron rod into my throat. I tried to clear my throat that was swollen to the point of bursting, but my breath remained stuck inside. I could feel the fluid rising in my ears and nose, and a nauseating whistling began in both. But the watery cold collected in my eyes refused to flow out. For some reason, the cold discharge had suddenly frozen. It seemed as if ice was forming in my entire body. I felt giddy.

I felt my frozen body would explode like a bomb, the way water freezes in the water pipes during winter and causes them to burst.

No – this is not the cold, this is not that cold. I seemed to have lost my nerve, and just then buffalo brain began to be fried in fenugreek seeds in the kitchen. The pungent smell of fenugreek combined with the stench of the brain began to fill the house.

'I get it now.' I suddenly got my breath back. The water collected in my eyes seeped out. The phlegm collected in my throat slid back to the dark shadows of the lungs. I found my nose and ears clearing. My head didn't seem so congested now. The ice of the cold began to melt.

'I've understood now. Today, as the Friday prayers got over in the mosque, buffalo brain shouldn't have been cooked in the house,' I spoke to myself.

Anjum came out of the kitchen. Her upright cruel nose was red due to the cold; it seemed like the tip of a burning log of wood peeping out of the ashes of a chulha. She placed a brass bowl of sweet porridge before me (it was Anjum who had brought all these ugly-looking bowls from her parents' home). I sat down and began to eat the porridge. But my hunger had vanished. I couldn't eat the porridge; my shaking teeth refused to chew it. I picked up the bowl, which looked as if it was meant to feed a Pomeranian, and put it aside. I started going through a pamphlet for a medium-range restaurant lying on the table. Its menu read:

Peas pulao
Veg biryani
Qorma (spelt korma)
Dum aloo
Zeera aloo
Shahi paneer
Kadhai gosht
Chicken changezi
Mutton nahari
Qeema kaleji (spelt keema qaleji)
Kashmiri stew
Dal makhani
Roomali roti
Tandoori roti
Missi roti
Butter naan

It was a long list. Somewhere far in the distance, two firecrackers went off one after the other.

I'm not afflicted by synaesthesia that I lose coordination between the five senses. However, I can hear the voice of colours. The secret voices of green-, yellow- and red-coloured foods. I also listen to the colour of blood. When I see the word biryani written on a piece of rough paper, I begin to eat it. This is how I eat all varieties of food, from the names of dishes written on a piece of paper or on the bills paid after eating the food. I consume the names of the different varieties of dishes with relish. Therefore, I'm well aware of all the conspiracies of food, since I have eaten the word 'food' and not the food itself. The word which hides within it all the destructiveness of the world and its times, its misapprehensions and fears.

I know that it all started with a poisonous lizard falling into the milk. It was probably from there that a worm was born inside me and introduced me to the new worlds of insight of the mind. This worm is the source of the vision of my eyes. A mysterious, invisible glow-worm which is connected to our hunger and greed and to all the dishes we eat through the day. This worm awakens and begins to wriggle frantically in my intestines once the food has been cooked over the chulha and reveals to me all the cardinal points of misfortune and ill omens. Only a worm can perform this task. The intestinal worm, not a gigantic beast. I have a suspicion that if this worm were to be ejected from my body – stuck in my faeces, flown down the drain – my very existence would be transformed into a properly useless thing. Like a useless throwaway object.

'The two haven't come back after the prayers?' I ask Anjum, or maybe myself. A din can be heard outside. Police vans blaring sirens pass one after the other. Anjum opens the window and peers outside. I too go to the window. There is no sun and far away in the east, the fog looks darker than usual. I can figure out that this isn't the fog; it is smoke, dense, black and fresh smoke.

There is a knock at the door. Anjum opens it and Alauddin enters, panting and wiping his nose due to the cold, producing sounds of shoon shoon. His bloated stomach is shaking vigorously.

'Hafeez! Hafeez! Thank God you're here.'

'What happened?' I'm mentally prepared to hear the bad news.

'Two bombs have exploded in the courts one after the other just now. At least fifteen people have died and there is no estimate of the number of injured people.'

'Where were you?' I ask.

'I wasn't in the courts. There was a lunch at Gulbarg Hotel on behalf of the Bar Council. I came here straight from there as I was worried about you. How are you at home today afternoon?'

'I was saved by the arhar dal khichdi.' I lit a cigarette.

'What do you mean?'

I don't say anything in reply and begin to think about the spicy fried buffalo brain.

Both the sons suddenly come running in, their faces white with fear.

'What's the matter? Anjum and Alauddin ask worriedly.

'The police is patrolling. The mosque is also surrounded by the police,' says the elder son, gasping for breath.

'Both of you don't go out anywhere,' Alauddin warns them. 'Regardless of who is doing it, we will have to bear the brunt.'

'Okay, Apa, I'll take your leave, Shabnam will be waiting for me at home. Take care and don't get nervous even if the police conduct a house search. I'll speak to the DIG that the police should not even look in the direction of my flat.' Alauddin made a show of being a well-connected person in his usual lowly manner and left.

The biggest drawback in Alauddin's character is his cowardliness, and I think that there is no other group of people more dangerous than a group of cowards. I was never a member of this group, which is why I feel that compared to Alauddin, I am much less dangerous.

I look at both my sons in silence. They seem extraordinarily nervous for some reason. Their faces have turned yellow with fear. Their lips are parched and they are sweating in this biting cold. These two are cowards too.

My elder son is called Zafar. He wears very fitted jeans, inside which his heavy buttocks move up and down shamelessly. In addition to glimpses of a merciless obscenity, he displays a nakedness even under such thick clothing. He normally walks with his legs far apart, which seems very unattractive. It feels as if he has a boil between his legs. He often talks about jihad, although he doesn't even know the meaning of the word.

My younger son is called Adnan. He doesn't wear jeans or tight clothing, but he too is crazy about religion. His voice has a feminine quality which lends his clean-shaven face a mysterious mercilessness. If his voice had not been so thin and feminine, the mercilessness and brutality may perhaps not have been there. He wears an earring in his left ear and colours his hair golden.

I wonder about having some similarity with my sons. Maybe not at present but there must definitely have been a time when I was the blueprint of one or both of them. When? At what age?

I'm sure that I was like them, but in some other place. Behind innumerable hills of time, I must have resembled the two of them in all certitude. I don't know when.

And now the running cold is not allowing me the time to ponder over all this.

At this point it should become clear that my memories are not merely my memories. They also include the memories of all those people who are not there in this world any longer, but through whose eyes I saw something or through whose tongues I heard something. All the cells of the left portion of my brain are subsisting by sucking the blood of the brains of all those dead people, especially while presenting my memories in the form of an appeal or petition when my most reliable witnesses are the memories of these dead people. It's difficult to rely on living people, but one can rely and believe in the dead. The dead are the kind of witnesses who can never change their accounts.

These days I have also come to realize (and this realization is dreadful) that it was not in my power to write down my memories, my joys and sorrows, my love and hate and my revenge. In fact, I'm perhaps only a medium. I'm a scrap of carbon paper in the garbage bin, on which someone's aggressive pen has inscribed this writing and these letters which apparently are not decipherable.

I always felt a kind of pressure while writing. The dreadful pressure of a mysterious pen. This pen which had no obvious relationship with me. There was a clean white paper over me and a similar one under me. That mysterious pen wanted to imprint its writing on the paper under me that it had written already on the white paper above. All its letters, words and sentences. I'm an extremely dark paper caught between the two white and clean sheets capable of becoming serious documents; I was to be torn into pieces like a useless thing and thrown into the dustbin later. The two white sheets of smooth high quality paper were determined to be reliable. The compulsion of that invisible mysterious pen's memory, the letters getting erased or mutilated on my dark complexion. I try to write or narrate something only through these words which are under erasure. This is exactly my appeal, this is exactly my petition.

I have perhaps crawled out of the garbage bin of time like a worm and I am in search of the court of law where I can confess my crimes and also seek recompense for the helplessness and ironies in which I have been imprisoned all my life. I don't know where such a court of law exists, and if such a court should convene.

I have no information about where the white sheets of paper

kept above and below me have been placed with the utmost care and protection, where they have been archived taking into account their importance.

This is according to each thing's destiny; nothing can escape destiny and go anywhere. This condition may perhaps prevail till my death, or even after my death.

The mention of death reminds me that although I have been carrying the burden of ill omen, curses and evil intent on my head since childhood, the ill omen which will introduce me to the time of my death is unknown. The smell of which food will persuade the insight-carrying worm which has been finding sustenance in my intestines to start wriggling vigorously?

But I don't want to die just yet. I don't want to return home now, so soon, although I dream of my ancestral home and the river of the fort every night. The river of the fort has changed its course and started flowing against the wall of my house. Its water is serving to decay the foundations of the house, gradually weakening them.

There will come a day when the entire house, along with its foundations, will emerge in the river like a small island and will float on the heart of the river with the force of the wind and the water.

It's one thing to miss one's home and another to return home. I'm not ready to go there yet. No, not at all.

One can't get good sleep at night due to the cold. The coughing wakes you up again and again and the phlegm collects in the throat. I have to clear my throat with force to get rid of the phlegm. I can't sleep for very long, but when I do, I always see my ancestral home in my dreams. It seems as if the house has turned into a dream. In this period, I have probably seen my house in dreams more than I have for real.

I look at the clock on the wall. It is three-thirty in the morning. My nostrils are hurting. The water of the cold has bruised the skin inside my nostrils and small eruptions have emerged there. It felt as if someone were poking my nose with the sharp tip of a knife. I have contracted a slight fever due to the intensity of the pain. I go up to the small white washbasin in the room to spit out the phlegm. I clear my throat with all the strength in my lungs. I sound like a distressed neighing horse. There's blood in the phlegm. The white basin has many red spots in it.

'Your cold is ripe. Did you hear, Hafeezuddin Babar? Your cold is ripe.'

It won't be long now before the cold departs. The lungs have finally filled with blood at the persistent coughing.

I come back to the room.

I want to sleep. I actually fall asleep for some time. I'm seeing my ancestral home. Before the front door of the deserted house, there is a strange, unruly din in the gher. I go to take a look. What kind of noise is this? It is a highly distressing scene.

Numerous wide-bodied eunuchs with kohl in their eyes are making obscene gestures and shaking their false breasts as they dance and sing in harsh voices, which sounds like the cracking of bamboo sticks.

*Kankariya maar ke jagaya, kal tu mere sapnon mein aya*
*Balma tu bada woh hai, zalima tu bada woh hai*

'You threw a pebble at me and awakened me, you visited me in my dreams yesterday

My love, you are sly and mischievous, my cruel beloved, you are sly and mischievous.'

The eunuchs are dancing in front of the silent and deserted house falling into ruin as if there had been a birth in the house recently. There is no one around except the eunuchs, not even a neighbour from the mohalla. There is nobody in the house either except me. I'm alone, alone to a pathetic degree. The eunuchs wink on seeing me and join their hands together to make the most obscene gesture. These terrifying eunuchs want to enter my house.

I feel like crying. There are tears in my eyes. I'm about to weep loudly. I'm scared. Someone is shaking me violently by the shoulder. I wake up with a start.

Anjum is standing with her eyes full of muck and her hair spread around her shoulders like a witch.

'You spoilt everyone's sleep. You've started producing horrible animal sounds while sleeping nowadays,' she yells at me and leaves, stomping her feet.

It's five in the morning. My teeth begin to chatter.

Exactly at noon, the postman brings a sealed envelope in my name. I look at the envelope carefully. It is from my town and the address is of my mohalla. The name of the sender is new to me. I open the envelope, my hands shaking. There is a folded piece of paper inside. I fish it out and begin reading:

Guddu Miyan! I hope you are well. You may not be able to place me, but I was a close friend of your Bade Mamu. You have played in my lap a couple of times. I'm writing to give you a piece of bad news. You have probably not visited your home in many years. Things are not good here. Your house has been taken over by a notorious fellow from our mohalla. He has even bribed the people in the lower court and gotten the house registered in his name. Such things are common these days. I have grown very old now. My house is very far from yours and it is beyond my capacity to do anything now. I'm giving you this information as part of my commitment to your family since I have been so close to them, with a complaint that if you had cared to come and read the fateha at your ancestors' graves or visited your home during Eid, Baqrid or Muharram, things wouldn't have come to such a pass. Neither would your house, which was a remembrance of your elders, have fallen to ruin. Nobody who acquires a higher education and becomes a lawyer or a doctor or a very rich man forgets their home the way you did. Anyhow, I'm hopeful that you will come soon after reading this letter. Since you are a well-known lawyer of the high court, perhaps you can sort this matter out. I obtained your address with great difficulty; please see to it that nobody gets to know that I have informed you of this conspiracy. They are highly dangerous people.

Your well-wisher,
Shakir Ali.

I tear up the letter into shreds and throw it into the dustbin. I get out of bed and stand up, my foot slips and I collide with the full-size mirror on the wall and fall face downwards on the floor. Lying flat on the floor, I open my eyes and raise my head to see myself in the mirror. The hair on my head has turned white. I can't believe my eyes.

I stand up. My wife and both my sons are standing at the door like statues, staring at me. My wife's hair has also greyed. Both my sons are looking much older. They are fully grown men.

I use all my strength to draw my breath in through my nose; the cold is gone. The cold has done its job and left, no water in the eyes, no phlegm rustling in the throat, no blood, no cough, no fever, no cold. The cold's flood has carried everything with it. There is nothing now. I gently stroke my head with my hand. Just these few grey hairs remain, memorials to a cold whose duration spread for centuries.

# Part IV
# Noises

Now
    There is no strength left in me
    Under this dirty sheaf of papers
    I'm suffocated
    The ugly smell of this ill-omened black ink
    Has rotted my nose
    I will fall into a deep sleep for some time
    And then he'll come
    My clerk – my scribe
    My copier
    He will wake me from my deep sleep
    Though he himself walks in his sleep
    He will catch me by the shoulders and shake me
    My ghost, my counterpart, my scribe
    Will ask me for my memory
    Which while I'm sleepy
    I will pawn and place in his hands
    Then I will sleep
    Then the sleepwalker
    Will move from the dark night towards a shining morning
    And will forward my appeals

He will copy my manner perfectly
No one will have even a grain of suspicion

Who is Hafeezuddin Babar?
And who is that deception, that ghost, that scribe and clerk
Who controls Hafeezuddin Babar's memory
No one will know
That it is the sleepwalkers who awaken the sleeping ones

As I may or may not have said earlier, apart from roaming around uselessly in the court, I also go to the library there to read books, although reading books is also a kind of loafing. I would loaf around in books of science, philosophy, history and geography like white ants do. And after having come to know that books are nothing but paper and whatever is written in them is incomplete and can neither come in useful for living one's life nor dying, I try to destroy these books in some way or the other. If I had my way, I would have turned into white ants and showed the books their place, destroyed their pride and reduced them to dust.

Having wasted my time in this manner, I set out for home towards evening. I was feeling hungry. I had not had anything apart from two biscuits and tea in the day. These biscuits and tea were not capable of helping me in any way now; they only created flatulence. Let's see what Anjum has cooked today. When I reached home, the first thing I did was to get into the toilet to urinate. The toilet was completely wet and smelt unpleasantly of mangoes.

The mother and sons hog mangoes all day like beasts and keep going to the toilet again and again. They are incurable, I thought resignedly. Emerging from the toilet, I rushed to the kitchen.

'Arey, arey, why have you come straight to the kitchen from the toilet? You barge in without washing your hands and face with your shoes on,' Anjum screamed. Her eyes contained such a glint of loathing that can be found only in the eyes of a malicious snake and not any human.

'Tell me what you're cooking today.' I ignored her comments and the glint of hatefulness in her eyes and asked drily.

The pressure cooker on the gas chulha was whistling softly, as if it were quietly sobbing.

Anjum's sharp, tyrannical nose began to swell and subside. The skin of her white neck began to turn smoky, as it happens to women who cook on chulhas which use wood as fuel.

'I'm asking you, what are you cooking?' I said somewhat loudly.

'Kadhi,' Anjum spoke, grinding her teeth.

'Kadhi.' I began to think, and my body gave a jolt. It's Thursday today, and cooking kadhi on a Thursday can prove destructive. An unknown kind of wave of lightning passed through the hair on my head. For a moment, the hair on my head stood on end. I felt a molten fire flowing from my throat down to my chest. I was about to experience a fit of awareness. I experienced once again today a mysterious and ill-omened spiritual capability which presents evil portent as a simple game of the creator before me. That moment passed. My senses and consciousness came back to their usual form.

'Kadhi shouldn't have been cooked today. It's not a good omen,' I mumbled.

'You old uneducated man, you are out of your mind. Get out of the kitchen. Zafar and Adnan want to speak with you,' Anjum screamed in anger.

I know from experience that there is no better place to break someone's head than the kitchen. There was no blowing pipe in this modern kitchen but there were still some heavy objects which I could bang on my wife's head, for instance the iron griddle right in front of me, but I remained silent just for the simple reason that kadhi–rice was my favourite food. My mouth began to water. How does it matter, I thought. Why should I deprive myself of eating my favourite dish because of the fear of some other people's deaths or terrible accidents? If something is to happen somewhere, let it, in any case, the news of death that usually came was of distant relatives or old neighbours in the mohalla, or it could be some world or national political leader. I was used to this ill-fated spiritual capability since childhood. And the truth of the matter was that the death of others was actually a very desirable dish of food for me which would mingle and dissolve in the saliva of my mouth and then disappear the way a thought does.

But I didn't know that it was a slightly different state of affairs this time. Not slightly but actually quite a different situation. I came out of the kitchen and Anjum got down on the floor and began to mop the spot where I had been standing.

I stood still when I got out of the kitchen. My memory has really lost all anchoring with my advancing age. I recalled Thursday was the day on which only meat should be cooked in the house because it is the day of fateha for all our ancestors and they must be waiting outside their graves for their share of food to arrive.

I went back to the kitchen.

'Is there just kadhi, no meat curry of any kind?'

'You have been stuffing your face continuously for the last four days with thick meat slices. You should not be eating so much meat in your old age.' It had been quite a while since I had even set my eyes on a piece of meat.

Anjum would never let any chance of taunting me about my age slip by. She doesn't look at her sagging, out-of-shape breasts which, if not supported, would touch the ground. The mean old woman, I thought to myself, but didn't say anything knowing that it doesn't take long for the kitchen to turn into a battleground.

I controlled myself and spoke with utmost patience. 'It's Thursday and we have to perform the fateha, did you forget this?'

'Can one perform the fateha only on meat? And your family members are known for their liking for kadhi. They would pounce on even the most rotten kadhi sent by someone or the other.' I could see Anjum's half-broken tooth. I have intense loathing for it and I have given serious thought to breaking it with the grinding slab.

'You are against the ritual of fateha itself, but remember, fateha and niyaz and nazr will continue systematically in this house till the time I'm alive!' I didn't want to aggravate the spat because it was the time when afternoon merges into evening and everyone's spirits must either be waiting for their food in the graveyard or roaming in the house. The house! Yes, the house which is eleven hundred and four miles away from here.

'Right, at least fry an egg quickly and serve the food. Time is short.' Saying this, I went to change my clothes. Time was indeed short. The maghrib call to prayer would be heard soon. When I passed my hands over my face after reading the fateha over the food which was almost clothed with the smoke of incense, the two-day stubble on it reminded me of my age. This was an old beard which made my fingers feel the old age sticking to them like a kind of leprosy. It was the very beard, I thought, when I first stepped into adolescence and down began to appear on my face. Then as I ran my fingers and palms on these little soft hairs, currents of youth, power, desire and intoxication ran through not only my fingers and palms but also through my body.

The maghrib call to prayer was heard.

'Where are Zafar and Adnan?' I asked Anjum, who was grumbling as she put away the food. 'What kind of a holy favour is this, cooking the food and then devouring it. It never got down to giving food to someone poor,' said Anjum under her breath.

'Where are Zafar and Adnan?'

'Are there fifty rooms in this house?' she spoke sardonically.

I admit that it was stupid of me to have asked this question. They must have been in the inner room where there is a TV right in front of the bedstead. I was feeling hungry, but I thought it would be better to listen to what they had to say and then I could have my food peacefully.

I went to the inner room. As expected, the two were seated on chairs, watching a religious channel on TV. They didn't pay any attention to me. I sat on the bed.

Zafar has done his engineering and has a long black beard. He wears suits and ties, and once in a while, jeans. He was wearing a suit and a tie today. There is nothing objectionable in this, but I find this look a little odd and out of place. If a person with a beard has a cap on his head and is in kurta–pyjama or kurta and lungi, he seems more gentle and kind than usual. This is just my own feeling. It's quite all right if you look at it from Zafar's point of view, but religious rules of dress and fashionable dressing are two separate things, and a man can observe both at the same time. What's the problem in this? I didn't want Zafar to be an engineer, but it was my wife's heartfelt desire. In my opinion at least, engineers, especially engineers of today's generation, should not even be regarded as educated. Engineers don't even have a remote connection with history, psychology, sociology or any such discipline that has to do with human sciences. Religious fundamentalism and an inscrutably cruel and tyrannical attitude towards humanity are markers of engineers now. And if you were to study this carefully you will see the obvious truth that the departments of technology and engineering in universities are becoming more and more narrow-minded and orthodox. This is a very strange contradiction, but it can be understood easily by considering that departments which don't have any human element in them are bound to end up like this. This is why these people can't understand the true spirit of religion either. And as for Zafar, I have my own suspicions about him. I fear that some night the police may knock at our door.

Adnan is an MBA and has a diploma in computer science. He hasn't grown a beard yet but his attitude towards religion is seemingly fanatic. The absence of a beard is probably due to the presence of some non-Muslim girl in his life. I'm quite sure that he will soon convert that non-Muslim girl into a Muslim and marry her, and thus earn some merit for good deeds in the process.

I lightly cleared my throat twice. Adnan switched off the TV. Both my sons took a good look at me first, as if examining me. Then Adnan spoke, 'What have you decided?'

'About what?'

'About that which we have told you many times.'

'Son, I can't exactly recall at this time, you tell me.'

'We are going to take up residence in Dubai. We can't stay peacefully in this country any longer. Ammi is also agreeable.'

I began to feel angry. Such severe anger that I started scratching my back with my left hand to control my fury. I had recently read in the newspaper that one way of gaining control over one's anger is to try to use your right hand for some important function if you are left-handed and vice versa. There was nothing more important for me at that time than scratching my back.

'What have you decided?' This time it was Zafar who asked the question frostily.

'What problem do we have here?' I asked softly.

'There is a permanent hatred for us and our community here. Our life is getting more and more difficult and threatened by the day over here.' Zafar spoke loudly.

'But this is our country, and everyone is not alike. Such things are routine. It's not proper to leave the country. And there is no country which will accept us as its own.' My tone was loud too.

'You are mistaken. This country is not going to last. I have no hopes for this country's survival. Not at all, and a country whose politics and leadership has become so hollow and insensitive, and where there is no end to atrocities against minorities, we don't want to have any emotional connect with such a country.'

'What are you saying, you gained your education here, you also do a small job here. You will be promoted in due course. Our country's constitution is very clear in this matter.'

'Keep the sixties mentality to yourself. The fact of the matter is that you have never had to face those conditions. It's going to become difficult to earn one's daily bread. Little do you know,' Adnan almost shouted.

'Belly...belly...to fill the belly, food, kitchen, food cupboard,' my mind suddenly became disconnected and began to repeat only these words. Adnan and Zafar were still saying something but I couldn't really follow.

'Hungry dogs of the belly – food. Kitchen. Battleground, action ground,' I mumbled aloud.

'What?' The two of them looked at me as if I had quite lost it.

'Nothing ... Raees Chacha in the 1962 war, Raheemuddin Mamu in the 1965 war and Feroz Phupha in the 1972 war, all lost their lives for this country, and even in Siachen ...' I spoke softly, but both of them exploded at me together.

'Don't teach us your history. We are not interested in the history, culture and customs of this country or of your forefathers. We don't regard this country as our native land. In any case, the concept of motherland has become outdated and ridiculous in the present times.'

'They all died for the belly, for the kitchen. For their intestines and the digestive system – they were cannibals, then they learnt how to cook. Then how to build homes. And to build a kitchen in the home.'

I couldn't hear the loud voices of my sons. I was hungry. The sugar level in my blood was probably going down. Was I dozing off?

'We can't understand your words. Keep them to yourself.' I suddenly came back to my senses as Adnan's eyes reddened.

'My words? You aren't capable of understanding my words at all, because you guys are the representatives of technology.' I again tried to scratch my back with my left hand.

'You'll try to pose as a philosopher now. You don't know that technology has endowed human beings with grand protection and safety.' Zafar now addressed me as 'tum' instead of 'aap'.

'I know that what technology is most used for is to exclude human consciousness from all its hypotheses, but what should one do with the fact that it is the product and result of human consciousness itself? The denial of human consciousness and human emotion sometimes becomes the cause of human destruction and this happens only because technology is a system within itself. All these weapons and bombs are a system within themselves which certainly deny human sense or any other emotion. What is to be kept in mind is that they themselves are destroyed first. Their destruction is not limited to them alone, the way a poisonous lizard which falls into boiling milk dies first and then poisons everyone else who drinks that milk. This is the mathematics of destruction, and this system is actually like a locked dark cell. It's a typical characteristic of a sealed system that it is always a slave to its own conditions and its own moralities. A system can view everything outside itself with its own eyes. It's clearly jaundiced. It can look at terrorism, exploitation, violence, cruelty, terror and pain only with the eyes of the system, to the extent that its senses and powers of understanding don't remain capable of sensing or distinguishing between politics, injustice, defamatory practices and duplicitousness. This is a kind of blindness which can't sense fluidity. Consciousness is fluid and the quality of consciousness is that though it creates a system, it refuses to become a system itself. A long and decisive refusal. I know, I know everything.'

I was short of breath. Both my sons smiled sarcastically. I became unexpectedly conscious of my increasing age and weakening body, but I immediately dismissed the thought reviving the memory of arguments and debates that I had indulged in during my youth.

'Listen, Zafar and Adnan, my children! Listen, technology is a result of human beings' great rational urges, but the very first thing that it wounded was the grand emotion of being human. Your technology is committing suicide. This suicide is its destiny because it has accepted the dreadful nature of its satanic, ghastly child who delivers a hateful kick at its mother's womb the moment it is born. The first breath of such a thankless creature is actually its suicide.'

'You could never do anything all your life but spout rhetoric, and this rhetoric couldn't help you earn anything substantial. Neither did you acquire a practice in the courts nor could you get a job in a college or university.' Adnan spoke with his innate insolence and rudeness.

An intense feeling of anger and sadness tried to suppress me completely, but today was a day of judgement. I couldn't possibly lose to these two-bit boys. I had to speak. I tried to do something with my left hand again and resumed speaking.

'This is not mere rhetoric. These are my opinions and my thoughts. You, Adnan! You have been a student of computer science. See how technology pushes us into a war against memory, and for that the first thing that is required is putting restrictions on thought and understanding, which you call rhetoric. Your computer works only on the binary system, that is, it knows only zero and one. Does anyone want to remind you that a learned man by the name of Pythagoras in ancient Greek thought had acknowledged absolute reality to be nothing more than a unit of one? Today, when your computer tells you that there is nothing by the name of hundred and in reality it's only one which you count a hundred times, does your mind induce you to think about it? But technology regards these apparently useless questions as signs of weakness in the spirit of science, and it's possible that this is right, but the inclination to put restrictions and boundaries on thought and questioning is akin to shamelessly ignoring the power of human memory. Your technology gives an inferiority complex to man. It depresses his moral ambition and looks with demeaning eyes at man's independent, illogical, creative attitudes.'

'For God's sake, we don't want to listen to all this, everything you say is incoherent nor is there any connection of cause and effect in your exposition.' Zafar got up from his chair.

'The connection of cause and effect? Haha, haha.' I deliberately burst into a crude laughter. Tiny particles of spittle began to form between my teeth. I wiped them with the sleeve of my kurta. Both my sons looked at me with revulsion.

'You haven't read Hume. You don't know antimatter. Where there is a centrality, the formal connection between cause and effect becomes meaningless. And this is also a defect of your science, which has been pointed out by most of the prominent physicists like Heisenberg, Neumann, Max Born and even Lee Yang. And Popper says very clearly that the action of cause and effect is evident in the material world, but the moment we step into the virtual world of electrons and protons, we are confronted with unbelievable and uncertain situations at many places. These two statements are in contradiction with each other, or there is something in between them which is contradictory. It is difficult to get rid of this contradictory element.'

'Just keep quiet, keep quiet, we weren't waiting for you here to listen to your nonsense. We don't want to live in this country. We want to go from here very soon and will come back only when the caliphate is established here. Your country's secular democracy is yours to enjoy. Go! Go and lick the feet of those who demolished the Babri Masjid.' Adnan stood up, clenching his fists.

I too got up from the corner of the bed. 'You both are denying yourselves. You are denying your science and technology. Have you ever read Joseph Conrad? Joseph Conrad says that terrorism is very close to the imaginative mind. And Shakespeare says in *Macbeth* that life is a tale told by an idiot, and Walter Benjamin says that technology is not meant to go along with the basic strengths of society. And it's obvious that technology can't do this because it denies social structures and their sense of understanding as well as human emotion, which is why it is not surprising that it becomes short of breath in the process.'

'Take care of your own breathing right now, crazy old man. It seems you will collapse,' Adnan said softly, but the words 'crazy old man' made me truly old suddenly. Anjum would often call me an old nut but I hardly paid any attention to that. I felt giddy. Will I become fully old today? For these children too whose sight had helped me maintain my youth?

'Good that you didn't get employment in the university or else sick of listening to your stupid and incoherent references, the students would have broken your head.' This was Zafar who was standing in front of me, but I felt that the voice was coming from afar. I could feel my pores breaking out into sweat. My sugar and blood pressure levels were falling fast. I must eat something now, I said to myself. I quickly started moving towards the kitchen.

'Take off your slippers and go in. Your slippers always have earthworms stuck to their soles.' Anjum emerged from the other room with the prayer mat in her hands.

I looked at Zafar and Adnan carefully. Throwing a filthy abuse at the earthworms and the earthworms' mother, I barged into the kitchen with unsteady feet. I encountered the same mango smell that was in the toilet. The moment I lifted the lid of the cooker to serve myself food, I recalled that I hadn't yet taken my half antidiabetic pill. I fished out the tablet from the pocket of my kurta and tried to break it into two with my frail and old fingernails, when I noticed the two of them standing at the door of the kitchen. I realized with regret that I should not have engaged with the two and felt defeated. I had actually lost to the microscopic bodies within me, for what else were these two but my own microscopic bodies?

Seemingly inattentive to the presence of those two and without looking in their direction, I continued to make the unsuccessful attempt of breaking the blue tablet into two. My nails had become so weak that there were greater chances of the nails breaking than the tablet.

'We came to tell you only this much: sell your share of the ancestral house. We are badly in need of money right now.' Adnan's merciless voice entered my ears like that sharp, chilly wind of the winters which gives me a severe cold. This wind always proved extremely painful for me. Now perhaps a gust of that wind blew away the little blue antidiabetic tablet off my palm.

'What? I should sell off the memory of my ancestors?' My voice contained extreme anger and shock.

'You just sell your portion. We are not talking about others.'

'But I don't have any demarcated share. The house was never divided.'

'So go now and get it divided and sell your share to some relative there.'

'No one lives there; that house must have turned into a ruin by now.'

'There must be some friend or relative who lives somewhere. Go and meet them and find the property papers and hire a lawyer. We have to leave this country, and we desperately need money for it.'

I heard the growl of a beast within me. I acted on that snarl and picking up the cooker from the gas stove, I smashed it against the floor. The cooker's lid fell open with a loud bang and the yellow kadhi and its yellow fried balls scattered all over the floor.

The two of them felt intimidated for a moment. The yellow-coloured kadhi spreading itself over the white floor of the kitchen cast its reflection on their faces which seemed jaundiced now.

Anjum came holding the prayer mat in her hands.

'What happened? Did the old man strike you?' Nerve-racked, she began to feel the faces of the boys.

Then Zafar spoke. 'He doesn't want the property to be divided.'

'The division must take place. You must go. Go you must, or your life and survival in this house will become difficult,' Anjum pronounced coldly.

'This is my decision. The property won't be divided in my lifetime. I can't perform this shameful act. And what are you guys threatening me with? I'll stay right here. I know this is not my house. But I have been living here since before you two were born. I can spit on this wretched flat and leave whenever I want to, but not because you want me to. How dare you imagine that you can throw me out?' I spoke in measured tones.

'Then listen carefully, you old fellow.' Zafar's tie, which was loosely hung around his neck, touched his beard. He stepped forward with some harmful intention. Both the sons had become even more bold on seeing their mother.

'Ramzan, the month of fasting, is beginning tomorrow. We can't live with an infidel. Let your socialism go back where it came from. You'll have to fast through the month and offer the five prayers every day. You'll also have to offer the taravih. In this home we will no longer allowed niyaz, nazr, fateha or any such things. No newfangled religious observances. You have had your will for a long time. Now things will go the way we want,' Adnan roared and his eyes began to redden with rage.

'No mother's son can compel me to do all this. Whatever I do, I'll do by my own will,' I said this without any apparent qualms, but an inscrutable weakness gripped me. I thought of Alauddin. Should I call him over at this time?

'Worry about your day of judgement; you have your feet right there in the grave,' said Anjum, rolling the prayer mat under her arm.

I felt extremely dizzy; I began to sway as I stood. I looked at my wrists. Wrinkles had appeared on them and all the soft down on them had suddenly turned white. I have grown old, I have grown completely old today. I imagined a toothless mouth and a weak, sick and insignificant old man going into the jaws of death.

But I tried to restore myself one more time. I tried once again to stand erect with my head held high. Struggling and fighting my giddy head, the wrinkles which had appeared on my skin, my gaping toothless mouth and my death, and the three of them. I looked at them and asked, 'What if I don't do any of this?'

The pressure of the blood in my body became so intense that it didn't want to remain concealed in it any longer. I was bleeding from my nose and from the ears, and the blood was trickling down to my neck. I wiped it with the sleeve of my kurta.

The three of them replied in unison; although their collective voices resembled the dangerous hiss of a serpent, their words were clear.

'Then we won't let you live.'

'It is a religious duty to kill you, you old infidel.'

'Old infidel? Deserving to die?' A father deserving death at the hands of his sons. I felt a severe blow on my heart. My heart began to sway like the sandbag hung on a tree by young men to practise boxing.

There was darkness before me, and my head was flying somewhere far off from my shoulders. My feet slipped on the sticky kadhi spread on the floor. I probably shouted for the last time as I tried to catch hold of the kitchen door frame, 'I'm not old; I'm Hafeezuddin Babar alias Guddu Miyan!'

'I'm a child.' I screamed hysterically. 'A very dangerous child. What you are going to do to me, I have done long back. Not once, but twice, yes twice.'

Swaying to the tune of the waves of my own deep and echoing voice, I finally fell to the floor of the kitchen like an old and weak tree and frantically tried to grasp my heart, which was hurting badly, with both my hands. But my heart eluded my hands. I don't know where my heart was. In my stomach, my intestines, my feet, or perhaps it had gotten stuck in the blood beginning to congeal in my body. And then, as I lay on the floor, overcome by pain, my eyes suddenly felt a strong light beam.

I saw, I saw. The rains have come, and along with them a number of crows have collected in the kitchen.

# Part V

# Dead Silence

It's a very old kitchen. Older than childhood. Wooden beams in the ceiling blackened by smoke. Cobwebs hang in every corner from the walls and from the beams. If the wind had a passage here, the cobwebs would have been cleared too like the sky. There are many yellow-and-black coloured lizards clinging to the walls and the ceiling. The brick floor has come undone in places and small red ants are crawling across it in long lines. Between the coal tar painted beams on the smoke-tortured ceiling is a naked forty-watt bulb suspended from an electric wire whose shine as well as light have been dimmed by the layer of smoke deposited on it. There are so many flies sticking to the red wire that it seems like a thick string of flies rather than a wire. This is an ancient kitchen. He knew it. Here was the skylight opening towards the palm tree and here was the brick screen in the direction of the staircase and there, to the other side, was the tiny dark storeroom.

He has fallen on the upright brick floor and is lying sideways with his left hand pressing on to his left cheek as if it were stuck in a quagmire.

The blackish-yellow light from the bulb, which was covered with smoke residue, suspended from the ceiling is falling right over his head. Both the sons want to kill him. Both are moving in his direction but are in a fix. They don't know how to commit a murder. Both of them look like him in his childhood. He has been able to find his lost things easily. He feels a surge of affection at the innocence of the sons. He teaches them a unique and fine method for murder. Both are intelligent and grasp the physics formulae quickly.

The one with the beard, who is wearing a tie and is clad in jeans, picks up the small but heavy grinding slab and moves slowly and carefully in his direction. His buttocks are wriggling in his tight jeans. He walks with legs opened wide as if he has a boil on his thigh.

He looks at his son's wrists on which the veins have popped out because of the heavy weight. His wrists and fingers are trembling in exactly the same way. These are the very same hands of his son which used to be his and then were lost somewhere. Or he had put those hands somewhere and forgotten where? He has suddenly found his hands back today.

He was advancing towards Aftab Bhai's bald head, holding this heavy grinding slab in the same hands. Aftab Bhai's bloodstains and specks of brain are still stuck to the stone grinding slab. Spices were ground on it so many times, but the spots didn't leave the grinding slab.

'Move ahead, not that way, this way. Put your right foot forward first and then the left foot.' He speaks but he doesn't even hear his own voice in the dense and deep silence outside.

The second son emerges, crawling out of a corner, like a giant chameleon emerging from behind large stones. He sticks out his thin mud-coloured tongue again and again and passes it over his lips. His gait is exactly the same. Perfectly like his own. He is happy that his gait will remain on this earth for quite some time. It has come back from behind the old hills of time.

The younger son is now slowly crawling towards a discoloured canister of kerosene oil kept on a small platform. He observes his face carefully. His face is screwed up, the same action, the same surreptitiousness.

It was the same manner, secretive and silent, with which he had burnt alive Anjum Apa's husband.

'Here, pour it, open the lid of the canister softly, very softly, the chulha has fire in it. Don't delay . . . now don't delay, pour, pour.'

He tries to explain but the noise of the wretched silence beating down incessantly stops the words in his mouth.

Both the sons are moving forward to murder him in their own respective manners, through their own respective routes and in their own respective time and space.

Both the brothers are now amazingly seeming like each other's twins as well as his own. They are two faded copies of a clear inscription. Carbon copies, photocopies!

The murder looks exactly the same as before. Both the murders have got muddled into each other, like two dangerous snakes intertwined.

The elder son crushed his head with the heavy stone grinding slab. And the younger son dropped the canister of kerosene oil on the fire burning in the chulha. He burnt to death.

And then it began raining outside. A gigantic gust of wind moving in the rain shower hurled a large copper cooking pot, which was very heavy, at his knees. Standing against the blue doors of the kitchen, his wife Anjum is staring at him.

Without any expression or emotion on her face, Anjum continues to stare at the leg bones in the huge cooking pot until they come to a boil.

Anjum Apa and Anjum Baji both jumped into the kitchen

through the skylight opening towards the palm tree, like two wet cats.

A white cat and a black cat.

Both of them sit on the floor meekly and watch him being murdered. They are full of greed and expectation that once the bones come to a boil, his wife will extract the marrow and throw the empty bones for them to lick and suck.

He's being murdered slowly. As he lies sideways on the floor, Anjum's white salwar is being stained by a trickle of blood flowing from her lower abdomen which reaches the floor and spreads over it. Within her salwar, the mouth of her uterus has opened the way a toothless suckling infant opens its clean and pure mouth before beginning to cry.

The trickle of blood on the floor reaches close to his head. Then it enters his right ear after making a half-circle at his temple. Inside the ear, it weeps. A little girl cries inside his ear.

'Papa, Papa, my Papa.'

The little girl's voice then falls silent.

Buried forever inside his ear, he heard the little girl's voice like a pure and holy call to prayer.

He's being murdered slowly.

'Guddu Miyan, what are you doing? Are you sleeping, Guddu Miyan?'

There's no problem anywhere, there's no pain anywhere. A network of lines drawn with a knife has formed on his body. Thousands of images tremble at the tip of the knife. But he can't see anything now. Once again, a darkness has descended over his eyes.

And when the darkness had descended fully, the age-old half-sliced moon covered his eyes on which blood from ancient unknown times had congealed and turned black.

One doesn't know when he got up and after how long.

He left his 'murder' lying on the floor the way one leaves trash lying around, carelessly.

He thought of taking a bath now.

'I will have a bath now. I will rub myself with green-coloured soap. I will rub off all the dirt from my body.'

He went into a dark bathroom and scrubbed himself with a loofah and covered himself with the soap suds. The dark bathroom brightened with the white soap suds. He paid proper attention to purification rituals since he was giving a bath to his own dead body, but when the flood entered the bathroom and frogs, fish and earthworms started nibbling at his ankles, he came out of the bathroom naked.

It was a moonlit night in the courtyard. He went into the tiny storage room with trunks. He took out his red sweater from his old iron trunk. A brand-new red sweater which Anjum Baji had knitted for him. And then the camel-coloured khaki pants which were part of his school uniform. His perfectly white canvas PT shoes were under the trunk. He quickly wore them, making a tight flower-shaped bow with the shoelaces.

His favourite shirt was under his sweater. The same sad blue shirt which he had brought back from the Eid fair. He stood erect and dusted his hair to remove the sawdust from the angithi, which remained stationary in spite of so much washing.

'So come now, Guddu Miyan. Come Hafeez. Come home. Enough is enough.'

Home, which was eleven hundred and four miles, and a journey, dangerous and full of serious troubles, away.

When he was ready to set out on the journey, a woman, who resembled every other woman in the world, handed him an earthen pot containing rasawal which was covered with red-coloured paper. She also gave him a crumpled piece of yellowing paper on which the recipe of spice biryani was written. Holding both in his hands, he began to quickly walk away. On the way, he came across his childhood friend, the jagged-eared rabbit. The white jagged-eared rabbit walked with him.

Right at that moment, a familiar age-old cockroach flew up to the collar of his blue shirt like a butterfly and perched itself there.

His sin, his crime fastened itself to the sad blue collar of his shirt.

Stopping at a spot, he lifted the red-coloured paper of the earthen pot containing rasawal. The earthen pot was teeming with the red worms fishermen use on their fishing rods to catch large-sized fish.

He unfolded the decaying piece of yellow paper and read the recipe for the biryani in the dark. They were the property and inheritance papers of the house.

He walked mostly with his bier on the journey which was very long, and in the beginning full of only black muddy rivers and thorny bushes, though at places he abandoned his bier and flitted around, wandering like a flaming piece of fire and will-o'-the-wisp.

He stopped at places and ate mouthfuls of muck which tasted just like chocolate and refreshed the taste in his mouth so much that he felt like singing an old film song, but then he was reminded that his dead body was close by. He postponed the idea of singing out of respect or affection. He walked along, swaying, absorbed in his own affection. It was Diwali in the wilderness, the way a musical note drops out of music and is alone and sad yet complete. Little diyas of Diwali were floating on streams and tiny rivers. Tiny bulbs hung from the branches of trees.

He was ready. To dance in the terrifying and ill-omened winds accompanying his dead body like a solitary musical note.

He floated around in the air like a crumpled piece of paper on God's entire earth, over mountains and the vast and full mountain forests, over the icebergs floating in the sea, over highlands and their sleeping volcanoes which had emitted fire before, but were silent now, like graves.

God knows how many tunnels were under his feet. How many streams had changed their course and how many rivers had dried and converted into deep sandy ravines. Which is why his feet produced a pounding in his chest and sank into it and his teeth came out of his mouth to scoff at him. The journey of evolution must have been like this. This is a different evolution, the lonely evolution of a single entity which goes back as much as it goes forward and also goes round and round towards the darknesses of the left and right.

Beneath his feet in the darknesses of the left and right is the wet quagmire where many streams are merging underground, losing themselves, going into extinction. He looks only for the river of the fort among these rivers. His foot is alert even in the quagmire, like the sleeping eye of a dog, because it has to feel the dampness of the rotting moss of the fort river. He has to drown in it.

God knows when it began to rain, then a wave of grief rose from his feet and surged till his heart to settle there. It didn't go any further and formed its whirlpool there. He didn't stop in the rain and continued walking. Out of the four women pall-bearers three had black umbrellas. They didn't want to get wet. He recognized the three of them. Anjum Baji, Anjum Apa and Anjum, his wife. He did not know the fourth woman who was getting wet in the rain; he might have seen her in his dreams.

Seeing the unknown woman getting wet, a deep sadness crept over him. This was an attack of sadness, a headless sadness which didn't have a face or a head. There was only a movement filled with a feeling of guilt and defeat. The way a brave soldier continues to wield his sword even after his head has been severed from his body, because his body is no longer a body but a meaningless motion and an infructuous activity. He bore the assault of this faceless, headless sadness and the awareness of crime and terrible sin and the inner consciousness of being mean and insensitive brought the bones of past times and threw them under his feet. His dead body was before him and on the other side the times gone by, seated on a jute string bed, were laughing at him. His legs had grown stiff because of the kicks he had delivered on the bones of the past. So, did everything happen only to make him sad?

The jagged-eared rabbit walking behind him trembled and shook in the rain. He would have taken the shivering rabbit in his arms had he not been carrying the pot of rasawal and the biryani recipe in his hands. The cockroach on the collar of his blue shirt had shrunk in size due to the rain, but his sins became even heavier and protracted. Then did everything happen only to make him sad? He saw everything with the eye of a puppet for whom joy is also a shadow or imitation of grief. Life was like death and death was not different from life too.

Now a silent wilderness, an unending wilderness which only a puppet's eye could discern. The puppet's eye became sleepy and fell asleep to the lullaby of the aged wilderness.

His shroud began to swell, drenched in the rain. The wind began blowing it up from within and it started going up like a white balloon. Gradually, the bier became heavier and heavier.

They reached a point where a wall obstructed the funeral procession. This was a burnt wall adjacent to a muddy hole full of black water, which was gently dashing against the burnt wall again and again. Joyfully, he descended from the bier with his wet shroud swollen like a balloon.

The bier was now empty and light. The four women waded into the viscous water and crossed the burnt wall with the bier over their shoulders. He went and lay down in the bier comfortably.

This was a journey based on centuries. We don't know after how many aeons he felt hungry again. He stopped along the banks of a narrow sad stream and ate some of the muddy earth on the riverbank. There was a fast but very familiar breeze blowing across the bank – the breeze of his childhood? The collar of his blue shirt began to flutter vigorously but the cockroach perched on his collar didn't budge. He recalled that, long ago, maybe in some other birth, he and a girl with desolate eyes ate pieces of cheese on the bank of some river like this one and in a breeze which was like the breeze that was blowing now. The cheese tasted like the mud that he ate a few minutes earlier. Then he burst into tears, perhaps he wept remembering those desolate eyes.

He thought he must weep now, immediately. How long had it been since he wept? He is accompanying his bier, after all. It seems necessary for him to weep and lament a little bit.

What a pity that there was no lament left now. He raised his eyes to the sky. The lament was there, caught and entangled in the blue haze.

His eye couldn't pluck that lament and weeping from there. The eye was not unsuccessful in making the lament. Actually, it lost to the blue pitiless net of the sky.

There was just the mud melting in his mouth, like soft pieces of cheese, like soft pieces of cheese. Right at that moment, a laughter brimming with mean and base joy echoed everywhere. Then a harsh, furious voice. A kite flew across the sky.

Now he knew.

The river of the fort was there in front. This indeed was the river of the fort – far away, across the river, he saw tiny houses just like those found in human settlements. These weren't the houses of snakes and fish. There was a familiar reddish-brown light shining on the far side of the river as if the sun was setting.

His bier left him at that spot and wandered off in some unknown direction, losing itself somewhere.

When he reached the other side of the river, he bent to clean the wet moss stuck to his feet and saw a clear line, a schism beneath his wet, moss-ridden feet. The earth had split there.

So was the journey over?

One dark continent of the spirit separates from the other continent and bids farewell. Turning back, he tried to see with his dry and farewell-bidding eyes all the rivers, the quagmires, the thorny bushes, the rotting leaves and seeds and the sand dunes, the black umbrellas, the biers and his own pall, along with his footprints, and failed.

Finally, he leapt over the crevice – as if the river Nile had been crossed. He became empty after crossing it.

Darkness began to overcome his body that revolved like the earth. His body fell on to the dark side behind the light of his brain.

The continent that he had traversed with his feet was now rapidly going away from him. He heard the sound of this departure.

God knows how many solar years will pass before this part of the earth receives light.

How many ages will pass before his sinful body illuminates itself in the light of his brain.

The brain which is extricated through the nose to prevent a corpse from rotting, leaving both of them to wander in their separate worlds.

He hadn't forgotten to carry the earthen pot of the rasawal and the biryani recipe very carefully when he crossed the gap in the road.

He reached the other side.

The eternal innocence and eternal sins of man managed to come along with him across the schism in the form of earthworms stuck to his canvas shoes.

He felt that his emptiness was suddenly filled by something – he has found something he had lost during the time the darkness had fallen on his body. This was certainly the case – he had found the lost geography of his spirit once again. The sad and complicated geography of his spirit on a piece of fresh and crisp white paper in the pocket of the khaki pants of his school uniform.

He is beginning to find all his lost things – the process continues.

Casting a cursory glance in the dense darkness, it is somewhat difficult to say if the object in front of you is a house under construction or a house dilapidating into a ruin. The reason is, that in either case the condition of the house is hardly any different, and equally pitiable. The same kind of rubble, the same scattered and broken look, similar looking piles of junk and a similar kind of darkness and suffocation beneath a roof under construction or tottering down, a similar kind of darkness and suffocation.

In both conditions, the earth has to put up with similar sorrows.

More than half the night had passed when the three shadows entered the house.

The first was the one whose shadow was walking on two legs and resembled a human being. The second was a shadow of a rabbit walking behind him. A rabbit who was leaping a bit, limping a bit, the rabbit with a jagged ear. The third shadow was that of a butterfly-like cockroach in the shape of a huge but trembling and shivering sin on the collar of his shirt.

They were shadows and it was like shadows that they had entered the house, but it's difficult to really call it an entry because there was neither a door nor an entrance with a threshold. There were just cords, beams and planks. There were mounds of large and small bricks and grass as tall as a man's height.

The darkness there was woven by the invisible straws of the dampness of the earth, the sand, the soil, limestones and wooden beams and ropes and wooden poles, which is why it was not a black darkness but a grey one. A grainy stone-coloured darkness, avoiding which left and right, above and below he walked carefully for a long time.

Despite being so careful, his left foot suddenly sank into the wet earth.

This was a sticky mound of thick slimy mortar. His foot went deep inside the glazed and sticky yellow mortar.

Did someone say 'Guddu Miyan has come'?

He tried very hard but couldn't extricate his foot. The tensile strength and the clinging power of wet earth defeated his foot. His leg was plastered with mud halfway up to the knee.

He screamed. He screamed softly; the scream was unfamiliar to him. He was a stranger to himself, so strange and disconnected that he could have been a being from another planet having no connection whatsoever with even the tiniest of insects in the process of evolution. He did not pay any heed to the shadows of the monkeys wandering all over the deserted house.

His jagged-eared rabbit began to jump and scamper around searching for grass, which he found soon enough, between the dark piles of brick and rubble.

The cockroach perched on the collar of his shirt sprang and joined his innumerable companions running around in the dark.

That sin didn't remain solitary and sad now. There was a whole assembly of sins. The brightly shining light of sins everywhere. And then suddenly he understood that it was useless to proceed any further and the business of building or demolition was scattered all around, everywhere.

These fallen beams, these swinging planks, these logs of wood suspended crookedly here and there, the broken glazing, these bricks lying around and the age-old decaying knives and man-high grass which had been thrown up by the ancient earth. This was the destination supported by whose scent he covered his journey without losing the way like a migratory bird.

This is home – his home.

'Guddu Miyan is here, Guddu Miyan.' Who spoke these words?

His left foot was still stuck in the mortar. When he couldn't maintain his balance on one leg, he made over the earthen pot containing rasawal to the mud. He bent a little and tucked the biryani recipe in his fist into the canvas shoe he wore on the right foot.

He now spread out both his hands to gain support.

Were these his hands?

Though these hands were indeed his, at that time they were like the arms of an octopus, each arm and each foot of which is different from the other, but the octopus's arms are its feet and its feet are its arms. Each arm of the octopus thinks differently. The nervous system of each is entirely distinct from the other.

The bat perched on one foot extended its wings. His right hand touched something.

A brick?

A plank?

A beam?

No – this is not wood, this is none of the above.

It's iron.

His right hand knew that it's iron. It was probable that the left hand wouldn't have known, which would have been sad. Yes, iron it was. The thick pipe of the handpump. An indulgent black, strong iron filled with magnetic power. There was a tap here. The moment you moved the hand of the pump, a thick stream of clear, pure water would gush out from a depth of a hundred and twenty feet and pour itself into the small tank under the tap. It would sprinkle drops of water here and there like a fountain. The same old tap of his childhood.

Standing by the tap, one could clearly see the scene inside the kitchen, just like a movie being viewed from a distance.

The chulha, the smoke rising from it, the dish meant for kneading dough, the chapatti basket, the griddle and the tongs and so many other things.

He beat his hand against the tap forcefully, not a sound. He walked so much and wandered so much, stumbled at so many places and collided with so many things. Not a sound echoed.

There was only silence. An eternal silence. The silence of the time before the universe came into existence. He heard the sound of the silence as if it was water flowing in a river.

At which shore was he? It wasn't the shore of life or of death. This was just the outline of a bygone water. The shadow of the water emerged from the pipe and grew longer and higher. One doesn't know if there was a roof or not, if there was a sky or not, but it began to rain. His head began to soak in the silent rain. The wind blew too, a very strong wind.

The ashes of time fly off from his body in the wind sometimes, and at other times accumulate on him even more. Who will rid him of the dirt and purify him if the wind behaves in this manner? This stranger wind. Those sins which couldn't be washed even on the washerman's station at the river, how could they be washed now? Such huge stains. The huge stone-like sins, which he had collected in his courtyard playfully, had turned into huge statues that wore terrifying masks and had been brought to life by some secret sculptor and had now followed him here.

But the rain continued to fall. The wind also continued to blow and he continued to get wet. Along with the left leg which was buried in the earth, his feeling changed into confidence. He had finally reached his destination.

'Guddu Miyan is here . . . Guddu Miyan is here . . . Guddu Miyan, Guddu Miyan.'

And this time around, his ears were able to recognize the voice of his parrot who was speaking the language of silence. The lisping tongue of Sunbul the parrot, like a green chilli.

He tore his eyes wide open in the darkness.

From which ring in the roof, which beam, from the top of which door frame was the parrot's cage hanging?

He was tired.

Is there any wall remaining somewhere against which he could rest his back?

He thought about the frightening tiredness with an unnecessary sadness and disappointment.

He died after growing old, but what did growing old mean?

Age increasing in the body, gas increasing in the balloon – what after that?

But everything doesn't end with age. Everything doesn't perish. Many new things also get added. God knows from which ancient sources do water, stones and ice keep sliding in this direction. The actions, movements and pauses of people of God knows which ancient ages have begun to dwell in him. They have come here to come alive once again. The manner which didn't exist earlier, neither in childhood, nor in youth. They were coming now. The vibrations of a new spirit were changing the earlier lineaments of his body. The corporeal frame was changing. He chewed his food in a new manner and sucked at the bones in a different style and the intestines in his belly spoke in a new idiom.

This newness wasn't an intention of his body. It had come from far-off ancient worlds. From the bones of the ancestors lying in graves, from chimpanzees and fish.

So what does growing old mean? What does continuity mean? Could anyone ever determine in a true sense the definition of mathematics? There was a promise of recovery of lost things, and this promise, which was a secret till now, was now open upon him. Death was also a lost property; what was it apart from a faded and poor copy of the drama of past times, their manner and attitudes?

It was the same death, rotten and decayed, older than centuries, and it was that which was coming in a renewed form. A metamorphosis into a third-rate and evil-intentioned play of a weak short story or defective novel. Death too was after all confined in the prison house of time, just as life was. Death and life are both unaware that a terrifying eternity without end is soon going to land a sound kick on the back of time. Life and death should both go down on their knees before eternity – eternity without end which does not consume the human body, but the flesh of its soul.

Yes, but there is surely an aspect of sadness in this. There is a blue shirt which flutters and moves under the power of the desolation.

But silent wilderness is never alone, never weak. There is a mysterious and shattering energy behind it which continually creates the universe. And the universe can never be complete because the belly of human beings is not empty of intestines yet. There won't be any place for intestines and a stomach in a complete universe.

So long as this doesn't happen, this eternal silence and wilderness will continue to change human bodies into walking shadows and swallow the raw flesh and bones of spirits with its mysterious and inscrutable strength.

The earthen pot of rasawal on the wet earth cracked against the pounding throb of the silence and the worms wriggled out and began to crawl up his legs.

The biryani recipe tucked in the canvas shoe on his right foot emerged in the shape of property documents and wrapped itself around his knees.

The intestines inside his belly scrunched themselves in shock.

The odour of sleep in the darkness.

The pounding of the silence was also the sound of their footsteps. Feet walking in a single file. Such pounding can cause cracks even in strong river bridges.

They were coming, arising from slumber.

Right in front of him the lantern hanging from the wooden beam lit up. And it became visible. The kitchen became clearly visible.

This was the kitchen. The old kitchen of his childhood. The dead ones were standing at the threshold of the kitchen.

Smoke began to emanate from the chulha.

All the dead ones were seated there on their respective wooden stools with their enamel plates before them. White plates with blue borders.

He knew them. These were all members of his household. They had woken up from sleep. Each of them had bitten their tongues with their own teeth while sleeping. A trickle of blood flowed from their mouths to their chins.

They sat, heads bowed. They resembled the crows which had gathered on the parapet of the kitchen to mourn the death of a companion long ago.

Their shadows swayed slowly on the kitchen walls. Like pictures made of smoke.

The enamel plates contained sooji halwa and chapattis. They all began to eat the halwa–chapatti.

He heard the smacking noise that their teeth and jaws were making. The way each one of them was producing noises while chewing and grinding the teeth was different and distinct from the other. He recognized every single sound. Every mouth and every set of teeth. The calls of the noises of quickly chewing and swallowing halwa with chapatti became even more ancient in the light of the smokiness of the bulb hanging by a wire in one of the rings on the ceiling.

But they couldn't recognize him. They didn't even look at him. They seemed to be eating in their sleep.

Was this the place of resurrection? He didn't even remember his mother's name.

No one looked in his direction. There wasn't even a hint of familiarity in their eyes.

Nobody saw that he was right in front, holding the iron pipe of the tap, one of his feet stuck deep in the mud. No one raised their head to see that one of the pots in the kitchen was empty and there was an enamel plate containing white-coloured dry sooji halwa and stale chapattis.

They were only eating, chewing and swallowing, and blood was now dripping from their chins into the white enamel plates.

They didn't even look up to see each other. They all, who were the parents, brothers and sisters, close and distant relatives, didn't even recognize each other. There were only two things common to all of them.

One was the chapatti and halwa and the other was the trickle of blood.

Was this a scene from the day of judgement?

And then he heard, in fact, his aged, turtle-like, dry and discoloured skin heard, and his octopus-like two hands which were spread out in the darkness and had different nervous systems heard . . . someone was giving the call to prayer, far away. The fajr azaan.

But this call to prayer was not the azaan of his sect. There was still some time left for that one to be given.

He didn't realize that death had thrown down a trick at them and had succeeded in fooling all the duds. And he was still standing in the place of resurrection like an idiot.

Even after his death, he wasn't able to figure out how elegantly and cleverly death is able to pull out human beings from accidents, diseases, total destruction and old age and keep them for itself. And then it is time for a court to be called to order.

There were so many deaths collected in the kitchen. And time had, along with nibbling at the dead ones, become used to feeding them halwa–chapatti too. And why not, after all, time too had to dissolve itself like halwa in the huge and terrifying gaping mouth of eternity without end.

Everyone will have to go and unite with people who are like him one day. It doesn't make any difference whether they are able to recognize him or not. Is this what they call coming alive once again or is it a second death or is it a legal case in the court of death? A case that has been filed against the human intestines, which is eternal and will continue forever?

Ultimately, leaving behind his left foot, which was stuck in the soil, and carefully holding the intestines in his stomach with both his hands, walking on one foot or hopping ludicrously, and leaving behind the merciless unfamiliar wind and the soundless rain, he too entered the kitchen, and sitting down on his wooden stool in one corner against the wall, he bent his head and began eating his share of halwa–chapatti from the white enamel plate.

The white wheat chapatti became roiled with the blood from his mouth, like dark, blackened blood on a half-moon.

Far away the azaan sounded again from another mosque and after that the calls to prayer started in different mosques. The interval was over. The sounds of the call to prayer intersecting each other announced the rising of the new sun once again, in the East.

*Allah-o Akbar Allah-o Akbar*
*Ashhado Alla Ilaha Illallah*
*Ashhado Alla Ilaha Illallah*

God is greater God is greater
I bear witness that
There is no god but God
There is no god but God.

# juggernaut

# THE APP FOR INDIAN READERS

*Fresh, original books tailored for mobile and for India. Starting at ₹10.*

### juggernaut.in

# CRAFTED FOR MOBILE READING

*Thought you would never read a book on mobile? Let us prove you wrong.*

juggernaut.in

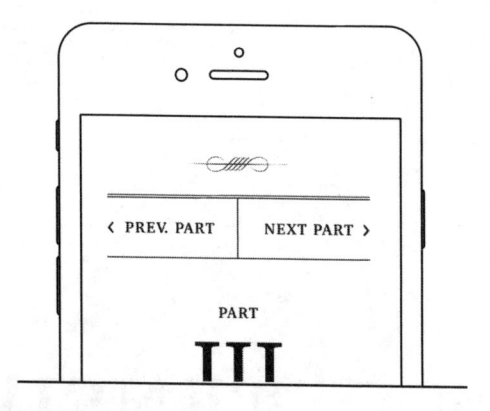

## Beautiful Typography

The quality of print transferred
to your mobile. Forget ugly PDFs.

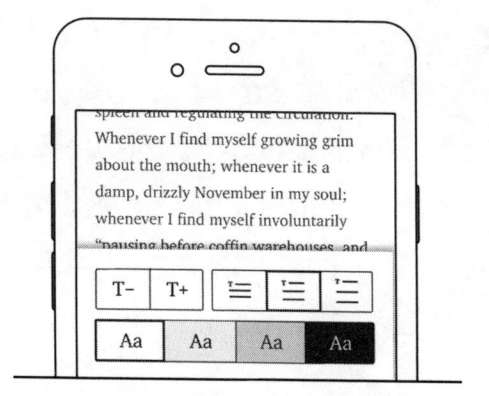

## Customizable Reading

Read in the font size, spacing
and background of your liking.

juggernaut.in

## AN EXTENSIVE LIBRARY

*Including fresh, new, original Juggernaut books from the likes of Sunny Leone, Praveen Swami, Husain Haqqani, Umera Ahmed, Rujuta Diwekar and lots more. Plus, books from partner publishers and loads of free classics. Whichever genre you like, there's a book waiting for you.*

juggernaut.in

juggernaut.in

# DON'T JUST READ; INTERACT

*We're changing the reading experience from passive to active.*

juggernaut.in

## Ask authors questions

Get all your answers from the horse's mouth. Juggernaut authors actually reply to every question they can.

## Rate and review

Let everyone know of your favourite reads or critique the finer points of a book – you will be heard in a community of like-minded readers.

## Gift books to friends

For a book-lover, there's no nicer gift than a book personally picked. You can even do it anonymously if you like.

## Enjoy new book formats

Discover serials released in parts over time, picture books including comics, and story-bundles at discounted rates. And coming soon, audiobooks.

juggernaut.in

# 4

## LOWEST PRICES & ONE-TAP BUYING

*Books start at ₹10 with regular discounts and free previews.*

juggernaut.in

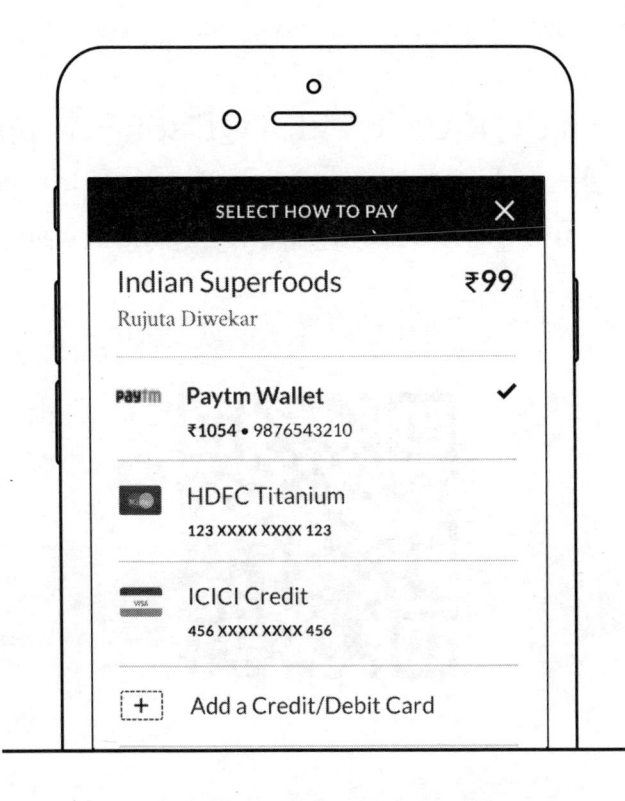

## Paytm Wallet, Cards & Apple Payments

On Android, just add a Paytm Wallet once and buy any book with one tap. On iOS, pay with one tap with your iTunes-linked debit/credit card.

Click the QR Code with a QR scanner app or type the link into the Internet browser on your phone to download the Juggernaut app.

For our complete catalogue, visit www.juggernaut.in
To submit your book, send a synopsis and two sample chapters to books@juggernaut.in
For all other queries, write to contact@juggernaut.in